The Predictable Heartbreaks
of Imogen Finch

ALSO BY JACQUELINE FIRKINS

*Marlowe Banks, Redesigned*
*How Not to Fall in Love*
*Hearts, Strings, and Other Breakable Things*

# The
# Predictable Heartbreaks
# of Imogen Finch

## A NOVEL

## Jacqueline Firkins

ST. MARTIN'S GRIFFIN
NEW YORK

First published in the United States by St. Martin's Griffin, an imprint of St. Martin's Publishing Group

THE PREDICTABLE HEARTBREAKS OF IMOGEN FINCH. Copyright © 2023 by Jacqueline Firkins. All rights reserved. Printed in the United States of America. For information, address St. Martin's Publishing Group, 120 Broadway, New York, NY 10271.

www.stmartins.com

Designed by Jen Edwards

Librarasy of Congress Cataloging-in-Publication Data

Names: Firkins, Jacqueline, author.
Title: The predictable heartbreaks of Imogen Finch : a novel / Jacqueline Firkins.
Description: First edition. | New York : St. Martin's Griffin, 2023.
Identifiers: LCCN 2023016835 | ISBN 9781250836526 (trade paperback) | ISBN 9781250836533 (ebook)
Subjects: LCGFT: Romance fiction. | Novels.
Classification: LCC PS3606.I734 P74 2023 | DDC 813/.6—dc23 /eng/20230413
LC record available at https://lccn.loc.gov/2023016835

Our books may be purchased in bulk for promotional, educational, or business use. Please contact your local bookseller or the Macmillan Corporate and Premium Sales Department at 1-800-221-7945, extension 5442, or by email at MacmillanSpecialMarkets@macmillan.com.

First Edition: 2023

10  9  8  7  6  5  4  3  2

*For the boy who left. And never came back.*

The Predictable Heartbreaks
of Imogen Finch

# Prologue

## HEARTBREAK #17

I've heard it said that knowing what's to come ruins the joy of surprise. If this wasn't a commonly held belief, the giftwrap industry wouldn't net nearly $20 billion annually. I agree that a flutter of anticipation can feel pretty damned amazing. The dizzying held-breath of an uncertain *What If* or an even giddier *Maybe This Time*. However, knowing what's to come has also prevented me from getting caught in the rain without an umbrella. It saved me from plummeting into crushing disappointment when a birthday card I hoped would contain concert tickets I'd hinted about to *everyone* turned out to hold a ten-dollar gift certificate for a recently foreclosed novelty sock store instead. And now, it's protecting me from sobbing over a half-finished plate of spaghetti while the only relationship I've held on to for more than a few months implodes with one short but gut-punching confession, a confession my now ex-boyfriend could barely articulate.

"For how long?" I ask once I finally find my voice.

Greg buries his face in his hands, his posture so slumped I can almost smell the guilt, though maybe that's the cheap powdered Parmesan I spilled a moment ago.

"Two months," he mutters into his hands. "Maybe more like three?"

"Wow." I lean back in the booth opposite him, letting the second gut punch land. For at least a full minute, I remain speechless. I'm too busy mentally replaying the last few months of our year-long relationship, wondering which business trips weren't really business trips. Which smile-inducing texts weren't "something funny his brother said." Which workouts weren't for his benefit. Or mine. "All this time. Why tell me now?"

He scrubs his face. Scratches at his sandy-blond hair. Shifts. Shifts again.

"I just . . ." He swallows. Looks away. "I want to give things a real shot with her."

I wince as gut punch number three lands, and the stark articulation of his preference for another woman rips through me—hard, sharp, and full of thorns. Nothing about it feels good. It hurts. A lot. And yet, it also feels so deeply inevitable, my brain has space for coexisting thoughts like, *I always disliked that overpriced suit he's wearing* and *I wonder if we should get the rest of our dinner to go?*

Maybe I shouldn't have that space.

But I do.

For the next ten minutes or so, while I sit with my brow furrowed and my fists in my lap, Greg explains how he came to this crossroads. The explanation morphs into a list of the many reasons he likes this other woman more than he likes me. He's trying to help me understand. He wants us both to find peace with his choice. I get that. But also . . .

*Really, Greg?! REALLY?!* The last thing I need is more evidence of why I will only ever be a guy's second-best option. Even if he pretended otherwise for months.

I let that thought fan the flames of anger. Inevitable or not, he betrayed me. This is my moment. I need to leap up from this table, fling what's left of my shitty red wine in his annoyingly handsome and guilt-ridden face, say something acerbic that will make him feel small and me feel powerful. Gain control. Drop the mic. Walk out. Don't look back.

I rally my ire and my nerves, gripping the stem of my wineglass.

And then Greg starts crying.

"I'm *so* sorry," he says. "I can't believe I did this to you. To us. I feel awful."

My anger fades. My wine remains un-flung. We both go quiet.

"You can't help what you feel," I eventually hear myself say. "If this is what you really want, it's better for all three of us if you stop pretending with me, right?"

He nods, barely, before choking awkwardly on a mismanaged swallow that has the unfortunate effect of sounding like a tragic sob. People we know are watching us. Our waiter avoids our table as she refills water glasses. I probably look like an ice queen for sitting here so stoically. I'm not stoic at all. I'm anything but. I just . . . knew this was coming. I didn't know when or where or how it would all go down, but I knew.

"Greg." I reach across the table, careful to avoid sweeping my elbow through my spaghetti sauce. I set my hand on his, drawing his eyes to mine. "It's okay. Really."

"Y-you s-sure?" he blubbers.

"Yeah." I tip my chin toward the parking lot. "Sitting here like this, hashing out every detail won't do either of us any good. Why don't you go ahead and take off?"

He nods while studying our unfinished dinner, now idle and unwanted. I'd like to think he sees a metaphor, but I'm pretty sure he's sorting out what we do about the bill.

I wait, hoping he'll pull out his wallet. He should at least pay for dinner if he's going to dump my ass in public on date night. But he doesn't take out his wallet. He just stares.

I can't help it. I feel bad that he feels bad. For the past year, Greg has been my partner. My person. It's been my job to take care of him, to lift him up when he's down. To make him smile. To assure him things will be okay. I can't change that in an instant. Caring about someone doesn't come with an off switch, which is a major design flaw.

"I'll get the check," I say. "Seriously. Just go."

He hesitates again, shifting and sniffling, but eventually he heads out, leaving me to flag down the waiter, text my best friend, and wonder where the fuck I left my spine.

# One

**W**hy do I always run out of clean underwear on the mornings I'm running late? The pair I find bunched up at the back of my drawer says *Happy Holidays!* but they might as well say *Human Catastrophe*. After nursing last week's breakup over way too many beers with Franny last night, I lost track of how many times I hit *snooze*. I left myself no time to put on makeup or dry my unnecessarily long hair after showering. Instead, I dig a pair of jeans and a wool pullover out of my laundry pile, yanking them on before making a mad dash from my disaster zone/basement suite up the stairs to the kitchen. If I hurry, I can make toast to go and get to the florist's without eliciting questions from my boss, Kym. Questions I will invariably answer because—as has recently been proven for the millionth time—I have the backbone of a single-celled amoeba. One hint about my raucous night and I'll be spilling every detail, even the most embarrassing ones.

I'm flying across the kitchen so fast, beelining it to the toaster, I don't see my mom standing by the glass doors to the backyard until she speaks, halting me midstep.

"Seven herons," she says in a tone so ominous even Stephen King would tremble at the sound. "Seven herons and six grebes."

"Six grebes," I repeat, instantly aborting my hopes of making it to work on time. This is life with my mom. One minute I'm an average twenty-eight-year-old woman who isn't living up to her potential. In the next, I'm dropped into an eerie convo about ducks. "The black and white ones with the funny little mohawks?"

"The cresteds, yes." My mom nods as she turns toward me. A frail hand rises to her lips and rests there, almost as though she's trying to silence herself. "A change is coming, Imogen. A shuffling of expectations. A surprise." Her eyes widen, though I can't tell if that means the surprise she just referred to will be good or bad.

It'll probably be bad. Few of my mom's prophecies fall into the Happily Ever After category, though the range of predicted catastrophes is broad, from minor friend spats to lifelong curses. She swears this is simply the way of things, and has been for countless generations. According to her stories, prophesying runs in our family, popping up every third or fourth generation, manifesting in early childhood, and only in the women. One of my ancestors milked it in the carnival circuit, shrouding herself in black lace veils and delivering doom and gloom from the back of a dusty old caravan. Another was a secret military advisor to Napoleon. It's a colorful family history, if also an embellished one.

My mom watches as I resume my attempt to throw together a hasty breakfast, pulling a bread loaf from a turquoise tin breadbox we inherited from my grandparents, along with half the contents of this house. A few of the items are vintage chic, but most are old, ugly, and in need of replacement. Not that we will replace them because A: my mom has assigned profound importance to everything we own and B: we don't have much money to spare. Too bad my mom can't foretell a windfall.

"A surprise, huh?" I ask when I can't stand the silent staring any longer.

"The directions they were facing suggested an unexpected loss. A severing. A transformation."

"That's a lot of information for one flock of birds."

"It's the grebes," she says as though this explains everything.

"What if one was a piece of driftwood? Hard to tell when it's so foggy."

"No, no. There were six. I counted them over and over." My mom turns toward the glass doors again. Outside, beyond a motley collection of wind chimes and a pair of beat-up lawn chairs, a pale sun is trying hard to burn away the morning fog. We only live a block from the beach, though our ocean view is obstructed by a three-story stucco apartment building that went up the year I was born, painted in a dull green that was probably supposed to blend in with nature but has yellowed with age, making it look like regurgitated pea puree. It's the perfect symbol of life in Pitt's Corner. Something transcendent is always close by, but it's obscured by a cheaply manufactured eyesore.

"And the herons?" I ask, unsure why the grebes are getting all the credit.

"Yes. Exactly. The herons." My mom fails to take in my look of confusion as she continues staring through the doors, though whether she's staring at the ugly building, the fog, or a horizon in her mind's eye, I can't tell. "Thirteen birds. *And* a shift in the wind. I felt it in my bones, just like when your father died."

The mention of my dad slows my movement with the toaster. This is the problem with my mom's prophecies. Despite how batshit crazy she often sounds, finding omens in whatever elements of nature she's paying attention to on any given day—birds, frogs, flies, clouds, ripples in puddles, stripes on a caterpillar, the reeds that poke up through the Oregon sand dunes—all of her prophecies come true. Not that she knows exactly what will happen, and the details are *just* general enough to allow room for skepticism. They're also accurate enough to support the theory that she might, in fact, be a witch.

She knew when my dad's fishing boat would sink in a squall, taking him and most of his crew with it. She knew when my brother, Antony, would wreck his friend's uninsured sports car and hemorrhage his college fund paying off the cost. She knew my sister, Lavinia, was destined to travel to Europe at age twenty-three, and then stay there, finding contentment as a literary researcher in Oxford. And she knew on my sixth birthday that I would never be first at anything.

Naturally, I was devastated by her pronouncement. I sobbed. I screamed. I railed at the world, furious that I was doomed to a lifetime of mediocrity I had yet to wrap my naïve little brain around. I only knew I hated limitations. I also had a fierce determination few could reckon with. My tears shed, I turned my attention to proving my mom wrong. Over the following years, I entered poetry, art, and baking contests. I played every sport I could find the time for. I auditioned for plays and talent competitions. I joined debate and math teams. I busted my ass for top grades. I ran for student offices, even ones I didn't want, as long as I had even the slimmest chance of getting voted in.

Twenty-two years later, after accumulating countless red and white ribbons without ever nudging past second place, I've long since stopped fighting my curse. I wish I could say that means I've found peace with it, but I can't. Underneath a light veneer of cynicism about my lot in life, I've never stopped yearning, just once, to be more than a nominee, a runner-up, a forgettable name among the ranks, or a girl a guy dumped once he met a hotter, smarter, funnier, more interesting girl he really wanted to be with. Case in point: Greg's spaghetti confession. Predictable by now, but still . . .

As I lean on the counter and wait for the toaster to work its magic, my mom slides into a chair at our rickety 1950s chrome dining set. She's wearing two sweaters today, one maroon Fair Isle and the other teal cable-knit, with two different shirt collars peeking out underneath. I don't tally her skirts, but I'd guess three. She always wears an odd number of garments. Even numbers are supposedly unlucky. Also on her unlucky list: unripe crabapples, silver spoons, broken egg yolks, and foxes. I try not to feed my mom's eccentricities, but since I can't totally dismiss them, I strike a conversational balance.

"So, that wind," I prompt. "This upcoming change isn't going to be good?"

She smiles softly, no longer trancelike. Just kind of slumpy and sad.

"It'll be"—she pauses, thinks, thinks some more—"complicated."

"Yeah, but good complicated or bad complicated?"

She studies me for a long moment while I try not to fidget under the intensity of her gaze. Her eyes are a deep umber with copper, gold, green, and blue speckles, a color combination she passed down to all three of us. But where my siblings and I see only what's in front of us with our marble eyes, our mom sees *everything*. It's unnerving.

"How much do you want to know?" she asks.

"I'm not sure." I consider the million-dollar question as I hunt for butter and realize I forgot to thaw any. "Will you still be here when I finish work tonight?"

She nods, her smile lingering, her every-color eyes full of reassurance.

"Will *I* still be here?" I ask.

She nods again, watching while I mangle my toast with rock-hard butter.

"Perhaps we should leave the matter there," she says. "For now."

These last two words send a shiver down my spine. I can't help but sense that this upcoming change will impact me. I'd solicit more information but I don't have the time or energy this morning. Besides, with my breakup wounds still raw and my optimism about my love life at an all-time low, I'm more eager than usual to write off my mom's predictions as elaborate delusions with a coincidentally high rate of fulfillment. Anyone can find a link between a shadow and a storm. The less I look for that link, the better.

With a slow, languorous sigh, my mom accepts my willful ignorance and shifts the subject, rattling off a few details about a scarf she's knitting and a new reality show she plans to watch. I don't fully process everything she says, thanks to a brain that's still bleary from too much alcohol and not enough sleep. Instead, I tell my mom I'll see her later. Then I run out the door with my toast in hand and the vague sensation that she mentioned something about needing to dig out her old black dress.

By the time I get to Amelia's Bloomers, word of my raucous night has already traveled. This is what happens in a town of 347 people. It's barely 8 a.m. and Kym already knows I climbed onto a bar last night and belted out an impassioned rendition of "I Will Survive" with a touring group of bikers, even though I can't hit a note and O'Malley's doesn't host karaoke nights. She also knows I spent much of the night flirting with Dutch, the super-hot, yes-I've-thought-about-it bartender, and subject of endless Pitt's Corner gossip. Thankfully I had the wherewithal not to go home with him, much to Kym's disappointment.

"He's a much better catch than Greg," she presses.

"He's not a fish. And Greg was great."

"Greg was—" She catches something in my expression that makes her stop short. "Sorry! Sorry. Overstepping. None of my business."

She waves away the conversation with a flutter of hands. Three seconds later, she redefines *none of my business* to mean *totally my business* by listing a dozen things she never really liked about Greg, and several things her husband, Eugene, didn't like about him, either.

I lay out daisies and assorted filler greens without engaging in Kym's diatribe. She means well. She always does, but I don't want to hear about Greg's perceived lack of assets. Being dumped by a smart, funny, sensitive guy is hard enough. Being dumped by a narcissistic, under-tipping, micromanaging, casually sexist man-toad would be a serious blow to my already shaky self-worth.

"You're better off without him," Kym says by way of punctuating her rant.

I muster a cheerful tone. "Let's hope so."

"Move on and move up."

"Or comfort eat and binge-watch bad TV for a while?"

"Get back in the saddle."

"Can I get 'back in' something I haven't previously used?"

"Put yourself out there."

"Out where, exactly?"

"I'm just saying," she says in that way people never *just say* anything. "Maybe this is a good time to have some fun. And Dutch could be the perfect rebound."

"He could be," I concede because, well, no argument there. He has deep dimples, full lips, impish blue eyes, and thick blond wavy hair that belongs in a shampoo ad. He also has big, strong hands that *really* know how to grip a beer pull or squeeze a lime. I don't even like lime in my beer, but sometimes I order it just so I can watch him squeeze.

"That man is practically built for sex," Kym continues, stepping up close enough to pick toast crumbs out of my sweater. "*Someone* should be sleeping with him."

"Not sure that someone should be me." I wedge another Gerbera daisy into a blue glass vase, jamming it in harder than necessary. I don't know why people love daisies so much. They look like kindergartener drawings, over-bright and oversimplified, as if Mother Nature was trying out the idea of a flower before she dug deep and got it right.

Kym gives my shoulder a squeeze as she shines a sympathetic smile on me. She has a perfect customer service smile, one that always looks genuine, probably because it is. She's naturally cheerful and she likes everyone, even when she's silently cataloguing ways to improve us all. She was a beauty queen when she was a teenager, and she's still stunning at fifty-something, with jet-black hair she wears in a sleek braid, and skin so smooth I could almost swear she doesn't have pores.

"Too worried about your curse?" she asks.

"My curse or my consistent dump-ability. Either way."

"Maybe it's one of those curses that only *seems* to work because you believe it."

"Or because all seventeen of my exes left me for other women."

"All seventeen? Really?"

"Close enough. Fifteen left me for other women. One left me for a man. The seventeenth left me to join a cult and give his body over to collective carnal worship of a love goddess I'd never heard of and have staunchly refused to google."

"Hard to argue with that." With a rueful sigh, Kym heads behind the counter and sets up the register while I continue with the day's arrangement orders, a task I was hired for because Kym's flower arranging capabilities top out at shoving a dozen carnations into a narrow-necked vase and wondering why they look like they're choking. Sometimes she adds a fern. While I'm proud to bring a more artistic eye to the shop, I often suspect Kym actually hired me because she wanted someone to talk to, someone whose life is far more sordid than hers, what with my doomed relationships and my off-kilter mother. I do spice things up around here. "It's such a shame though," she adds, because dropping the topic would be too much to ask. "There are so few single people in Pitt's Corner."

"I'm aware," I say, my tone impressively free of irritation. "Doesn't mean I want to add another ex to my already extensive People to Avoid list."

"Would Dutch count as an ex?"

"You mean if we only have meaningless sex?"

"Of course. I wasn't suggesting you fall in love with him."

My body tenses. I attempt a passive expression but I fail miserably.

"What's wrong?" Kym asks.

"It's those words. *In love.*" I fight a frown as I tie a bow on the vase of daisies.

Kym chuckles, taking in my expression, which is still far from impassive.

"Something wrong with falling in love?" she asks.

"More like something unachievable." I trim a length of ribbon, planning to leave the matter there, but Kym has stopped counting out change. Her perfectly arched brows are raised and she's waiting for me to continue. One way or another, she's getting this story out of me, so I might as well cut to the chase. "I cared about Greg, like I cared about all of my exes. When I was in the relationship, I was a hundred percent in. I committed. I did the work. I learned the Five Love Languages and I made sure to use them all. Greg's decision to walk away from all of that sucks. I haven't felt great this week, but I haven't felt as not-great as I should after the sudden demise of a year-long relationship. In fact, I shook off most of my heartbreak in one rousing night at a bar."

Kym eyes me quizzically. "So . . . you want to feel worse?"

"I want to feel *more*. My relationships might be doomed from the start, but shouldn't at least one end with more than a low rumble of resentment and a temporary blow to my ego?" I set aside the daisies and start in on an October-themed arrangement with fake autumn leaves and even faker baby pumpkins.

Kym resumes counting out change, but she keeps a curious eye on me.

"Maybe you've developed effective coping mechanisms," she suggests.

I snort out a laugh, suspecting very few therapists would recommend inebriated public humiliation and persistent emotional remove as "effective coping mechanisms."

"Or maybe I can't fall in love anymore," I say. "Not really. Not fully."

Kym perks up. "'Anymore'?"

*Shit. She caught me. She always does.*

I hedge as I work on the fall bouquet, but Kym asks a lot of probing questions and soon enough I cave, until I'm telling her about the loss that truly crushed me, the one that suggests that yes, I have been *in love*. Once. Only once.

I was a teenager at the time, back when my emotions were still messy and untamed, and back before I understood the full limitations of my curse. That boy. *That. Boy.* Even now, thinking about him makes my chest seize and my brain go fuzzy with wistfulness. We never even dated, but my heart leapt whenever he entered a room or brushed my hand or looked at me a second longer than necessary. Everything about him mattered *so much*. His tastes. His passions. His smile. His frown. His presence. I counted every minute together, and every minute apart. When he left town and we fell out of touch—or rather, when I finally accepted that he'd fully ghosted me—coping with the loss didn't require a beer. It required a lifetime.

Honestly? It's still requiring a lifetime.

But that was then, I guess. Apparently love is different as an adult. As a cursed adult, anyway. So unless my mom has something to say about the matter—unless a few grebes and herons mean *my* life is about to change—this is all I can hope for. Another relationship. Another breakup. Another night of drinking with Franny while shaking off my resentment about being tossed aside for a woman who outshines me. Another piece of evidence that I'll only ever be second best, so I might as well settle in for the ride.

# Two

From Amelia's Bloomers, I head to the Hound and the Fury, where I pick up house keys for the dozen or so dogs I'll walk before lunch, taking my unruly charges out in two batches of five or six at a time. Vera, my boss, runs the operation out of an old house she rents with seven roommates. Based on the pungent cloud that greets me when I arrive for key collection, I'm pretty sure she spends most of her earnings on weed. She's nineteen and says *dude* a lot. It's mildly humiliating to accept a wad of wrinkled cash from her once a week, knowing she's my direct superior. She's running a business. I'm working six part-time jobs while letting my art school degree desiccate in a shoebox. Vera also has furniture that isn't from another century and a steady boyfriend who didn't leave her for a leggy lawyer with one of those deceptively simple ponytails that shake out instantly into fuck-me hair.

Basically, she's living my dream life.

"Heard about Greg." Vera hands me a zippered pouch full of keys and a printed town map with X's on several houses. I keep wondering if we should be using an app, but not wondering (or caring) enough to pursue the idea. "Joanie said he didn't even pay for dinner. Just dropped the bomb, walked out, and left you with the bill. What a loser."

I respond with a noncommittal "Mmm" as I count keys and scan the map so I know where to head from here. As with Kym, I appreciate Vera's attempt at solidarity, but if Greg is a loser, then I'm an even bigger loser for dating him. And for not throwing my wine in his face while he detailed another woman's superior assets. My instinct to take care of *his* feelings during that conversation was— and still is—disconcerting.

While I try not to dwell on those thoughts, Vera twists a lock of hair around her index finger, watching me with a charming combination of boredom and disdain.

"You sleep with Dutch yet?" she asks.

I choke out a laugh. "I've been single for a week."

She blinks at me through a fog of confusion. "Is that a *yes?*"

"Some people might consider a week a rather short recovery period."

Vera scoffs. "Some people who aren't getting laid."

I force a smile, reminding myself that while Vera looks like she got out of bed about ten seconds ago, and she probably smell-checked her T-shirt on her way to the door, she is my boss. As with Kym, I can't tell her to shut the hell up and mind her own business. Instead, I jangle the key pouch and flee the scene as though the dogs will dock my pay if I don't arrive precisely when they expect me. I don't need sex advice from my teenage boss any more than I needed it from my middle-aged boss. I also don't need it from the quartet of octogenarians who hang out on Lyle Lee's front porch every morning, but they offer a few helpful tidbits as I pass, waving me over from a rotting sofa, under the guise of asking how I'm doing. I should probably get a T-shirt that says KEEP YOUR GOSSIP OFF MY VAGINA, but knowing my luck, I'd be wearing the tee when I bumped into Greg's new girlfriend. She'd look fabulous in a sexy suit and heels while I looked like I was going to great lengths to advertise my niche sense of humor.

Thankfully, my company for the next two hours will be entirely of the canine variety. I grew up surrounded by dogs. Everyone in my family is a softie, so we took in pretty much any stray or ancient shelter dog who needed a home. I adored them all at a bone-deep level, but the last of the family pets died shortly after I moved back home. By then I knew my mom was too lost in her meanderings and I was too busy trying to take care of her and the house and a backlog of unpaid bills to add another responsibility.

So here I am, walking other people's dogs to get my fix. This would easily be my favorite of my six jobs, except for Jack, the oh-so-creatively named Jack Russell terrier who's determined to chase every squirrel, car, leaf, or speck of dust that passes, tangling the leashes of the well-behaved Labs and spaniels who trot along by my side. He also barks at babies and pees on unsuspecting dachshunds. I keep trying to convince him the Evil Villain Hall of Fame isn't real, but thus far he's still aiming for induction.

As I'm leashing him up, distracting him with a biscuit so he'll stand still long enough to let me put on his harness, an ambulance passes. A hound I've already picked up howls with the siren while a spindly pointer cowers against me. I watch the ambulance until it rounds a curve between some reedy dunes and disappears from view. I'm on a really quiet street, and while ambulances are hardly unheard of in Pitt's Corner, this one's coming from a secluded residential area with only eight or ten houses, all of them grand old mansions with enormous lots that overlook a picturesque cove.

My mom's morning prophecy comes to mind and I wonder if one of the rich people who live nearby choked on their caviar. I don't wish any of those people ill-will, but if someone in town is about to die, I'd prefer they be a member of the Old Money Crew, a tight clique of multi-generationally wealthy families who inherited their massive properties and now use them as vacation homes. Meanwhile, the rest of us scrape by and pray our crappy little working-class town never gets gentrified to keep up with the one-percenters who can afford to own multiple homes. Even if a decent coffee shop would be kind of amazing.

I'm on the beach half an hour later with the dogs when my phone pings.

Franny: Are you sitting down?
Imogen: Standing actually. 2 dogs swimming. 1 rolling in
    seaweed. 1 herding. 1 terrifying seagulls (Jack). 1 peeing
    on what I think was someone's sandcastle
Franny: Sit down. I have news

I stare at the screen, wondering if Franny's simply being her usual dramatic self. I adore her, but the last time she "had news," she wanted me to know she'd finally found a lipstick that worked with her red hair. Granted, the lipstick was an excellent color on her, but I'm pretty sure I could've borne the news while standing. I also fully realize I could fake sitting down and Franny would never know, but the combination of the ambulance and an eerie image of thirteen birds makes me find a beached log where I can keep an eye on the dogs while I absorb Franny's news.

Imogen: Sitting. What's up?
Franny: Mr. Swift just died. WHILE HE WAS FUCKING HIS
    MISTRESS!!!!

*Wow. WOW. Okay.* That *is* news, and I'm glad Franny warned me to sit down. Mr. Swift owns one of the Old Money mansions.

He and his wife moved to the outskirts of Portland about eight years ago, presumably to separate residences, though on the rare occasions they're both in town, they put up a pretense of being together. For most of the year, they alternate weekend use of their coastal property. I've been cleaning it every Wednesday so neither Mr. nor Mrs. has to see signs of the other's presence, nor the presence of either party's extramarital partners. Out of sight, out of mind, I guess.

Until now. Holy shit.

Franny: You still there?
Imogen: Yeah. Just in shock
Franny: Not as shocked as she was!
Imogen: Dark, Franny. Real dark
Franny: Joe got the scoop from Sandy who heard it from
Eugene who got it from the EMT who arrived on the
scene. What a way to go, right?

I try to imagine dying while a guy's inside me, and it hardly conjures a euphoric picture. More like intense trauma that would force the survivor into a lifetime of therapy. Or at least a lifetime of celibacy. I feel awful for Mr. Swift's mistress, even if I suspect she'll eventually be better off without him. He wasn't the nicest man, though he paid me well for my attention to detail, and for my discretion.

As I consider the likelihood that I'm about to lose that income, I force Jack to stop humping an impossibly tolerant Saint Bernard. Jack's ego truly knows no bounds. He lost his balls years ago but he still assumes he can populate the world in his image.

Imogen: Think they'll sell the house?
Franny: Probably. Unless Mrs. Swift wants it
Imogen: It does have that gorgeous widow's walk

Franny: Can you imagine? Black veil. Long dress. Looking out
   to sea. Pining

Imogen: She doesn't strike me as the pining type

Franny: More like the pop the champagne and celebrate her
   freedom type?

Imogen: More like the take the inheritance and quietly slip
   away type

Franny: Fair. Think Eliot will come back for the funeral?

My chest tightens and I have to sit down again. The name practically blazes from my screen. *Eliot.* Eliot Swift. Quiet, sweet, smart, soft, beautiful, outwardly fearless but inwardly tortured Eliot. The third member of our childhood friendship trio. Also, *that boy*, the one I told Kym about earlier today, though I somehow managed to withhold his name. He was my first major crush, and the only one I kept completely secret, even from Franny. She and Eliot meant everything to me when we were growing up. I couldn't mess up our friendships. Besides, I always suspected that if any of us busted through our strict friend-zone boundaries, it would be Franny and Eliot. I never felt excluded from our trio, but as with every other part of my life, I could only ever come second to either of them. Any doubts I nurtured about the matter vanished when Franny and Eliot went to prom together, losing their virginity to each other later that night. I had to hear about it from both of them, gritting my teeth and acting like I wasn't shattered. Twice.

It's all ancient history now. By sheer dumb luck, Franny and I both ended up back in Pitt's Corner, but we lost touch with Eliot years ago. Still, he's the one I think of when I hear the words *in love*. Not Greg. Not any of the other guys I've dated. I think of Eliot.

Imogen: He won't come back

Franny: It's his dad's funeral

Imogen: He hated his dad

Franny: IT'S HIS DAD'S FUNERAL!!!

Imogen: Your point?

Franny: Only an asshole would skip a family funeral

Imogen: An asshole or someone hiking in Kyrgyzstan

Franny: Is that where he is now?

Imogen: It was a random guess. I stopped watching after his
    Mongolia trip

Franny: Was that the one where he almost fell from the frozen
    waterfall?

Imogen: I think that was somewhere in Norway. Mongolia
    was the fever

Eliot's Mongolia trip was about three years ago, one of the many
solo journeys he films for his YouTube channel, *The Un-lonesome
Wanderer*. I used to watch every video, even the early ones when he
had no filming skills and I was one of his only followers, but eventually I couldn't handle seeing him almost die anymore. He'd obviously survived his fever because he made it out of the mountains to
post the video, but for weeks I couldn't stop picturing him sweating
through his delirium, talking brain-garbled nonsense to his camera,
alone under the stars. In my imagination, he was dead by morning
and his body was found months later, half eaten by wild dogs. I don't
know if that part of Mongolia has wild dogs. It just looked like an
environment where fresh meat wouldn't last long.

Franny: Did your mom predict anything this morning? About
    Mr. Swift?

While I chase down an errant terrier, I think back to my mom's
eerie mumblings. Franny's one of the few people who fully believes

in my mom's prophecies. Most of our community engages in the prognosticating through sheer curiosity, the way people often read horoscopes even though they don't think everyone born in a given month will face an identical fate. Others respond with ridicule, some couched, some not so couched. A few simply don't care. But Franny's convinced my mom knows *everything*.

> Imogen: She mentioned a sudden loss
> Franny: Bingo
> Imogen: Also a severing. A transformation. A change of
>     expectations. A surprise
> Franny: SOMEONE was definitely surprised!

I laugh a little, but in an uneasy way, because I'm not positive everything my mom said was about Mr. Swift's death. She didn't like the man any more than the rest of us did. His death alone wouldn't have put that faraway look in her eyes, or made her stare at me as though she was worried about how I might respond to whatever unfolded in her prophecy. It wouldn't have made her put that weighty pause before the word *complicated*.

As I consider the possibilities, I pull up my old text thread with Eliot, which I saved and back up a couple times a year so it doesn't vanish the way he did. The dates are jarring. Our most recent exchange was over eight years ago, around the time his parents turned their giant house into a weekend getaway.

> Imogen: When are you coming back to visit?
> Eliot: When icicles form on Satan's testicles

I drew him a cartoon of naked, freezing Satan, an excellent use of the artistic talents I parlayed into the illustration degree I don't otherwise employ. He replied with a polite request to stop sending him dick pics. Followed by a winking emoji.

The rest of the text thread is notably one-sided. A few *How are you?* texts I sent over the months that followed, check-ins on his whereabouts, comments on whatever I saw on his YouTube channel, a random funny GIF or two. Nothing at all from Eliot.

As I scroll through the thread now, I wonder if he kept his number. He might've changed it years ago. Still, I should at least try to reach out, offer my condolences. Then again, even the thought feels like I'm opening Pandora's box. Feelings I've kept locked away for years are already sneaking out. Longing. Envy. Insecurity. Maybe even fear. I have to force myself to take slow, deep breaths as a jittery ache surges in my chest.

I can deal with getting dumped. I can ride out the uptick in town gossip. I can even cope with a life of predestined mediocrity, one in which I cobble together a living in my working-class town and wonder what my life would be like if I was *one* notch better at any of the things I've tried. But if my mom's prophecy has something to do with Eliot Swift coming back into my life—and coming back in a *complicated* way—I am going to lose my mind. Despite a persistent wish to feel something more, to fall in love without protective walls and lowered expectations, I can't be second best to Eliot. Not again.

My thoughts spiral. The jitters in my chest speed up. My sweat glands join in the fun. The dogs blur into black and tan blobs.

Am I shivering? I shouldn't be shivering.

In my growing haze, a solution strikes me. Rather than wait for the rest of my mom's prophecy to unfold, I'll find a way to fulfill it myself.

# HEARTBREAK #12

Two months into my relationship with Quentin Bowers, I felt like I knew him, and I liked what I knew. He was funny and charismatic. He had great taste in music. He worked six days a week, running a successful charter fishing service out of a town just north of Pitt's Corner. He was terrified of premature baldness despite having a full head of hair. He also *really* loved blow jobs, especially if I gave his balls a tug when he was about to climax.

The guttural groan that escaped him one lazy afternoon made his cat leap from its nearby perch. That cat always watched us. I always tried not to care. I always failed.

"That's so fucking good, babe." Quentin dug a hand into my enormous messy bun as his hips rose off the bed in one last thrust, though the sharp tang at the back of my throat suggested he was already well and truly finished. "God, I love Sundays."

I *mmm'ed* in agreement as I inched back far enough to let his dick slide from between my lips and settle between his legs. Then I snuck in a nibble on his inner thigh, hoping to indicate that although he was done, I was just getting started.

Working my way up his stomach, I planted kisses while he bit down a grin, urging me forward with a beckoning finger. I was *so* turned on by then—high off the power of knowing I could pull feral and delirious noises from him—but I'd barely made it to the base of his ribs when his phone buzzed on his bedside table. I assumed he'd ignore it while I prowled up his naked body like a comically ravenous panther, but he glanced at the screen. Whatever he saw made him jerk backward, his breath catching.

I stopped planting kisses. He scooted into a sitting position as he grabbed the phone, his eyes wide and his thumbs fluttering away, texting at an impossible rate.

"Everything okay?" I asked. "Was someone in an accident?"

He looked up at me, but only for an instant before his thumbs were at it again.

"Shit. Sorry. No," he said. "No accident. But I have to go. Now. Like, *right* now."

"Okay?" I sat back on my heels, still positioned between his legs, stripped bare and feeling newly exposed. Especially since the cat was staring again.

Quentin leapt to his feet, scrambling to collect the clothes we'd left strewn around his apartment in our haste to get naked. I followed suit while watching him warily, wondering what the hell had happened. But I didn't press. He was obviously freaking out. He'd tell me when the situation was less urgent. Everything would be fine.

A few minutes later, as he drove me home before heading to his destination, he explained what was happening. He wasn't driving to a hospital or a police station or the scene of an accident. He was driving to the apartment of the girl he'd been in love with for years. She'd broken up with her long-term boyfriend and was finally single. Quentin tried to soften the news, balancing it with apologies, but his fingers were tapping out tunes on his thigh and despite obvious effort, he couldn't repress a grin. He was even humming, though he kept catching himself and stopping, only to start again.

He wasn't freaking out at all. He was beside himself with joy.

At least he had the decency to drop me off on his way to her place. Small consolation, and I was fuming when he drove away, but he married the woman a year later and they're clearly very happy together. Also, that cat was a pervy menace. I may have lost the guy, and my confidence took a serious hit that day, but now Quentin's wife has to yank his balls while that furry little feline asshole watches. Pretty sure, when all the pros and cons are tallied, I came out ahead on this one.

# Three

My plan to fulfill my mom's prophecy has backfired, adding an extra layer of awkwardness as I set down a lunch order at the corner booth, which happens to be occupied by Quentin Bowers and his beautiful wife whose name I can never remember, though I probably could if I gave it an ounce of effort. Right now, all I can think about is her gorgeous chestnut beachy waves, the way they catch the light and cascade over her slender shoulders. This time yesterday, I had hair down to my ass. It was thick, healthy, and let's face it, probably my greatest asset. Today, it's a travesty.

Last night, in my fit of angst about Eliot and Franny and a seriously crushing heartbreak on the horizon, I chopped my hair short and Franny helped me bleach it blonde. Officially it fits my mom's prophecy. It's a sudden loss, a severing, a transformation. I've also raised enough eyebrows to confirm that it's a surprise. However, I was *not* meant to be a blonde. Especially a blonde with a bad kitchen-shear pixie cut. Also, now that I've slept on the choice, I'm pretty sure I'm not altering any portentous futures by dipping into a bottle of peroxide. I'm simply reinforcing my ex's life choices.

"I almost didn't recognize you," Quentin says as I set down his burger. A logical response, since he spent most of our relationship with a direct view of the top of my head.

"I used to be a brunette," I tell his wife, even though she knows what color my hair was. We might not be besties, but she and Quentin eat here a lot. It's super awesome to see them together, his arm around her shoulders, her head tipped against his chest.

"The blonde looks nice on you," Mrs. Bowers says, a sweet but obvious lie.

I force a friendly smile. "Change is good, right?"

"Yeeeeaaah," Quentin says, in a tone that confirms my suspicions. I am a ridiculous disaster. His wife is perfect. I was never meant to be more than a hookup.

I set down the rest of the order, make the minimum amount of obligatory small talk, and return to the prep area, where Franny's gathering condiments. We're working our Wednesday lunch shift at Ed's Corner Diner. Franny's here full-time but I only do three afternoons a week, alternating with afternoons at the hardware store next door.

"Stop playing with it," she scolds as she catches me patting the back of my neck, seeking length that's no longer there. "You swore you wouldn't hate it."

"I thought I'd look like Gwyneth Paltrow in *Sliding Doors*." I scratch my hairline again, recalling how the character transformed when she chopped off her mousy-brown locks and went blonde. She became bold, confident, more herself than ever. I can't stop scouring Etsy for hats. "Dumb thought, since I've never looked like Gwyneth Paltrow."

"That's probably a good thing," Franny assures me. "She sells mud for vaginas."

I laugh, even though I'm not sure vagina mud is on the Goop menu. I should check, because fake-shopping inane health and beauty products might get my mind off the flaccid hay bale perched atop my head. It's on the yellow side of platinum and the cut has revealed my hidden ability to manifest cowlicks. We also sapped every ounce of moisture from the follicles last night. Franny kept saying the bleach wasn't done yet. I never should've believed her. She does everything in excess, which is charming when it doesn't involve frying my hair. Thank god I handled the scissors myself.

She carries a tray of burgers and fries to a quartet of rowdy teens while I grab a pot of coffee and a menu for a slim, elegantly dressed woman who just sat down at a booth near the back. She removes the cardigan from her twin-set but keeps her giant Sophia Loren sunglasses on, lending her an air of mystique. Then again, maybe she only seems mysterious because I don't recognize her among the regulars and townies. We don't get a lot of unknown faces in here. They stand out.

I cross the diner, which is clean but virtually undecorated, save for a bouquet of noticeably fake flowers stapled to a chunk of un-painted lattice behind the register. Ed told us he got the idea from a home decorating show. I don't watch home decorating shows, but I assume he nailed the concept. Beyond the register, the diner has fourteen tables: eight booths and six two-tops squeezed together on the opposite side of a narrow aisle. Around noon, every table is full and we have a line out the door. It's madness. But by late after-noon, like now, it's an easy gig for a waitstaff of two, plus Ed in the kitchen. When business is especially slow, I get released early, but Ed knows I take care of my mom and I need the cash. Like most of the community, he thinks of my mom as an integral part of life in Pitt's Corner. She adds character, something highly prized in a town best known as a place people drive through on their way to somewhere more interesting.

"Coffee?" I ask as I set the menu on Sophia Loren's table.

"Yes. Thank you." She turns over her mug. It rattles when it hits the saucer. Despite a distinct air of self-assurance, her hands are shaking.

I pretend not to notice as I pour, but I steal a look at her face, or what I can see of her face behind the smoky lenses that practically swallow her. She's petite, with sharp cheekbones and a narrow chin that gives her face a heart-like shape. Her coral lipstick is perfectly applied and matches her recently manicured nails. Her honey-blonde hair is combed into a tidy bun while tiny silver ballet dancers dangle from her earlobes.

I've seen those earrings before, tucked in a gift box, when I was cleaning the Swifts' house. I've seen a photo of this woman, too. It was on the floor by Mr. Swift's desk, as though he'd dropped it and not realized. I slipped it into his drawer, but not before taking a peek. The couple was posing for a selfie in front of a cute alpine lodge, skis in hand. Mr. Swift and Not Mrs. Swift were both smiling, but in a vacant we're-taking-a-photo-so-we-should-probably-look-happy kind of way, which is the only way I ever saw Mr. Swift smile. Like it was an obligation.

Before me, the woman glances at the menu without picking it up.

"What do you recommend?" she asks.

"We do staples better than specials." I turn around to make sure Ed isn't listening from the kitchen, taking my remark as a slur. "Burgers. Pancakes. That kind of thing."

She nods as if considering. "Is there a salad?"

"We have two. The chef salad with meat and cheese, which is only negligibly a salad. Or the Greek, which actually has vegetables besides lettuce."

"The Greek, then." She hands me the menu, her hand still shaking.

I offer her a sympathetic smile before crossing to the service station.

"Who's that?" Franny whispers as she refills a Coke. The teenagers are like sieves with our free refills, but we were, too, not that long ago. "She looks like a movie star."

"Not sure what a movie star would be doing in Oregon's armpit." I feign disinterest while I pass the order slip to Ed. He frowns when he reads it. He only put salads on the menu because his health-conscious husband strong-armed him into it. Ed lives by the three B's: butter, bacon, and bread. Also, if it isn't fried, it barely counts as food.

Franny nudges me with a hip. "What are you not telling me?"

"What do you mean?" I ask, my usual dead giveaway.

"I mean . . ." Franny leans in closer. "Who. Is. She?"

This is how I get suckered into town gossip, by having *no* poker face.

"Let's just say she had a challenging Tuesday."

Franny's eyes widen. "The fatal fling?!"

"Apparently she stayed the night."

I start prepping a new pot of coffee while Franny cranes around me to get a better look at our unfortunate customer. Thankfully, Franny has *some* discretion so her eyes are soon back on the soda machine, where she tops up the umpteenth refill.

"That woman must know everyone here will be talking about her," she says. "If I'd screwed some dude to death, I'd get the hell out of Dodge."

"Maybe she's sticking around for the funeral."

Franny cringes. "Awkward."

I mirror her grimace as I picture the scene: a row of well-starched upper-class women in black designer dresses. Some of the women weep. Others gaze stoically at the coffin. They all put up a good front of not knowing who the others are.

"It's probably for the best that Eliot has no intention of ever returning to Pitt's Corner," I say, still hoping his resolve on the matter hasn't changed. I could kill my mom for this. Without her grebes, her long-held stares, and her "complicated," I would've been elated at the possibility of seeing Eliot again. Now the idea is keeping me up at night.

"He only has two parents," Franny points out unnecessarily.

"Yeah, and they were both awful. He doesn't owe either of them anything."

"I guess not." She sets aside the soda to slump against the counter, tucking a red spiral curl behind her ear before blowing out a sigh. "I texted him to say I was sorry."

"I did, too. Seemed like the right thing to do."

"Yeah, though I probably should've stopped at *I'm sorry*." Franny rolls her eyes through a quiet, self-effacing laugh. "I practically wrote him a novel about how much I miss him and I hope he's surrounded by people who love him and is there anything I can do and on and on *and on*. Total word vomit. What did you say?"

I pull out my phone and show Franny my text.

Imogen: I heard about your dad. I'm so sorry

She shakes her head at me as I lower my phone. "I wish I had your restraint."

"More like intense paralysis about what else to say." Truthfully, that pathetic text took me hours to write. I typed and deleted a billion others first. I couldn't even decide on an emoji. In the end,

I went without. Even a simple heart felt too personal. Now that I know what Franny sent, I feel like I might as well have been a condolences bot.

No wonder Eliot was always closer to Franny. She gushes with light and love. I self-edit to the point of soullessness. But I can't let myself obsess. I doubt he got our messages, and even if he did, he'll have more important things on his mind.

While I restack coffee filters and Franny takes the teens their refills, Ed barks out, "Takeout order up," sliding me a large paper bag with a receipt stapled near the top.

I read the name scribbled on the receipt, muttering a few curses before spinning around to see Parker Kent standing by the register, his construction gear muddied from work, with a hard hat dangling from a loose fist. Ex number fifteen. Why Kym thinks I should date anyone else in this everyone-knows-everyone town is utterly beyond me.

Parker waves as he catches my eye. I wave back, but I don't cross the room with his order. I'm too struck by the glint of gold on his ring finger. I shouldn't care. We only went out for five months and we had *nothing* in common. He was always making me playlists of monotonous trance music he said I should try harder to appreciate, and then quizzing me to make sure I'd *really* listened. He also gave me epic Russian novels he thought I should work harder to like, and he cooked me unnecessarily spicy food I'd expressly said I didn't enjoy, with the aim of helping me "cultivate my palate." For whatever reason, while we were together, I considered these benevolent gestures.

Still . . . *The woman he left me for is now his wife?*

The takeout bag slides from my grip as Franny sweeps past and grabs it.

"I've got this." She sneaks me a wink. "Go ahead and restock silverware."

I mouth *thank you* and make a beeline to the dishwasher, where

I shake off all thoughts of my sordid dating history by checking the cleanliness of every single fork tine.

When I drop off blonde Sophia Loren's salad a few minutes later, I can't help but notice as she slyly tucks a wadded tissue into her purse. I feel like I should offer my sympathies or otherwise acknowledge that I know who she is and that she's hurting, but she might prefer to be left alone, so I simply ask if I can get her anything else.

"Yes, actually." She finally removes her sunglasses, revealing red, puffy eyes. "I was told the girl who cleans the Swifts' house works here. Is that you or should I talk to the other one?" She tips her chin toward Franny, who's over at the prep area, restacking already-stacked napkins in an obvious effort to look like she's not watching us.

"That's me," I say. "Though I assume my services aren't required this week."

"Actually, they are." Sophia sort-of smiles, the same way she did in her skiing photo. It's almost painful in person. "I'm staying in Newport until the funeral. Mrs. Swift arrives Friday evening. The house will be empty until then. Would you mind continuing your routine for one more week? She doesn't need to see . . . to be reminded . . ." She swallows, looks at her salad, looks back at me. "Maybe swing by the house tonight?"

"Of course," I say, sincerely grateful I can do something to help her out.

"Thank you. You're very kind to do this." She reaches into her purse and hands me what I quickly realize is a thick envelope of cash.

I try to hand it back. "You don't need to—"

"Oh, yes," she says. "I think I do."

We share a moment, one in which she knows what I know, and I know she knows what I know, but neither of us needs to come right out and say it. We're just two women who accept that life is sometimes more challenging, or, perhaps, more *complicated* than we want it to be, and at those times, a little bit of cleaning can be a useful step forward.

# Four

The house looks different when I pull up. It's still massive, a late-nineteenth-century collection of dormers, wrapped porches, spindly chimneys, and green tiled roofs. A large turret anchors one corner while ornate balustrades and finials add a level of detail that would seem excessive if they were painted in anything other than a uniform shade of upper-class ivory. An immaculate lawn stretches toward the beach, creating a clear, open space for croquet or badminton, both of which I played—and lost—here years ago. As a kid, this was a house from a fairy tale. As a teen, it felt like a movie set from *The Great Gatsby*. Now, it's the place where Eliot's dad died, leaving two ghosts instead of one.

I enter through the side door, flip on a few lights, and do a quick scan of the ground floor. As expected, Sophia—or whatever her real name is—vacated quickly. The kitchen's a mess, with an array of brunch items left out. An omelet pan is crusted over on a back burner. A loaf of partially sliced bread is going stale on a cutting board. In the living room, newspapers and magazines litter the sofa. Blankets and throw pillows are askew. Men's dress shoes look like they've been kicked off near an armchair. The rest of the floor is similar. Nothing's a disaster. Mr. Swift was about a nine and a half on a ten-point tidiness scale. It's just weird to see signs of life when the actual life is gone.

With a few bracing breaths, I head into the laundry room to gather supplies and put on my sound-canceling headphones. This house is old. The heaters clank and the floorboards creak. High winds can make trees click against the windows. A man just died here. I don't want to start debating whether or not I'm actually alone.

I put on an excessively cheerful playlist and hike up to the fourth floor so I can start my usual bathroom routine, bucket of cleaning supplies in one hand, squeegee mop in the other. Despite the mess in the kitchen, and despite the creepiness of tackling the master bedroom a day after someone died there, cleaning bathrooms is the worst. What's more, this house has nine of them. Thankfully, they don't all get used on each visit. Only two or three usually need scouring, but they all require a quick check.

As I reach the top of the stairs, I notice someone left the lights on in one of the guest suites. Entering the room, I also find the bed's been mussed and a few pieces of clothing have been dropped on the floor. A T-shirt, a bulky fisherman's sweater, and some balled-up socks.

*Fabulous.* Now I not only have to picture Mr. Swift and Sophia having death sex, I have to imagine them christening multiple rooms while they did it. They also left the bathroom lights on. I step inside and—

I stop short, my breath catching.

Someone's using the glass shower stall. It's steamed up, so I can't see much, but the figure inside is tall and fit. Tan. Tattoos. Long dark hair hanging down her back. Sophia was blonde and pale, and staying in Newport for the week, so Mr. Swift must've invited another woman here. A woman who might not realize he won't be making his booty call. I should probably tell her what happened. After she's showered and dressed, of course. God, I hope this isn't the "surprise" from my mom's prophecy. If it is, she did a bang-up job at hiding her sense of humor. She didn't even break a smile.

I turn to flee, hoping mistress number two doesn't notice my gross invasion of her privacy. My bucket catches on the door handle. While attempting to free it, I drop my mop. It clatters to the floor, announcing my presence as clearly as a bugle drone at dawn.

The figure in the shower spins toward me.

"Housekeeping!" I blurt out like a maid at a hotel. "Sorry! So sorry. Leaving now! Like, *right* now." I grab the bucket and mop. Then I scurry out. Fast.

As I barrel down the stairs, I realize I leapt to a hasty conclusion. Maybe the woman in the shower isn't Mr. Swift's mistress. Maybe Mrs. Swift hired her to do the same job I've been assigned, not anticipating her husband's mistress would assume the responsibility. Maybe she's a squatter, or a relative or friend of the family who's been granted permission to use a guest suite, assuming no one else would be by. Whoever she is, hopefully she'll come find me so I can apologize for my intrusion, ensure she knows Mr. Swift won't be making an appearance, and schedule a new cleaning appointment, one when I can arrive without risk of seeing anyone naked.

I set aside my headphones and start cleaning the kitchen, assuming the noise will travel and the woman in the guest suite will eventually wander down. Sure enough, I'm scrubbing grease splatters off the stove when I hear sock-covered feet pad down the main stairs. I look up to see not a woman, but a wiry, weathered guy in a faded gray T-shirt and ripped jeans that accordion at his ankles. His arms are heavily inked. His long dark hair is piled atop his head, wet from the shower and hastily secured with an elastic. His tanned face sports thick-rimmed glasses and a full beard with a few months of growth. It's not a face I know, but it resembles a face I used to know. At least, I think it does.

"Eliot?" I ask.

He squints at me. "Imogen?"

I flick a hand at his head. "You have a man bun. And a beard."

He flicks a hand at my head. "You're blond. Ish."

I blink at him, so stunned he's here, I'm at a total loss about how to proceed.

"You came back," I say, because stating the obvious seems like a better beginning than *I was just thinking about how you might be the great love of my life but I spent years assuming I'd never see you again and I'd never come first to you anyway so I've been serial dating since we finished high school and it's been predictably unfulfilling and I'm sorry your dad just died but I'm also terrified you're coming back into my life to break my heart again unless we can find a way to end my curse and love each other forever?*

"You're cleaning my parents' house," he says, so same, really.

"It's good work if you can get it."

"Didn't you go to art school?"

"Didn't you swear hell would have to freeze over for you to return?"

"Yeah, well, if my dad's there now, it won't stay warm for long." He draws a hand down his beard while he stares at me as though he can't reconcile the woman before him with the girl he used to know. At least that's what I assume he's thinking since that's pretty much what I'm thinking about him. Except for the woman/girl part. Obviously.

"Last time I saw you, you were . . ." I close my mouth, unsure where I was going with this. Pale? Preppy? Indoorsy? Adorably pudgy? Averse to the concept of someone putting a needle in your skin? "Different," I finish. Understatement of the century.

"Last time I saw you, you were crying at a bus station." He steps farther into the kitchen but he halts on the opposite side of the island I'm wiping down. It's weird to not hug him after all this time apart, but I guess the moment's passed.

Of course it's passed. I skipped the hug and started in on his man bun. Because I am slick like that.

"Franny should've taken you that day," I say. "I've always sucked at goodbyes."

He smiles a little, just enough to make him look more familiar, even though he was never much of a smiler. How could he be, growing up in this house with that family?

"I think you did okay," he says. "They were important tears. I didn't mind."

"I soaked your shoulder."

"You gave me something to remember you by."

"And got snot on your shirt."

"Two things to remember you by." His smile inches higher and I feel us easing out of our stilted surprise into something more like the warm friendship we once knew.

*I should really hug him. Why in the hell haven't I hugged him?*

"I thought our goodbye might be forever," I say instead.

"It wasn't meant to be. Not from you. Or from Franny. Just from this place. This town. This horrible house." Eliot looks around as though he's taking in his childhood home, seeking something familiar in the cold, unforgiving surfaces: stainless steel, dark marble, and whitewashed wood, thickly varnished to hide all hint of natural texture.

As he runs a tattooed hand along the edge of the island, I fight a powerful urge to ask why he didn't stay in touch if he didn't intend our goodbye to be forever, but the question feels like an accusation, and I don't want to put more distance between us. A marble island is enough. And eight years of silence. And a secret crush. And a curse.

"So, why did you come back?" I ask instead.

"I was hiking in B.C. when my mom called." He grabs the crusted-over omelet pan and carries it to the sink. "I was only a bus ride away, so she guilted me into coming. Something about duty to the family, which is a funny thing to say to the son she shipped off every chance she got, drilling in a message about independence." He turns on the faucet, finds a scouring pad, and scrubs so hard his knuckles whiten.

I gather dishes and hand them off for him to wash, even though I could halt his efforts and do all the cleaning myself. I'm getting well paid for it. The kitchen also has a high-end dishwasher that would easily fit everything, but Eliot was always calmest with an activity. Sitting still wasn't his style. It isn't my style, either. We suited each other that way. It's weird though. Of all the ways I imagined greeting him if I ever saw him again, cleaning his parents' kitchen together didn't make the list.

"I've seen your channel," I say. "You nailed the independence."

"I found a lifestyle that suits me," he says to the pan in his hands.

"*The Un-lonesome Wanderer.*" I pause my gathering to watch him scrub, and I can't help but notice the squareness of his shoulders as they shift under his thinned-out T-shirt. I used to think of him as round, soft, anti-athletic, easy to sink against. His dad was always trying to get him to play golf and tennis, partly for the exercise, but also for the country club culture. *It's how you get to know other people like us,* he used to say. Eliot was never sure if *people like us* meant rich, white, Republican, or emotionally repressed. Probably all of the above. He never did play golf or tennis. He didn't go to college, either. Instead, he scaled mountains, crossed deserts, trekked hundred-mile pilgrimages, and swam across fjords. It shows. "All those trips. Alone. You really never get lonely?"

"I don't need company," he answers without missing a beat.

"Everyone needs company."

"That's not true. I was never very good with people. You know that."

I don't know that, but I find a dish towel and take the pan from him, still marveling at how we've fallen into this strange task instead of grabbing a drink and heading into the den to catch up. It's been so long. He's been around the world. He has fish and elephants and swirls of smoke inked into his arms. I want to know everything, not through a YouTube channel, but directly from him. I want to tell him how much I've missed him. Mostly, I want to hold him. I want *him* to hold *me*, as though we can erase the distance that's grown between us by pressing our bodies close together, even if only for a moment. Even if I'll never be to him what he was to me.

What he still is to me.

"So, you live in Pitt's Corner?" He frowns at a spatula he's now scrubbing, though I get the sense he's actually frowning at the idea of anyone living here by choice.

"My mom kept getting fired. People tried, but you know what she's like. And she's a lot worse than she used to be. Barely a week goes by without another supposed disaster on the horizon. After enough scary omens, no one could rationalize keeping her on staff. Who wants their pancakes served with a side of impending doom?" I smile in an awkward, it-isn't-really-funny kind of way. Eliot simply nods, never one to mask hard truths with humor. That was always my trademark. "She refused to move into any kind of care facility. She loves her house. I love her. The solution was obvious."

"What about Antony or Lavinia? Why couldn't they help?"

"You know how they feel about the predictions. It's easier to stay away than it is to tune them out. Besides, they both have full-time jobs and families to support." I take the spatula as Eliot moves on to a pair of coffee mugs with birds on them, one with a blue jay, the other, a swallow. The Swifts had a set of twelve, though Eliot snuck me the mug with the finch when we were kids. I still use it to hold my toothbrush. And to remember.

*Two birds with one stone.* Eliot Swift. Imogen Finch. Franny Rockwell.

Eliot pauses, staring at the mug with the little swallow, rubbing a thumb over the wing while water runs down the back of his hand. Maybe he's remembering, too, though as was so often the case, I can't tell how he feels about whatever's on his mind.

"Is Lavinia still in England?" he asks.

"Yep. Living her dream life at Oxford, proving Marlowe was a better playwright than Shakespeare, which means our dad is turning over in his grave."

Eliot shakes off a twitch in his shoulders as he resumes his efforts with the mug.

I silently chastise myself for jumping right in there with *dad* and *grave.*

"And Antony?" he asks, politely breezing over my gaffe.

"In Boston with a husband, two kids, and a corner office at an architectural firm that researches and restores historic properties. He's swamped but happy."

"Swamped but happy," Eliot repeats, more to himself than to me. His eyes stay trained on the mug that's obviously clean by now as he asks, "And you?"

"Semi-swamped. Semi-happy." I hold out my hand for the swallow mug, which Eliot reluctantly relinquishes before moving on to the one with the blue jay. The one he handed me is chipped and the color has faded, making it feel out of place in this kitchen full of shiny surfaces, though the same could be said for Eliot. Or for me.

"Your childhood curse," he says. "Still think you'll never be first at anything?"

"Hard to deny over twenty years of cold, hard evidence." I laugh, but Eliot doesn't laugh with me. Instead, he studies me through his thick-rimmed glasses, which look both resolutely practical and trendily chic, even though nothing about him indicates he cares about fashion. His jeans are threadbare. His T-shirt is one wash away from disintegrating. His hair looks like it hasn't been cut in years. A *lot* of years.

"All this time," he says. "And not one first?"

"Not at anything, not to anyone." I attempt a smile but it fades fast as Eliot continues watching me like he knows damned well I'm trying to make light of something that isn't actually funny. "I know you've never believed in curses or prophecies."

"Maybe not, but I believe in belief. That counts for something."

"People are always saying that, but I'm not so sure." I stow the mug with its mates, tucked away in a cabinet where they won't be seen now that they're flawed. Funny that they're still here at all, with their chipped paint and cracked handles, though the Swifts always valued their collections. Limited-edition ceramic mugs. Cars. Art. High-end décor. Designer clothes. Watches and jewelry. Wine. Anything that told people—without having to *tell* people—how much the couple had achieved in life.

Eliot pivots to face me, blue jay mug still in hand. "So your belief that you don't deserve to be first has absolutely no bearing on your inability to edge past second place?"

"Considering how many years I spent believing I *did* deserve to be first, only to be met with the same results, *no*." My response comes out sharper than I intend.

As patient as ever, Eliot doesn't recoil or get defensive. He simply watches me as his forehead furrows, rumpling in a way that seems etched into his skin, like smile lines for the un-smiley. It's a look I remember well, though the lines are deeper now. The furrows greater in number. He's still beautiful, whether he's eighteen or twenty-eight, pale or sun-darkened, soft or lean, freshly shorn or boasting thick, long hair I can't help but envy, hair that looks a lot like mine did until I destroyed it twenty-four hours ago. His coppery-brown eyes haven't changed. They're sadder, maybe. Tired, distant, wary, something I can't put my finger on, but still just as warm. Just as kind.

"What?" I ask when his silent scrutiny starts to make me twitchy.

"You *know* what." His eyes brighten a little with his open reliance on our familiarity with each other, his implication that a look communicates everything, because our shared history fills in the rest. The implication shrinks the distance between us, until that distance feels less like a decade apart and more like . . . like a momentary step away.

"I've tried," I say. "I've really, *really* tried."

Eliot shifts a shoulder. "Doesn't mean you can't try again."

"How? Why? What would be different? More belief in myself?"

"More belief. Some creative strategizing. A redirection of effort."

"You seriously don't remember?" I ask through another laugh. "All of those contests and races? The endless sports practices and study sessions. The campaigns. The music lessons. The audition preparation. The baking. The all-nighters with my sketch pad or poetry notebook. The pointless nurturing of hope. What's left to 'redirect' to?"

"I don't know." He considers for a moment, brow still furrowed. "Have you ever entered a coloring contest?" His lips twitch and I'm relieved to realize he's joking.

I give him a look while fighting a smile. "I have *not* entered a coloring contest."

"What about worm charming?"

"Please tell me that's not a real thing."

"Wife carrying?"

"I lack the requisite counterpart."

"Bog snorkeling? Cheese wheel chasing? Toe wrestling?"

"Clearly, I don't get out enough." I roll my eyes as yet another laugh sputters out of me. "What's your point? That unless I try *everything*, my curse could still be bullshit? Just a self-perpetuated inferiority complex standing between me and true happiness?"

Eliot blinks at me as the words *true happiness* sit between us, dense and weighty.

"Not *everything*," he says. "Just check under a few unturned stones. I'll check with you." He bumps my hip with his. That bump is all it takes to make a few butterflies take flight in my chest. Well, that and the implication we might hang out beyond tonight.

"Because you want to bog snorkel?" I ask, though I'm not even sure what that is.

"Because I'd love to witness your first big win, and because maybe I can help." He catches the obvious question in my eyes before his gaze drops to the blue jay mug in his hands. "I'll research competitions, cheer you on, keep you company, believe in you even when you don't believe in yourself. It'll be fun. Like old times. Besides, I need something to do while I'm in town, something besides creep around this mausoleum and avoid my mother." We're hip-to-hip again and I have no idea if the contact is an accident, or how to react if it isn't an accident. "What do you say? Should we give it a shot?"

I toy with the towel, still stuck on that thing he said about believing in me.

"'We' being you and me?" I ask. "'It' being an attempt to break my curse?"

"Exactly. Unless you really, *really* don't want to." He leaves me an opening to reply but I don't use it. I'm too busy leaping ahead to yet another collection of failures, though other thoughts also creep in, as the little seed of hope that's always present begins to sprout, needing only the slightest encouragement to bloom. Because what if Eliot's right? What if I simply wasn't good enough to win anything yet? What if I wasn't the right match for any of my exes? What if thirteen ducks only cause an ample supply of green poo to collect on the rocky shoreline? What if—as I've told myself on and off for years with no absolutely irrefutable answers—I have no limitations at all?

When my hesitation turns into a weirdly long silence, Eliot leans closer.

"Don't worry," he says in a wink-wink, nudge-nudge kind of way. "If we enter a coloring contest together, I promise to color outside the lines so I don't beat you."

"Ha-ha." I give him a light flick with the towel. It's a bit flirty, but I can't take it back now. "And when we both lose to a six-year-old who's more deserving of the prize?"

"Then we'll try something else. Maybe not the worm charming, but we'll find a few fun contests." He hands off the blue jay mug for me to dry. "Bet one of the bars in the area has a dartboard or a trivia night. We can organize a foot race or tug-of-war. If Ed's still running that hole-in-the-wall diner, he might host a pancake or pie competition. Whatever." He bumps my hip again, which he seriously has to stop doing, because my butterflies are multiplying. "It only takes one variation to turn *never* into *sometimes*."

"Yeah, but how long are you willing to wait for that *sometimes*?"

"A week, I guess? Or five days." Eliot casts me a quick glance before resuming his cleaning. "I told my mom I'd stick around through Monday so I could accompany her to the reading of the will. I think she assumes she'll look more sympathetic with her kid there, because we both know my dad left her as little as possible, and she's going to fight it."

I stop drying dishes as I watch Eliot scratch at something crusted onto a plate. Despite our talk of silly contests, and despite my preoccupation with curses and crushes, my heart aches for him. This has to be hard. After ten years away, he came back to watch his dad get buried and his mom fight for a house she doesn't even want. *This* house. This cold, creaky, beautiful but home-less home. People thought I was crazy to return to this town, to set aside my big city dreams of becoming a professional illustrator so I could walk dogs and pour coffee while everyone within a ten-mile radius invests in my love life. But at least I came back for a mother who loves and needs me, a community that embraces me, a sense of purpose, and an incontrovertible knowledge that for all of Pitt's Corner's quirks and annoyances, I belong here. Eliot doesn't. He never did.

"What happens after Monday?" I ask, already guessing the answer.

"I go back to B.C. to get my gear. Maybe finish the hike I'd planned. Then I might return to the Kalahari. It's so peaceful there." He finally smiles. *Really* smiles, not a flicker of the lips that indicates a smile is possible, should something ever happen that's worth smiling about. Goddamn, he is *so* beautiful when he smiles. Not because he has perfect white teeth or cute dimples or some other physical attribute that transforms his face, but because happiness suits him. It looks so right on him, I feel it in my gut, a glow, a warmth, a tenacious stirring of another kind of hope, the kind it would be even more foolish to nurture. "You'd love it so much. I can totally picture you sketching the long, low horizons. Red sands at sunset. Trees like knob-knuckled bones. Meerkats."

I swallow a lump that seems to have formed in my throat without warning.

"That sounds nice," I manage before turning away to busy myself by organizing an already-organized cupboard. I'll never go to the Kalahari. We both know it. I have as many reasons to stay as Eliot has to leave. "So, Tuesday morning, you're off?"

Eliot nods as his eyes drift to the window above the sink. The ivory linen curtains are parted. A faint remnant of daylight dusts the immaculate lawn where we used to laugh over lazy croquet games and smack badminton birdies anywhere but where they were supposed to fly. Where he and Franny and I ran laughing toward the private beach to dive under the waves and bolt out again, shrieking from the cold. Where we curled up together in a tethered rowboat and got drunk under the stars, sharing our hopes and dreams with each other. Where I now see only grass and mist.

What Eliot sees, I can't be sure.

"The longer I stay," he says, "the more I'll unearth resentments I thought I'd left behind. This house is like a trigger factory. If my mom does get it in the will, maybe I can convince her to burn the damned thing down." His eyes skim across the ceiling and I wonder if he's imagining it covered in flames. "I almost got a hotel room but the idea felt ridiculous when all of these bedrooms are empty. It's only a bed. Four walls. A shower. If I don't give any of it more meaning than that, it's fine." He scratches at the plate again until it comes clean. "But I can't stay here, Imogen. I can't *stay* anywhere."

I nod, and then I keep nodding, as if pretending to understand will make me actually understand, but I find the task impossible. I need a home where I can put down roots. I need people who love me and places where I know precisely how the pancakes will taste or which beer to avoid. I need the familiar sound of a dozen wind chimes all playing their own melodies. The smell of salt in the air. The whisper of wind in the reeds that poke through the dunes like thick strands of hair. I need to not be a stranger among strangers. I need to be needed. Eliot needs the opposite. Which means . . .

"So, we have five days to break my curse?" I ask.

He hands me the plate. I let it drip without drying it. He notices.

"I bet we can do it in four."

I smile at that, though my smile is forced, and I can tell by the steadiness of Eliot's gaze that he knows. I'm in no rush to cross off tasks and send him on his way again. Now that he's here, the last thing I want to do is accelerate our next goodbye.

We clean the rest of the kitchen while brainstorming games and contests we can enter. He finishes the dishes and I scour the countertops until everything shines. I also do a sweep of the house and return with a half-empty champagne bottle and a pair of crystal flutes I find in the master bedroom. Eliot raises a brow but he doesn't say anything. He simply pours out the remaining liquid and washes the flutes.

When we're down to the last few pieces of silverware, I stand beside him, utensil drawer open, towel in hand. I take in his sun-kissed skin, the art he carries on his body, the dark hair that's trying to form waves as it dries, the clothes that look like they've been around the world with him, laundered and repaired on repeat. I think about the boy I knew and the man I'd like to know, even if I only get to know him for five days.

"Eliot?" I wait until he looks up from the fork he's scrubbing. "For the record, you were good with some people."

A ghost of a smile plays with his lips, causing a rush of longing to flow through me, pure, intense, familiar, but also not, like an echo of a feeling I experienced long ago.

Several seconds pass before he rinses the fork and hands it off.

Then he reaches for another.

# HEARTBREAK #6

I noticed Orion Jones the moment he slid onto the stool next to mine in life drawing class during my fourth and final year of art school. I'd seen him around campus over the past few years, but we didn't talk often, and I hadn't sat by him in classes. He was tall and a little bit gangly, with long fingers and a wicked smile, one he was swift to shine my way.

"Ready for three hours of naked time?" he asked.

I choked out a laugh. "Excuse me?"

He nudged his chin toward the dais at the center of the room, where a voluptuous woman in a terry cloth bathrobe was trying out poses with a bamboo pole.

"Right. Yeah. Ready." My entire body flushed as I fumbled with my charcoal.

Thankfully, Orion seemed charmed by light embarrassment. So charmed, we kept sneaking glances at each other throughout the class period, glances that grew more heated as I watched him finesse the shadows under his sketch's breasts or as he watched me correct the shape of a roughly drawn inner thigh with the side of my thumb.

We were drawing, sure, and studying the figure, but we were also engaging in some intensely hot foreplay.

This became a pattern. For the next few weeks, we took the same seats, each of us with a view of the other's sketch pad. He'd work on the curve of a buttock until he was certain I was watching. I'd do the same with the highlight and shadow of a nipple. His breathing would grow more rapid. I'd pat sweat off my brow and neck. And the glances between us? They were long. They were loaded. They could burn down the building.

At around week four or five, when class let out, we both stayed behind. I thought we were about to verbally acknowledge our flirtation, but the instant we were alone, his hands were on my body, and mine were on his. He pressed me up against a wall of art cubbies. Charcoal got everywhere. Blackened fingerprints on necks, cheeks, arms, waists. I'd never taken words like *scorching* seriously, but goddamn if Orion's kisses didn't light something inside me on fire, and soon enough I was popping the button on his jeans.

"Wait." He set his hands on mine, pulling back far enough to meet my eyes.

"What's wrong?" I glanced around, worried someone had entered the studio.

"I like you, and I like *this*." He snuck in a quick but intense kiss. "But I think sex should mean something. We don't need to move so fast. We should go on a date. Get to know each other. Let this be more than a quick bang in the studio."

I melted at that, even while a voice in the back of my head warned me to be careful. A "quick bang in the studio" had a known termination. There was safety in that.

"Okay," I said. "Let's get to know each other."

For several weeks, Orion and I dated. We went out to dinner

and gallery shows. We drew each other's portraits. We watched Bob
Ross on YouTube while spooning on Orion's sofa, both of us tipsy
from cheap wine. He met some of my friends. I met some of his.
We kissed *a lot*, but every time we progressed beyond kissing, Orion
stopped us.

"Let's make it last," he'd say, or something to that effect.

I told myself he was being romantic. He wanted to make sure I
didn't feel like I was only a hookup. Whatever we were building *was*
going to mean something.

Late one night, as I ran into the drawing studio to grab the pencil
case I'd left behind during class, I found Orion lying on the model's
dais, with the model. They were naked, entwined around each other,
and fast asleep. Several empty beer bottles littered the floor beside
them, along with at least three used condoms.

Orion texted me the next day to tell me he'd met someone else,
someone he felt more "chemistry" with. I didn't respond. We didn't
need to get into it. I dropped the life drawing class though. I also
texted Eliot, not to bitch about Orion, but because I was desperate
to connect with someone I knew would always be honest with me.

Eliot didn't reply.

# Five

*E*liot Swift!" Franny flings her arms around his neck without restraint, right in the middle of the lunch rush at the diner. When she's practically hugged the life out of him—because that is how you're supposed to greet a long-lost friend when he shows up back in your hometown—she gives him a big, loud kiss on his cheek before pulling back to assess him at arm's length. "Oh my god! You have more hair than I do!"

He flicks at his bulky topknot while she examines it from all angles.

"I should get it cut," he says. "It's not really a choice. Just laziness."

Franny pivots her grin from him to me, where I stand a few feet away, finding a small pocket of space between the packed tables. I'm not working here today. I'm on a short break between dog walking and my shift at the hardware store, but Eliot timed his visit to the diner so I could catch his reunion with Franny.

"I told you he'd come back," she says to me, still grinning.

Eliot turns around to face me. "Did you place bets?"

I shake my head. "I took you at your word. That's all."

"Your mom didn't have anything to say about it?" Eliot gives me one of his almost-smiles, as cynical about prophecies as ever, though he's as curious as anyone.

"My mom mentioned a sudden loss." I keep my voice low, though with Lyle Lee and the Front Porch Gossip Gang at the nearest table, my mom's latest prediction will be all over town by day's end. "She also mentioned a transformation. And a surprise."

Franny takes Eliot's face between both hands, gazing at him with open wonder.

"No kidding about the transformation." She flashes him another grin, glowing without reservation in a way I've always envied but never been able to emulate. "Look at you, Swiftie. You got all rugged on us." She squeezes his shoulders and lets her hands trail down to his forearms, making me rue, yet again, the weird distance I kept from him last night, handing off silverware instead of drawing him close. "Travel suits you. I don't know if it's mountain air or eating bugs or whatever but you're fucking gorgeous."

Eliot shuffles and shrugs and looks altogether uncomfortable, not so much with Franny's enthusiasm. He had to expect that. But everyone is looking at him now, ready to judge the prodigal son returned, and to make him the hot topic of their conversations. He left town as a privileged trust fund kid, wearing khakis and Top-Siders, with most people predicting he wouldn't last a month without his parents' bank account. He returned as a scruffy nomad in busted-up jeans, completely self-reliant. Of course people will talk.

"Imogen told me you came back to raise your goddaughter," he says to Franny. "I'm sorry about your sister and her husband. I should've checked in more often."

Franny takes a deep breath and lets it go. Six years have passed, and she's too cheerful by nature to dwell, but the grief is there, tucked in the margins of her smiles.

"Who would've guessed I'd be raising a kid?" She laughs before shooting me a wry purse of her lips. "Don't answer that. I know your mom saw the plane crash."

She did see it, though she didn't tell anyone until the news broke. She just shuffled around the house while tapping her lips and muttering, *That poor, poor girl.*

For the next few minutes, Franny and Eliot exchange a rapid-fire catch-up. She tells him about Anika, her brilliant but boundary-pushing fifteen-year-old goddaughter. He rattles off highlights about recent travels to Samoa, Ethiopia, and the Outer Hebrides. The two of them fall into their old camaraderie, totally lacking the stilted pauses and uncertainty that colored my time with Eliot last night.

They've always been like this: comfortable, uninhibited, the best of friends. Franny's also beautiful, with great curves and a thick mass of copper corkscrew curls that prevents her from ever having a bad hair day. As I watch the two of them together—laughing, touching, coming alive at the sight of each other—my excitement about this reunion dims. I don't think Franny has been pining for Eliot for the past ten years, not in the way I have, anyway, yet I can't help but sense we're about to repeat history.

"We *have* to go out tonight," she gushes to Eliot, her hands now linked in his.

"As long as we fit in a game or contest." He sneaks me another almost-smile.

I try to return it, but his attention's already on Franny again.

"I want to hear *everything*," she says. "Fave places and what's left on your bucket list and are you vegan and hyper-healthy now or can you still down a pint of B&J faster than either of us and didn't I read somewhere that you're running marathons and are you, like, a monk or a pilgrim or whatever or do you leave a girl behind everywhere you go?"

Eliot chuckles and I try not to look too interested in this last piece of information. I try not to look too interested in Franny's interest in the information, either.

"Fave place," he says. "Too many to name just one. Bucket list, same. Also, definitely not vegan. I eat pretty much anything, and if you bring the pint, I'll bring the spoons. Marathons, yes." He pulls up his shirt hems to reveal a *26.2* in thick black ink right above his hipbone. His very smooth, very traceable hipbone, which falls out of view as his shirt drops into place. "Six so far and hoping to do the Great Wall next May. As far as monkhood . . ." He scrubs at the back of his neck while his eyes sweep across the faces of the lunch crowd. "Let's just say I'm not celibate and leave the topic there."

"Oh, hell no." Franny laughs. "You have stories and we want to hear them."

Ed hollers from the kitchen for Franny to stop gabbing and come grab her damned orders before his damned customers leave without their damned food. For a skinny guy in his seventies, his voice carries, even if he fakes his cantankerousness for humor's sake.

"I should let you get back to work," I tell Franny. "Eliot also needs to eat and my shift is about to start at the hardware store, but we'll all catch up tonight, right?"

"O'Malley's at eight?" Franny collects nods from Eliot and me as she stacks dirty dishes from a nearby two-top on her forearm. "Can you believe the old place is still in business?" she asks Eliot. "Dan took it over from his dad. They have a shitty dartboard and a shitty pool table, but we can also bring cards or something. And the first round's on me, unless Imogen uses her sexy wiles to get us free beers."

Eliot's brows inch up as he gives me an *oh, really* look that makes me squirm. I'm not sure if I'm squirming in a good way or a bad way but I definitely can't stand still.

"I don't have sexy wiles," I say.

"Bullshit." Franny slides me a playful smirk before clearing the rest of the table and motioning for Eliot to take a seat. "Our dear friend here has a thing going with the bartender. It's the slowest burn of the century but they'll consummate it at some point."

Eliot resumes the *oh, really* look while I continue scooching toward the door at a glacial pace, hemmed in by diners, tables, and a reluctance to break eye contact.

"I ran into Kym Green on my way over," he says. "She updated me on half the town but she made a special point of ensuring I knew you just went through a breakup. She didn't mention the bartender. Maybe she got her stories confused?"

"More like selective recall with a heavy dose of meddling." I make a mental note to have a strong word with Kym before I touch another sprig of baby's breath. Whether she connected the dots or took a stab in the dark, with Eliot in town for a few more days, she'll suss out the full details of my secret high school crush soon enough. "I should . . . hardware, hammers, work, single, whatever." I point over my shoulder at the door.

Eliot smiles a little more broadly this time, making the skin crease beside his eyes. For a few heart-fluttering seconds, I feel like we might be sharing a moment, but he cuts off eye contact as Franny offers him coffee and a laminated menu.

He doesn't look up again.

❦

"It's better." My mom lowers the scissors and hands me a mirror.

I take a look, turning my head side to side. I bought a cheap box of hair dye on the way home and my mom trimmed away my choppy, uneven ends. One of her many jobs over the years was working in a salon. She was good, and she enjoyed the work, but she kept telling clients things like, *I'm so sorry about your sister* or *That man didn't deserve you anyway*, things the clients didn't understand until truths unfolded hours or sometimes days later. The salon owner couldn't keep her on.

Thankfully, my mom's still a skilled stylist, making my multitude of cowlicks look less like an unfortunate accident while the renewed lack of platinum prevents me from flinching at my reflection. The box said *French Roast* but really, it's just brown.

"You know my prophecies don't work like this," my mom tells me.

"I know." I lower the mirror and brush off the back of my neck. "I panicked."

"You thought I'd seen *your* loss? *Your* transformation?"

"I thought a lot of things, all at once." I take another look at my hair, frowning while I attempt to finger-comb the front into a more deliberate-looking disarray. I aim for Sexy Bedhead but settle for Recent Nap. "You saw his return, didn't you?"

"I did." She sets a hand on my shoulder. "I saw his departure, too."

"Tuesday morning, apparently. The wanderlust is strong in that one." I chuckle as though I've made a grand pronouncement like a stoic mentor in a superhero movie.

My mom squeezes my shoulder without breaking a smile. In that squeeze, and in the worry I see in her eyes as I crane my head around, I realize she knows.

"I never told you," I say.

"You didn't have to."

"You saw signs?"

She shakes her head. "I watched you grow up together. I didn't need signs to know how you felt." She releases my shoulder and reaches for her scissors. "I also sat with you on prom night, and I witnessed the tears you shed after he left town, the hopeful message checking and refreshing of emails. I watched you struggle for years about how often to reach out and when to accept that it was time to stop trying."

"Well, I did stop trying. And for good reason." I get up and find a broom while my mom packs away her haircutting kit. As we tidy, I try to shake off her mention of prom. It was one stupid night, and yet, it was the night that brought everything into focus, the night I confirmed that if my curse was real—and, frankly, even if it wasn't—my biggest challenge in life wouldn't be a lack of titles or trophies.

I continue sweeping, but before long, I notice my mom has gone still. Her tools are packed up and she's watching me with a familiar look on her face, a look that says she's holding something back, something she's not sure I want to hear.

"You're worried I'll get attached again," I say.

"I didn't say that."

"Only to watch him to fall for Franny. Or some other woman."

"I didn't say that, either. Only that things will be complicated."

I swallow a swell of exasperation. It's that word again.

*Complicated.*

"But you know he'll leave," I say.

"Yes."

"And I'll stay."

"Yes."

"So getting attached would be pointless."

My mom watches me sweep as she stands nearby in umpteen layers of clothing, with her graying hair and her every-color eyes, part seer, part ragpicker, all mom.

"Under what circumstances have you seen attachment be pointless?" she asks.

I open my mouth to say *my relationship with Greg, for one*, but it isn't true. I wasn't unhappy in that relationship, even if it ended on a sour note. The same could be said for all of my romantic relationships. Those attachments kept me from feeling like I was floating through the world with my part-time jobs and my trunked career ambitions, unsure what to anchor my choices to. They gave me a *before* and *after* without everything feeling like it was only in the *now*. A history we built together. Anticipation. Inside jokes. Overlapping tastes. Connective tissue that tied one life event to the next. A sense—even if it was a delusional one—that I mattered to someone outside of my own tiny existence.

People *need* people. The only person I know who believes otherwise is Eliot.

Or at least, he says he believes otherwise.

"Maybe my attachments aren't pointless," I concede. "But Eliot's not like me."

"People look for things in different ways. Doesn't mean they're not looking."

"Or that they're looking for the same things." My grip tightens on the broom handle as I finish sweeping. I know my mom's trying to be helpful, and Eliot probably is looking for *something* as he travels the world, but he has as much right to not want a relationship or a home or a connection to other people, as I do to crave those things.

My mom flips the hand mirror faceup before setting it facedown again. It's a quick gesture, the simple occupation of a restless hand, though where my mom is concerned, nothing is simple. And mirrors don't always show us what we want to see.

"Your father laughed when I told him on our first date that we'd have a family together one day," she says. "Partly because I'd made a prediction about something I couldn't possibly know, but more because he had always wanted a quiet, orderly life, with his books lined up *just so* on his shelves, and weeks on end spent with only the open sea for company. Years later, he loved this house as much as the rest of us did, with the chaos of three active children and your half-finished art and science projects taking up shelf space that used to hold his library. Plus a busy kitchen, an open invite for friends to visit, and six or seven dogs circling our ankles at any given time." She grips a chair back with a bony hand, glancing around as though she pictures every seat occupied by someone she loves. "He stopped laughing off my predictions, too."

"I know." I toss the hair clippings and put away the broom and dustpan, flooded with nostalgia. My dad was endlessly patient with my mom's prophecies, even as they grew more frequent and catastrophic. "But what does all of that have to do with Eliot?"

"People change, Imogen. And in ways they can't always anticipate."

I almost laugh but I stop myself in time, softening a guffaw into a wry smile.

"Please don't tell me you think *I'm* supposed to change Eliot," I say.

"No one can change anyone if they don't want to change themselves."

"He gave me no indication that he wants to change."

My mom shrugs a little. "Maybe he doesn't know what he wants."

I battle another swell of exasperation. "But you *do* know?"

She doesn't answer right away. Instead, she lets her gaze drift to the glass doors that face toward the ugly green apartment building, beyond which lies the ocean.

"It's the grebes," she says, because of course she does, and this is why Antony is in Boston and Lavinia is in Oxford and I'm left trying to sort out whether our mom is a witch or if her ramblings are so hard to parse, she simply *seems* to know things.

"Eliot was pretty definitive last night," I say. "He has more solo travel plans. He speaks of other places in ways he never used to talk about Pitt's Corner. Color, texture, and an open sense of awe. He also has something like four million followers awaiting his next video, people who revere him as an iconoclast. That's a big obligation."

My mom gives me another of her quick shrugs. They're little more than a flinch or a shudder, but they deliver a clear *I know otherwise* message.

I try to brush off that message as I finish tidying, make my mom tea, and get ready to head out for the evening. The last thing I want to do is try to change someone who's happy with himself as he is.

Actually, that's not true. The last thing I want to do is try to change someone who's happy with himself as he is *and* get heartbroken in the process.

Eliot's only in town for a few days. Despite my panic on the beach on Tuesday, and despite some unavoidable anxiety about another looming separation, I'm not a hormonal teenager anymore. I'm a rational adult. I can enjoy Eliot's company. We'll have fun with a few games and contests I won't win. He and Franny and I will wander down memory lane. Maybe the two of them will repeat prom night while I hang out with my mom on our rotting sofa again. Maybe I'll learn what the hell bog snorkeling is.

Whatever happens, next Tuesday, I'll let Eliot go.

With a little caution, maybe I can even manage it without sobbing this time.

# Six

I slide onto a stool at the end of the bar, facing the entryway. Since it's Thursday, O'Malley's is only at half capacity, but I might as well keep a lookout. Besides, this is the best seat for watching Dutch pull beers, with an unobstructed side view of his rippling forearms. Am I objectifying him? Absolutely. But they are some seriously nice forearms.

Unsurprisingly, I arrived before my friends. Franny's always late. Eliot used to be the most punctual of the three of us, but he's operating on Rockwell time tonight. They're coming together, of course. I had to check on my mom after work, while Franny was free to pick him up anytime, maybe even take him to dinner before heading here. Despite some unavoidable envy, I'm glad they're coming together. Eliot was never comfortable in social settings, especially ones where he barely knew anyone. We're all so different. I sometimes used to wonder if we only became friends because we grew up together. If we'd met when we were in high school or as adults, we might not have talked at all.

I make a quick scan of the familiar faces and familiar scenery. In a bigger town, O'Malley's would probably be the bar no one went to. Its décor, menu selections, and general ambiance are almost aggressively uninteresting. The place isn't gritty enough to be a dive or stylish enough to be anything other than ordinary. A country song twangs at low volume through a quartet of dusty speakers while a row of neon signs advertises local microbrews against dark navy walls. By Oregon standards, Pitt's Corner has very few beer snobs, but I appreciate having options besides Miller and Bud Light.

Halfway down the bar, Dutch is serving Carl Prendergast and Jaime Marquez what looks like whiskey on the rocks—the usual for Pitt's Corner's friendly real estate rivals—but he soon catches my eye. He flinches, and my hand instinctively rises to pat down my hair.

"Look at you." He saunters over, a blindingly handsome grin stretching across his face. I love that he saunters. I bet he'd be totally at home on a ranch teeming with wild horses. His thick blond waves would flutter in a dusky, sunset breeze while he straddled a stallion in jeans that should be illegal to fit so well. His strong hands would grip the reins while his powerful thighs would press against . . .

Okay. Maybe Vera was right about getting laid. And maybe sleeping with Dutch would help me shake off my irritating preoccupation with Eliot. Dutch and I might not have a long-term future, but we'd probably make it more than five days together.

"New day, new look?" he asks.

"Something like that." I continue patting my shorn head. "It's too short."

"What? No way! It's sexy," he counters, embodying the word as he speaks it, with his low rumbly voice and long-held eye contact. "Is the color different, too?"

"I bleached it. Then I tried to dye it back. Badly."

"Not badly at all. It's cool. Arty." He reaches out to graze his fingers over a cowlick by my temple, and my heart rate kicks up a notch. He is stupidly hot. I am stupidly human. "That was quite a night on Monday. You make it home okay?"

"One of the key advantages of living in a town this size is the ability to stumble to pretty much any local destination without the need of a car."

"Any local destination, huh?" His smile tips on one side, his implication clear.

"Like my mother's house," I admonish, though without bite.

"Oh, *that* destination." He nods as though he's letting a profound revelation sink in. "You sure you weren't suggesting a stumble back to a certain beachside bungalow? Warm lighting. High-quality sheets. Breakfast in bed. No checkout time."

Damn, that sounds appealing, and I'm tempted to tell him I'll take him up on the offer now that I'm not wasted and I can take full responsibility for my choices. But something stops me short. Maybe the knowledge that Eliot's about to walk in the door. Or maybe the feeling that I'm not ready to be another guy's second-best option. I really like O'Malley's. I don't want to start drinking in my mom's basement. Not yet, anyway.

"Yeah, I'm sure," I say, though my reluctance to say it is clear.

Dutch flashes me another devastating grin and I'm forced to doubt my sanity.

"You're a hard sell, Finch."

"I have high standards."

"That so?" He narrows his pretty blue eyes at me, like he knows I'm aware they're pretty. He walks a line between confidence and smugness but he never crosses it, which is why flirting with him is so much fun. "You know I knew Greg, right?"

"Of course. Your point?"

"That I question your definition of high standards."

I shoot him a scowl, unsure why everyone in town is suddenly so anti-Greg—or if they were always anti-Greg and I'm only noticing now—but Dutch waggles his brows in a cute but ridiculous way, turning my scowl into a sputter of laughter.

"Game, set, and match," I tell him.

He laughs with me as he grabs a pint glass and deftly flips it upright.

"Consolation drink?" he asks. "It's on the house."

Franny's words from earlier ring in my ears. *Sexy wiles* still feels like a stretch, but I do get a lot of free drinks here, even when I haven't taken the time to put on makeup or pick out my most flattering tank top and my favorite pair of boyfriend jeans, ones that have been softened through countless washes and ride low on my hips. Thank god the skinny jean trend is finally over. I feel sexiest when I'm comfortable. Not when my body has been squeezed into fabric that wasn't designed to stretch.

"I'm not really feeling the beer tonight," I say, Tuesday's hangover too fresh.

"Whiskey?" Dutch nods toward Carl and Jaime. They're immersed in a heated conversation about a big client they're competing to represent. Since Pitt's Corner is hardly a real estate hot bed, I assume they mean an out-of-town client, but then I catch the words *widow* and *Harrow Drive*. They're talking about the Swifts' house, which means Eliot's mom is already planning the sale before she even knows if the house is hers. Poor Eliot. No wonder he wants to get out of town as fast as possible.

"I'm not feeling the whiskey, either." My gaze snags on a dewy martini shaker. I don't usually order cocktails, but as I consider my mom's wisdom about change, I decide it's time to try something new. "How about something muddled?"

"You got it." Dutch grabs a handful of berries from a mini-fridge. I watch his forearms flex while he mashes fruit against the side of a glass. They look good, as always, but as he gathers ingredients and deftly mixes them into something I already know I'll enjoy, I start to wonder if I've been objectifying him deliberately, determined to label him *Fantasy Only* and put him on a shelf I can't reach. Maybe he's more than a fantasy. And maybe my drink order isn't the only thing I should shake up.

Dutch keeps me company for a while, but eventually he needs to attend to other customers. I'm halfway through my mint-berry-gin-something-something-something when Franny and Eliot bustle in, holding open the door long enough to let in a burst of brisk October air. She spots me right away and I wave her over. The stools to my left are both open. I silently will Eliot to take the one closest to me, but Franny plops onto it, slapping a pack of cards onto the bar and rambling breathless apologies about being late because Anika had homework questions and then the fire alarm dead battery noise went off but Franny didn't have any extra batteries and then she couldn't find the cards and when she finally *did* find the cards, she forgot how far the drive was out to Eliot's house.

He stiffens as she says this last bit. When we were kids, he asked us not to call it his house, but to only refer to it as his parents' house. I don't expect Franny to remember that after all these years, but I get why he still hates the association.

When she finally stops for air and flags down Dutch, I catch Eliot's eye.

"How was your first day back in Pitt's Corner?" I ask.

He shrugs as he shuffles off a worn canvas jacket and drapes it over his stool. He's wearing jeans, a dingy crewneck undershirt, and a faded henley that looks like it used to be bright blue but is now only a shade off slate or stone, a color that fits right in to our seaside town.

"I'm surprised how many people remember me," he says. "I

couldn't make it a block without someone offering condolences or asking about something they'd seen on my channel or commenting on my appearance. I feel like the daily special."

"You undersell yourself," I say. "You're at least the *weekly* special."

He tips up his chin and almost smiles, a trademark Eliot Swift move, and one that slays me every time. Dutch's smile may be more conventionally handsome, but Eliot's is harder to earn.

Apparently, I prefer to work for it.

Dutch comes over to take orders. Franny gets a beer but Eliot eyes my glass and says he'll have whatever I'm having. I tell him it's muddled. He says it sounds perfect.

The drinks soon arrive and the three of us play blackjack while settling into an easy conversation, though it's probably only easy because Franny's in the middle, chatting amiably and asking Eliot about his travels and his YouTube channel and how he finds the various local jobs he takes so he can afford to keep traveling and what it's like to stargaze from a mountaintop or ride out a sandstorm in a patched-up tent.

Story by story, he fills in the blanks on how a bus ticket out of Pitt's Corner with no plan beyond getting as far away as possible led to his grabbing the first international flight he could book out of Portland. He ended up in Copenhagen, where he got a job scraping barnacles off boat hulls. There, he met a group of hikers with room for one more in their minivan. While he liked the people he started traveling with, he quickly realized he was happiest following his own route, in his own time. He also realized he enjoyed making a video journal, one people he met along his route kept asking him to share. So, he set off with a backpack, a camera-phone, and a YouTube link. A year or so later, one of his videos went viral through a random celebrity mention, and the channel took off.

I hang on every word while marveling that Eliot is the same guy who used to fake a limp or an allergy attack to get out of gym class. I also lose every hand of blackjack.

Every. Single. Hand.

When Eliot begs for a break as the evening's storyteller, Franny and I fill him in on a few of Pitt's Corner happenings, all of which sound preposterously trivial in light of his worldly travels, but they're our happenings, so they hold a place in my heart. Jim Kettering renovated the shabby little single-screen movie theater, where people now show up on a Friday or Saturday night at 7 p.m. and vote on what Netflix show to watch together. Patty and Veejay Chowdhury won a statewide zucchini growing contest last year. Olive Curtis snagged her eighth husband after number seven left her for a twenty-two-year-old gymnast. We sound like a town in a cozy murder mystery, though the cozy version of our town would be called something picturesque like Oar's Landing or Gull's Cove. We'd also have fewer potholes and a much lower unemployment rate.

Midway through our second round of drinks, Franny excuses herself to take a call from Anika, who's panicking about something to do with a cute girl she likes. As soon as Franny steps out, Eliot slides onto her stool and taps my knee with his. I return his tap. He taps back. I do, too, and before I know it, we're both biting down smiles and shyly exchanging glances that suggest we're reliving the same memories. We used to do this a lot, lying side by side in the tethered rowboat or on a picnic blanket, each of us immersed in a book, until one would alert the other with a soft tap-tap of a knee. The other would tap back, as though we were speaking in Morse code. We didn't know any code at all, though somehow, we always sensed each other's meaning. *Are you awake? How's the book? Want to head in?* Or my favorite, *Just making sure you're there.*

"What?" he asks, causing me to realize I'm shaking my head.

"I still can't believe you're here," I say.

"I can't believe *you're* here." He digs in his pockets and sets a pile of change on the bar, flipping a coin into a shot glass and indicating it's my turn to do the same. "I thought you'd be in L.A. or New York, or that once you made a name for yourself, you'd buy a picturesque artist's cottage in New England. Vermont, maybe. Someplace green with covered bridges and with lazy cows you made into kids' book characters."

I warm at the thought, and also sadden. He thinks of me as I was. Not as I am.

"My mom got her foreclosure notice right as I finished my degree in L.A." I flip my coin toward the shot glass and miss. Of course. "I was single and unemployed with no immediate career prospects. I'd applied for several internships and assistant positions, interviewed at galleries, attended networking events, but nothing had come through yet, and I already sensed that I didn't want to stay in L.A. or move to New York, places that promise their residents the comfort of anonymity and deliver tenfold. Turns out, for all of my complaints about Pitt's Corner, I don't actually like disappearing into a crowd. I hadn't thought about New England. Shortsighted of me, now that you mention the cows." I smile again. Eliot doesn't smile again, but his brows twitch and his chin tips up so I know I've amused him a little. He also flips a dime into the shot glass without really trying. I flip a nickel—trying my hardest—and it rolls off the bar onto the floor.

Eliot lines up a third coin. "Then you really didn't mind coming back?"

"Career-wise, it was an adjustment." I picture my closet full of art supplies and half-finished projects. Some days they haunt me. Other days they feel like they belong to someone else entirely. "But honestly? It was nice to be home. And to be needed."

Eliot nods in understanding, though I get the feeling he's just being polite.

"Are you still drawing, at least?" His coin misses the glass, probably on purpose.

"Not really. I'm pretty busy most days."

"Cleaning houses?"

"And walking dogs, arranging flowers, serving burgers, selling screws, delivering pizza, impulse-ruining my hair, and making sure my mom's taken care of."

Eliot nods again, taking in the information. "And you're happy with that?"

"Semi-happy," I remind him, referencing last night's conversation. "It's funny how as kids we're so often told to follow our dreams. We draw pictures and write essays about who we want to be. Artists. Politicians. Athletes. Inventors. Movie stars. The great leaders of tomorrow. As we grow up, life throws us problems to solve, so we start solving them, and before we know it, we're too busy trying to pay the heating bill or ensuring our mom doesn't fall out of a tree to pause and think about our dreams, let alone to chase them." I flip my coin and surprise us both by making it into the glass, putting our score at two to one. "Do I miss making art? Absolutely, but only when I stop to breathe long enough to remember why I pursued it in the first place."

Eliot fumbles with his fourth coin. It hits the rim of the glass but bounces out. I take ages to line up my fourth coin, determined to even the score, at least temporarily. Sadly, my shot is way off and lands in a dish of cocktail olives. I pluck it out before Dutch notices, laughing off my incompetence at even the simplest competition.

As usual, Eliot doesn't laugh with me. Instead, he watches me with a characteristic air of thoughtful gravity, grazing his knuckles over his bearded jawline.

"It's only a game," I tell him. "I didn't expect to break my curse with quarters."

"It's not the game. Or the curse. It's what you said about no longer chasing a dream." He lowers his hand, but his eyes stay locked on mine, steady and serious. "Back in high school, you were so ambitious, with a million projects going. The graphic novel series you started with all the magic doors. The retro punk tarot deck you were designing. The long list of picture book proposals. What happened to all those ideas?"

I feel a sigh coming on but I smother it by finishing my drink. As I set down my glass, Eliot tap-tap-taps my knee again. It's sweet and I sense that his inquiry is coming from a place of care, even though it feels like criticism I don't want to hear right now.

"Priorities change," I tell him. "And Pitt's Corner isn't exactly the cultural mecca of the West Coast, or an economic boomtown. A lot of people are out of work. I'm lucky I can cobble together an income." I flick at the frayed edges of a hole in his jeans, revealing an inch of tattooed thigh. "We can't all be YouTube stars."

"I don't care about being a YouTube star." Eliot smooths his frayed threads, letting his fingertips rest in the spot mine vacated, set against skin I *almost* touched.

"How can you not care?" I ask. "*Millions* of people follow you."

He shifts in his seat as though my comment has made him uncomfortable.

"I don't track numbers or read comments," he says. "I just like making a public record of where I've been. If I pull a Chris McCandless, I've left something behind."

His words land like a punch to the chest. I don't know how we got from knee-tapping and silly games to my aborted career and his potential death, but Eliot has never shied away from grave topics, so here we are.

Rather than respond, I flag down Dutch for another drink. He nods in understanding before using a series of silent gestures to confirm that Eliot wants another drink, too. Dutch is a skilled bartender. He's observant, good at multitasking, easy to talk to. He's also staying in Pitt's Corner. Words I should brand on my brain.

As he starts mixing our drinks halfway down the bar, my gaze drifts to his forearms, like usual, but I can't seem to keep it there. It sneaks back to Eliot's weathered hands as they rotate his empty glass. His cuticles are ragged. The knuckles on his left hand are scabbed over. A whitened scar crosses his wrist bone. Another wraps his thumb. A black ink tendril curves over the back of his right hand and loops his index finger, the end of a tentacled octopus arm I saw snake down his entire forearm when he was in short sleeves last night.

Eliot notices my staring and swivels to face me, leaving his glass to idle as his hands spread across his thighs, palms down. They inch forward but stop short before reaching his knees, and before reaching mine.

"You're right," he says. "Priorities adapt. I didn't mean to be a snob about your jobs, or your choice to live here. I just wish you could enjoy being needed, and living in a place that feels like home, while still finding time to chase a dream once in a while. Even a small dream. Even the teeny tiniest dream about a few cute New England cows."

"Oh, Eliot." I don't bother smothering my sigh this time, because I share his wish, so much, even though I haven't admitted that to myself in a lot of years. Instead, I buried all thoughts of my creative passions eight fathoms deep, convincing myself I'm happy enough with life as it is. I suspect my packed schedule isn't the only reason, but I don't feel like examining the matter too closely right now, so I simply tell Eliot, "If I ever decide to chase a dream about cute cows, you'll be the first to know."

His eyes brighten at my words, taking me back to a time when we did tell each other everything—or almost everything. When he was *always* the first to know.

"Promise?" he asks, and I swear I can hear a deep need for a *yes* in his voice.

I draw an X over my chest. "Cross my heart and hope to moo."

Eliot's smile slowly builds. This time it doesn't flicker and fade before it reaches half-mast. Instead, it grows to its full height and width, causing my heart to swell to the point of bursting. For all of Eliot's impenetrable seriousness, in the rare moments when he looks truly happy, it's like the entire world opens up, like there's a side of him that's been dying to emerge but it needed to be told it was okay to come out.

"Are *you* chasing a dream?" I ask, still lost in his smile, and in his eyes.

His brow flickers and his hand returns to the hole in his jeans, where he toys with the dangling threads, circling that annoyingly seductive inch of bared skin.

"Sometimes I *feel* like I'm chasing a dream," he says after what must be at least a full minute of serious contemplation. "But when I let myself go still, *really* still, I wonder if I've never learned how to run toward anything at all. Only how to run away."

My chest constricts again as I search his no-longer-smiling eyes.

"What have you been running away from?" I ask.

His gaze drifts to the door, beyond which lies the sea, the town where he never belonged, and the house he slammed the door on the day after we all graduated. Beyond which also lies a morgue, and within it, a man who shares little with Eliot besides a last name.

When Eliot's eyes travel back to mine, he tap-tap-taps my knee with his, slowly, stilling, until it's not a tap at all. His hands also inch forward until the edge of his pinky rests against my knee, not quite an invite, but not quite an accident, either.

"When I sort out how to put it into words," he says, "you'll be the first to know."

My breath snags at his echo of my words. *You'll be the first.* Words that are so easy for me to say to him and so hard for me to believe for myself. But I love that he said them, and that he wouldn't say them unless he meant them, so I push past my usual reticence and set my hand on his, gently curling my fingers to encase his hand in mine.

Surprise flashes through Eliot's warm brown eyes, forces a dip in his inky brows. We don't have a history of holding hands, but he doesn't withdraw his hand from mine. He doesn't look away, either.

Maybe it's just a look, and just a touch. A few inches of skin against a few inches of skin. A hand against a hand. A knee braced against a knee, twinned in faded denim. But nothing was ever *just* between Eliot Swift and me.

Or rather, it was never *just* to me.

His lips part as though he's about to say something. Mine do, too, because our silence is growing more awkward by the second, but before either of says anything at all, Franny bursts in and flings an arm around each of us, causing us to jerk apart.

"Sorry that took so long," she says. "That poor girl can hold a crush *forever*. So much sighing and crying. It's not that complicated. If you're in love with someone you tell them. Then you mash faces or you eat your feelings. That's all there is to it, right?"

Dutch chooses that moment to set down our drinks.

I prod a mint leaf.

Eliot wipes a streak of muddled blackberry off the rim of his glass.

Neither of us says a word.

# Seven

It's almost midnight when we decide to call it a night. I came in third at blackjack, second at coin flipping and darts, dead last at a round of pool Carl and Jaime joined in on, and second again at a trivia game Dutch found behind the bar and played with us, steadily holding the lead despite an obvious and amusing attempt to fake ignorance so I at least had a chance at winning, a chance I lost when he drew a question about microbrews he couldn't possibly lie about. In other words, my curse is not yet broken.

However, Dutch and I kept the flirting to a minimum and Franny didn't get *too* cozy with Eliot, so we all had a good time without too many uncomfortable emotional undercurrents. Carl and Jaime also confirmed that Eliot's mom is already planning the house sale. Eliot took the news surprisingly well, grateful the house would soon belong to someone else, even if he wouldn't get a chance to burn it down.

As we finish our drinks and Franny answers her umpteenth anxious text from Anika, Eliot tips his chin toward the opposite end of the bar, where Dutch is chatting with two hyper-fit forty-something women I've seen around but don't know by name.

"So that's the guy," Eliot says, adjusting his position where he now sits on the center stool.

Franny glances up from her screen and gives her thumbs a momentary rest.

"The guy patiently hoping Imogen will get naked with him?" she asks.

"I was going to say the guy we pay for the drinks, but whatever." Eliot's tone is bone-dry, but I catch a twitch at the corner of his mouth. The twitch is hard to see beneath his beard, but I know what I'm looking for.

"He's definitely the one we pay for the drinks," I say, matching his tone.

He tap-taps my knee, lips still twitching. "Unless you get them for free."

I open my mouth to deny the suggestion, but I'm the world's worst liar. Besides, is it really so terrible if Eliot Swift knows a hot guy is interested in me?

"We *might* get a substantial discount on the first round," I admit.

"And the second round," Franny adds as she resumes texting. "And the third."

Eliot looks over at Dutch again, like, *really* looks. Thank god the women are holding Dutch's attention because Eliot might as well be cataloging the number of hairs in Dutch's carefully cultivated stubble or the thread count of his tight black T-shirt. This is what he meant about not being good with people. He's fine with people, but he doesn't censor himself for politeness' sake. He doesn't edit in order to be more likable.

"He's great at trivia," Eliot notes.

"A rousing endorsement," I joke through a laugh.

"Friendly, too."

"Hard job for anyone who isn't."

"Attentive without hovering, attractive, great sense of humor."

"But?" I ask, because there's obviously a *but*.

Eliot shrugs a tense shoulder. "But he doesn't seem like your type."

"My *type*?" I reel, taken so off-guard I nearly fall off my stool. I turn to Franny for assistance but she looks as baffled as I feel. "What in the hell is 'my type'?"

Eliot inches up another shrug, this one even more tense than the last.

"Artists," he says. "Writers. Musicians. Creative sorts. Seekers of muses."

"Are you kidding?" I gape, still reeling. "That's complete and utter bullshit."

"It didn't used to be." Eliot barely blinks, his expression unreadable, but I have to assume he's serious. Invention for provocation's sake has never been his style.

"First of all, still bullshit." I attempt another laugh but it comes out forced, stilted, more like a cough. "Second of all, even if I did 'used to have a type,' how would you know what it was? I never even went on a date until you were long gone."

Franny drapes an arm around Eliot's shoulders. "She has a point, Swiftie."

"Thank you!" I say, ignoring her embrace and focusing on her reinforcement.

"Also, her last boyfriend was an accountant," she adds. "His hair was basic. His clothes were basic. His taste in music, books, and art was definitely basic."

I lean around Eliot, trying to catch her eye. This is the most she has said about Greg, ever. She tends to change the subject whenever I mention him, even when we were out drinking the other night. Now I wonder if she felt more than she let on.

"Basic isn't always a bad thing," I say, watching closely for her reaction.

"Sure. Just helping to prove your point." Her tone is placating and she's obviously holding something back, but Eliot speaks before I can press her to say more.

"Maybe you didn't date in high school," he says, still stuck on this topic for some unfortunate reason. "But you were always crushing on someone." His eyes travel around my face as he takes in what I assume is a perplexed expression, because the only person I crushed on in high school is sitting beside me right now. "Weren't you into the guy who made those collages out of found objects? Joey? Jimmy? Jason?"

"You liked Johnny Kendell?" Franny looks to me for confirmation.

"Johnny was a pretentious ass." I choke out another laugh. Eliot's suggestion is absurd. "He once told me illustration was to art like mayonnaise was to haute cuisine. I liked his work though. All that beach glass and driftwood. The way he found a use for any old junk that washed up on the shore." I look to Eliot. "I thought you liked it, too."

"I did, I guess. He wasn't afraid to go weird. I respected that." He studies me for a long moment, as though he needs time to process what I just said. Now I need time to process why he'd need time to process, but he soon follows up with, "What about that tall guy from English class? The one who wrote the baby bird story you liked so much."

"Ian Washington?" Franny supplies, looking to me again with a face full of confusion that mirrors my own. She's no longer even glancing at her phone, swept up in our conversation. "Ian? Really? The quintessential teenage mansplainer?"

"Right?" Another chuckle slips out of me. "He tried to explain what menstrual cramps felt like after the subject came up in sixth grade health class. 'Because he had sisters, so he *knew*.'" I share an amused eye roll with Franny but Eliot continues watching me without breaking a smile, which is . . . starting to feel weird. "I never had a crush on Ian. I swear. I liked his writing. I liked that story in particular because it was about birds, and birds were a symbol I shared with *you*, you idiot." I swat his thigh with the back of my hand, hoping he's starting to sense that this conversation is ridiculous.

Whether he does or not, Franny jumps in with a prolonged *awwww* as though our bird bond is adorable. She even pinches Eliot's cheek with the hand that's been resting on his shoulder, the hand I'm still trying to ignore. He brushes her hand away while flashing her a light smirk. She feigns indignance at his brush-off, and his smirk widens in response. They're not flirting, exactly, but the energy could tip that direction any second, so I wave Dutch over and ask for the bill. He confirms he's on it with a wink and a grin, taking in our group dynamic and sliding away again without another word. I'm not sure what all he saw, but Eliot left out *perceptive* when he listed Dutch's strengths. Apparently, he was too busy cataloguing my supposed crushes on guys I haven't thought about in years.

"Anyone else?" I ask as we all stand and put on our coats.

Eliot jams his hands into his pockets. "Only the obvious."

I squint at him in confusion. "The obvious being . . . ?"

"Ryan Heckerling."

"Emo guitar boy?" Franny and I say in unison, making us burst into giggles before she flicks her copper curls off her forehead in a distinctly Ryan Heckerling fashion.

"Remember that song he wrote for the senior talent show?" she asks.

With more laughter, the two of us manage to recall a few painful lyrics about homespun hearts and hand-sewn love. We're so busy trying to sort out how *shadow* and *shallow* were supposed to rhyme, it takes me a moment to register that we're completely in our own world, while Eliot stands stock still, his hands still firmly wedged in his pockets and his serious expression unchanged.

"I thought you loved that song," he says when we finally pause for breath.

"Why would you think that?" I ask, still sputtering.

"Weren't you dying to take him to prom after you heard it?"

My laughter drops away as a ten-year-old lie comes back to haunt me.

*Right. That.*

Ryan was the first guy I saw after Eliot told me he was going to prom with Franny. I didn't want my friends to know I was barely holding myself together. I would've claimed I wanted to go with anyone at all and made that claim convincing.

Thankfully, Dutch slides us the bill, saving me from answering Eliot's question. Eliot drags a beat-up wallet from his back pocket, but Franny and I convince him he's the guest of honor and shouldn't have to pay. Also, the bill is notably low. At least one of us is drinking for free tonight. Franny and I split the remaining charges while I shake off my newly jogged memories of prom, all of which I want to keep buried. Deep.

Dutch flashes me a grin as I follow Franny and Eliot out the door. It's a hell of a grin, igniting sparks of desire all across my skin. I still don't want another ex in town, especially an ex who works at my favorite bar, but if I make it through Eliot's entire visit without combusting from this distinctly agonizing blend of longing and prophetic apprehension, I'm giving Dutch's breakfast-in-bed offer the consideration it deserves.

My friends and I stop by Franny's running-on-willpower rust-bucket of a truck. She offers me a ride, even though I only live a few blocks away. I accept, because even after only a few drinks, I don't want to wander home alone from this bar again, my mind swimming with questions I can't seem to shut down through sheer willpower. Questions about art, priorities, attachment, crushes, running away, and the word *complicated*.

We climb into the cab, with Eliot in the middle since he'll get out after me. As we buckle up, he asks if either of us wants to keep him company a little longer.

"I thought you said you didn't need company," I tease.

"Doesn't mean I don't want it," he says. "If it's the right company."

Franny leans in and sets a hand on his shoulder, making me wonder yet again why she finds it so easy to reach for him—to reach for anyone—while I withhold and retreat.

"Your visit's so short," she says. "I'll take every second I can get."

Eliot shines a warm smile on her before pivoting my way, the question still brimming in his eyes. I think about my mom at home alone, and the four jobs I'll do tomorrow, and my sluggishness after Monday night's breakup beers. I also consider my profound desire to end this night on a high note, before I have to witness anything more-than-friendly between Franny and Eliot. They're practically cheek-to-cheek right now, and not for the first time tonight. A kiss feels almost inevitable, if not more than a kiss. But his visit *is* short, and god knows when or if I'll ever see him again.

"What did you have in mind?" I ask.

"My parents' house," he says. "It isn't just four walls, a bed, and a shower. It's creeping me out. Any chance you want to stay over? There's plenty of ice cream. Wine. Lots of unused beds. We can play a few more games. Keep trying to break that curse."

"I'm in," Franny says with enthusiasm. "Though I have to check on Anika first."

"And I need to check on my mom." My heart sinks as I say this. I rarely spent the night with Greg, or with any of my exes. My inclination for prioritizing my mom's care has been a constant source of tension in my relationships, and I've never found a good balance.

Eliot's forehead furrows in concern, as though he senses I meant more than I said.

"How much supervision does she need now?" he asks me.

"It varies," I say. "Most nights she goes to bed around nine or ten and sleeps until dawn, and most days she's just Mom, knitting, watching TV, taking walks, and visiting with friends. Other days though, and other nights, her behavior is more . . . unpredictable, which I recognize is ironic for a woman who makes so many predictions."

My friends send me twinned looks of sympathy, and I can almost see Eliot replaying our discussion about adulthood and getting stuck in an endless cycle of barely met responsibilities, to the exclusion of chasing one's dreams.

"Whatever you need to do," he says, shame-free words I could kiss him for.

"Let's see if she's even up," Franny offers. "We'll go from there."

With a sharp groan of the gearshift, and a raspy engine cough that I'm used to but that makes Eliot wince, Franny pulls out of the parking lot and drives to my place, where I confirm that my mom's in bed and everything's in order.

She wakes when I check in on her, scolding me soundly for worrying. I don't argue the point. We both know she's given me plenty to worry about, but she promises she'll stay put all night. I make her repeat that promise twice more, looking me straight in the eye. I also make her swear that if she leaves the house for *any* reason, she'll take her phone. I turned on location tracking about a year ago. It irritated her at first, but she soon accepted that it was a necessary precaution, thank god. Hunting her down was the worst.

I'm still conflicted about leaving my mom alone all night, but my guilt ebbs as Franny cheers when I get back into the truck, while Eliot flashes me an unrestrained smile that makes my heart rate spike, proving that even at age twenty-eight, I'm still capable of being silly about a boy. He just has to be the right boy.

Eliot and Franny keep up a steady conversation until we pull into her driveway. She steps out to check on Anika and grab a few things for our sleepover, leaving Eliot and me alone in the cab. We're quiet, unspeaking, which feels okay for a minute or two, but I soon sense we're both looking for a way to end the silence.

I'm about to ask for details on Eliot's upcoming hike, but he speaks first.

"You never answered my question," he says.

I turn to face him. "Which question is that?"

"High school? Ryan Heckerling? Prom?"

*Okay. Wow.* I thought that conversation was over, or maybe I just hoped.

"It doesn't matter," I say, forcing a casual tone. "Prom's overrated."

Eliot gives me a dubious look, seeing right through my evasion. Of course.

"Seriously," I say through a breathy chuckle. "I didn't need to go."

"But you could've gone if you wanted to," he presses. "If not with Ryan, or Ian, or Johnny, then with someone else. You were in so many clubs. Plus all of those sports teams. Everyone knew you. And they all liked you."

A snort of laughter slips out of me. People liked me, yes, but in a part-of-the-crowd kind of way. Not a you're-the-girl-I'm-dying-to-date way. Once I knew Franny and Eliot were going to prom together, I did try to get a date, mostly to ensure I didn't spend the night wallowing. I had to ask seven guys before one said yes. Two days later, he told me the girl he really wanted to go with was available after all so was it cool if he went with her instead? Thus began my tragic dating pattern, not that Eliot and Franny knew about all that. It was too humiliating to share. It's still too humiliating to share, though perhaps I can risk a small truth, now that it's so far in the past.

"Turned out the only guy I wanted to go with already had a date," I say.

Eliot cocks his head, making his floppy man bun switch sides. The motion's new, and I like it, even while he continues to look dubious behind his thick-rimmed glasses.

"Why didn't you say something?" he asks.

"Because you could've forced him to change his mind?"

"Because I could've talked to Franny. All three of us could've gone together." He says this so simply, like a self-evident truth, but he has *got* to be kidding.

"What, so I could watch your coats while you and Franny slow danced?"

"It wouldn't have been like that."

"Then what would it have been like?" I flash Eliot an amused smile, desperate to keep the mood light, but he frowns at me with all the gravity in the world.

"Different than it was," he says, his voice low, quiet, subtly apologetic.

My smile fades. *Different* isn't much of a stretch, considering he was dining, dancing, and having sex with Franny that night while I withheld tears and binged *Golden Girls* episodes with my mom. Pretty much anything would've been *different*.

"Why are we even talking about this?" I ask. "It was ages ago."

"It's this town." Eliot looks out the driver's side window to a dark stretch of bland, working-class suburbia. "It dredges up old memories. And old regrets."

"Like not inviting me to be your third wheel at prom?" I nudge his side.

Predictably, he doesn't break a smile, not even a twitch and a chin tilt.

"Like letting fear dictate one's choices," he says. "Like missing opportunities."

"'Missing opportunities'? Didn't you and Franny have sex that night?"

Despite my attempt at a teasing tone, Eliot goes all shifty, running his tattooed hands down his thighs and looking everywhere but at me. For several seconds, we sit in awkward silence, jammed side by side in the too-small cab of a salt-eaten pickup, parked in a run-down, low-income neighborhood with mass-produced housing and a tinkling sand dollar wind chime within earshot, waiting for Franny, while a giant unanswered question hovers between us. It might be the most Pitt's Corner moment of my life.

"We were seventeen," Eliot says at last. "We were best friends. We were curious. High school was ending and neither of us had ever done it. We knew I was leaving soon. We also both knew no matter how it went, we wouldn't be jerks about it."

I mull this over as I recall Franny telling me about their night, and later Eliot. Though they were both positive about the experience, neither of them gloated. Neither of them said it was the best night of their lives. Neither of them indicated that having sex was the start of a deeper relationship between them. None of that mattered to me at the time, not when it was overshadowed by the most essential point: he didn't pick me.

"Doesn't sound like a missed opportunity to me," I say through another laugh, one that does nothing to disguise the childish petulance that laces my tone.

Eliot studies me again, seeing through my slim attempt at humor, as always.

"My point is . . ." He pauses, furrows his brow. "My point is . . ." he repeats in a distinctly Eliot Swiftian way, weighting simple words with complex meaning by forcing them to land a second time around. "When Franny asked me to go to prom with her, I assumed you'd be going with someone else. It had nothing to do with a curse."

I swallow, hard, letting his comment sit without my usual snarky reply.

*Right. Okay. Interesting.* And yet, how does Eliot know his choice to go to prom with Franny had nothing to do with a curse? Did he really say yes because he thought I was interested in someone else, confusing my love of art with a love for the artists? Or because Franny asked him first, reaching for what she wanted while I've always assumed every request for shared space or time is an imposition? Maybe that's all there is to it. Chance. Life. Timing. Personalities. Mistaken assumptions. Or maybe my curse set those assumptions in motion. I appreciate Eliot's point, but how do we identify our limitations with any sense of certainty unless we find a way to push past them? And when do we simply accept our limitations for what they are and get on with life?

"Well, thanks," I say, because it's all that needs to be said. "That's nice to hear."

Eliot responds with one of his barely-there smiles. After a pause, he also slips an arm around my shoulders, inviting me to settle against him. The gesture's as new for us as my handhold at the bar, but I accept, with only a second's hesitation, letting my head tip onto his shoulder as I breathe him in. He doesn't smell like musk or sandalwood or some other hyper-sexy man-aroma. He smells like blackberries, since he spilled some of his drink on his shirt at the bar. The scent is nice, and it reminds me of summers gone by.

"One more thing," he says.

"Oh god." I shake my head against him. "Please don't let it be about prom."

"It's about this hair, actually." He lightly tugs at a few short, fried locks.

I pat down my hair, cursing my decision to destroy it. "It's awful. I know."

He traces one of my more prominent cowlicks while I prepare for him to pander to my vanity by saying it's not so bad, or that it's edgy, fun, different, creative, or any of the other sweet but implausible euphemisms people have been tossing at me all day.

"It is awful," he says instead, because Eliot Swift is not a bullshitter. He's a truth teller. It's one of the things I loved about him, one of things I probably still love about him, even after all this time. "It feels like plastic. I mean, you *really* torched it."

"Screw you, Swift." I edge out of his embrace, checking my reflection in the visor mirror. He's right. The color's acceptable, but this grow-out will be *rough*. I'm about to say something to this effect when I catch Eliot watching me through the mirror. He's smiling ever-so-slightly, as if he's having a private laugh with himself. "What?"

He shakes his head, still semi-smiling. "Nothing."

"*Some*thing."

"Yeah, maybe."

I turn to face him, willing him to spill with the power of my stare.

"You just . . ." He tilts his head, considering. "You still look good. That's all."

I pat down my cowlicks again, to little effect. "I don't."

"You do, Finch. You really do." He's still smiling. A bit. I'm 99 percent certain he's only trying to make me feel better about what was obviously an impulsive and erroneous choice, but if I can accept the criticism, I should be able to accept the compliment, too.

"Well . . . thanks," I say again.

"You're welcome." He stretches out his arm, inviting me back in.

I hesitate for more than a second this time, feeling like I should tell him he looks good, too, but if I say it, it'll mean something *way* different than when he said it. So, I keep the thought to myself, flipping the visor up so I can't see my reflection. Then I nestle against Eliot's side. He gives my shoulders a light squeeze, drawing me close.

We sit together without another word, two old friends more at home teasing each other than we are with any form of sincere intimacy, though I get the sense we're both working on it. And so, we do, as best we can in the moment, settling into a side embrace as a late-night breeze blows in off the ocean, making reeds rustle and sand dollar wind chimes clickety-clack, while we wait for Franny to join us.

# Eight

*E*liot unlocks the front door and Franny enters first, flapping her arms and shouting for the ghosts to take cover because the live-people party has arrived.

"You're ridiculous," I say from the front steps.

She spins toward me, grinning from ear to ear. "Would you have me any other way?"

I shake my head at her. "Absolutely not."

Eliot follows Franny into the foyer, flicking on lights as he enters. I enter third, holding back while I take advantage of the amazing Wi-Fi to check my mom's location.

"Everything okay?" Eliot asks.

"Her phone hasn't moved," I confirm. "I'll take that as a cautious *yes*."

He nods before turning to Franny. "And Anika? She's all right til morning?"

"She's bingeing old *Star Trek* episodes with a friend. They'll be ranting about the blatant sexism and impenetrable techno-babble for hours. It's her favorite therapy." Franny spins around under an enormous crystal chandelier, taking everything in as though she's re-familiarizing herself with the house. Behind glass doors, a traditional study sits sentinel to our right, lined with floor-to-ceiling bookshelves and the kind of dark, heavy furniture that makes me think of bankers in Dickens novels. A sweeping staircase with polished mahogany railings curves upward straight ahead. Neatly-framed photos rise with the staircase, simple black-and-white landscapes without any people in them. Without any family in them. A prim-looking parlor collects moonlight on the left, all dusty pastels, tiny florals, and china collections that look like they could break just by glaring at them too severely, though if that was true, Eliot would've broken them years ago.

"Home sweet home," he says dryly as he unties his battered hiking boots.

Beside him, Franny slides off her high-heeled ankle boots, revealing a pair of vivid rainbow-striped socks Anika bought her last Christmas. She's in a flirty little black dress and her favorite cropped satin bomber jacket. It's her usual going-out look, simple but sexy, with a few stylish accessories. Franny knows she's attractive. She's aware that she draws certain kinds of attention, envious glances from women and desirous ones from men. Because of that, she's deliberate about how and when to display her body. She also stays on trend. And yet, her socks say she doesn't care about any of it. It's very Franny and it's the kind of thing I love about her. It's the kind of thing Eliot loved, too.

"You keep this place spotless," she tells me. "I forgot how much stuff was in here. All the glass, the books, the china figurines. Cleaning it all must've taken ages."

"I only dusted once a month." I fumble with the knots on my red Converse to avoid making eye contact with Eliot, uncomfortable with the reminder that I basically became his housekeeper during his absence. Not that he ever made me feel lesser for being working class, but the divide between us has always been there, shaping our lives in different ways. "The job wasn't bad. Really. Mostly dishes and linens."

"Linens. Right." Eliot turns on his heel and marches from the foyer toward the den and kitchen, likely fleeing my boneheaded reminder that his parents both brought their lovers here. I might as well have called it their sex den.

Cursing my lack of smoothness, I kick off my shoes and leave them in a heap with the others, pausing to recall how Eliot's mom used to make us line up every shoe *just so* in the coat closet and ensure the door was shut. Nothing out of place or alignment. No signs of life allowed. The memory makes our current haphazard pile of shoes seem deliberately rebellious, suggesting a serious scolding is seconds away. Weird how that feeling lingers. Maybe the house really is haunted.

By the time I banish that thought and catch up with Eliot and Franny, their coats are tossed over the back of a kitchen chair with the same lack of precision as our shoes. He's uncorking a bottle of wine and Franny's setting glasses on the island's countertop.

"I grabbed this from the cellar earlier today," Eliot says. "I don't know anything about wine, but I guarantee nothing down there cost less than eighty bucks a bottle, so it'll be better than whatever we drank in those last months of high school."

"Pretty much anything would fit that category." Franny pulls a stool up to the island and looks around the kitchen the same way she looked around the foyer, wide-eyed and with slow, incredulous shakes of her head. I see this place every week. She hasn't seen it in years, and it's eerily unchanged. Her gaze passes over a marble mortar and pestle and a stainless-steel bowl of vivid green ceramic apples before landing on Eliot's struggle with the cork. "Eighty bucks a bottle, huh? Should we pitch in?"

Eliot huffs out a humorless laugh as he yanks out the cork with a sharp *pop*.

"We'll let my dad foot the bill for this one," he says. "God knows he didn't earn it any more than we did. Not honestly anyway."

As Eliot lowers the cork, Franny reaches across the island and sets her hand on his. The two of them hold a look while I stand nearby, twisting the stem of a wineglass and trying not to feel third-wheel-ish. Out of respect for the dead, none of us says anything further about Mr. Swift's shady business practices. As far as I know, he never did anything illegal, but he wasn't known for prioritizing job satisfaction or employee welfare. People were always suing him for one thing or another. And always losing.

Franny's hand slips away and Eliot pours three substantial glasses of wine. As we each take an appreciative sip—because no matter how it was paid for, it's *way* better than what any of us are used to—we decide on three contests that will let us continue pursuing Eliot's grand curse-breaking plan. I propose a storytelling contest because I still want to hear more about Eliot's travels. Franny proposes *Name That Tune*, a game she's certain to win, but since it's late, and she doesn't think my curse is breakable, and she loves to sing, I don't mind at all. Eliot—dear, sweet Eliot—proposes a drawing contest.

"There are only three of us," he says. "Two of us can't draw. You've got this."

I smile at him without contradiction. I love his tenacious belief in me, and that he knows—he just *knows*—that curse or no curse, I'm happiest with a pencil in my hands.

We start with our stories. Franny gets us all laughing by telling us about Anika sneaking a few beers, claiming she wasn't drunk, and promptly walking into a wall.

I follow up by relating a now anecdotal and highly comedic

version of visiting a boyfriend at his corporate office, dressed in sexy lingerie, heels I could barely manage, and a trench coat that wasn't fooling anyone, only to be told by his secretary that he was out at his weekly marriage counseling session with his wife. Reeling in shock, I stumbled into a potted ficus, ripped my coat, broke a heel, and flashed the secretary my barely-there lace thong. In sympathy, she loaned me the sneakers and track pants she had in her gym bag so I could get out of the building without incurring more humiliation. It was one of the only times I wasn't officially "dumped" for another woman, but I definitely didn't come first in that situation. I'm not even sure I came in second.

Eliot is horrified by my tale, but I promise him the sting has long since softened and it's okay to laugh. In fact, it's vital. If I can't find any humor in my past relationships, I'll have a total breakdown, stuck in constant analysis about how I let myself date guys who cheat on me or criticize my relationship with my mom or end up being married and never even offer me an apology for lying about it. I still sometimes wonder how that guy's wife is holding up though, and if she knew, and how many times he cheated. I suppose at least they were working on something with all that therapy.

Eliot takes his turn last. As at the bar, it's obvious as he speaks why he has such a huge following on YouTube. His appreciation for the world around him colors every word, like in his description of a running antelope or the differences between the Atlantic, Pacific, Indian, and Arctic Oceans, or the way darkness becomes palpable deep inside a cavern where no light penetrates, where fear gives way to a profound sense of peace because only in complete and utter darkness can the self fully disappear.

Prompted by us both to continue, he also tells us about being stung by a jellyfish and about sliding down a cliffside to outrun an avalanche, as well as lighter tales like being locked in a hostel bathroom for seven hours in Hamburg. By the time someone fixed the lock, a crowd had gathered to welcome him back to civilization, a spectacular irony for someone who spends most of his time as far away from civilization as possible.

I feel heady with wine and stories by the time we finish, and Eliot's so clearly the winner, nothing he says will convince either Franny or me otherwise.

We combine the next two contests, each of us with a pencil and some gilded stationery Eliot finds for scratch paper. He also recalls his promise of ice cream, setting half a dozen fancy mason jars on the island, with flavors like black currant praline and lavender rhubarb. As a staunch B&J fan, I want to hate the rich-people brand, but I don't. It's delicious. Secretly, I've always envied the Swifts' ability to buy whatever they want without a second thought. I don't need a house with nine bathrooms, or a cellar full of ridiculously expensive wine, but barely scraping by week after week is exhausting.

We doodle away while humming out tunes the others try to guess. Franny's the only natural performer present, and the only one with any musical talent or knowledge. She took a lot of singing lessons when we were growing up, and she fronted a band in college, but they all went their separate ways after graduation. Now she contents herself with singing in the car or joining the local choir for holiday carols.

As she hums an entire pop song I can't quite place, and Eliot listens in quiet admiration, I focus on my drawing, which I'm slow to start. I tell myself I'm just rusty but I know my inertia is more complex. I keep thinking through everything I said at the bar about why I set aside my art. It was all true. I've been busy, preoccupied, juggling too much, but I can't claim I've had no time at all to draw. So if making art is so important to me, why did I need Eliot to put this pencil in my hand? Why couldn't I do it myself?

I can't answer that question, not without more time and consideration, but I manage to block out shapes and lay in shadows while we take turns guessing song titles. My friends laugh when I attempt a few notes of "Blister in the Sun." Despite my off-key humming, Franny guesses the song right away while Eliot shakes his head at me.

"Good thing we're also drawing," he says. "Singing *really* isn't your talent."

I scoff. "And softening the truth isn't yours."

He fakes offense. "I thought that was what you loved about me."

"I loved you for your—" I cringe, biting back all the ways I could end that sentence. *Your heart,* comes to mind. *Your big, beautiful, do-no-harm heart.*

Eliot raises a curious brow but I clamp my mouth shut and resume my drawing.

"She loved you for your posh hand-me-downs," Franny interjects, thank god. "None of our parents ever bought us cashmere. Or anything that had to be dry-cleaned."

"My parents had very specific taste. Nothing easily cared for was worth owning. Besides"—he sneaks me the barest hint of a smile—"I preferred the sweaters you made."

I warm at the memory, and gasp audibly when he takes out his phone and shows me a selfie from several years ago. He's about twenty-two or twenty-three in the shot, bronzed and lean from his outdoor adventures, standing among snow-capped mountains with a giant backpack and a walking stick, wearing a hideous every-color sweater I made from my mom's leftover yarn bits shortly before he left. I took up knitting at age eight so I could enter an annual kids' crafting contest. I never came close to winning, but Eliot wore whatever acrylic monstrosities emerged from my faulty needlework, no matter how itchy or asymmetrical. At first, I thought he did it to piss off his parents, but eventually I realized he did it for me. So I wouldn't feel like a failure.

The sweater's threadbare in the photo, with several patches and more holes than yarn. Good lord. He not only took it with him when he left, he kept it for years. Ten bucks at a thrift store would've bought him something warmer and less of an eyesore.

"Okay, that's adorable," Franny says, peering over my shoulder at the screen.

"That's insane," I counter. "Please tell me you don't still have it."

Eliot takes his phone back and pockets it while shrugging sheepishly.

"I had to downsize in Nepal about four years ago," he says. "Essentials only so I could carry enough food and water. There wasn't much left to the sweater at the time."

While he tips back his wineglass, Franny sets her hand on her heart and mouths *Oh my god*, to me. I give her an *I know, right?* look, but honestly? I'm not that surprised. Eliot has always been sweet, thoughtful, and far more sentimental than most guys we know. Still . . . his choice to keep my sweater for so long makes my heart pinch. A lot.

"I could make you a new one," I offer, watching Eliot while I draw.

He does his trademark chin lift/head tilt. "Really?"

"Of course. I'd love to. Though I might not finish by Tuesday morning."

"I'll give you a mailing address in B.C. Same guy who's holding my gear."

"Or you could extend your visit," Franny suggests, exuding hope through a grin.

He looks back and forth between us while spinning the stem of his glass. Franny. Me. Franny. Me. Franny again. His expression remains impassive, as it so often does. I'd give *anything* to know what's going through his mind right now, even though his gaze has firmly settled on Franny and shows no signs of drifting back my way.

"I suppose an extension could be arranged," he says. "For a day or two."

My heart practically leaps out of my chest. I thought this was nonnegotiable.

Franny cheers, "Hell, yes!" while I eke out a painfully desperate, "Really?"

Eliot shrugs. "An Imogen Finch original is on the line. Can't turn that down."

I beam at him, unable to hide my joy, but while I only manage to smile, Franny jumps to her feet, flings her arms around his neck from behind, and plants a loud, mushy kiss on his cheek, still draped around him while he leans into her embrace, laughing.

"Knit slowly," she tells me. "Let's keep our boy around as long as possible."

I maintain my smile, but my joy dims. Because there they are, cheek-to-cheek again, so at ease with each other. And sure, he kept my sweater. He also said nice things tonight, and prom wasn't as much of a brush-off as I thought. I just . . . don't know how to be like that. Openly warm, affectionate, and full of enthusiasm. Seeing them together, it's impossible to imagine anyone *not* picking Franny. Not then. Not now. Not ever.

It's Eliot's turn in *Name That Tune*, but since Franny's so obviously winning, we decide to wrap up the contests for the night. We gather close to set our drawings on the island, making room by shoving aside the now empty wine bottle and mostly melted ice cream jars. Eliot reveals his drawing first, a hasty stick figure holding a sign that says LOSER. He probably spent ten seconds on it, determined to hand me the win. Franny sets down her sketches next. She drew a bunch of dogs. They're wonky and the proportions are bananas but they're also adorable. I'm pretty sure one of them is Jack, my least favorite terrier, though the evil side-eye in the drawing could be an accidental smudge.

I give my own drawing a final perusal, still gripped in a tight fist. I drew three kids, holding hands and leaping off a dock into the ocean. It's a sweet, nostalgic image, full of details like Franny's errant corkscrew curls and Eliot's glasses flying off his head. The shading and textures aren't my best, but the bones of a resonant illustration are there, suggesting the image belongs in a children's book, like so many drawings I used to do.

For a moment, I think maybe I've got this. Maybe Eliot's right after all and my curse really is bullshit. We are about to break it. Right here. Right now. As soon as I set down this sketch, I'll be free of limitations. I can stop predicting failure and anticipating break-ups. I can let myself fall in love again. I can let myself do anything at all again. Even the most grandiose dream in the world will be possible.

And then . . .

And . . .

Then . . .

As I lay down my sketch, my elbow knocks over the nearest mason jar. A puddle of melted chocolate ice cream forms on my page. Franny leaps up and tries to wipe off the ice cream, but she knocks over the wine bottle. It breaks, and the last dregs of wine spill out. While Eliot picks up broken glass, he cuts himself, not badly, but enough to make us stop trying to save my drawing, using it instead to gather up the glass and the spillage, tossing the whole lot in the trash.

By the time Eliot locates the Band-Aids and Franny and I clear away the rest of the mess, my drawing is buried under soiled paper towels and broken glass, seen only by me. And this is why I still believe I'm cursed. It's not just the relationship rejections and the lack of blue ribbons. It's the multi-hour traffic jams or sudden-onset illnesses that prevented me from attending a Quiz Bowl or soccer match on the days my teams won. Or the way my college art portfolio went missing right before the grad showcase, when I was the frontrunner for at least one of the prizes. A bird once shat on my face during a track meet. An elaborate cake went flying from my hands at the county fairgrounds, seconds before I placed it on the judging table. My name and photo didn't make it into the *Most Likely To* section of my senior yearbook even though *every* other senior had a mention.

With enough willpower, and enough hope, I can let myself forget these things. I can tell myself to believe my perpetual second-rate status is all about luck and timing. My mom's prophecies have nothing to do with the actions that follow. My only limitations are self-inflicted, brought on by personal doubts and insecurities. But right now . . .

"Looks like Franny takes this one, too," I say as I stare at the trash can.

She tips her head onto my shoulder and lets out a rueful sigh.

"I'm so sorry," she says. "What was it meant to be?"

"The three of us. Age seven. At the end of the dock." I nod toward the window.

Franny follows my gaze, as does Eliot, stepping up beside us to set the Band-Aid box on the counter. Beyond a light glow from the house, the yard is dark, but we all know what lies beyond the yard, even if it's been obscured in my drawing.

For a moment, we're all quiet, each lost in our own thoughts. Then we straighten up as one, exchanging questioning looks that suggest we're all thinking the same thing.

Franny grips my wrist. "We *have* to do it."

"We don't *have* to," I say, but her eyes are alight and she's practically dancing.

"It'll be fun!" she says.

"It'll be freezing." I send Eliot a pleading look.

He merely shrugs. "One more contest before we call it a night?"

Before I can get out a quick but decisive *no*, Franny is whooping with joy and dragging us toward the back door, a fierce and unstoppable woman on a mission . . .

# Nine

The three of us stand near the end of the Swifts' long floating dock, staring at the gently lapping waves. The shoreline curves around us, creating a cove that calms the strongest currents, the ones that bash against the rockier coasts immediately to the north and south. A row of hanging lanterns provides soft illumination, picking out the edges of a rowboat and a small sailboat tethered to our right. The rowboat looks newer than the one we used to lie in, wedged like sardines, staring up at the stars. I smile at the memory anyway, the closeness, the togetherness. The feeling that the world was still unfolding and anything was possible, even for a girl with a curse.

"It's the middle of October," I say, now on my umpteenth argument about this.

Franny waves away my objection. "Yeah, and?"

"And I'd rather be curled up under cozy blankets."

"Those blankets will be even cozier after a brisk, refreshing swim!" Franny starts undressing, never one to hesitate when fun beckons. I'm usually only a step behind, happy to follow her lead, but not tonight. And not because I'm worried about the cold.

"Maybe eight games are enough for one night," I say.

"Last one," Eliot says. Then he steps up close and whispers, "Once we're in the water, I'll distract her. You make a break for it. Let's wrap the night with a win."

I spin on him, arms folded across my chest. "Cheating negates victory."

"Says who?"

"Says over twenty years of experience. And a functional moral compass."

He casts me a dubious look, but soon we're both watching Franny. Within seconds her socks, jacket, and dress are in a heap on the dock next to the towels Eliot had the wherewithal to grab before we ran down here. She's wearing a black satin bra and hipster underpants that basically double as a bikini. She looks gorgeous, all hips and boobs with a cute little lizard tattoo that circles her belly button.

"Shirt off, Swiftie!" She waves for him to start stripping. "Show us those tats!"

With a quick eye roll for my benefit, he yanks off his henley and undershirt in one clean motion, revealing a tautly muscled back and strong, lean arms inked with linked tattoos. They cover about half of his skin, all in monochromatic black linework. An ornate eight-pointed compass that could've been copied from an old treasure map. A surging wave. A baobab tree. Clouds. Fish. Flowers. The octopus that undulates from his bicep to his knuckles. What I think might be da Vinci's flying machine. Several words and phrases I can't make out without a closer look. Maybe even a bird or two?

Franny lets out an ear-piercing whistle. "Holy thirst trap, Eliot!"

He shoots her a look of pure annoyance. "I'm only doing this if you promise to never, ever say that again. Seriously. Pain of death. Excruciatingly slow, torturous death."

"You show up here with *that* body"—she flaps a hand at him—

"and all that ink, and we can't objectify you? Not even, like, a lip bite and a single drop of drool?"

He looks to me for reinforcement, but I've got nothing. It's all I can do not to stare. Franny stifles a laugh, sputtering through a balled-up fist she presses to her lips, accurately reading my silence for what it is. Thankfully, her sputtering draws Eliot's attention away so he can't see the blush that's taking over my neck and face.

*Shit.* What I wouldn't give right now for an ability to be chill under pressure. And the strength of conviction to avoid situations like this in the first place.

Franny promises to rein in the objectifying, so Eliot tugs off his socks, unbuckles his belt, and drops his jeans, leaving him in heather-gray knit boxers. They hang off his hips, stretched out and thinned with over-washing like the rest of his clothes. They're not the least appealing men's underwear I've ever seen, but they're in the bottom three for sure. And yet, he still manages to look so breathtakingly sexy, I might be muted for life.

He removes his glasses, pocketing them in his jeans. Then he rubs his arms as he joins Franny at the end of the dock, where the two of them watch the incoming waves together until she cranes around, shining her infectious grin on me.

"C'mon, Mogi! The faster we do this, the sooner we can huddle under blankets!"

My eyes dart from Franny in her sleek black underwear to Eliot in his shabby boxers. My friends both look cold, but also comfortable, natural, standing there half naked with no hint of self-consciousness, which is . . . not how I operate.

I take a step back. "Actually, I'm going to sit this one out."

"You're going to *what*?!" Franny glares at me, mock-appalled.

"I didn't dress for swimming." I take another step away, a slow but steady retreat.

"And we did?" Eliot gestures at his too-loose, too-thin boxers. So not helpful.

Franny plants her hands on her hips. "We don't care if you're in granny panties."

"It's not that." I grimace and take another step back.

Franny's eyes widen. "Polka dots? *Star Wars*? Knee-to-navel Spanx?"

"Not that, either." Another step.

Eliot furrows his brow at me, quietly curious, but Franny takes a more aggressive approach to my lack of participation, circling me to plant herself in my flight path.

"Imogen Finch!" she says, all scoldy but also laughing a little, like she's trying to play the stern school marm but can't quite manage it. "We are jumping off this dock together whether you strip down or not. So will you please accept that we're all friends and we don't give a shit if you have *Wednesday* glitter-printed across your ass?"

I look to Eliot for help but he responds with a predictable shrug, still rubbing his arms. His very fit, very tan, very inked, very thirst-trappy arms.

"Whatever you're going to do, do it quickly," he says.

Franny argues with him that there's no "whatever" about it. He insists that I have a right to make whatever choices feel good for me. She counters, noting our limited time together and how I'm ruining a perfectly good opportunity to make an amazing memory. The two of them argue until I can't bear it anymore.

"Fine!" I say, already yanking off my socks. "You win. But no jokes, okay?"

They both agree as though they're astonished I even have to ask. Before I can talk myself out of it, I shove my jeans down and rip off my sweater and tank top, only to look up and find Franny and Eliot gaping at me. Because of course they are.

"Holy shit," Franny says. "Were we supposed to leave you with Dutch?"

"I didn't wear it for him. I wore it for me." I glance down at my navy and pink mesh lingerie. I'm in sheer underpants that cut high on my butt cheeks and a demi-cup bra that leaves little to the imagination. I bought the set because I loved the details: sharply contrasting colors, piped seams, tiny velvet bows, and beautiful scalloped lace that softens the edges. However, my friends can see pretty much everything, from my nipples to my landing strip, and I'm not sure how I feel about that.

"You didn't, I mean, you just, um . . ." Eliot blubbers.

"I've had some struggles with sexual confidence," I say, only because I'm several drinks in and already feel exposed so I might as well confess everything. "Nice lingerie helps. I like the way it makes me feel, even if I'm the only one who sees it."

"Yeah, but—" Eliot runs a hand down his face, his mouth ajar.

"But Dutch would lose his mind if he knew he had this to look forward to," Franny finishes for him. "If you're still turning him down by month's end, I'm raiding your underwear drawer and sending him a care package."

"Isn't that sexual harassment?" I ask. "And a gross invasion of privacy?"

"*That* is the helpful nudge of a friend who cares about your sexual well-being."

I open my mouth to argue the point, but I'm distracted by a splash at the end of the dock. Eliot's gone, but his head soon pops up from the waves. He looks like a cartoon merman with his long dark hair slipping out of its elastic and draping over his shoulder.

"Sorry!" he shouts up as he treads water. "Couldn't wait any longer."

"The siren's call of the ocean?" Franny asks.

"Something like that." His eyes meet mine for the briefest of seconds before he ducks back under and swims a few strokes toward shore.

Before I can fully consider what his glance might mean, Franny lets out a yelp of excitement and grabs my hand. A second later, we're leaping off the dock together and plunging into the ocean.

The cold water jolts me, hard and fast. My body goes stiff. My toes and fingers curl. My jaw clenches. My shoulders jerk toward my ears. However . . .

Slowly, gently, as it always does, the rhythmic motion of the waves offsets the shock. I settle into the calming undulations before kicking upward and breaking through the surface. Despite the continued chill against my skin, this ocean is home. It will always be home. The smell of salt and seaweed. The slow *hush-hush-hush* sound of the waves. The way the water moves at its own pace, the way it always has and always will, despite the trivial concerns of a woman who feels appropriately small in its presence.

As I catch my breath, I spot Franny and Eliot a few yards away. She's shrieking and swearing at the cold while he sends a flat-palmed splash her direction. She retaliates by dunking him under, forcing him down with both hands on his head. I'm not sure if Eliot's fulfilling his promise to distract her or if they're just having a bit of fun together. Either way, their antics feel so familiar, in the best possible way, bringing back memories of a dozen summers gone by.

Franny was right. This was a good idea.

The water's too cold to linger in for long so we promptly line up equidistant to the shore and countdown to *go* together. Then we take off, drawn by thoughts of dry towels and warm blankets. I lose track of my friends as I swim, so I'm not sure who's winning, but as I check the depth and find I can now trudge through sand and seaweed, only waist-deep in the water, Eliot surprises me by locking his arms around me from behind and flinging us both sideways. We fall together, gulping in a breath before we're submerged. I don't even pretend to fight him as his entire body presses against me, his chest to my back, his groin to my ass, our legs tangled. I relax into his embrace/vise grip. While the undercurrent tugs us sideways, my bleary brain registers strength. Warmth. Skin. Long hair floating past my cheeks. Thighs sliding against thighs.

Eliot's hold loosens right away so my arms are no longer pinned to my sides, but he doesn't fully let go. Instead, his hands splay over my belly and he continues drawing me against him. He's only extending his throwdown in a way that won't completely disempower me, but his touch feels surprisingly intimate, probably because I'm not struggling against him so he doesn't need to hold me at all.

And yet, he does.

As his palms shift against my belly, I can't help myself. I arch into him, letting my head sink backward onto his shoulder so my cheek brushes his beard. I also set my hands on his, curling my fingers as though I'm about to pry his hands from my body. Only I don't do any prying. I let a rush of fantasies overtake me instead. Our linked hands sliding lower. His strong forearms gliding over my hipbones. His fingers inching past my waistband, lower, ever lower, teasing me with a painfully slow approach until they finally, finally, *finally* slide between my legs. His mouth on my ear. Teeth, too. And an unmistakable sign of his arousal pressing against my barely-clad ass.

None of this happens, of course. With the next wave, Eliot lets go and we stagger to our feet, wiping salt water from our eyes. I'm breathing more heavily than I should be. We weren't underwater for very long. Eliot must be wondering what my problem is. He's watching me, unsmiling, which may be his default expression, but he looks even more serious than usual. I swear I only leaned into him a little bit, held on a second longer than necessary, kept my thoughts firmly lodged in my head, but I worry I still crossed a line.

"I'm sorry," Eliot and I say, practically in unison.

I blink at him in confusion. "Why are *you* sorry?"

"I shouldn't have . . . you know." He frowns down at his hands.

"Tackled me? I think it's a pretty fair part of the game."

"The game. Right." He nods but his frown deepens. "And you?"

"I shouldn't have—" I stop there, searching for a lighter confession than *I got carried away by lust for a few seconds and will eventually turn those few seconds into weeks, months, maybe even years of highly effective masturbatory fantasies.*

"Imogen?" he prompts when my silence stretches on too long.

"Eliot?" I reply, because mimicry seems like a solid tactic right now.

"Tell me," he says, a gentle, earnest plea. "Tell me what you think you—"

"You guys okay?" Franny interjects as she joins us. "What's with the staring?"

Eliot looks to me as if he's seeking direction. At least that's what I assume he's doing since I'm doing the same with him. I'm so confused right now. But if we're both sorry about something the other didn't notice, maybe nothing needs an apology at all.

"Eliot surprised me with the throwdown." I manage a limp smile, first in Franny's direction, then in Eliot's. "I'm a little winded. That's all."

Franny snorts out a laugh as her eyes drop to my chest.

"You mean you're a little cold," she corrects. "Hello, Nipples McGee."

"Oh my god." I lock my arms over my chest and spin away from her, trudging shoreward. "You promised," I call back. "No jokes about my underwear."

She catches up and flings an arm around my shoulders.

"I'm only teasing," she says. "You look crazy hot in that set. And no one cares if we can see your nips. We're all friends here." She cranes around. "Right, Swiftie?"

He follows after us, a fist knotted in his merman hair.

"Friends," he says. "Absolutely."

# Ten

An hour or so after our swim, the three of us are stretched out on the big U-shaped sectional in the den, tucked under blankets, having wrapped the final game of the night by calling it a draw. We're all wearing Eliot's T-shirts and boxers, though I also kept my bra and underpants on so Franny couldn't steal them and give them to Dutch. I'm pretty sure she wouldn't actually take that step, but pretty sure isn't dead certain. She's half-asleep to our right, snuggled into a corner, her feet kicked up on Eliot's lap while he rubs one of her arches with his thumb. He's reclining in the middle, a remote in his free hand, searching for a movie to watch, a task that's taking forever because he rarely watches TV and he's overwhelmed by the streaming choices. I'm on his left, nestled in another corner while trying to recall how to do a basic rib stitch with the yarn we scavenged before settling in for sleep, TV, or in my case, general restlessness.

"This wool is gorgeous," I say as Eliot's eyes skim over the description of yet another movie we're not going to watch. "I didn't know your grandmother used to knit."

"Why would you? My mom gave the blankets and scarves away

to 'people who couldn't afford nicer things' as she liked to say." He flips to another movie description, and then another. "I have no idea why she kept her mom's old crafting stuff. I only knew it was in the attic because I went hunting for photos of my dad this morning. My mom's request. She hired someone to make a slide show for the funeral."

I lower the knitting needles. "She didn't want to do it herself?"

"Oh hell no." He rolls his head toward me, his expression wry. "If there's one thing this family consistently excels at, it's outsourcing acts of care or compassion."

I slump against my corner of the sectional, newly reminded that Eliot didn't come back to visit with old friends. He's here for his dad's funeral, and to watch his mom fight for an inheritance without shedding a tear. I search for words of consolation that go beyond *I'm sorry*, but I can't find any, so I *look* the words instead.

Reading my expression, Eliot shrugs as he turns back to the TV.

"It's fine," he says, though it's obviously not. It never has been.

"You sure?" I ask, hoping it sounds like an invite, not an accusation.

He flips to another movie description, one he doesn't appear to read.

"No," he says, still flipping. "It's an emotional minefield that sent me to the opposite side of the world with ten bucks in my pocket and a teeth-grinding habit when I should've been immersed in intensive therapy. But you know: tom-ay-to, tom-ah-to."

I lower my knitting, still desperate for something comforting and meaningful to say, something that can ease even the tiniest fraction of the pain Eliot carries with him, but when he keeps his gaze locked on the TV, I get the distinct sense he'd rather I say nothing at all. So I resume my knitting and he continues his movie search.

After scanning countless titles, he settles on an alternate-history film that's based on a book he read while hiking the Western Ghats last year. He describes that trip while I manage a few rows of stitches in what I hope will become at least a marginally wearable fisherman's style sweater. The yarn is a soft, squishy wool in a deep navy blue with the barest hint of green to it. My knitting won't do it justice, but judging by the photo Eliot showed me earlier tonight, he won't turn up his nose at my imperfect work.

While the movie plays and Franny drifts into a lightly snoring slumber, Eliot and I continue catching up on the past few years. I tell him about the summer my mom spent lying on our roof every night, watching for falling stars. I also describe the time I caught her up a giant oak tree, examining a robin's nest, counting the spots on the eggs. The fire department had to get her down, like a scared cat in a cartoon. The whole town watched it happen, drawn by the sirens. I was mortified, though thankfully my mom was uninjured.

I have dozens of similar stories, but I choose the ones that don't involve getting calls from police in other towns, asking me to pick up my mom for obstructing traffic or trespassing in nature preserves. I also leave out the one where she wandered off without a word and by day two, half the town was out searching for her. We found her walking along the shoulder of a road halfway to Portland, with a dandelion crown on her head and a jar of spiders clutched in both hands, oblivious to the panic she caused by going on her un-announced walkabout. She carries her phone with her now, and I haven't lost track of her in over a year, but still, better Eliot thinks of my mom as a charming eccentric than as a responsibility rife with challenges to manage. He has enough going on in his own life right now. He doesn't need to take on my problems.

"I always liked your mom," he says after I tell him about a mother-daughter kite project that was meant to test something about the wind but only tangled a ton of string. "I'm glad she has you." He doesn't toss this out like it's the right thing to say. He says it like he means it deep in his heart, which means I feel it deep in mine. "I'm not sure if you've considered this, but don't you think you're first to her?"

I smile a little. I have considered this. And quickly refuted it.

"Being someone's emergency contact doesn't qualify as a first place," I say. "Also, my mom has three kids. It's not a competition. She loves us all."

Eliot rubs his beard in that way he does, like he's reminding himself it's there.

"Funny, isn't it?" he asks with a distinct lack of humor. "How some people have enough love to share with three or ten or a thousand people. Others can't manage one."

I pause my knitting again, giving Eliot my full attention, just in case.

He catches me watching him out of the corner of his eye.

"Sorry," he says. "Pretend I didn't say that."

"You're allowed to feel shitty about having shitty parents."

He nods, still rubbing his beard and not looking directly at me.

"Maybe," he says, and again, after more rubbing and more nodding, "Maybe."

"If you want to talk about it, I'm happy to listen."

He responds with a tip of his chin and an almost smile that suggests he appreciates my offer, but he doesn't say anything. I remind myself he made it very clear. The only shoulders he wants to lean on are his own.

However, after a breath or two, he surprises me.

"My dad swore I'd be back, you know. He said I was only sowing wild oats or whatever." He adopts a clipped, paternal tone that implies a wagging finger, even though his hands rest in his lap. "'You're young, Eliot. Naïve. You read all those books so you think you're so smart but you don't know anything. You certainly don't understand what matters in life. When you finish all that rambling, what will you have to show for it?'" He looks at the bookshelves that flank the flat-screen, full of leather-bound book sets with uncracked spines and ostentatiously large geode bookends. He also takes in the original art on the walls, the Tiffany lamps, the decorative eggs, and the huge Persian rug that probably cost more than my mom's entire house. "I never got my dad to understand that was the point. To live. To be *in* the moment. And to have nothing 'to show for it' at all."

I give this a few seconds to land, knowing it wasn't easy for Eliot to say.

"Except your channel," I offer, not as an argument, but as a concession.

"Sure, I guess, but I can delete it anytime. One click. No questions asked. There's no bullshit claim to land rights. No walls to keep things in or people out. No collections that require monthly dusting or combination locks on cellar doors. Nothing that can be bought, sold, or fought over. If I can't carry it with me, I let it go."

I consider this, with my knitting in my lap. I've never needed fancy things, per se, but I do crave little benchmarks of the life I've lived so far. Souvenirs, I guess, or places and people on whom I've left a mark. A language of familiarity that can only be built through shared experience, a language that says, *We were here. Together. Witnesses to each other's lives. More than witnesses. Active, willing, invested participants.*

Also, something doesn't quite gel about Eliot's Live Only in the Now stance. Not that I question his views on the accumulation of wealth and impressive possessions, but for a guy who claims he doesn't give a shit about *things*, he kept that hideous sweater for a *really* long time. The art on his body also suggests he's interested in some kind of record of his experiences. And he definitely wanted to be with friends tonight.

"What about relationships?" I ask. "What about a life that has nothing to do with walls and wine cellars. Just people who know you and love you?"

He offers me a particularly Eliot Swiftian frown, all plunged eyebrows, thoughtful eyes, and tight lips, so familiar even with his thinned-out face and scruffy nomad beard.

"Honestly?" he says. "I'm not sure how to have one without the other. How do I let someone love me if the idea of sharing a few walls with them makes me want to grab the first bus out of town, terrified I'm becoming my parents? That's a horrible offer."

"Unless you find someone else who hates walls. And loves buses."

"No one loves buses."

"Fine. Stick with 'someone who hates walls.' It's a pretty high bar already."

He almost laughs, and I feel the weight of the conversation ebb, though his serious eyes practically burn through me, as intense as sunlit pine tar.

"Someone who doesn't care if I want to be alone most of the time?" he asks.

"*Most* of the time. But not *all* of the time?"

"No." His frown softens further. "Not *all* of the time."

"Then the bar might not be so high after all."

We share a subtle smile, and a silence underscored by the TV and the soft rhythm of Franny's sleep-relaxed breathing. Eliot tips his head onto the sofa back and takes a deep breath while I wonder if "someone" is out there for him. I also wonder if he'll ever accept the kind of love Franny and I offer him without lumping it in with the trappings of a life he's never wanted. Whether he accepts it or not, it will always be there for him.

Always.

As our silence stretches on, I get teary so I switch topics, probing about the YouTube channel Eliot treats as if it's no big deal even though over four million people would argue otherwise. Predictably, he jumps on board with the conversational shift. He tells me about the constant pressure to promote products on his channel, which he refuses to do, though he could apparently make a ton of money. He takes up local jobs instead. Farming. Factory gigs. Transportation of goods. Adventure guide work. With my cobbled together jobs, I'm a little envious that he can make easy money and he chooses not to, but I also respect that he sticks to his principles. At least he let us drink the fancy wine and eat the fancy ice cream tonight without worrying that we've morally corrupted him.

It's after 4 a.m. when the movie ends. Franny's completely knocked out, curled up in a ball in her corner, mouth agape, hands tucked under her cheek. Eliot and I are still too wired to join her. He's weirded out being in this house. I don't want to sleep through our increasingly limited time together, not that I'd admit that out loud.

Eliot locates his phone and invites me to scooch closer, much like he did in Franny's truck. I settle in against his side as we scour the internet for contests to enter. We find an online coloring contest that doesn't list an age limit but definitely should, dozens of quick-entry giveaways and games, a corn-shucking contest in a nearby town, a cocktail-themed cupcake recipe contest, and an amateur square dance competition that's unlikely to lead to my first victory but would definitely get us laughing. We discuss schedule, too. We can fit a few things around my work shifts tomorrow, and Sunday's open for both of us, but Saturday's the funeral and Monday Eliot will be with his mom.

"The drunken cupcake one is open all month," I read off the site. "If we can't do it this weekend, I could give it a shot next week and post the entry after you leave."

He blinks as though surprised. "You'd enter on your own?"

"We can only fit in so much. And you'll be gone by Tuesday."

He flicks at the swatch of knitting that's still in my lap, letting his hand rest agonizingly close to mine, octopus tattoo, climbing scars, ratty cuticles, and all.

"Unless the sweater isn't done," he says.

"Right." I study my wonky knitting. "Though if I keep at it, I think I can finish."

"Hmm," he says, and then again, "Hmm," doing that repeating thing he always does, layering the echoed word with twice the weight of the original. I'm still staring at the navy rectangle in my lap, wondering what he's hmm-ing about, when he inches his hand closer, grazing my knuckles with his. "I've been meaning to say. I'm not sure why I keep waiting to say it. Maybe because the words sound so insufficient. I keep hoping better ones will come. But I'm sorry I ghosted you all these years."

I flinch, startled by the subject change, and by the heartfelt apology I've been craving for *so* long. The sheer sound of it rushes through me, obliterating a million tiny resentments I've accumulated over the years, knotted into muscle memory I didn't even realize I was holding on to.

*Goddamn.* The power of a well-delivered and sincere apology. It's magical. But as the sting of tears threatens, I lock my eyes on my knitting.

"It's all right," I manage with an impressively steady voice.

"No, it's not."

"People grow up and grow apart."

"Not people like us."

I glance over to see Eliot looking at me as though he has no patience for the kinds of polite evasions that get me through an average day. *How are you? Good. How's your mom? Never a dull moment. How's work? Same*

*old, same old. Heard from Eliot lately? You can find him on YouTube.*
*(I.e., no, and asking me yet again is crushing my soul.)*

"You're right," I say. "It's been hard. I didn't understand what I did wrong."

"Nothing. Nothing at all." He hooks my index finger with his, barely, but it's sweet, like our old knee taps, a quiet way of letting me know he's there. "I was a total mess in those first years after I left town, haunted by my dad's big speech about what I still had to learn. Too focused on where I'd been and not where I wanted to go. I was completely aimless, hopping any train that came into a station, scraping together money for hostels or campgrounds. Meanwhile, my parents were hounding me to return, to get 'a real education,' to settle down and choose a career path, to build the kind of life we're all told to want from the day we're born. A life with a house, a family, a corner office, and a two-car garage that's packed with so much stuff only one car fits.

"After a while, I started to entertain the idea, to give space to the pull to return, but I couldn't tell if I was doing it because some part of me actually wanted the things my parents described or because I was susceptible to the hype." His middle finger nudges forward. I'm not sure if he's twitching or sneaking his way into a handhold. Either way, I shift my fingers just enough to let him know his hand is welcome in mine.

"So you cut all ties?" I ask. "To lessen the pull?"

He nods, easing into what might even be a caress now.

"I won't claim it was a brave move. Or a smart move. Just a way of simplifying."

I watch our hands shift against each other, making the tiniest of movements, a fingertip against a fingertip, a knuckle sweeping the side of a thumb.

"And now?" I ask.

"Now I recognize the hype for what it is."

"Meaning the pull is gone?"

"The pull is . . . different."

"Different how?"

His forehead furrows, forcing his dark brows to plunge behind his glasses.

"Can we be totally honest with each other for a second?" he asks.

I tense, but not as much as I might if he wasn't tapping my knuckles.

"Okay?" I say, though it comes out squeaky and uncertain. I keep my eyes on our hands, worried he's going to draw out more truth than I'm prepared for tonight.

"Back in the ocean," he says. "I wasn't apologizing for tackling you."

"Okay," I say again, eyes still trained downward.

"I was apologizing for holding you the other way. The this-isn't-a-game way."

I suck in a breath, my heart pounding, *still* unable to look him in the eye.

He taps again. "What were you apologizing for?"

I don't move. I don't even release the breath I just inhaled. I simply stare at his knuckles where they're pushing past mine to link our hands together. Or maybe mine are doing the pushing. Either way, our fingers curl around each other, testing, exploring. Every movement is slow and tentative, soft, simple, but *so* not simple.

"I was apologizing for enjoying the way you were holding me," I say at last.

His forehead rumples again but he doesn't flinch, withdraw his hand, or make any other gesture that might indicate my comment is unwelcome.

We sit in relative silence, side by side, our hands loosely linked in my lap, as though neither of us knows where to take the conversation from here.

While our confessions hang in the air without capitulation or epilogue, Eliot slips a knitting needle out of the patch of ribbing I made tonight.

He gently unplucks a row of stitches.

Then he eases the needle back into place.

## HEARTBREAK #4

I met August Han, appropriately enough, in August. We had one of those can't-be-real meet-cutes where we both tried to buy the last available flourless chocolate cake at my favorite L.A. bakery. It was the one request a friend of mine had made for her birthday. It was also, apparently, the one request August's friend had made of him. We were equally determined to walk out of the bakery with *our* cake, and we made our feelings known.

In the end, we split the cake. And exchanged numbers.

Over the next three months, I introduced August to free museum days at LACMA. He got me into concerts at the Hollywood Bowl, where he worked as a sound technician. We hiked. We thrift shopped. We tried surfing. We rented Rollerblades together. We had *lots* of great sex. And we laughed. So much. Even though my first few relationships hadn't ended well, I embraced the possibility that this time, things would be different.

And they were different. They were great, in fact, except for one problem. August clammed up the moment words like *relationship*, *dating*, or *boyfriend* slipped out. He liked me, but he "didn't want to put a label on it." I craved a little more certainty.

After a particularly tense conversation on the topic, I decided I'd been putting too much pressure on him. On us. He was right. We didn't need labels. What did I care what we called each other? So, I packed us a surprise picnic the following weekend, complete with a flourless chocolate cake. I put on my cutest, brightest sundress and braided my long hair into an Instagram-worthy coronet, wedging in tiny flowers. I showed up at August's apartment on a sunny afternoon, the image of no-stress, no-need-for-labels fun.

He frowned as he cracked his door and saw me on his landing, grinning away.

"Did we have plans?" he asked. Not *hello*. Not *nice to see you*. Not even *hey*.

My grin fell away. "I've been thinking about our argument."

"Yeah. Um . . . me, too." He stepped onto the landing with me, shutting the door behind him. I realized then that he was only wearing a loose pair of jeans. And the belt laced through the loops wasn't fastened. Also . . . was that lipstick on his neck?

"What were *you* thinking?" I asked, suddenly very, *very* still.

"You were right. If I'm really in this, I shouldn't freak out about the word *boyfriend*."

"'If'?" I squeaked out.

"Yeah, well, that's the thing." He scratched at a thin patch of black hair on his chest. A very thin patch. "I was at work last night, and this new girl on the crew started flirting with me. It got me thinking, and I figured if I *was* really in this"—he waved a hand between the two of us—"and I slept with someone else, then I'd wake up, like, *knowing* I'd made the wrong choice and it was time to commit. For real."

I squinted at him, otherwise unmoving. "So . . . you slept with someone else to test whether or not you were ready to commit to me?"

He shrugged, scratching at his chest hair again. "I guess?"

I willed myself not to ask, but I asked anyway. "And?"

"And . . . well . . . I learned what I needed to learn."

I went home and poured my heartbreak into my art. I also periodically stalked August and his new girlfriend on social media, wondering if he'd eventually "test" their relationship the way he'd "tested" ours. A year later, they were still together. With labels. Funny that I thought our relationship could be strengthened with a picnic. He thought it could be strengthened by boning his cute new coworker. Guess we were both wrong.

Good thing I had cake in my picnic basket. I ate the entire thing that night, all in one sitting. And I never returned to that bakery.

# Eleven

## FRIDAY

"I knew it the instant I saw him yesterday," Kym gushes, a ray of well-assembled morning sunshine in her J.Crew coordinates and perfect French braid.

"He's a friend," I say, a phrase I suspect will become a common refrain in days to come, since Pitt's Corner gossip channels operate faster than our highest speed Wi-Fi. When Kym doesn't reply right away, I look up from the enormous mass of white lilies I'm sorting to see her watching me with impatience, her arms folded and her toe tapping. I roll my eyes as I gesture at the flowers. "He's here for a funeral. Not a romance."

"Who says the two are mutually exclusive?"

"I don't recall 'Love and Death' being a popular Netflix category."

Kym purses her lips at me, but only for an instant before heading into the back room to gather greenery and filler flowers for the funeral arrangements we're making this morning. Mrs. Swift sent a hefty check with the instructions: *tasteful shades of ivory only, no white; three elegant bouquets, no tacky wreaths; keep the look traditional; don't skimp*. Basically, she wants us to make sure the arrangements look expensive while indicting nothing about her husband's tastes or personality. Pretty predictable.

"He looked pleased when I told him you broke up with your boyfriend," Kym says as she returns to the main room with her arms full of roses and gladiolas.

I flash her a second of side-eye, unsure where to start unpacking her statement. A, Eliot rarely looks "pleased" so that's probably a lie. B, on the off-chance he did look cheerful about my breakup, that would be kind of an asshole reaction, and poor incentive for dating him. C, I didn't break up with Greg. He broke up with me.

"Eliot's not even the same guy I knew in high school," I say.

"Oh? How has he changed?"

"He's"—*totally the same guy I knew in high school*—"he has a beard now."

Kim huffs out a light laugh at my expense.

"So buy him a razor and tell him how you feel about him already!"

I set a pair of glass vases on the counter with unnecessary force.

"I thought you were on Team Dutch," I say.

"That was before you told me you were in love with someone else."

"*Was* in love," I emphasize. "Past tense. Like, way, way, *way* past tense."

Kym positions herself on the opposite side of the counter, where she checks rosebuds for flaws and sorts them into three piles, one for each vase and a third for the casket. I start trimming the lilies that will center each arrangement. I'm not sure why I'm being so cagey about Eliot, except that whatever sparked between us last night was so brief, so fleeting, I can't let my imagination—or Kym's, or anyone else's—run wild. I know he wanted to hold me. He knows I wanted to be held. That's it. End of story.

"Does he have a girlfriend?" Kym asks.

"I didn't ask."

"Has he *mentioned* a girlfriend?"

"No."

"A boyfriend?"

"Nope."

"Marriage? Divorce? Children?"

"Also not mentioned, and therefore unlikely."

"Crimes or misdemeanors? Skipped parole?"

"His public travelogue would make skipping parole uniquely challenging."

"Drug addiction? A tendency toward violence?"

"Also long shots."

"What about castration?"

"Kym!" I jerk to attention and come perilously close to beheading a lily.

She waves off my indignation with another laugh.

"I just don't see what the problem is," she says.

"Yes, you do."

She sighs, watching me with a parental sort of sympathy, one laden with concern. She also stops plucking imperfect rose petals while I stop snipping lily stems. We face each other across the counter, separated by a mound of macabre foliage. Funny that death gets marked in our culture with black clothes but white flowers. Or in this case, ivory.

"You know I take your mother's wisdom seriously," she says, and I can't help but love her choice of words. Not *visions*. Not *omens*. *Wisdom*. "I got our airbags checked just in time last year. And Eugene will be forever grateful he didn't take the kids camping after she warned us about those high winds a few years back. So many trees down."

I nod as I resume my work, unsure where she's going with this.

"I also know you've had a run of bad luck with men," she adds, an unexpected shift in her faith in my mom's *wisdom*, and a unique take on seventeen consecutive non-mutual breakups. "But what's wrong with having a little fun? Your friend only being in town for a few days could even be a good thing. A chance to have a quick fling without worrying about other women or adding to your . . . what did you call it?"

"My extensive People to Avoid list?"

"Exactly! That!" She waggles a rose at me. "He'll be gone before you have to avoid him. So flirt a little. Work up to a kiss. Find out if the fluttery feelings come back."

*The fluttery feelings have already been noted,* I think. *Noted, permanently catalogued, and analyzed to the point of extreme irritation.*

"The funeral's tomorrow," I remind Kym unnecessarily. "I should probably skip 'Want to make out behind the pulpit?' and focus on 'I'm so sorry for your loss.'"

"Okay." She dismisses the conversation with a flap of her hand. "But if you need to come in late next week, I can take care of the arrangements for a few days."

I glance at the pile of flowers before her, picturing them crammed into vases with a few hasty sprigs of baby's breath. Also, next week, I'll be desperate to stay busy.

"Thanks," I say. "But I promise I'll be here on time."

An hour after leaving Amelia's Bloomers, I'm on the beach, pulling Jack off the back end of a thirteen-year-old chocolate Lab who's too nice to tell him to leave her alone. I aim him toward the water, hoping he'll go find a length of kelp to molest, or maybe he can annoy a few seagulls with his attempt to dominate all living species. I don't know if the Lab has the ability to fully register my assistance, but I swear she looks at me like she owes me one. The patriarchy blows. Us girls have to stick together.

I have eight dogs today, which is more than usual but manageable since three are old and mostly lean against driftwood while staring at the sea, dreaming of halcyon days of yore. A whippet rubs its head in something I'm grateful I can't smell from here while a scruffy little mutt prances along the beach with a stick he's been carrying around for twenty minutes now. What a gift, to fall in love with something so quickly and completely, utterly fearless about the potential consequences of its loss. Dogs are the best.

My phone buzzes in my pocket. I check that all of my dogs are accounted for and occupied before finding a log to sit on, piling up leashes beside me.

Franny: On a quick break. How are you holding up?

Imogen: Tired. Overcaffeinated. But okay

Franny: Did you guys sleep at all?

Imogen: We had a lot to catch up on

Franny: I'll say

Franny follows up her text by sending a selfie of Eliot standing shirtless in front of a waterfall. His torso is slightly twisted as he points over his shoulder, and while the pose looks relaxed and natural, as if he's simply pointing out something about the falls, it also manages to perfectly display his lean, inked body, like I could count his abs if I wanted to, which I totally don't. The shot is a still from one of his travel videos. I assume Franny found it by googling him since that was how I once came across it. Among others.

Franny: He's not the boy next door anymore, amirite?

Imogen: He never was the boy next door. He was the boy in
    the enormous mansion five miles away where all the other
    rich people lived

Franny: You know you have hang-ups about class, right?

Imogen: You know I've been scrubbing his toilets, right?

Franny: Fair point. Still. I think one of us should make a move

I stare at the screen, fingers hovering and stomach sinking. After watching Franny and Eliot together for the last twenty-four hours, this is hardly a surprise, but—

Franny: I think it should be you

I jerk upright so fast I drop my phone. It falls in the sand, just missing a pile of crab shells. I brush off the sand and reread Franny's last text several times before I reply.

Imogen: Why me?

Franny: He's too broody for me

Imogen: Since when?

Franny: Since always

Imogen: What about prom?

Franny: Oh, he DEFINITELY brooded at prom

I laugh to myself, drawing the attention of an ancient husky who's sleeping near my feet. I'd suspect Franny of deliberately evading my point, but she and Eliot really did go to prom as friends, even if their night out ended up in more-than-friends territory.

Imogen: Eliot's a deep thinker. That's a good thing

Franny: Some of his thoughts aren't so deep

Imogen: Meaning?

Franny: Meaning he totally got a boner over you last night

I drop my phone again. The sudden movement alarms the husky.

Imogen: Excuse me?

Franny: Why do you think he jumped in without us?

Imogen: He was cold?

Franny: And the ocean would warm him up?

Imogen: It might. If he was moving

Franny: He was "moving" all right!

Imogen: You're ridiculous

Franny: Love me anyway?

Imogen: Always

She sends me a video clip of Eliot hauling himself out of a body of water onto a dock. He's shirtless, *again*, and whoever extracted the clip from his travelogue slowed it down so water droplets cling to Eliot's body as they trickle downward. His wet swim trunks do their fair share of clinging as well.

*Good lord.* My entire body flushes. I'm pretty sure even my toes are red. Despite my obvious attraction, I'm not "making a move." I couldn't even manage a hug this morning before Franny and I got in her truck. I was afraid to indicate I'd read too much into our 4 a.m. confessional. So, I shuffled before Eliot like an idiot, flashing a choppy wave and saying I'd catch him later tonight. Where Franny gets the idea that I have "sexy wiles" is beyond me. I might as well be a character from Richard Scarry's *Busytown*. Just a friendly pig in overalls with a wave and a cheesy grin.

> Franny: You're thinking about it, aren't you?
> Imogen: Absolutely not
> Franny: Absolutely bullshit
> Imogen: You don't know that
> Franny: You forget. I know what your lust face looks like
> Imogen: Please tell me that's an autocorrect error
> Franny: Hardly. Also, there's this . . .

Another photo pops up. This time Eliot's in The Sweater. As beautiful as he is shirtless among rain forests and waterfalls, this is the shot that makes my heart clench.

> Franny: I'm such an idiot
> Imogen: Highly arguable
> Franny: How did I not see it?
> Imogen: Temporary blindness? Even orbiting astronauts could see that sweater
> Franny: Not the sweater. The crush! Back in high school!

*Shit.* She knows. A lifetime of carefully maintained silence washed away in one night of blotchy blushes and stolen glances. And whatever else comprises a "lust face."

> Imogen: Please don't tell him
> Franny: Wait. YOU had a crush too?

*Oh. Oops. Hmm. Okay. New angle.*

Franny: This just gets better and better

Imogen: Can we pretend I didn't text that?

Franny: No way. This is perfect

Imogen: Define perfect

Franny: You were into him and he was into you!

Imogen: Evidence suggests otherwise

Franny: *I asked him to prom. *I suggested we have sex. *I
made all the moves

Imogen: Moves he embraced though, right?

Franny: Whatever. I was afraid to miss out on anything. He
was easily persuaded. We were both dumb kids who
didn't know what the hell we wanted

Imogen: Exactly. See above text RE: lack of evidence of what
Eliot was "into"

Franny: Hello? The sweater? He didn't keep anything I gave
him

Imogen: Your parting gift was pot brownies. Doubt they'd
have made it to Nepal

Franny responds with a laughing/crying emoji. I take a moment to count my charges and pull Jack off the Lab again. Read the room, jerk. And get the lady's consent.

Franny: I'm just saying. You could be part of Eliot's
transformation. Or he could be part of yours. Maybe
this is a second chance for both of you. You're good at
seconds!

Imogen: Don't remind me

Franny: At least think about it. And know I'm rooting for you.
     Both of you

I indulge in a wistful sigh, with only the dogs and the seagulls to hear me. No matter what happens over the next few days, I have Franny. I have dogs. And I have the ocean. Life could be so much worse.

Imogen: Consider it thought about
Franny: Good. Keep thinking. Gotta go. Ed's threatening
     to fire me if I don't get the damned side salads on the
     damned plates with the damned burgers for the people
     who should've ordered fries because salads are a waste
     of plate space
Imogen: Be there by lunch rush
Franny: xoxo

She goes back to work while I get up to toss a ball for a miniature dachshund who's afraid of the water and only ever wants to play fetch in dry sand. He scurries after the ball on his stubby little legs, dodging tufts of beach grass and empty crab shells left behind by greedy seagulls. Between ball tosses, I reread my text convo with Franny. I love her enthusiasm, and I'm relieved to stop assuming I'll come second to her again where Eliot's concerned, but at least I know Franny. I adore her. I can picture her with Eliot and find *some* joy in the image. Bracing to meet an unknown woman at an unknown time feels like a much bigger challenge, one even a decade of being unceremoniously dumped can't prepare me for. Best not to go down a road I know can only end badly.

I'm talking myself down from picturing Eliot's perfect match— tanned, fit, inked, climbs mountains in sexy cargo shorts, vehemently hates walls—when I notice a jogger approaching from the south end of the beach. Few people jog here since the terrain is so uneven and the public shoreline is periodically interrupted by private properties. Plein-air painters pop up easels once in a while, but with more striking sandy beaches and rock formations to both the north and south, Pitt's Corner is a bit of a no-man's-land.

I start corralling the dogs, but as the figure gets closer, I realize it's not a random jogger. It's Eliot, because while I'm barely standing after a sleepless, muddled night, he has propelled himself more than six miles from his parents' house. On foot. An excellent reminder that I'm unlikely to be his second-chance soulmate. Still, I pat down my ugly hair and rub muddy paw prints off my jeans, assembling myself the best I can.

Eliot slows to a walk as several dogs trot over to greet him (or in Jack's case, bark as though Eliot's invading his private sanctuary). He pats the dogs on their heads as he weaves his way over to me, wearing a dingy, sweat-soaked T-shirt and a pair of ill-fitting running shorts that should be off-putting but hit his muscular thighs at a *really* good spot. I tell myself I'm only noticing because Franny encouraged me to notice, but that's a lie.

"Marathon training already?" I ask.

"Just keeping in shape. Running's also a good way to tour a place. I can cover a lot of ground at a steady pace and see everything without a pane of glass in the way."

"What's 'a lot of ground'?"

He shrugs while scratching at the back of his neck, incidentally displaying his arm muscles to perfect advantage à la the waterfall photo I've completely forgotten about.

"I don't know," he says, all sheepish and adorable. "Sixteen or eighteen miles?"

A gust of laughter bursts out of me.

"I mean, I did an Ironman before breakfast, but whatever."

He smiles at that, not full-out, but more than his usual tip-and-twitch.

"I've seen you swim," he says. "Not sure an Ironman's in your near future."

I sucker punch his arm. He laughs as he rubs the point of impact, faking injury.

"Keep up that sass and I'm not sure another sleepover's in *your* future," I tease.

His smile flickers and fades as though my teasing hit harder than intended.

"Noted," he says. "No more Ironman jokes."

"Well, you know, unless they're funny."

His face scrunches up in exaggerated concentration.

"Nope," he says after a long pause. "I've got nothing."

"Niche genre."

"Very niche." He tips his chin and I consider it a win.

A shower of flying sand halts our banter, kicked our direction by a recognizable set of Jack Russell terrier paws. Jack side-eyes us as we step out of the spray, and I swear he's calculating a redirection of his efforts so he'll hit us *just so*, but a seagull swoops down nearby and distracts him. I toss the gull a few dog treats in gratitude.

"You still up for company on your pizza delivery shift later?" Eliot asks.

"As long as you're still okay to spend three hours in an old Honda hatchback that smells like onions, pepperoni, and an occasional tang of soggy pineapple."

"I can handle it. We have giveaways to enter. You drive. I'll type."

"Sounds like a date." I choke on the word. "Not a date. Just a drive. Work. Contests. Curse. Whatever. I just mean my shotgun seat is all yours."

He flashes me a rare full-out smile that makes my heart perform distinctly non-heart-like contortions.

*Goddammit.* I could text myself hourly reminders that Eliot's leaving in four days and I'll only ever be second to him anyway and I'd still crave his hard-earned smiles, his untempered truths, his unwavering belief in me, and his support for my dreams, even the dreams I shoved in a closet years ago.

I eventually rein in my infatuation and blather out something about leashing up the dogs. I'm about to tell Eliot I'll pick him up at six when my phone buzzes again. I assume it's Franny, sending me another thirst-trap shot of Eliot, but the text is from Kym's husband, Eugene. He runs the local history museum, which is basically an old railroad car with some gold rush photos and rusty tools. The text on my screen barely registers—*Hi. Are you working?*—but the one that follows makes my breath catch.

> Eugene: I'm at Coastal Medical with your mom. She doesn't want you to worry. Made me promise not to call you, so I'm sneaking in a text. She fell on the rocks near the museum. She's okay. Nothing broken. But the doctor won't release her without an escort to make sure she gets home safely. I'd see her home and stay with her but Kym's parents just flew in to PDX and I need to go pick them up. How soon can you get here?

"Oh, god." I frantically clip a leash to the nearest dog. "Not again."

"What's the matter?" Eliot holds out a hand and nods at my tangle of leashes.

"You don't know which one belongs to which dog," I say, a bit shrill now.

"Give me that one's." He tips his chin toward Jack's resumed manic sand spray. "He looks like he might be your biggest challenge."

"You have no idea." I extract Jack's leash and hand it to Eliot while rapidly relaying Eugene's text and trying not to freak out. "I need to get all of these dogs home. Return keys to Vera. Call the diner to let Ed know I'm not coming in today. Notify—"

"I'll deal with the dogs," Eliot says in a calm, authoritative voice that's precisely what I need right now. "I'll also text Franny about the diner. You go get your mom."

I leash up the dachshund and beckon a pair of terriers over with treats.

"It's complicated," I say. "Every dog goes to a different house."

"Okay. Then you drop off the dogs. I'll get your mom."

"You don't have to d—"

"Imogen. Seriously. Let me help."

I pause just long enough to meet his eyes, and to read the assurance in them.

"Really?" I ask. "You wouldn't mind?"

"Of course not." Eliot somehow out-alphas Jack, forcing the little demon to sit while he clips on the leash and I wrangle the mutt and the Lab. "Take your time. Do what you need to do. Breathe. I've got this. I'll see you back at your place."

"Okay. All right. Yes. Great. Okay." I spin around, counting dogs while I will my thoughts to return to order. *Six. Seven. Eight.* That's all of them. The dogs, that is. I can't even begin to count my thoughts.

I tighten my grip on the leashes, jogging away to start my drop-off loop. When I turn back around to thank Eliot, he's already running in the direction of the hospital.

# Twelve

H ello?" I call from the front door when I finally get home.

"We're in here!" My mom's voice reaches me from the din-ing room.

I rush through the living room without removing my shoes or coat, halting as the adjacent dining room comes into view. Eliot's seated in one of our heavy 1940s dining chairs. He's still in his running clothes, but a faded pink and orange floral towel is draped around his shoulders while a ring of long, dark, wavy locks sur-rounds his sock-clad feet. My mom stands behind him, electric clip-pers in hand, a proud smile on her face. A gauze square is taped to her temple and a rash-like red patch stretches from her cheek to her chin. Her nose is also scraped up, her free hand is bandaged, and her left eye is lightly bruised. She looks like she face-planted on the rocks, a piece of information Eugene conveniently omitted from his texted description of her fall. But also . . .

"What do you think?" Eliot runs a hand over his head. Not his hair. His head. His glasses are off and he's fully shorn, down to about a quarter-inch of even dark growth. He mentioned yesterday that he wasn't attached to the length, but *wow*.

"It's short," I say with my usual talent for pointing out the obvious.

My mom steps forward and lifts his face with a scabbed knuckle under his chin.

"You look very handsome," she says. "Like an action hero."

I snort out a laugh before I can stop myself.

"What?" he asks through the tiniest twitch of a smile. "You don't see me whipping out an automatic or gritting my teeth through a high-speed car chase?"

"It's a stretch," I admit, still picturing him as the shy, bookish boy I knew years ago, despite his YouTube persona and increased muscle mass. "But give me time. I'll adjust to the idea." Now that I know I can stop panicking, I peel off my coat and toss it onto our ugly chenille sofa, a mustard-colored 1970s relic that's almost hideous enough to become chic again. Then I step into the dining room, taking a closer look at my mom's battered face. "I didn't take you for a *Fight Club* fan. Ouch. Are you all right?"

"Fine, fine." She flaps a dismissive hand. "A little tumble. Nothing to fuss about."

I open my mouth to protest but I catch Eliot's eye before speaking. He offers me a subtle shrug, one that suggests maybe we do have reason to fuss, but if my mom's downplaying her accident, we should at least consider following her lead.

"A little tumble," I concede, sneaking Eliot an eye roll. "Duly noted."

My mom shoots me a scowl, recognizing my concession for what it is. I'd defend my subtle snark, but she already knows nothing's "little" about another fall, and neither of us wants to fight in front of Eliot. She'll be okay. That's the most important thing.

Eliot takes in our silent standoff before locating his glasses on the dining table and slipping them on. Then he checks his reflection in a nearby hand mirror.

"Any chance you have a razor around?" he asks. "I should probably ditch this beard. Otherwise I'll have to learn how to wear hipster neck scarves."

I squint at him, with his shorn head, full beard, and inky tattoos.

"A cleverly knotted posh scarf might suit you," I say.

"Nah. I'd look like a total faker."

"A seersucker suit jacket?"

"I haven't worn a suit jacket since high school."

"Pegged trousers? Novelty socks? What about a banjo?" I flash him an eager grin.

His eyes twinkle as he gives me a chin lift, inching toward a full smile.

"Let's start with the razor," he says. "Hipster props can be part of plan B."

We share a look of understanding as he slides the towel off his shoulders. As always, Eliot read the situation correctly, not only chattering on about unimportant nonsense to ease the tension in the room, but sacrificing his beautiful Samson hair to distract my mom from her injuries. The word *gratitude* doesn't even begin to cover what I'm feeling right now. I suppose that's why someone invented the word *love*.

I lead Eliot to the hall bathroom where I dig through bins of crumbling bath salt cubes and dog grooming supplies until I find a bag of disposable razors. They probably should've been tossed years ago when I shifted to waxing, but like so many things in this house, they've remained well past their point of usefulness.

"Men's. Interesting." He turns over the package. "For your overnight guests?" He waits for my reaction and I can't help but enjoy the implication that he might be jealous.

"Just avoiding the pink tax," I say after a deliberate pause. "Same razors. Different color. Half the price."

He nods, removing a razor and examining his reflection from multiple angles. As he starts the faucet, filling the sink, I position myself in the doorway.

"How is she really?" I ask, my voice hushed.

"The doctor confirmed mostly surface wounds, though she's hiding a knee brace under her skirts. Honestly, I think she's more embarrassed than hurt. We got here and she couldn't sit still. Kept offering me tea. Cookies. Asking if I needed anything."

"So you gave her a task to do." My gaze lifts to his newly sharpened hairline.

Eliot averts his eyes, checking the water temperature. "I kept her busy."

My chest pinches so hard I have to lean against the doorframe until I can confirm my heart is beating normally. I'm not used to this level of support, not from the men in my life. If Greg had been here, he'd lecture me about putting my mom in a home since she's incapable of going two minutes unsupervised, a complete distortion of the truth. My previous two exes wouldn't even come over, too weirded out by the prophecies. The boyfriend before that might've brought her home, but then he would've ignored her while he sat in a corner with his attention locked on his phone, claiming he "wasn't good at stuff like this" as though that was reason not to try. Eliot intuits what's needed and takes care of it. No resentment. No clever avoidance of anything resembling caretaking. And no accusations about how a situation could've been prevented in the first place.

*How can I let someone love me?* he asked last night.

But how can he not?

"Thank you," I say. "For everything. Taking charge. Picking her up. The hair."

He starts lathering his beard with a sliver of crappy hand soap.

"Does it happen it a lot?" he asks. "Her getting hurt like that?"

I shift a shoulder, still braced against the doorframe.

"Every few months, I guess. More often in recent years." I glance down the hall to ensure she isn't listening before I turn back to Eliot. "She doesn't usually end up at the hospital. I find her at home trying to Band-Aid scraped knees or pick gravel out of her palms. But she's sprained a wrist a couple of times. An ankle once. Fallen on the ice in the winter or into blackberry brambles in the summer. She had a nasty run-in with a wasp's nest last year. A cyclist also knocked her over when she wasn't watching where she was walking, too busy tracking a murmuration of swallows." I kick at the doorjamb with my sneakered toe, working back through the memories. "Most days she's fine. Honestly. Everyone in town helps keep an eye out. She's healthy both mentally and physically, but she gets lost in her own meanderings, and she forgets to be careful."

Eliot watches me through the mirror as he drags the razor down his cheek.

"And she prefers to 'meander' on her own?" he asks.

"Not necessarily. She has friends in town who take walks with her or drive her up the coast for bird-watching expeditions. She likes company. She just wants to be free to experience the world in her own way. And she wants to live in her own familiar space. I promised her I'd give her that. Even if it's not always easy."

Eliot nods, rinsing the razor before removing another strip of his beard.

"So she needs a companion," he says, and I could kiss him for not saying *nurse*. "Someone to go on these meanderings with her. When you or her friends can't be there."

"Finding a dedicated companion would be amazing. But easier said than done."

While Eliot shaves, I fill him in on various efforts my siblings and I have made to find additional care for our mom. Most services require a medical diagnosis, which we don't have, and at this point, even if we could get a diagnosis, it would be considered a preexisting condition and not covered under most insurance plans. We found a great place last year after the wasp's nest incident. Less focused on medical care and more on being present and capable in case of a crisis, but it was way out of our price range, even with all of our resources combined. Lavinia makes next to nothing at her literary research job and Antony's not bringing in huge figures restoring properties. They both contribute, but none of us can afford three hundred bucks a day for in-home care. Our mom is also fiercely independent, and totally fine most days. It's hard to rationalize spending that kind of money for someone who doesn't want the extra care, and doesn't always need it.

"Do you mind if I do a little research on my own?" Eliot asks, now down to the last bits of soapy stubble on his chin.

"That would be great," I say. "Probably best if she doesn't know though."

He mimes zipping his lips, inadvertently streaking suds across his mouth. He makes a face at the taste and we share a tension-relieving laugh. I don't know what Eliot will discover that Antony, Lavinia, and I haven't yet considered, but I trust him. He cares about my mom and about me. Anything he does will be kind and well-considered.

Eliot finishes shaving while I head back to the dining room, where I sweep up his hair and gently get my mom to explain that she was on the rocks because she spotted something reflective in a little tidal pool and she needed to know what it was. (I don't ask why it matters. For my mom, it just does.) While she attempted to identify the object, she stumbled and slid down the side of the rocks, banging her way to the sand. Thankfully, Eugene witnessed her fall as he was locking up the railway car.

"I'm sorry I interrupted your work," she says, her body sagging with contrition.

"Fridays at the diner are generally slow," I outright lie. "Franny can manage without me. And Nandini can get another pizza driver tonight." I set down my broom and dustpan so I can pull my mom into a gentle hug. "I'm just glad you're okay."

"I'm fine." She returns my embrace, settling against my chest with a deep sigh that pushes through all three of her sweaters. "Nothing that won't heal. Though I hate that I'll never know about that tidal pool. The ocean will have washed it clean by now."

I release my embrace, pulling back to tuck my mom's graying hair behind her ear.

"Maybe sometimes it's better not to know." I toss out the words conversationally, but a heavy silence falls as we both look toward the hall and the glow of the bathroom light. I'm not thinking about tidal pools anymore. Neither is my mom.

Words and images flash through my mind. *Loss. Transformation. Severing.* A boy getting on a bus. A man getting on a bus. *A change of expectations. Maybe he doesn't know what he wants.* Thirteen birds in an early morning fog. An underwater embrace. *A second chance for both of you.* Blood and broken glass on a pencil sketch of a childhood memory. A dead man's hollow house. A growing patch of deep blue knitting.

Not knowing suddenly seems unbearable. I start to form a question about my mom's prophecy, but the sound of running water indicates Eliot might soon emerge. I don't want to get into the nuances of "complicated" predictions with him in earshot, so I swallow my curiosity, pick up the dustpan, and finish tidying the dining room.

Minutes later, I'm staring into a cupboard, searching for snacks that are more enticing than stale saltines, when Eliot coughs behind me. I spin around and—

"Holy shit." I clap a hand over my mouth. "Sorry. Inside voice."

He runs a hand over his cleanly shaven face as his lips twitch into what I can officially call a smile now, even if it's only at half-mast. I never established a personal point of view about beards, but now that Eliot's beard is gone, I plant myself firmly in the anti-beard camp. His incredible bone structure is no longer hidden. His lips are in full view. His big brown eyes also look even bigger, warmer, like two spots on a painter's palette, where umber and sienna are only half blended. And yet, their coloring has never been their greatest asset. It's their profound tenderness. The way he looks at everything and everyone as though they *really* matter, even though he never holds on for long.

"Was that a good *holy shit* or a bad *holy shit*?" he asks.

"Good. Definitely good. I mean, I don't see a banjo anywhere so you're not my type, but, yeah. You're pretty dreamy when you're not hiding those cheekbones or that jawline." I cringe, my face heating to about a billion degrees, awash with mortification that I just said that out loud. "Sorry. Don't mean to creep you out."

"Consider me non-creeped." He shakes his head as if he's dismissing the idea, though he's flushing now, too, clearly embarrassed that I inadvertently ogled him.

That I'm *still* inadvertently ogling him.

I mean . . . I just . . . *fuck*.

Eventually I blink myself out of my stupor and register his running clothes.

"I'm so sorry," I say. "You've been sitting around in sweaty clothes all this time. We should get you back to your parents' place so you can clean up and change."

Without warning, I flash to an image of Eliot in the shower on the first night he was back in town, an image that's far more vivid than my actual memory of that moment. Steam. Naked skin. Suds.

Water running over shoulders that have squared out in recent years, biceps that haul him up mountainsides, abs I still refuse to count. Water running over the erection Franny completely invented but now I can't get off my mind.

"Are we still on for pizza delivery tonight?" Eliot asks, gloriously ignorant of the inner workings of my brain. "I have our list of contests all cued up."

"I, um . . ." I clear my throat as I shake off all thoughts of naked skin and erections. Hopefully forever. "I'm going to stay in tonight. Keep my mom company. My boss has a long list of teenagers she can call, all of whom are more aggressive drivers and faster with deliveries. She only gives me the shifts because she knows I need the cash."

Eliot nods while grazing his inked knuckles over his newly smooth jawline.

"I don't mind sticking around for a bit," he says.

"You don't have plans for the afternoon?"

"Like entering a coloring contest?"

"Like taking a nap? Enjoying some peace and quiet?"

"I'll have plenty of peace and quiet next week."

"Don't you at least want to change clothes?"

"Did Antony leave anything behind I could borrow?"

"Yeah. Probably." I assess Eliot's frame. For strictly forensic purposes. Antony's taller and heavier, but a T-shirt's a T-shirt. "He keeps sweats here for sleeping in when he visits. Some tees and socks. But are you sure? I can totally drive you back."

Eliot peers toward the living room, where my mom is knitting in front of the TV.

"You should stay here. We both should. She could use the company." He stops grazing his jawline and scratches at the back of his neck, not as if his neck itches, but as if his hand needed to stay active and that's where it landed next.

Suddenly it hits me. Why he's not accepting my offer to drive him to his parents' place. Sophia said Mrs. Swift was returning to Pitt's Corner tonight. Eliot isn't suggesting he stay here as a favor to me. Nor is he suggesting he only stay for the afternoon.

"You *really* hate that house, don't you?" I ask, skirting any mention of his mom.

"Maybe I *really* want to watch you color," he volleys back.

"You mean you want to see me excavate my art supplies."

"Would that be such a bad thing?"

I consider the question as I picture my old tackle boxes filled with markers, paints, inks, brushes, palettes and papers, boxes of broken charcoal sticks, a full pastel set I barely used, the tools of a trade I was once so passionate about pursuing.

*I just wish you could enjoy being needed, and living in a place that feels like home, while still finding time to chase a dream once in a while,* Eliot said last night. Then he put a pencil in my hand. A pencil that felt like it belonged there. A pencil *he knew* would feel like it belonged there, even though I'd let myself forget for so long.

"C'mon." I nod toward the hall that leads to the bathroom and bedrooms. "Let's find you a towel, some soap, and a change of clothes."

# Thirteen

"It's terrible," I say with no attempt to soften my critique.

"It's supposed to be terrible." Eliot turns his page sideways, as though a new perspective will improve his scribbles. It doesn't. The picture we're each coloring is a line drawing of a scarecrow among pumpkins and corn stalks. Eliot kept his promise to color outside the lines. His pumpkins also have blotchy pink dots that make them look diseased while his scarecrow is bright yellow. The overalls are yellow. The hat is yellow. The face is yellow. The color bleeds off the body as though it's glowing from a uranium leak, a thought that makes the crooked grin read more like a pained grimace. In the upper right corner of the page, on the given blanks, Eliot has written his name and age.

"They're going to assume the twenty-eight is a mistake," I say.

"Doesn't matter. Let's see yours." Eliot leans over from his seat next to me on the sofa. He's wearing Antony's XXL Boston University sweatpants and a long-sleeved tee with anthropomorphized M&M's on it. Antony has always loved M&M's, and his shirt has been kicking around this house for at least twenty years. It's faded and stained, but Eliot donned the clothes without complaint, even while the sweatpants repeatedly slid low on his hips and I repeatedly told myself not to notice (while, of course, repeatedly noticing).

I pass Eliot my coloring page, still laughing to myself that he thinks *this* is the way to break my curse. No one in their right mind would hand the win to an adult, no matter how brilliantly I select and apply my colors, though with this particular contest, I also know winning has never been the point. The point is the marker in my hand, and the other art supplies strewn across the coffee table where we've kicked up our feet.

"This is amazing." Eliot's eyes skim over my added line work, which takes the image from a bubbly cartoon into dark graphic novel territory with sharper angles, the implication of movement, and a strong black-and-white contrast with only a few pops of purple and green. "How did you do this? It's like a whole different picture."

I take the page from him. "Training, I guess?"

"More like talent," my mom says from the armchair to my right. Her voice jolts me. I thought she fell asleep twenty minutes ago, around the time the umpteenth episode of her favorite reality show, *Good People, Bad Choices*, ended. I prefer scripted dramas where the plot threads all tie up neatly at the end, but my mom adores the messier side of humanity, probably because the futures she sees are so rarely neat and tidy.

Eliot and I have been enjoying the quiet as we colored beside each other, close enough to tap a knee or an elbow every once in a while. We printed out the pics after entering more than fifty random contests with minimal entry requirements. Comments on social media giveaways. Quick product reviews. Short questionnaires. We also polished off the pizza I ordered so I could tip the driver who took over for me tonight, a sixteen-year-old socially reticent skater named Hank who mumbled out, *Cool,* as he pocketed the extra twenty in his oversized hoodie and trudged back to his wreck of a Pinto. By the time he's my age, he'll probably be running a successful sporting goods shop, with a wife, a mortgage, an SUV, and a second kid on the way. For now, he's my coworker.

"Can I see some of your other work?" Eliot asks.

I wince before I can stop myself, catching a curious glance from my mom out of the corner of my eye. Or rather, a *complicated* glance. Suddenly I feel like I'm seventeen again, with strict rules about when boys are allowed to be in bedrooms.

"I don't know," I hedge. "I haven't looked at any of my work in ages."

"No time like the present?" Eliot smiles at me, full of hope, with a slow bat of his lashes, and just like that, all resistance is futile. He might as well be Tiny Tim, charming the grumpiest of Scrooges into giving his family a turkey for Christmas.

"How are you doing?" I ask my mom. "You okay if we vanish for a bit?"

She flaps a slender hand at me with a teasing purse of her lips.

"You two have fun. I'm going to tuck in early tonight." She hauls herself out of the armchair and straightens her skirts and sweaters, chosen through a logic entirely her own. I used to wonder how she didn't roast in her many layers, but she swore she was fine. All those clothes also help us keep the heating bill down, so I'm not about to push for change. "Extra sheets and pillowcases are in Antony's dresser. Towels in the linen closet across the hall. You know your way to the kitchen if you get hungry."

I confirm that I'll make sure Eliot has everything he needs. Then we all say good night and my mom heads down the hall toward her bedroom.

As soon as she disappears from view, Eliot leans in close, his arm brushing mine and his breath tickling my ear. "Was that a *yes*?"

*A yes to what?* I think, though I'd say *yes* to pretty much anything when he's this close to me, with his voice shooting sparks of nervous anticipation through my body.

"Can I see some of your art?" he prompts when I fail to say anything.

"My art. Right. Of course. Yeah. We can take a look." I blink myself out of my millionth wandering thought for the day, standing to clear away the pizza detritus while Eliot photographs our coloring entries and submits them on the contest site. I also put away the remotes, tuck our ugly avocado throw pillows into the corners of our equally ugly mustard sofa, pack up my art supplies, pick crumbs off the floor, and give the coffee table a full wipe-down. I'm obviously stalling—as nervous about being alone in my room with Eliot as I am about showing him my art—but before I know it, I run out of things to tidy, so I open the basement door and lead the way downstairs.

"Déjà vu, huh?" Eliot asks from a step behind me.

"Something like that." I send a quick smile over my shoulder before continuing my descent, recalling the days when Eliot would come over to hang out so he could avoid his parents' latest fight. They never yelled or threw punches. Instead, they iced each other out with disapproval so intense, and so cutting, anyone would wither in the crossfire.

During the extended bouts, Eliot sometimes stayed overnight, using the same bedroom he'll sleep in tonight, the one Antony vacated when he left for Boston. The house was built with only three bedrooms and one bathroom. I shared a room with Lavinia until she was sixteen and I was thirteen and we were both desperate for our own space. We all chipped in to renovate the basement. The reno isn't glamorous, and half the space remains unfinished, walled off for storage, laundry, and a curmudgeon of a boiler that still makes me jump in the night. But the open stairs lead directly into a good-sized bedroom with ample closet space and a full bath attached. The carpet is industrial, a low-pile gray remnant we got for almost nothing, and the furniture is an assortment of thrift store finds and embarrassing household rejects, but the walls are a beautiful shade of robin's-egg blue I picked out myself. It's my one source of pride in the space, and it still brings me joy, despite a gradual accumulation of clutter I now wish I'd tidied.

"I wasn't expecting company," I say, already gathering laundry off the floor.

"It's fine." Eliot spins around slowly, taking everything in, from the toppling stacks of shelf-less books to the high, narrow window, to the unmade twin bed in the far corner. "You should see some of the places I've stayed over the last ten years. Tents. Vans. Caves. Park benches. You won't scare me off with a few dirty clothes." His eyes drift over to my open lingerie drawer, which is currently vomiting bras, left in disarray from last night's search for the almost-naked mesh set I will now forever associate with Eliot and the ocean and a pair of strong hands pressing against my stomach.

"I should, um . . ." I toss my armload of laundry in a corner and attempt to close the drawer with a hip, an attempt that fails miserably, much to Eliot's amusement.

As he chuckles behind me, I cease my frenetic tidying and open the closet, removing my art school portfolio, the one that went missing right before the senior showcase and appeared in the studio the next morning in a location so obvious, it couldn't have been there when we were looking the day before. Everyone had a theory. Most people suspected Ursula Pritkin, the girl who won the prize that was most likely to be mine. She claimed she didn't know anything about it. I didn't press the issue. It didn't matter who took my work, or if it disappeared through forces none of us could explain in rational terms. One way or another, I was never going to win anything.

I hand Eliot the portfolio, suggesting he look through it while I at least clear some floor space. He sits on the unmade bed, folding his legs underneath him and laying the portfolio on his lap. I wait as he opens the cover, skims my résumé, and turns the page to reveal a spread from one of the graphic novels I never finished, with noir-inspired images of storm clouds, flocks of crows, and canopies of black umbrellas. He looks up to see me watching him and gestures for me to carry on with my cleaning.

I do so, and by the time I've hidden the adult acne medication and stowed my dirty clothes in a hamper, Eliot's looking at my final page, a spread from a kids' book I wrote and illustrated about a polar bear and a cute little piglet. The polar bear's unhappy so the piglet keeps bringing him things to make him smile. A balloon. A bouquet of flowers. A huge stacked sandwich as tall as the polar bear. The gifts get sillier and more extreme, but nothing makes the bear smile, so the piglet eventually stops bringing gifts, sitting down beside the polar bear and simply keeping him company. On the final page, they lean against each other and watch the sunset. The polar bear still isn't smiling, but he never needed to smile, or to be happy. He just needed to be with his friend.

I take a seat next to Eliot, chewing a nail in nervous anticipation of his response to my work. Not that he'll be unkind. In fact, he used to be my biggest supporter, but I know in one way or another, my work is all about needing other people, whether it's a stark graphic novel with creepy crows that absorb grief at funerals or a sweet little kids' book about a pig and a bear. Or, okay, a sweet little kids' book about depression, an affliction my dad suffered with in the years before his death. Regardless of the format or style, Eliot will know what my work's about, and I know we disagree on its central premise.

He runs a hand over the closing image of the piglet and the polar bear.

"Did you ever submit this anywhere?" he asks. "Agents? Publishers? Contests?"

"Contests? No," I say through a laugh. "For obvious reasons."

"And you didn't try to get it published?" he presses, not laughing with me.

I shake my head, glancing over at the work I've kept buried for six years.

"That was the plan when I finished school," I say. "Polish it. Send it out. See if anyone wanted it. Then everything went on pause with my mom's foreclosure notice and my move back here. I got immersed in loan applications, job applications, paying back taxes, real estate law, budget spreadsheets, negotiating payment plans with utility companies, long video calls with Antony and Lavinia as we sorted out our options."

"And once the options were sorted?" Eliot asks, because letting me stop there would be far too easy. We already covered this at the bar last night. He's not going to be satisfied with *I've been busy* again. He's not going to let *me* be satisfied with it, either.

I consider how to respond, having only recently begun examining this question.

"By the time the dust settled," I say, working out my answer as I talk my way through it, "and by the time I thought about my creative work again, most of my art school classmates had established social media presences. They were getting agents and gallery showings. I felt so far behind I didn't know how I'd ever catch up. I figured my curse was rearing its ugly head, dooming me to perpetual second-rate status."

Eliot flips to the beginning of the portfolio and the image of the funeral. I spent ages on the series, inking every raindrop and every last feather on the crows. It's the piece that would've been most likely to earn me a prize, if a win had been possible.

"So you think you're not good enough to succeed profession-ally?" he asks.

"Yes," I say, but as I say it, it doesn't ring true. "Actually, no. I don't know. I did think that, for a while, but after a few months of following my classmates' online parade of accolades, I sensed it wasn't making me question my *abilities* so much as making me ques-tion my *ambitions*. A life that required exhaustive self-promotion and career scrambling held little appeal. I didn't need to publish my art. I just needed to make it."

Eliot blinks at me in confusion. "But you *stopped* making it."

"Yep." I slide the portfolio off his lap and zip it up. If we're go-ing to dig deeper into this topic, it'll be easier if I feel less exposed. "Ironic, right? I figure out what I want and then I don't *do* anything about it. A classic Imogen Finch move if ever there was one." I laugh in that way I do, a smoke-and-mirrors attempt to ensure I'm the only one who knows a conversation has reached the place where I kept the messy, contradictory parts of myself I'm too embarrassed to share. The place where I'm ruled by jealousy, insecurity, shame, or confusion about things I feel like I should know by now.

Despite my attempt to lighten the mood, Eliot continues blink-ing at me from behind his hot nerd glasses, his expression impene-trably serious.

"I understand putting your dreams on pause for a while," he says. "And I understand how comparisons to others can make tak-ing action harder, even if *I* think your work is incredible, but if you weren't trying to compete professionally . . . ?" He ends the question there, as though even asking it is so baffling he can't possibly finish.

"I don't *know* why." I slide off the bed, no longer comfortable with stillness. No longer comfortable with anything. "Call it inertia. Intimidation. Exhaustion. Imposter syndrome. A nagging sense that making art was selfish or pointless. Twenty-plus years of never being *quite* as good as I wanted to be at anything. All of the above."

"And?" he says, because apparently, he's going to pick at this scab until it bleeds.

"And nothing."

"And *something*."

"Why can't that be enough?"

"Because it doesn't add up."

"You can't plug life into a calculator."

"You know what I mean."

"Do I? You sure about that?"

"I'd bet my life on it."

"Then you're taking a hell of a risk."

"I'm calling it like I see it." He folds his arms across his chest, showing no sign of relenting. Quite the opposite. "Curse or no curse, you know you're good. You know you love to draw. You know doing what you love isn't pointless. You've always pushed your limits, even while you assume you're cursed to hit them *every* time. So why—?"

"Because I was too focused on attending to everyone else's needs since they were all more important than my own." The admission bursts out of me, startling us both.

Eliot finally stops looking at me as though I'm a mystery to solve. The creases between his brows soften and he relaxes against the wall behind him. I appear to have provided an answer that satisfies his curiosity. An answer that feels like the truth. It's not an answer I like, but as it hangs in the air between us, it feels like the truth to me, too.

"I want the people I care about to feel valued," I say. "I don't want to let down anyone who relies on me. And I *like* being relied on. That makes *me* feel valued. Add in a few offhand comments I internalized. Or, okay, *a lot* of offhand comments I internalized.

Dismissive language about my 'hobbies' or 'little doodles.' Light but hurtful jokes about my useless or self-indulgent degree. A snide remark or two about 'all that time I wasted.' Rhetorical questions about how I didn't actually expect to make money drawing cartoons, did I? Pretty soon I believed making my art simply wasn't important, not in the grand scheme of things. Everyone else seemed to believe it, too."

"Everyone?" Eliot asks as though he already knows the answer.

"Not my family, of course. Or Franny. Just—" *The guys I dated,* I think, but I can't bring myself to say it aloud. It's too humiliating, knowing I let myself get talked to this way. And I stayed. "*Almost* everyone," I amend. "Until some nosy, pushy, long-haired, ink-stained know-it-all wandered into town and saw through that lie."

Eliot pats down his head. "I'm not long-haired anymore."

"Yeah, but you're still a know-it-all." I flash him a smile, grateful he *finally* seems to be dropping the interrogation. Then I turn away and attempt to shove my portfolio into my closet. It won't fit in the spot it used to occupy. The bins and boxes are wedged too tightly, with my disorganized clothes taking up every spare inch of space. I'm soon stuck leaning the portfolio against my dresser. Given the house I grew up in, this strikes me as a potential sign, as if my art refuses to be ignored any longer. From the lightly amused look on Eliot's face, he appears to share my thought. I'm about to make a joke about the matter, my usual M.O. when I want to escape conversations about big, weighty life choices, but I surprise myself. "How have you always known me better than I know myself?"

Eliot's forehead furrows, a look that's more pronounced now that his hair's gone.

"Have I?" he asks.

"I put up all these walls but you see through every single one of them. How?"

He shrugs against a background of robin's-egg blue, drowning in clothes that are far too big for him and plucking at the fringe on my ancient dirt-colored afghan.

"Maybe it's my general hatred of walls." He smiles, in that way he does. Look fast or it's gone. "Or maybe I know a thing or two about the lies we tell ourselves, the ways we convince ourselves we're fine when we're anything but."

I sit beside him again, drawing my legs to my chest and resting my cheek on my knees so I can watch him sideways. He rolls his head toward me, meeting my gaze. My body's jittery from his inquisition about my abandoned art, but I sense he knows I've said all I can on the matter, at least for now, and it's time to let the matter rest.

"What lies do you tell yourself?" I ask.

His brows rise above the rims of his glasses as he looks at me, at the ceiling, at my only marginally tidied room, and at me again, all while toying with the fringe.

"I tell myself I'm happiest in perpetual motion." His attention drifts down toward his fidgeting hands. "I need space. Freedom. New places. New people. New input. An ability to let go of everything behind me, and to make no set plans for the future. No anchors, tethers, or ties. No walls." He gives up on the fringe and traces the lettering on Antony's sweatpants. "I do want those things. That's not a lie. But I don't travel *only* because I want to keep moving. I travel because I don't know how to be still."

I let this land without an immediate reply, recalling what he said last night. *When I let myself go still, really still, I wonder if I've never learned how to run toward anything at all. Only how to run away.* I haven't figured out what he's running away from. I don't think he has, either, at least not clearly enough to tell me, but I sense him wanting to figure it out as his brows knit and he resumes torturing my ugly afghan.

"Stillness can be hard," I say, well aware of the effort I put into juggling six jobs, taking care of my mom, and doting on a steady string of boyfriends who—upon even the slightest reflection—didn't deserve that much of my attention. Some days I wish I had more time to myself, but I also appreciate that my busyness has left me little space with which to thoroughly examine my life choices. "It's beautiful when we can embrace it, but it's easier to forget our fears and anxieties when we're on the go."

"Exactly." Eliot flicks something off the bed. Toast crumbs, probably, because this room isn't embarrassing enough already. "What fears are *you* avoiding?"

"Spiders crawling into my mouth while I sleep," I say, blurting out the first random fear that comes to mind, hoping to get a smile out of Eliot, a real smile, not a conflicted half-master. "Also killer bees. Killer sharks. Killer tomatoes. Killer anything, really." I laugh, true to my character, while Eliot remains quiet and serious, true to his. After a moment, I tap-tap-tap his knee with mine. "And you? Biggest fears?"

"Not tomatoes, killer or otherwise." He flashes me a quick glimpse of wry side-eye. Frowns. Furrows. Breathes. Considers. Doesn't smile. "Honestly? Right now, in this moment, I have two main fears. Not sure which of the two is greater."

His gaze lifts to meet mine. In his unsettled eyes, I can see the battle warring within him, the struggle to sort fear from fear. I wait for him to say *becoming my parents* or *living a life dictated by other people's expectations.* Maybe even something related to his adventuring like *falling off a cliff* or *being buried alive under an avalanche.* Whatever he's about to say, it's *way* more serious than swallowing spiders.

"Number one." He frowns again. Pauses. Searches my face, though for what I don't know. "That I'll kiss you and then I'll leave you, only causing us both pain."

*Oh my god.* My breath catches in my throat. I swallow, and swallow again.

"And number two?" I ask. Barely.

"That I *won't* kiss you and then I'll leave you, only causing us both pain." His lashes flutter and his jaw tenses, but he holds my gaze, and I hold his, too stunned to do anything else. "All those years ago. I wanted . . . I felt . . . I didn't want to make leaving any harder than it already was. My friendship with Franny was always simpler, more straightforward. I didn't have to worry about what things meant with her. But with you, I knew that if I, if *we* . . ." He shakes his head. Presses his lips together. Gusts a frustrated sigh through his nose. "I don't want to hurt you or give you false expectations. I also don't want to spend another ten years wandering the globe, wishing I'd gotten over my bullshit and said something, or *done* something, before we said goodbye again."

I stare at him, speechless, while reminding myself to breathe. He stares back, his forehead furrowed while a conflict of epic proportions plays out in his eyes. I reach for my usual well-honed denials, my walls, my armor, my defenses, my reasons to keep my distance, but I can't find any reasons, not now that Eliot's words are out there, so solid and clear. He can't un-say them. I can't unhear them. I don't *want* to unhear them. Curse or no curse, expectations true, false, or otherwise, this moment could be all we have.

This moment could be all we have.

Slowly, cautiously, I unfold myself, pivoting around to slide onto Eliot's lap. I watch him closely, searching for signs he wants me to stop. I don't see any. Instead, his hands wrap around my hips as I settle into position, my heart hammering so hard I can't even follow my own train of thought, let alone speculate about Eliot's.

"So you're afraid to kiss me and then leave me?" I ask.

Eliot nods. "'Afraid' doesn't even begin to cover it."

"And you're afraid to *not* kiss me and then leave me?"

"The regrets will haunt me for the rest of my life."

"Then what if you don't do either?"

His expression grows wary. "You mean what if I stay?"

"No." *Hammer, hammer, hammer.* "I mean what if *I* kiss *you*?"

He doesn't answer but his breath comes hard and fast as his grip tightens on my hips. His eyes travel around my face and he bites his lip, letting it slide from between his teeth with a light sheen of wetness. Taking it as a sign that he's at least considering a kiss, I set a hand on his cheek, where my fingertips graze the tiny bristles of his newly clipped sideburns. How many times have I imagined touching him like this? Wanting him like this, without hiding it? And how many times have I done nothing about it? I feel like my entire life was leading to this moment. And I can barely breathe for the anticipation.

"Say yes," I whisper, because it's all I can manage. "Please, *please* say yes."

Eliot swallows. As he licks his lips again, I realize he's trembling. I might be, too.

"Yes," he says. "The answer has always been and will always be *yes.*"

His voice is so quiet but his *yeses* ring out like shots fired from a starting pistol. The instant they register in my brain, I lean in and set my lips against his.

Ten years vanish in an instant. Maybe even more than ten years. A lifetime of longing that sends a lion's roar through my body, a rush, a torrent, a cyclone, a primal scream, a tidal wave, a galloping stampede, as every moment in which I've thought of this, wanted it, yearned for it, surges, full force, through my blood and my bones.

*Yes,* I think. *The answer has always been yes.*

Eliot's lips part against mine. His tongue slides forward, warm, wet, wanting. I scoot toward him on his lap, holding his head against mine with one hand while the other hand presses against his heart, feeling it *pound, pound, pound* in time with mine.

We test. We taste. We allow our minds to catch up with our bodies, as if neither of us can believe we're finally doing this, but before long, I'm lost in a dizzying haze of hungry kisses, hot breath, and frantic hands. I grip Eliot's strong neck, tracing the lines of his tendons with my thumb. He untucks my shirt, pressing a palm against my back, skin-to-skin. We kiss. We gasp. We moan. We pant. We clasp and clutch. We plunge into each other, a mutual deep dive into an abyss made entirely of yeses.

Pretty soon I can't help myself. I start rocking against him, feeling him harden between my legs as our tongues and teeth clash, and as I inhale sheer, irrevocable desire with every breath he lets out and I take in.

His hand inches up my back, exploring the fasteners on my bra but making no move to slide the hooks free. I will him to go for it as I bury my face against his neck, pulling aside the collar of his already stretched-out shirt to plant long, lingering kisses on his tattooed skin. A leaf. A cloud. A feather, maybe. The northern tip of the compass that spans his right shoulder blade. He's salty with sweat, despite the dank basement air. His skin is practically blazing. The evidence of his desire is such a turn-on—his heat, his sweat, his accidental little groans, his erection—making me want to kiss every inch of his body, traversing a language of inked symbols I've only just begun to understand.

"Eliot?" I whisper against his neck.

His mouth finds my ear, resting there, ajar, his breath warm and fast.

"Imogen?" he murmurs, the heat in his voice practically volcanic.

"I don't want to stop with a kiss."

He exhales in a whoosh of breath that sends a shiver through me. As he draws in a new breath, his hand slides off my back and he scoots me away from him with both hands on my hips, watching me with flushed cheeks and a million questions swimming in his earnest eyes. I silently beg him not to ask the most obvious one. *Is that wise when I'm leaving soon and don't plan to return?* We both know. We already know.

But that isn't the question he asks. He asks me if I'm sure. He doesn't say the words. He doesn't need to. He asks only with his eyes. I answer with mine.

*Yes,* I tell him silently. *The answer has always been yes.*

Reading me correctly, he finds the hems of my sweater and shirt, drawing both garments over my head before tossing them to the floor. Then he drinks me in with his eyes, grazing a hand across the black and pink lace bralette that barely skims over the center of my nipples, leaving the rest to peek out from the scalloped lace. I've never been confident about my body, but I like my breasts, and a bra like this—with its intentional lack of coverage—makes me feel like I'm worth looking at. Eliot appears to share my assessment, staring with an appreciation that ignites my skin.

"Christ, Finch," he says. "You don't give a guy a fighting chance."

I bite down a smile, picturing him almost naked at the end of the dock last night.

"And you do?" I draw Antony's M&M's tee over Eliot's head and ease the sleeve cuffs over his hands. Then I get my own eyeful, taking in his sculpted body, which still astonishes me, even after knowing for years what he's been putting this body through.

As I begin tracing his contours, studying them as though I need to know their precise angles and proportions in order to draw them, he nudges aside the edge of my bra with his thumb and takes my nipple between his lips, circling it with the tip of his tongue.

A jolt of sensation rushes through me, leaving a throbbing ache between my legs. I grind against him with a newfound hatred for jeans and sweatpants and anything that bars me from feeling every inch of him against every inch of me. He runs a thumb over my lower lip. I take it into my mouth, licking it until he sets it against my other nipple, now circling both at once, one with his tongue, the other with the wet pad of his thumb, building a rhythm I *just* start to settle into when he breaks it with a sharp pinch or a nip of his teeth. The sudden changes of pressure shoot electricity straight to the pulsing flesh between my legs. He *mmmms* in satisfaction whenever I flinch, resuming his gentle circles. I don't know where he picked up his technique but I like it. I *really* like it.

My eyelids flutter shut and I arch into him, clawing at his back while he lavishes my breasts with more attention than they've had in years.

"God, that feels good," I gasp out.

He answers with another intoxicating *mmmm*, too busy with his mouth to offer more as I rub against him until I swear I'm going to shatter if I don't feel him inside me.

I'm not sure how I find the willpower to pull away, but somehow I manage to clamber off his lap and onto my feet so I can remove my jeans and socks, leaving me only in my now-covering-nothing-at-all bralette and matching black lace boy shorts. Eliot watches me strip, lazily reclining against the blue wall while running a finger back-and-forth across his kiss-swollen lower lip.

It strikes me suddenly that we're fooling around in my childhood bedroom, with my mom asleep upstairs. I know we're almost thirty, and she probably knows damned well what we're doing down here. But still . . .

"What's so funny?" Eliot asks, catching the smile I can't restrain.

I point at the ceiling, cringing slightly.

Eliot glances up. "Think she'd care?"

I shake my head. "Pretty sure she saw it coming."

"This time, I won't try to prove her wrong." He shines an un-restrained smile on me as he beckons me forward, but I shake my head.

"I lost *my* pants," I say, my implication clear.

Eliot's smile turns bashful, an unusual look on him.

"You know I took off all my running clothes before I showered," he says.

I give him a *yeah, and* look.

"And I'm going commando under these." He tucks a thumb inside the waistband of the sweatpants and inches them down, re-vealing a trail of dark hair against tan skin, and the top of a detailed orchid tattoo that must've hurt like a son-of-bitch so close to his groin. If he's trying to dissuade me, he's failing miserably, because getting that peek of inked flesh only makes me more interested in seeing the rest of him.

I pick my jeans up off the floor. "Up to you, Swift. On or off?"

"Yeah, um . . ." He shifts in his seat as his eyes drift down to where he's still holding the sweatpants. Below his hand is a bulge so obvious, I almost laugh.

"You know I know what's going on in there, right?" I ask.

"Yeah, but—" He cuts himself off with an awkward grimace.

"And this isn't my first time. I happen to know it isn't yours, either."

He concedes the point with a tip of his chin but the grimace remains.

"Maybe not," he says. "But it is my first time with *you*."

My entire body melts at that, and I have to hold myself up by the rim of my dresser. I should've known Eliot wouldn't take this lightly. We can fall headlong into passionate kisses. We can grope each other with reckless abandon. In days to come, we can call what we've done "casual," compartmentalize it with convenient words, tell ourselves we got carried away or we were "only having a little fun" as Kym suggested, but even if this is the only night we have together. It matters. To both of us.

"Tell you what." I drop my jeans and step forward, wedging a knee between his where his legs still dangle off the side of my rumpled, undersized, piece-of-shit bed. "If I show you what's going on in my pants, will you show me what's going on in yours?"

His cheeks flush a deep shade of pink. Also adorable.

"You're not wearing any pants," he says.

"You miss my point." I reach forward and take his hand, slowly guiding it inside the waistband of my underwear. After another *are you sure* look, he takes over from there, easing his hand lower until he's cupping me between my legs, curling two fingers just high enough to feel the clear evidence of my arousal.

"Fucking hell," he says, barely more than a breath. Then he's grabbing my ass with his free hand and yanking me forward until I'm kneeling on the bed, legs parted to straddle his while his fingers stroke me, gliding through wetness I'm shocked he didn't expect. He's certainly aware of it now, as evidenced by the look of open hunger on his face. "You always did know how to get your way around me."

I sneak in a breathless kiss, framing his face with both hands while my hips twitch and circle against his roving fingers and his grip tightens on my ass.

"Is that what I'm doing?" I ask. "Getting my way?"

Eliot gives me a chin tip and a twitch of a smile.

"Didn't say I was complaining." His smile widens and his fingers grow bolder, teasing my entrance with the suggestion of penetration he doesn't quite follow through on. He gets close and then retreats again, all while watching me with a mischievous glint in his eye. I'm about to show him precisely where I want his fingers when he removes his hand from my underwear and raises his ass off the bed. "Go ahead. It's only fair."

Inferring his meaning, I inch his sweatpants down on his hips, letting them gather around his thighs and revealing the rest of the orchid tattoo, a dense tangle of dark hair, and his very thick, very erect penis, its tip already wet.

Nothing is surprising about what I see, but I stare for a moment in astonishment, because I'm not looking at just anyone's hard-on. I'm looking at Eliot Swift's hard-on. The guy I spent all of junior high and high school fantasizing about. The guy who crept into my sex dreams in the years after he left town. I've spent countless hours imagining what this would be like. What he'd look like under his clothes. How touching him would feel. What he'd want me to do. What *I'd* want to do. And suddenly it's not a fantasy anymore. Eliot Swift is in my bedroom, on my bed, with his pants around his thighs and his saliva still coating my nipples, making me feel every draft.

"What?" he asks, shaking me out of my staring.

"I've thought about this," I say. "A lot."

"Me, too," he says, and then, in his Eliot Swiftian way, he repeats, "Me, too."

We could lunge at each other again, propelled by confessions of shared fantasies. Instead, he draws me into a tight embrace on his lap, an embrace I return. His erection presses into my belly, and I'm keenly aware that only a tiny slip of lace separates us, but even while my body overflows with craving, I savor the feel of his strong arms around me, and I let myself hold him as though I'll never let him go. Even though I know I will.

For several minutes we let tenderness override desire. He nuzzles my neck and I rest my cheek against his head, smiling to myself at his action-hero haircut, the result of his beautiful act of care. When I start planting tiny kisses on the side of his face, he draws back far enough to meet my eyes and trail his fingertips over my cheek, my nose, my lips, my jawline. His eyes are so serious, making me worry he's about to tell me he has a girlfriend, or several girlfriends, or a dozen children scattered across the globe.

"What?" I ask this time.

"This," he says. "You. Me. Here. All of this. It's just . . ." He shakes his head as though he's rejecting whatever words are coming to his mind. Perhaps because there are no words. There's a feeling of rightness, maybe even of inevitability, mixed with a mutual awareness that we always were and always will be . . . *complicated*.

"I know," I tell him. "Trust me. I *know*."

I kiss him then, because we don't need to search for more words right now. He kisses me back, and we release our embrace to let our hands roam. He grips my hair, my neck, my breasts, my thighs. I knead his shoulders and chest as though I'm molding them myself. Prompted by a tightly restrained twitch of his hips, I wet my palms and massage his erection. He pulses in my grip, groans against my ear, utters a fantastically filthy stream of muttered curses, until he halts me by setting his hands on mine and giving me a look that suggests if I continue, we won't be fooling around much longer.

I climb off his lap and root around in my overstuffed bedside table until I find a lone, unexpired condom, thank god. By the time I rejoin Eliot on the bed, his sweatpants are in a lump on the floor and he's yanking off his socks. I shimmy my underwear off, letting my bra follow. Usually I like keeping something on, but not this time. Not with Eliot. When we do this, I don't want anything between us at all.

We take a minute to look at each other, both naked, with nothing hidden, obscured, or cleverly dressed up to impact an onlooker's perception. *This is us,* I think, *our truest and most vulnerable selves, and there is no one I'd rather share myself with.*

I hand Eliot the condom. We swap yet another *are you sure* look, one that doesn't take long for us to answer. We're both brimming over with yeses. I can see them in his eyes. I can feel them in my bones. I tap-tap-tap his knee with mine—giving the gesture a whole new meaning—while he tears open the package and rolls on the condom. Then he guides me forward so I straddle him, and he places my hand around the base of his shaft.

"When you're ready," he says. "I want to feel you make that choice."

I can't help but smile. "Do you have any idea how sexy that is?"

"Sexy for both of us." He takes my face between his hands and draws me closer.

I lean forward to kiss him while I adjust my grip and lower myself far enough to feel him at my entrance. Our eyes meet and his breath comes faster, gusting against my lips. My heart resumes its hammering, pounding so loudly I worry it could wake the entire neighborhood. Eliot's hands slide into my hair. My horrible ruined hair. I shift slightly, feeling him against me, reveling in the anticipation. He's so close. So deliciously, deliriously close. He's right there and all I have to do is—

Eliot groans with pleasure, mouth ajar and lashes fluttering as I lower my body and take him fully in. I want to watch him, to mentally record every second of this with some kind of superpower of heightened awareness, but my body takes over, because Eliot Swift is inside me and he feels *so* goddamned good and we're really doing this and my heart is still hammering away and we're both gasping like idiots and I am made of fire.

I move slowly, with the tiniest roll of my hips, my eyes closed and my hands braced on Eliot's shoulders. He trails his hands down the sides of my body until he's guiding my hips, first in gentle circles, then in deeper thrusts. Together, we find a rhythm. The rhythm changes, and changes again, but remains slow and gentle, as if we're both doing our damnedest not to rush. The yeses I once thought in silence start slipping out between my lips, breathless and panted but unmistakable. Eliot starts muttering, too. My name, maybe. A curse word or two. I fit my mouth against his, fumble through another insatiable kiss, until his fingers dig into my ass and I push into him with a sharp, fierce thrust that makes the springs in my bed let out an ear-piercing *grrroooonk*.

Eliot and I freeze, instantly locking eyes before glancing toward the ceiling. After several seconds of tense silence, we burst into laughter. I thrust again, though at half-strength this time, and the bed springs let out another wake-the-block squeal.

Eliot continues laughing, his eyes bright with mirth.

"That's unnatural," he says.

"*That* is a sixty-year-old bed."

"How do you have sex in here?"

"Honestly? I don't." I glance around my room, which is *so* not designed for seduction with its ugly mismatched furniture, damp mildew scent, and lack of decent lighting. Eliot's the only guy I know who hasn't balked at any of that. The only one who hasn't suggested my choice to live in my mother's basement was a sign I haven't grown up yet, or a sign I haven't faced reality about her state of health. He's the only one who fully accepts me as I am, even while he pushes me to reach for the things that make me happy. And I can't imagine being with anyone else after he leaves. Ever.

The instant I have that thought, I'm struck with a profound desire to banish it. To force all thoughts of his departure from my mind, and any similar thoughts from his.

I rise up on my knees until we're no longer joined together. Then

I take Eliot by the hand and lead him off the bed, kicking aside the clothes we removed earlier. I lie on the floor, drawing him down with me. I let my knees fall open and he wedges himself into the space I create. Without another word—with only a look that suggests his thoughts mirror mine—he checks the condom and pushes back inside me.

This time we don't worry about bedsprings or savoring the moment or anything other than the intoxicating rush of our bodies moving together. He plants my hands on either side of my head, holding them there as he thrusts into me, hard, and my hips rise to meet his. I don't close my eyes this time. Eliot doesn't, either. We stare at each other as though we're composing a silent contract between us, a contract that says this isn't about love and longing anymore. This is a detonation. A collision. A crash of two bodies propelled by intense and untamable craving. And it's what we both want.

We slide across the floor in sharp jerks. I can already tell I'm going to have some serious rug burns later as our bodies slap together with such force I start to wonder if we're making too much noise again, but *good god*, the way he feels inside me and the way his eyes bore into mine as he hovers above me while his grip never wavers on my hands and we drive away our fears with a combined power of will and hunger. I could live in this moment for the rest of my life, just Eliot and me and the sweat on our skin and the fire in his eyes and this undeniable oneness that draws more yeses from my lips until he asks me if I'm close and I can only answer with another yes, and then another and another, but my words halt when my head hits my dresser, an impact Eliot must notice because he releases one of my hands so I can use it to cushion the top of my head while he uses his now free hand to lift my hips, and that slight change of angle makes him push farther forward inside me with every thrust until I start to cry out, and I'm too loud but I can't stop, and at my next gasp Eliot releases my other hand and covers my mouth, which I might find off-putting in other circumstances, but I could remove his hand if I wanted to or simply shift away, except I'm so turned on and I know he's only covering my mouth so we don't have to slow down, making it insanely hot, so instead of drawing his hand aside, I bite into his flesh, causing his breath to hitch as he pulses inside me, fighting a grimace he can't actually fight while he stutters out a groan, and as amazing as his body feels joined with mine, the knowledge that he's come undone becomes my undoing.

I convulse around him, sending muffled curses into his palm while my entire body shudders. And shudders. And shudders. Until it finally goes limp against the floor.

Eliot removes his hand from my mouth, his face flooding with contrition.

"I'm so sorry," he says.

I take his hand, kiss his palm, and press it against my hammering heart.

"Don't be," I tell him. "Not about any of it. Ever. Okay?"

He nods, searching my eyes for forgiveness he doesn't need. Whatever he finds in my expression must do the trick though, because he lies down, half on me, half off, as if he doesn't want to pull out yet but he doesn't want to smother me, either. He caresses my face with featherlight fingertips while our hearts and lungs settle. I am so full of love for him right now, I'm not sure how I'm keeping the words locked inside me, but I can see from the look in his eyes that his mind is already whirring and everything we kept at bay is creeping back in again.

*A transformation. A shuffling of expectations. A severing.*

"Can I stay?" he asks.

I skip a breath, thinking, *Yes! Please! YES!*

## HEARTBREAK #9

Lance Tipsword was the last guy I dated before moving back to Pitt's Corner. Given his name, I anticipated he'd either have a big dick he'd wield like a jousting weapon or he'd be a fan of Renaissance festivals. Lance, sadly, fit neither description. But he was fun, and at that time in my life—with school nearing its end and a boatload of uncertainty about what came next, I was craving something joyous and mindless. Lance fit the bill.

We got together the old-fashioned way: by hooking up at a party. Despite it being a less than memorable night, I stayed over at his place, an apartment he appeared to be sharing with four other guys. The following morning, while nursing our hangovers at a nearby coffee shop, Lance confessed that he was only in town for a week, visiting one of the guys I assumed was his roommate while "taking a break" from his studies somewhere in Utah. The name of the school didn't stick with me. He might've invented it.

I assured him I'd gone home with him with no expectations (other than my misguided assumption that he'd be hung like a piece of medieval weaponry).

Lance took a different point of view.

"I *really* like you," he assured me. "Shouldn't we at least give this a chance?"

I wasn't sure what "this" was, but I was flattered by his enthusiasm and I figured, why not? Might as well give it a week and see what happened.

We spent a lot of time together that week, and doing things I hadn't done with anyone else. We ran around town gluing googly eyes to objects that looked like they were faces. We took a free swing dance class in a park. We joined a flash mob. We got stoned at the observatory, where we also ate way too many fun-size Milky Way bars, a snack choice that made us giggle like idiots, given our view of the cosmos.

I drove him to the airport at the end of his visit, stepping out onto the curb to hug and kiss him goodbye. By then, despite our lackluster physical connection, and despite some natural skepticism regarding our long-term future, I found myself sad to see him go.

"I'll text you every day," he said while squeezing me in a tight embrace. "We'll video chat. Plan another visit. Stay connected. Figure it out."

"It's okay if you end up wanting to date other people," I said.

He drew back, brow furrowed. "Why would I want to do that?"

"Distance is hard. And we've only been together for a week."

"But it's been a great fucking week." He grinned at me then, and I grinned back. I couldn't help myself. He was so sure he wanted a relationship with me. He was willing to *work* to make that happen. He had no doubts. That kind of certainty was intoxicating.

For the next two months, we did stay connected. Video calls. Emails. Lots of texting. Phone sex. A visit planned for my graduation. I kept thinking, he can't really be this serious. Not after only a week together. But he kept coming through. So, I did, too.

A week before my graduation, he called to tell me he wasn't

coming after all. He'd slept with someone else shortly after getting back to Utah. And she was pregnant. And he loved her. And they were going to get married and raise the kid together.

The most amazing thing about that situation was that I *knew*, deep in my soul, the end was coming. We didn't have enough to go on. I gave him a million outs. He didn't take them. He *refused* to take them. And so, the end still managed to blindside me.

When Antony called a few weeks later, having been notified about the house foreclosure and my mom's need for increased care, I was quick to volunteer.

# Fourteen

## SATURDAY

I blink myself out of a dead slumber shortly after 5 a.m. when Eliot stirs behind me, nuzzling the back of my neck with his nose as though he's trying to wake me, but in the gentlest way possible. We're wedged together tightly, the only way we fit on my bed. He's playing the big spoon, with an arm and a leg wrapped over me. I swear my heart doubles in size as I confirm he's real and he's here and last night wasn't a dream.

"You can go back to sleep," I mumble. "We set three alarms."

"I know," he murmurs into my hair. "But I wanted a little time with you before I have to go. There are some things I want to say."

My drowsiness instantly evaporates. No one says *There are some things I want to say* and then says something anyone actually wants to hear. Instead, they say things like, *I'm going to be pretty busy for the next few weeks* or *When I mentioned I was divorced, what I really meant was . . .* or *You know I'm seeing other people, right?*

"Eliot, it's okay. We both knew what we were doing."

"That's not what I want to talk about. Well, sort of. But not exactly."

Fighting a growing knot of apprehension, I spin in his arms. My room is dark, other than a slight glow from my alarm clock and a hint of moonlight that finds its way through the narrow window above us. I can just make out Eliot's features, and see that his brows are knitted, though I could've guessed that from the tone of his voice. His glasses are off, folded next to my alarm clock. I wonder how well he can see me without them, and decide it's okay if I'm in soft focus. In fact, it's probably best for a lot of reasons.

"The next few days might be confusing for both of us," he says.

"Possibly." I manage a weak smile. "Probably. Definitely."

"My mom will insist on family only in the front pew today."

*Oof. Right. His mom. The funeral.*

"I'll still be there," I say. "Franny, too. And my mom."

"I know." He plants a sweet little kiss on my nose. "I just don't want you to feel like I'm blowing you off or pretending last night didn't happen."

"Oh, um, okay, thanks," I stammer out, surprised to hear he's thinking beyond a one-time collision of detonating libidos. It's a beautiful thought, and one I cling to with all my heart as I trace the contours of his lips, committing them to memory.

He takes a gentle nip of my fingertip as he slides a knee between my thighs, parting my legs and drawing me closer. Skin against glorious, soft, warm skin.

"And if we want to do this again . . ." he says.

I can't help but laugh. *"If?"*

He sort of smiles, but only sort of, inhaling deeply while adjusting his embrace.

"There's no one else, Imogen. I know you worry about your curse, and I don't want you to think I'm even the slightest bit interested in another woman."

I nod in his arms, grateful, relieved, despite some unavoidable doubts about how long his "interests" will remain undivided. I refuse to let that thought spiral right now, focusing instead on Eliot's skin. His heat. His closeness. The sleepy rumble in his voice.

"I've embraced a certain lifestyle," he continues. "Being in constant transience makes it easy for me to fall into a habit of casual sex, or short-term, no-strings relationships. I meet someone new. We have fun. We go our separate ways. Sometimes we stay in touch for a while, but usually not." He studies my face as he draws in a breath. "You haven't asked about my relationship history or my current relationship status. I understand why, or at least I *think* I understand why, but I want you to know I haven't been with anyone in about six months. And I've been tested."

*Wow. Okay. I was wrong. This is all stuff I want to hear.*

"I've been tested, too," I say.

Eliot's brows knit further. "Didn't you *just* go through a breakup?"

"Yeah, with a guy who cheated on me. Maybe he only slept with the woman he's with now, and maybe *she* only slept with *him*, but I didn't ask for details. Instead, I rapidly confirmed that my relationship was truly over, with no unexpected side effects." As I trace Eliot's lips again, I become more aware of how tightly our bodies are entwined, of how naked we are, of his thigh wedged between my thighs, and of how long it took me to find that one lone condom in my drawer last night. "I also have an IUD."

"Then we're doubly safe." He finds my eyes in the dim light, reading the question therein. He swallows a couple of times, as though he's debating what to say or how to say it. The pause is just long enough for me to suspect what's coming. "A few years ago, I got wasted on an overnight in Cairo and made some bad choices. The girl I met that night called me later, worried she might be pregnant. Turned out to be a false alarm, but I realized how reckless I was being. I also knew I never wanted to have kids." He pauses again, his face inches from mine on a shared pillow. "So I got a vasectomy."

He watches me closely, as if he's bracing for judgment, or for me to freak out about some imaginary life plan I made with him after a single night together. But I didn't make that life plan. I didn't make any plan. I just wanted to feel as close to him as possible.

"Listen to us," I say. "Being all mature about testing and birth control."

He responds by tucking my head against his collarbone and resting his cheek against my forehead, possibly because he wants a break from our eye contact, a choice I'm okay with. Despite my habitual attempt to lighten the mood, I recognize that a lot is happening right now, and that last night's intimacy is nothing compared to this. *This* is Eliot laying himself bare to me. Not only did he make a big confession about his life choices, he made it within the context of those life choices not really affecting me. The birth control, yes. The disinterest in fatherhood, no. Since we're only trying to navigate the next few days, he's trusting me to hear what he's telling me, and to hear *only* what he's telling me, which is harder than it sounds.

"For what it's worth," I tell him, because I feel like I should offer up *something* here. "I don't want to have kids, either. Greg and I talked about it a little. He's the only guy who stuck around for more than a few months, but by the time we were dating, my relationship pattern was pretty clear, and I wasn't interested in raising a kid on my own. My mom did it after my dad died. I've watched Franny do it, too. They're both amazing at it, and they love it, but it still looks *really* hard. Also, as much as I like taking care of people, my mom and my community are more than enough. Even if they weren't, I've always preferred dogs to babies."

Eliot finally laughs a little, which helps ease the worst of my tension. I sneak in a kiss while he's still smiling, as though a kiss can somehow prevent his smile from fading.

"You and your dogs," he says. "It's weird to be here without any."

"I know. And maybe someday I'll get one again."

"One. Or two. Or a baker's dozen."

"A baker's dozen. I like the sound of that." I sneak in another kiss. And another, as I picture this house full of noise and dog hair and donut beds and squeaky toys, all in the best possible way. "Thank you," I say as I pull away, though I don't pull away far.

Eliot blinks at me quizzically. "For what?"

"I expected this morning to be weird, with both of us trying to read each other's signals and sort out where to go from here. You know. The usual questions. Like, are we snuggling because we both want to snuggle or because you haven't figured out a polite way to extricate yourself yet? Do we talk about past relationships or do we pretend relationship status doesn't matter because it might only matter to one of us and admitting that is terrifying? If you say, 'I had a good time last night,' is that code for, 'thanks, bye!' or are you trying to subtly indicate interest so I'll take the lead and say I want to see you again? Do we act like nothing happened when we're around other people or can I hold your hand in public? It's like learning another foreign language every time I date someone new. But I should've known you'd meet the challenge head-on."

Eliot concedes the point with a look. "I've never been good at speaking in code."

"I know, and I've always"—I pivot just in time—"*appreciated* that about you." I catch something in his eyes that suggests he knows what I was about to say. I'm not sure how he *can't* know. I'm so obviously in love with him, but the word *love* feels too big to speak aloud right now, as if it rewrites the silent contract we composed together last night. Even spoken as an offering, the word so often feels like a demand.

Thankfully, Eliot diverts our attention by trailing a fingertip around the curve of my breast and lazily spiraling inward toward my nipple while he watches my body respond to his touch. And respond, it does. Every goddamned inch of it.

"For the record," he says. "I'm not trying to politely extricate myself."

"For the record," I echo, already a little breathless. "Neither am I."

He raises a brow, still caressing my breast. "So you *do* want to do this again?"

"I'm open to the possibility." I wrap his hip with my leg, making my meaning clear. "But only if you put on that *incredibly* sexy outfit you wore last night. It seems only fair when I've gone to such great lengths to create a seductive atmosphere in here."

The boiler on the other side of my wall chooses that moment to *clank* and *clunk* the way it does whenever the heating mechanism kicks in, making the overhead pipes rattle. I laugh at the ridiculousness of it all. Eliot doesn't laugh with me, but the corners of his lips pull up past his usual twitch point into a full-on smile, a rare, unrestrained one that makes me feel like entire gardens are blooming in my chest.

"Fuck the atmosphere," he says. Then his lips are on mine and our hands are exploring and our bodies are already in motion . . .

# Fifteen

Imogen: You on your way yet?

Franny: Still rallying Anika and trying to pick an outfit. You?

Imogen: Already here. I came early with Kym to sort out the flowers

Franny: I don't have as many black clothes as I thought

Imogen: Just wear whatever. Eliot won't care

Franny: Yeah, but his mom will. And she'll give me The Look

Imogen: Ugh. Right. The Look

Franny: What are you wearing?

Imogen: That 1950s satin cocktail dress I found at Goodwill last year

Franny: Now I REALLY feel underdressed

Imogen: Turns out I don't have many black clothes either

Franny: But you look amazing in that dress!

Imogen: I look like an extra in a smoky bar scene from Mad Men

Franny: Exactly! Va-va-voom!

Imogen: Whatever. Just get here already

Franny: On my way soon. I swear. Is Eliot there yet?

Imogen: Yeah. He's with his mom and his uncles

Franny: How is he?

Imogen: As expected

Franny: Utterly miserable?

Imogen: Nailed it

I glance toward the front of the church from the back pew where I'm sitting with my mom, a location I chose because I suspected Franny would be late and this is the easiest spot for her to quietly slip into. Eliot and Mrs. Swift are sitting in the front pew, facing forward, with a mile of space between them. Two men in their fifties sit to Mrs. Swift's left. I recognized them immediately as Mr. Swift's brothers. All three of them share the same angular features, severe brows, and sharply jutted chins, making them appear somewhat hawklike. Eliot lucked out and got his mom's chin and brows, which are far less formidable, though when he scowls, I can still see a paternal resemblance.

Mrs. Swift is in an impeccable black wool dress, with her dark hair pulled into a twist and an impressive multi-strand set of pearls around her neck. Eliot's in a black suit and tie that he keeps tugging on. The jacket's tight in the shoulders and short in the sleeves, making me suspect the clothes belonged to his dad. The choice is seriously messed up, though of course his mom wouldn't let him show up here in his travel clothes. I should've thought ahead and taken him shopping last night. I also should've stayed with him this morning instead of dropping him off at his parents' house before picking up the flowers and driving them here. He swore he'd be okay, but *okay* is always a relative term.

A few more people trickle in and take their seats, chatting in hushed voices while recorded organ music drones on in low undertones. The church is only about a quarter full, and almost everyone here is middle-aged or older. Most are probably Mr. Swift's employees or members of the country club set. I don't see a single child, making me wonder if Mrs. Swift banned them to ensure no one interrupted the service. I wouldn't put it past her. Children were always banished to zoned-off areas back in the days when the Swifts had house parties. God forbid anyone even mention a pet.

Sophia enters the church and exchanges a brief nod with me before taking a seat in the pew on the opposite side of the aisle. She's likely trying to keep a low profile, though judging by the glances people cast her way, her anonymity has already been blown. I think word spread on the day she came into the diner. Now, across from me, she pulls a tissue from her purse and dabs at the corners of her eyes. She's the only person here who looks truly, sincerely sad. I feel awful for her. She's here to mourn a man she cared about, and everyone will be whispering about how she screwed that man to death. Even I can't help thinking about it, and hoping she has a really, *really* good therapist.

Ten minutes after the service was scheduled to start, an ancient, bespectacled priest takes his place at a podium to the left of the casket. As he shuffles papers atop his bible, and as the murmuring crowd quiets, Franny bustles in with Anika in tow and slides into the pew next to me, ducking down and tossing her jangling keys into her purse. She's in an oversized black sweater that hangs off one shoulder, a black denim miniskirt, and several bangles that clink together. Next to her, Anika looks like Wednesday Addams, but with vivid magenta hair, by far the brightest thing in this room.

Despite Franny's attempt to be discreet, heads turn our way. Disapproval cascades off Mrs. Swift and her brothers-in-law but Eliot offers us a conflicted smile. He looks so alone up there. And so lost. I smile back and even offer him a little wave. Franny blows him a kiss. He tips his chin ever so slightly, and then faces front again, easing his head from side to side and clawing at the knot in his tie.

*God, I hope this is a short service.*

"Holy shit," Franny whispers, as irreverent as ever. "He looks like the Hulk in that suit. Let me guess, his mom's choice? And did she make him shave and cut his hair?"

"Actually, the haircut was his choice," I whisper back. "I'll explain later."

"I'm surprised she didn't force him to cover every last tat."

"She probably tried. Then decided gloves made him look like a murderer. Not the best choice with a body *right* there." I look toward the casket at the front of the room. Thankfully, it's closed, with the tasteful ivory flowers I arranged yesterday atop the lid. I understand why people want a chance to see the departed one last time, and to say their goodbyes directly, but in Eliot's case, I think a softer parting will be easier.

As I turn toward Franny, Anika sneaks her phone onto her lap.

"The sound's off on that thing, right?" Franny asks.

Anika gives her a look of unmitigated annoyance.

"I'm not an idiot," she says. "I *know* we're at a funeral."

"You didn't seem to know when you asked if you could bring a snack."

"You were the one rushing me out the door without breakfast."

"We were running late."

"No shit." Anika scoffs. "And whose fault was that?"

Franny throws up her hands and sneaks me an exasperated eye roll. Anika returns her attention to her phone with an eye roll of her own. A familiar tension simmers between the two of them, and I'm reminded of what I said to Eliot earlier this morning about how single parenthood has never appealed to me. However, as the priest clears his throat and begins rambling about love, loss, and cycles of life, Franny slips an arm around Anika and draws her in for a side-hug. Anika melts into her without hesitation, all signs of annoyance gone, replaced with a mutual need for comfort only the other can provide. No matter what stresses percolate under the surface, we've all said goodbye to someone we love, and those memories feel especially sharp today.

I take my mom's hand, knowing she's thinking about my dad. We listen to the priest, or at least sort-of listen while our minds wander and we each nurture our own individual griefs. But the sermon goes on *forever*, and by the time the priest invites anyone who wants to speak about Mr. Swift to step up and share a few words, I've dropped my mom's hand and I'm shifting in my seat, tugging at my slinky skirt and unable to get comfortable. Franny notices and flashes me a confused frown.

"Do you need to pee?" she whispers.

"Nope. I'm good."

"Then what's all the squirming for?"

"I'm not squirming." I am *totally* squirming. And the harder I try to sit still, the worse it gets, because now I'm not only uncomfortable, I'm aware I'm being watched.

"Thong up your ass?" Franny asks. "Tampon in wrong?"

Anika looks up at that. I glance back and forth between her and my mom, then back at Franny, who's staring at me like she's not dropping the subject until I reply. This is *not* the time and place to be having this conversation, but she'll find out eventually.

I lean close, cup my hand around my mouth, and whisper, "Rug burns."

Franny's eyes go wide and she claps a hand over her mouth to smother a squeal of joy. Naturally, Anika and my mom are now looking on with curiosity. My mom knows Eliot spent the night in my room last night. No doubt she also knows we didn't just look at my art and tell each other bedtime stories. Still, I don't need everyone in this pew to be thinking about my sex life right now, especially where it concerns the son of the deceased.

As the first speaker—one of Mr. Swift's golf buddies—starts waxing poetic about halcyon days on the back nine, Anika returns her attention to her phone and Franny finally gets over herself, lowering her hand to give me a quick flick on the thigh.

"Good for you," she whispers. "Dutch or Swiftie?"

"Who do you think?" I indicate Eliot with my eyes.

Franny beams at me, as though I've just made her greatest wish come true.

"So he helped deliver more than pizza last night?" she asks, thick with innuendo.

"Let's just say we had a change of plans." I tug at the open neckline on my dress, newly self-conscious about the amount of skin I'm showing now that my entire chest is flushed, along with my face, neck, and ears. I find blushes charming on other people, but I blush in blotches. It's not a good look. "Promise you won't give him a hard time."

"Sounds like he already had a 'hard time.'"

"Seriously? Here? Now?" I push through gritted teeth.

Franny waves me off while a teasing glint lingers in her eyes.

"We're here for Eliot," she says. "Not for an ode to putting greens. You two *finally* banged it out after over a decade of mutual long-distance pining, and you won't even let me make one teeny tiny joke about it?"

I concede with a sigh. "Okay, but only one."

She snickers silently beside me, then pretends to listen to the golf speech for a minute or two, but her eyes keep darting my way and eventually she can't stand it.

"So how was it?" she asks under her breath. "Besides abrasive on your ass?"

I check to make sure Anika and my mom at least *seem* to be focused elsewhere.

"Confusing," I say, though that barely scratches the surface. "Scary because I couldn't pretend it didn't mean anything. Not so scary because he didn't pretend, either. It was also intense. Raw. Real. Imperfect. Electric. Kind. Sweaty. Tender. Even funny."

"In other words, it was great?"

"Yeah." I stifle a laugh. "What you said."

Franny presses a fist to her heart and watches me like a proud parent, which is ridiculous when we're the same age *and* we're talking about a guy she had sex with, too, though he was probably a lot less adept at nipple play when he was seventeen.

"You know I never would've asked him to prom if I knew, right?" Franny asks.

"I do. Now. Not that I ever felt like you were trying to take him from me."

"And I definitely wouldn't have—"

"I know." I hold up a hand, catching a twitch of Anika's lips that suggests she's hearing more than she's letting on, despite her apparent focus on her phone.

Franny glances over at Anika before leaning closer to me.

"What happens now? Are you guys going to . . . ?" She bites her lip in a way that I think is supposed to imply *bang again* but really, her question could end with almost any words and my answer would be the same.

"I don't know. We'll have to see."

My mom emits a *hmm* so quiet I could almost swear I didn't hear it. Almost. Her eyes are locked on the speaker and her hands are clasped calmly in her lap, but she's obviously listening to Franny and me. She's also thinking about those damned ducks again, and what she told me about Eliot.

*But he'll leave. Yes. And I'll stay. Yes.*

As much as I love my mom, in this particular moment, I envy my brother and sister, who are able to live their lives without constant hints of whatever *complicated* future is yet to come. I also wish at least one of those stupid contests Eliot and I entered yesterday had come through with a win. We entered over fifty. Granted, they didn't all end today so a win is still possible, but so far, not a single message has reached my inbox.

I try to let those thoughts go while a dozen more people talk about Mr. Swift's acumen at business, golf, tennis, sailing, and bridge. They rhapsodize anecdotally about his taste in single malt scotch or art or Italian suits. They describe him as a benevolent employer, and as a devoted husband and father. Mrs. Swift listens to every word with an unflinching expression that makes her seem carved in stone. Eliot listens to most of the speakers with his head lowered and his tattooed hands linked around the back of his neck. Even from twenty rows away, I can tell his knuckles are white and he's drawing on every ounce of willpower to prevent himself from jumping up and calling bullshit.

When people stop volunteering to speak, Mrs. Swift takes the podium. She stands ramrod straight, with a placid smile that seems more appropriate for a keynote at a business conference than a memorial speech at her husband's funeral. She expresses gratitude for the ways Mr. Swift provided a loving home for his family, and she praises him for being an active member of his community. I tune out the rest, too busy watching Eliot dig his fingernails into his neck as though he wants to tear off his skin. I will him to feel my love from the back of the church, and Franny's love, and my mom's. This was never going to be a truth-telling ceremony. He just needs to get through it and move on.

Mrs. Swift eventually takes her seat. The priest asks if Eliot wants a turn. He shakes his head, burying his face in his hands. The priest looks on with sympathy, likely interpreting Eliot's posture as intense grief rather than barely restrained rage. Somewhere inside all that anger, I know there's a seed of sorrow, if not for what was, then for what might have been, but acknowledging that sorrow may be years off yet.

Just when I think the ceremony is nearing its end, the slide show starts. It's not long, maybe three or four minutes, the length of a monotonous hymn that plays in the background, but wow, is it painful. No hugs. No laughter. No goofy candids or awkward selfies. Just formal, stilted images of Mr. Swift golfing, or sailing, or posing next to his wife in front of their perfect, beautiful house. Eliot only appears in three shots. One as a baby, seated alone on a blanket in the yard, frowning at the camera while his dad reads a newspaper in a nearby Adirondack chair. One at age four or five, examining a tennis racket while his dad demonstrates a swing. One at age seven or eight, suited up for a studio family portrait. That's it. Fifty or sixty shots go by and Eliot is in three of them. Always looking miserable. Never being held or even touched.

As the pallbearers carry out the casket and the church begins to empty, Franny, Anika, my mom, and I slide out with the crowd, grateful for fresh air and movement. We stay near the base of the stairs, waiting for Eliot, while Anika shows Franny something on her phone and my mom waylays a skinny guy with a handlebar mustache, asking if his home insurance policy is up to date. The guy blubbers out that it's none of my mom's business. Then he scurries toward the parking lot with his phone pressed to his ear and panic in his eyes. My mom watches him depart with a rueful shake of her head.

"Is he going to be all right?" I ask.

"He'll be fine. It's the house he has to worry about." My mom's eyes drift skyward. "People should take better care of their gutters in the fall. All these leaves build up. Puddles form. Rot sets in. One heavy rainstorm and the water goes through the roof."

I follow her gaze. The sky overhead is totally clear, vivid cerulean from horizon to horizon, a sight that should be peaceful but leaves me uneasy. Of course, my mom *might* have wandered past Mustache Guy's house while he was outside, seen his full gutters, and made the kind of prediction anyone could make. With too much neglect, any house runs the risk of damages. And my mom didn't say *when* the house would be hit. A hard rain is bound to fall by month's end, or sometime in early November. However . . .

Too curious to leave well enough alone, I step aside and check the weather app on my phone. Chance of rain: none from now until midnight. The ten-day forecast also looks clear, with only a slight chance of showers by week's end. Since this is Coastal Oregon, weather forecasters should know better, but this time, I hope they're right. It would seriously change my outlook on life if my mom was wrong just once.

As I pocket my phone in my overcoat, my mom wanders over to chat with a trio of women her age, two members of her knitting group and a third who's been into the hardware store in recent weeks, working through an extensive home renovation. Not far past the group, near the corner of the church, I notice Sophia standing alone, watching the pallbearers and dabbing at her watery eyes. She looks less like a movie star without her giant sunglasses, but she's still striking with her sleek honey-blond hair, her blade-sharp cheekbones, and the alabaster skin that looks almost fragile in the bright sunlight. Or maybe it's not her skin that seems fragile. It's her aloneness.

Unsure how long Eliot will be, I tell Franny I'll be right back. Then I take the opportunity to approach Mr. Swift's final and most unfortunate mistress. She smiles when she spots me, flapping a hand at her puffy face.

"Get a hold on it," she says. "I know."

"Actually, I was going to say I'm so sorry for your loss."

"Oh." She blinks rapidly as new tears form. "Thank you." She sniffles and wipes her nose on a well-used tissue. "I know what people are saying. That I have no right."

"You cared about him. You have every right."

"I did care." She nods, fighting another round of tears. "I really did." She looks at me as if she's expecting me to express astonishment, but I don't have any to express. I might not understand how anyone could fall in love with Mr. Swift, but I do understand that love doesn't simply flow to obvious and easy places. If it did, I'd be planning a date with Dutch instead of further entangling myself with a guy I know is about to leave me. A guy I care about way too much for that prospect to not be excruciating.

I wait beside Sophia as she looks toward the hearse, and as people glance our way while trying to look like they're not glancing our way. I also check the church doors to see if Eliot's emerging, but there's still no sign of him.

"You're friends with his son, right?" Sophia asks.

I flinch, wondering if she read my mind. Stranger things have happened.

"I saw you wave at him inside," she says, catching my look.

"Right. Yes. Of course." I blink away my random jolt of apprehension and get ahold of myself. "We grew up together. Franny, too." I point over my shoulder, where Franny's holding Anika close and running a soothing hand over her magenta hair.

Sophia nods as she wipes her nose on the now disintegrating tissue.

"I always hoped I'd get to meet him one day," she says. "Obviously not today."

I smile at the bitter irony, though I make no attempt to look cheerful.

"He's pretty great, even if—" I stop myself, because saying *even if his dad didn't think so* sounds deeply insensitive. "Even if he didn't always stay in touch."

Sophia gives me a look that suggests she's well aware of the subtext here.

"I know Harris wasn't the easiest man to get along with," she says. "Call me crazy, but I liked the challenge. And I felt his love, even if he wasn't always gifted at showing it." She stops there, snagging on something in my expression, probably the *no kidding* I'm trying so hard to keep to myself. "Showing love is a skill," she adds. "It can be learned and developed. Yet we expect everyone to instinctively know how to do it, rarely accounting for the possibility of growth. The possibility of change."

I look at Franny and Anika, still locked in their embrace, and at my mom, who's now chatting with one of the pallbearers, resting a comforting hand on his arm. I think about Eliot letting my mom cut his hair and Ed hiring me when he didn't need another waitress and the whole town tracking down my mom when she went missing last year. And I consider the distinction Sophia's drawing between a feeling and its demonstration.

"I suppose people's instincts vary," I say, the best I can offer.

She pockets her tissue and locates another in her patent leather clutch.

"Harris liked straightforward cause and effect," she says. "A leads to B leads to C. People, of course, are far more complex than that. They frustrated him. But underneath that frustration, he *wanted* to understand them. He wanted to understand his son most of all." She looks at me as if she's willing me to comprehend more than she's saying, and maybe I do, because for all of Eliot's honesty, he's always been an enigma, with a busy internal life he keeps to himself. He's also by far the most stubborn of the three of us. If he decided he didn't *want* to be understood, that would be that.

The chattering behind me grows louder. I turn around to see Eliot and his mom step out of the church. Mrs. Swift is mid-conversation with the priest, but Eliot scans the milling crowd. He spots Franny first, stepping into the embrace she offers him while she rubs his back and chatters out of my earshot, probably trying to make him laugh. I'm about to excuse myself so I can join them when Sophia sets a hand on my wrist.

"I don't know if this is appropriate," she says. "But if it ever feels right to share with Eliot, Harris talked about him all the time. He watched every video. He bragged about how brave his son was, and how brilliant. He desperately wanted to make amends, but he never figured out how. He thought love was about protection and guidance. And about giving people the things he thought they should have. That worked well enough for us, but what was he supposed to do with a son who didn't want protection and who didn't need guidance? A son who wanted nothing from him? Nothing concrete, anyway." She pauses there as she lowers her hand and looks toward the hearse again. "I know none of this is any of my business, but we're past the point of what's appropriate." She smiles a little, and we silently acknowledge the unusual circumstances of Mr. Swift's death. "All I'm trying to say is that the lovely young man over there should know his father loved him, even if Harris never figured out how to say it or how to show it."

A lump forms in my throat, thick as overcooked oatmeal. I made it through the entire funeral service with only an occasional sad thought, but learning Eliot had more love in his life than he imagined nearly breaks me.

I crane around to see him loosening his tie and popping his collar button. Franny mimics ruffling his hair, even though he no longer has any hair to ruffle. Anika rolls her eyes as though adults are *so* embarrassing, but she laughs a little, too, drawing out a tiny smile from Eliot. A tiny, beautiful, sad smile.

"Today might not be the best day," I tell Sophia. "But I'll try to find a time."

She melts before me, already soaking her new tissue.

"Thank you," she says. "And thank you for making me feel like less of an intruder here. It was nice meeting you, or sort of meeting you. Though I don't expect I'll ever have reason to be back this way." With a conflicted smile much like the one we exchanged at the diner earlier in the week, she nods, turns, and walks away.

I watch her until she climbs into her car, my thoughts swimming. I never even learned her real name but I feel like I just parted from a kindred spirit, maybe because we both fell in love with members of the Swift family. More likely because we both know love isn't always what we want it to be, or shown the way we want it to be shown, but that doesn't mean it isn't worth having. Even when it leads to hard goodbyes.

With a bracing breath, I join Franny, Anika, and Eliot over by the church steps. Despite some uncertainty about how we're supposed to act around each other today, hugs feel like fair game, so I draw Eliot into an embrace and hold him tight.

"How are you?" I say as I pull back a few inches, brushing a hand over his cheek the way I might if I was sweeping away tears, even though he hasn't shed any.

"At least Act One is over," he says. Catching the question in my eye he adds, "Cemetery next. Then my mom arranged something at the country club. She didn't want people at the house. She said it was easier to leave a gathering we weren't hosting, but I think she's also keeping the place clean so she can list it next week."

"Wow." The word slips out of me before I can stop it. "Sorry. It's just . . ."

"Weird to arrange your husband's memorial around your real estate plans?"

"Yeah. Something like that."

Eliot drops his embrace, but he keeps a hand on the small of my back so I rest my hand on his shoulder, where his jacket seam is near to splitting from the strain. Franny takes in our sustained contact, sneaking me a *You go girl* look. This is hardly the time and place to revel in the way Eliot's touching me, but when his thumb sweeps in slow, rhythmic arcs across my spine, I can't help my little burst of euphoria.

*I'm here,* it whispers with each sweep. *I'm here and I'm glad you're beside me.*

"Eliot?" comes a sharp voice from behind us. "We should go."

We spin around as Mrs. Swift draws a set of keys from her purse. She's wearing a crisp, tailored black overcoat that perfectly matches her dress while the rest of us are in a motley assortment of whatever fall coats and scarves we had on hand. My coat is bright blue plaid, garish, outdated, made of cheap polyester, frayed at the cuffs and elbows, and earning me a potent helping of The Look. Making matters worse, I left the coat open, so my sexy dress and cleavage are in full view. Mrs. Swift notices and The Look intensifies.

"Do you mind if I ride with my friends?" Eliot asks his mom.

Her lips purse as she scans our little group, taking in our mismatched clothes and untidy hair, no doubt finding us wanting on all accounts.

"One. Day," she says to Eliot. "You promised me *one day* without a fight."

He tenses beside me. I lift my hand off his shoulder, sensing he might need some space right now, but he draws me closer, letting his hand slip further around my waist.

"I'll be right behind you," he says to his mom. "I just need a few minutes."

"I don't mind driving him," I offer. "We can follow your car."

Mrs. Swift's expression doesn't change. It rarely does.

"A moment please?" She draws Eliot aside, forcing us to break contact.

Franny edges closer to me, eyes wide. Even Anika steps toward us, as we all exchange wary glances, silently plotting a rescue should one be required.

"You are *not* arriving at the cemetery with our housekeeper," Mrs. Swift whispers, not quite out of our earshot, possibly by mistake but more likely, *not* by mistake. "The idea's absurd. What would people say?"

"I don't care what people say," Eliot tells her.

"Not today." She pinches the top of her nose. "Please don't do this to me today."

"Do what? Ask for a few minutes with my friends?"

"Ignore my wishes. And your father's. At his funeral. Are you really that selfish?"

Eliot lets out a sigh that can probably be heard in Siberia.

"It's only a ride," he says as the sigh abates.

"Absolutely not. Especially since she's dressed like a call girl."

Franny winces and Anika's jaw drops ajar while I force myself not to check my cleavage or button my coat. Besides, who even says *call girl* these days?

Eliot scrubs his face with both hands and I feel us all struggling not to intervene.

"One day," his mom repeats, her voice growing more strained

with every word. "Let's see your father interred. Make an appearance at the gathering—"

"Which my friends also can't attend."

"Members only. You know that already. At least put in an hour or two. Shake a few hands. Show an ounce of respect for your father's community so I don't have to spend the entire afternoon making excuses for you. What you do after that is up to you."

Eliot draws in a slow, deep breath, the kind people often count through when they're trying to calm themselves down. *One, one thousand, Two, one thousand . . .*

"Fine," he says. "But respect goes both ways. If you want it, you can give it, too."

His mom blinks at him in confusion, but Eliot's already spinning toward us and stepping our way. Franny blurts out an inane comment about Ed burning a pancake order yesterday. Anika and I act deeply invested in the outcome, but the look Eliot gives us suggests we're not fooling him. He knows we were listening. And it is what it is.

He cups my elbow with a gentle hand and draws me toward him.

"For the record," he says, a phrase we seem to be saying a lot lately. I'm not sure why. "You look beautiful. Apparently, I need to decline the ride, but if I'm lucky enough to see you later, I hope you're still wearing that dress. And I hope you feel great in it."

I set my hands on his chest as his arms wrap around me. Amid a million other thoughts about his mom's biting comments, his dad's inability to convey love, our class differences, and that stupid suit Eliot shouldn't have to wear, it fully sinks in that he's treating me like a girlfriend, making a clear assumption that we're on the other side of a line now. The side where we reach for each other, where we stand together in public as if we're a couple, where we talk about seeing each other again as though it's a foregone conclusion. So, I kiss him, chastely, not like I'm trying to prove anything to his mom or to anyone else, but because it's what I want to do and I think it's okay to do it.

"Are you going to be all right?" I ask him, quiet and close.

"Absolutely not," he says through a breathy laugh. "But it's only *one day*." He mimics his mom's intonation, following it up with his usual not-quite-smile.

"I'll keep my phone by my side," I tell him. "Text if you need me. I can hop in the car and come get you anytime. Anywhere. We can have a quiet night in." I turn toward Franny and Anika. "Or we can plan a night out. Or a slumber party. We'll make a pillow fort. Stock up on ice cream. Really bad wine. Board games I'm guaranteed to lose."

Franny throws her arms around us both, pulling us into a group hug.

"That's why we love having her around so much, right, Swiftie?" She winks, baiting him to compliment me in a way that reveals something about his feelings.

"I'm still determined to see her win," he says instead.

I snuggle in closer and pray with every ounce of my being that he's right. That I can win *something*. That I can finally rid myself of the constant weight of inevitable failure I carry with me. And that I can become more than a placeholder. Soon.

We hold our group hug—two birds with one stone—until someone clears their throat nearby. It's Mrs. Swift, of course, tapping her diamond-encrusted wristwatch. We drop our group embrace, but Franny sneaks in another hug with Eliot, along with her usual loud, mushy kiss on his cheek. Anika awkwardly waves goodbye from a few feet away. I steal one last kiss on Eliot's lips, whispering, "Anytime, anywhere," before backing away. Then I turn to Mrs. Swift with her pearls and her pursed lips.

I want to say so many things to her right now, but I bottle my anger and irritation, reminding myself that her husband just died, and no matter how unaffected she seems, grief is complicated. Today can't be easy for her. For a lot of reasons.

"I'm so sorry for your loss," I say, and I mean it.

"Thank you," she says with obvious effort.

Eliot gives my arm a light squeeze before joining her.

"Wasn't there something else you wanted to say?" he asks her.

She glances back and forth between Eliot and me. She looks, in turns, curious, angry, confused, annoyed, and disappointed. It's like watching the stages of grief play out all at once, but on someone who's really skilled at hiding that grief. I know what Eliot's asking of her. We all do. He's asking her to offer me the same kind of respect she's asking of him toward his dad's country club buddies, a respect she's reluctant to give.

"Mom?" he prompts as the silence drags on.

Her expression softens slightly and I'm *just* starting to wonder if he's going to get an apology out of her when she says, "The flowers looked lovely."

Then she takes Eliot's arm and guides him away.

# Sixteen

Eight hours after leaving the church, I'm home alone, working on Eliot's sweater in front of the local news. I've been knitting since I got home, so I have most of the body done. I'm still in my sexy cocktail dress, which is starting to feel ridiculous, but I keep hoping Eliot will text and I'd rather not take off the dress before I see him. Meanwhile, the news is displaying stats on the "unexpected" torrential rainstorm that hit about two hours ago, flooding nearby alleys and fields. It also damaged a few properties, including the house of a guy they're interviewing right now. A large section of his roof is caved in and he has a distinctive handlebar mustache I wish I hadn't noticed earlier today, but I did.

Score one for my mom.

Minus one for my hopes of shedding my curse.

My mom is out at book club, which is code for wine night. She never gets drunk, but she's always a little rosy when she comes home complaining about how no one else read the book they all chose. After three years, she should know what to expect by now, but she has fun with her group regardless, and once a month, I get a Saturday night to myself with no concerns about my mom's whereabouts or activities.

My phone buzzes on the coffee table. I snatch it up, hoping it's *finally* Eliot.

Franny: Any word yet?

Imogen: No. You?

Franny: Not a peep. I'm getting worried

Imogen: His mom probably locked him in at the country club

Franny: She can be rather insistent

Imogen: That's a nice way of putting it

Franny: Do you think the pillow fort is out at this point?

Imogen: Maybe we raincheck it? Try again tomorrow?

Franny: That works. We have way too much ice cream for
     only two of us

Imogen: There's no such thing as too much ice cream

Franny: Fair. But Eliot's the only one who likes Chunky Monkey

Imogen: Frozen bananas are an abomination

Franny: True fact. But I'm stuck with them now

Imogen: Should we go look for him at the club?

Franny: You think they'd let us in?

Imogen: For a few minutes, yes. Unless they assume we're
     "call girls"

Franny: I still can't believe she said that

Imogen: Can't you? Really?

Franny: How in the hell did Eliot turn out so kind?

Imogen: Probably by knowing how awful it feels to be treated
     unkindly

Franny: Yeah. Probably

Franny and I debate the rescue plan and decide to go for it. Better to do it now, before the flooding gets worse and Eliot's trapped with the golf and tennis set all night.

I turn off the TV and text my mom to let her know where I'll be. She texts back that she doesn't understand how anyone can read only the first five chapters of a murder mystery. I debate several snarky replies about how life is different for those of us who are accustomed to not knowing how everything turns out, but I decide not to engage, signing off with a promise to be home by 10 p.m., when her club usually wraps up and her friends drive her home. Then I give my makeup a quick refresh, scrub a hand through my useless hair, and grab my coat, buttoning it up this time so no one can see my cleavage.

I'm plucking my car keys from their usual hook by the door when someone knocks. I swing open the door to find Eliot standing in the pouring rain, still wearing his black suit pants and white dress shirt, though his tie and jacket are gone and his shirt's partly unbuttoned. He's completely drenched, with his clothes clinging to his body and his tattoos showing through his translucent shirtsleeves. I'm so stunned by how insanely hot he looks, it takes me a second to register he's panting and hollow-eyed. And here.

"You're going somewhere," he gusts out, chest heaving.

"Yeah, to get you." I peer out into the rain. "How did you—I mean, did you—?"

"Run here from the club? Yeah."

"That's, like, fifteen miles away. In the dark. In the cold. In the rain."

"Worth every step if you'll get me out of these fucking clothes."

"Oh my god. Sorry. Of course." I grab him by the shirt front and drag him inside, feeling stupid for not doing so right away. As I shut the door behind him, a puddle forms around his soggy black dress socks, and I realize he's not wearing any shoes. He's not limping or anything but the image still freaks me out. I can't imagine the circumstances that would impel me to run shoeless into the night.

He's also shivering, so I set a hand on his back and usher him toward the basement. "Your feet. Are they okay?"

"My dad's shoes were too small. I could barely stand in them, let alone run. I ditched them on the roadside with the jacket and tie." He stumbles down the stairs with me, his wet socks slapping against the uncarpeted two-by fours that make up the treads.

"Why didn't you text me? I could've picked you up."

"My phone died. I didn't have a chance to charge it this morning. I know my mom has your number but I couldn't bear to ask her. We both know what she would've said. I didn't want to hear it or fight about it. I just wanted to get the hell out of there." He takes a few quick breaths, still winded from his run. "I thought I was just going to take a walk. Escape the noise. Clear my head. Circle back. Get the club to call me a cab. But the walk turned into a run, I realized I was heading this way, and I didn't want to turn back."

"Of course." I follow him across my room, which, thankfully, I took the time to tidy today. I didn't add any glamour, but the space is mildly less embarrassing than it was yesterday. "We'll get the shower going. I'll find you some clothes while you warm up."

We cram into my tiny bathroom together. I start the shower, taking off my coat so I can hold a hand in the spray to monitor the temperature, which takes *forever* to heat up. Eliot leans against the sink, lacing his hands behind his neck the way he did at the service this morning. He's still catching his breath and I'm still marveling that he ran all the way here. Sure, he's in incredible physical shape, but he must've been running for at least two hours, along dark roads, with terrible visibility. If a driver chose the wrong moment to adjust the radio or sip a beverage, he would've been flattened.

"Did something happen?" I ask. "At the club?"

He shakes his head. "It's those people, with their hors d'oeuvres and assumptions, all looking down their noses at me, sneaking their disdain into polite conversation. *Where did you end up going to college? Oh, really? How unusual. Your dad was so sure he'd have another Harvard man in the family. Guess we all face disappointments. You do what for a living? How does that even work, not having a permanent address? How do you get a credit card or enroll in a phone plan? Where do you keep everything? My kid watches those little videos you do for YouTube. Too bad we all can't go on vacation forever. Getting it out of your system before you have a family? Surely you won't deprive your mother of the joy of being a grandmother? So many young people these days, setting aside traditional family values. It's all so selfish. What happens next? Never too soon to start a retirement plan. Or begin building equity. Ever consider working for your dad's company? He would've loved that. It's not too late to make some changes."*

The water finally warms up a bit, so I let it run while I start unbuttoning Eliot's shirt. The fabric is cold and wet, and the buttons stick in the little holes.

"I'm sorry," I say. "And I'm sorry you had to face that alone."

His brows plunge together as he removes his glasses and sets them on the sink.

"It doesn't make sense," he says.

"What doesn't make sense?"

"I do everything else alone. Why did that feel so different?"

"Because you had a *really* hard day. And because people suck?"

"Not all people."

"No," I say through a laugh. "Not all people."

The final button refuses to give way, but Eliot takes both my hands in his and raises them to his lips, planting a slow, cold-lipped kiss on my knuckles. I smile at him, grateful we're at a place where we can openly share affection with each other, but his forehead remains furrowed as his brain churns through thoughts I can only imagine.

"I don't know what to do with this," he says.

I free a hand and brush rainwater off his cheeks, mentally noting that I've never seen him cry, even when we were kids. Even when we said goodbye all those years ago.

"You don't know what to do with what?" I ask.

"You. Me. *This*." He squeezes the hand he's still holding, resting it by his lips. "Initially I was so shocked to see you again, I wasn't thinking about what could happen between us while I was here. Then all these memories came flooding back, things I'd locked away in a misguided attempt to diminish their importance. Now I've spent an entire day wishing you were with me. Knowing I would've been able to handle things better. You would've found a way to cut through the snobbery. Turned the whole infuriating affair into a game of some kind. Made me laugh with a really bad Ironman joke. Played keep-away with my mother. Hidden with me in a closet. Something—*anything*—that prevented me from standing there in a sea of faces, explaining my life choices to people who were predisposed to disapprove of everything I said."

I catch a drop of rainwater before it falls from the tip of his nose.

"It's okay to want support," I say.

"I'm not sure *want* is the right word."

"It's also okay to *need* support."

"Actually, it's terrifying."

*Oh, Eliot,* I think, as my heart breaks for him for the millionth time.

"It doesn't have to be terrifying," I say. "Does it?"

"I don't know." He shakes his head, forehead furrows deepening. "I don't know."

In the mirror over his shoulder, I notice steam is finally drifting out from behind the shower curtain. We can't eradicate his fears right now, simply by wishing them away. They're too deeply ingrained. But we can at least warm him up and then get him dry.

"As requested, let's get you out of these clothes." I start in on his bottom shirt button again but when it *still* doesn't pop open, Eliot draws my hands away.

"Whatever. They're already wet." He steps toward the shower and shoves aside the curtain. It's flimsy and hanging from only half of the plastic loops, the others having long since broken, but Eliot doesn't register my lack of upkeep as he steps into the shower, still fully dressed, letting the hot water hit his face.

With a sudden recollection that Franny's expecting me in her driveway any second, I find my phone in my coat pocket and fire off a quick text, letting her know Eliot's at my place and I'll circle back once I know how he wants to spend the night.

"Take your time," I tell Eliot. "I'll go find you clothes and fresh towels."

"Don't." He turns to face me. "Just stay with me. Please." He goes rigid, as though his plea surprises him even more than it surprises me, but he doesn't withdraw it or do anything to lessen its weight. The need in his eyes is almost palpable, as is the fear of that need. He also looks a little unhinged, standing in the shower, wearing his father's too-small, too-formal clothes. Seeing him like this, so uncertain, so vulnerable, it strikes me that my mom was probably right when she suggested Eliot was searching for something. And maybe we do want some of the same things.

"Okay. I'll stay," I say, and at the tiniest uptick at the corner of Eliot's lips, I kick off my shoes and join him in the shower, drawing the curtain shut behind me.

"Your dress," he says, though it's too late for cautionary measures.

I wrap my arms around his neck. "It's only a dress."

"Yeah, but it's a hell of a dress." His hands skim down my sides. In the next second his lips are on mine and I no longer regret spending the entire day in this outfit.

For several minutes we drown our fears in steam and wet skin and the kinds of kisses that banish unwanted thoughts to the outskirts of our minds. We step into a world where it's okay to leave our problems at the door, not forever, but for now. I find my way to Eliot's last remaining shirt button. When it *still* refuses to budge, he yanks it from its threads and wrenches the shirt off, leaving it in a wad at our feet. I follow rivulets of water down his bare chest with my fingertips, studying the trees and clouds and swirls of smoke that stain his skin. It fascinates me, all of this ink, each image drawn by a different hand. If we had more time together, I'd ask Eliot to tell me the story behind every tattoo. Instead, I lodge the images in my memory so I can revisit them in days to come.

As Eliot's lips drift along my neck and over the swells of my breasts, I unfasten his trousers. He shimmies out of them, along with his boxers, this time without hesitation about showing himself to me. I'm soaking in the sight of his naked body when my gaze snags on the black dress socks he's still wearing. I sputter out a laugh before I can stop myself. He looks down, rolling his eyes through a head shake before bracing himself against the wall and yanking off the socks.

"Fucking socks," he says. "This is the unsexy part."

"You are *so* wrong," I say, still laughing a little. "It's all sexy."

He lets out a self-deprecating groan, tossing his socks to the shower floor with a punishing *thwack*, but underneath his show of annoyance, I think he gets it. Those silly socks are what make this moment feel real. And nothing is sexier than that.

I spin away from him and reach over my shoulder to indicate the top of my zipper.

"No way," he says. "I've been thinking about this dress all day. Though I had no idea I'd get to see you in it like this. I should've run here hours ago."

I start to turn and face him, but he halts me, gripping my hips and rotating me away from him again. While the shower rains down on us, he nudges my head sideways, elongating my neck so he can paint it with more kisses. He sneaks in a few nips as he presses his groin to my ass, grinding against me and gusting low growls of pleasure across my neck. I'm not sure why, but knowing he's stark naked while I'm fully clothed is a serious turn-on. Less surprising, his uninhibited enjoyment of my body is also a turn-on, and soon every inch of me is quivering with anticipation.

Using one hand to brace myself against the wall, I set the other on his, curling his fingers under the hem of my dress and guiding them upward. Inch by agonizing inch, he scooches my tight, soaked skirt up my thighs until my ass is bared to him and I can part my legs wide enough to let him slip between my thighs. I feel him there, against the inside of my thigh, hot wet skin to hot wet skin, but he's not moving anymore.

I crane around. "What's wrong?"

He shakes his head at me, brows raised, eyes glassy. "Just taking in the view."

I glance down, reminding myself what I put on this morning. I went for bold magenta, a hidden rebellion under my somber black attire, or, my *semi*-somber black attire. The scalloped lace rides high on my cheeks, cut perfectly to flatter my minimal curves. I take advantage of the choice, wiggling a little for Eliot's benefit.

He mutters something unintelligible under his breath. I don't ask what he said. I get the gist. Even if I didn't, he makes his sentiments clear a moment later by reaching around to wrench aside my underwear and fondle me, dancing his impressively skilled fingers

around the places where I'm most sensitive, fitting his strong, lean
body around mine, and responding to every twitch and tremor until
I'm gasping and my legs tremble.

"I want to feel all of you," I tell him, though I can barely get the
words out.

"Now? You sure?" His fingers keep moving and I am losing my
mind.

"The answer has always been and will always be yes," I quote
back to him.

He lets out a low, appreciative *mmmmm* as he retracts his hand
and shifts his stance behind me. He guides himself this time, holding my underwear off to the side and running the head of his shaft
through my wetness while I bend forward and basically present myself to him for the taking. This is new territory for me, since displays of sexual confidence aren't exactly my trademark, but the move
doesn't go unappreciated, earning me another admiring *mmmmm*. I
love that noise. I want to put it on repeat forever.

Despite a few steamy shower fantasies I've entertained about
Eliot over the years, and despite how this particular shower started
out even hotter than I'd imagined—with his wet clothes clinging to
his amazing body and the open lust in his eyes as he checked out my
ass—it's all a little awkward from here, trying to find the right angle, maintain our footing, and enjoy the hot shower stream without
washing away the wetness that helps us fit together smoothly. We
laugh as we fumble through it. However . . .

*However . . .*

When we do find the right position and he guides himself inside
me, filling me up and hitting a spot that turns my knees to jelly, the
awkwardness vanishes and all I can think about is how right this
feels. How inevitable. As he slides forward and back with his strong
hands gripping my thighs, the intense physical pleasure rips away

any last lingering anxieties and plants me in the present moment like nothing else, with no questions left to ask, let alone answer.

Only now. Only this. Only us.

The shower rains down. Steam fills the room. My palms slip lower on the tiled wall. My breath quickens. Eliot's does, too. The delicious friction between us builds as my nerve endings seem to multiply every time he eases back and pushes forward again.

"Tell me when you're close," he practically growls in my ear.

*I'm already close,* I think as he thrusts against me, but I don't tell him that. I want this feeling to last. And since I can't finish first— not something I'm going to tell him while he's fucking me and skeptical about my curse anyway—I heave out a breath while I tell him he feels good, *so* good. Then he's moving faster, thrusting deeper, one hand planted on the shower wall beside my head, the other reaching around to finger me again in tight, almost ticklish circles that spark sensation to my toes and back.

I start making little sex noises I can't seem to hold in anymore. He stops bracing himself on the wall so he can loop his hand through my underwear where they're already pulled sideways on my ass cheek, now gripped in a tight fist as our bodies slap together and our momentum builds and my noises get louder and he asks if we're home alone and I tell him, *Yes!* and he practically shouts, *Thank fucking god!* and my own impassioned noises grow louder and I bend deeper, pressing the side of my face to the shower wall, and he stops fingering me to fist that hand in my bunched up skirt, holding me against him so we move as one, and we reset our rhythm, rocking together until I feel him surge inside me seconds before my body unfurls and . . .

*Yes,* I think. *There. That. This. You. Us. Yes. Yes. Yes.*

We pant together, both unmoving, letting the aftershocks ripple through us as the shower hits our backs. When my body finally stops trembling, Eliot presses a palm to my chest and raises me upright, holding me against him in a tight embrace, hand-to-heart.

"Is this okay?" he asks.

"Holding me after sex? Um, yeah? It's kind of perfect."

He shakes his head and plants a lingering kiss on my neck.

"I mean all of it. Even being here right now. If we're not . . . if we won't . . ."

His unfinished question slices through the haziness of my orgasm-induced brain fog. I spin in his arms. The fear in his eyes has returned, though maybe it never really left. I cup the back of his head with a gentle hand while dusting his cheeks with tiny kisses, drawing back when I think he's ready for me to answer him.

"I know you're not using me for sex," I say. "Or for anything else."

"Even after what you said last night? About putting everyone else's needs before your own? I don't want to be one more guy who makes you do that."

"You're not. At all." I search his eyes, willing him to believe me. "This was a brutal day for you. Not just because of what people said at the country club. I want to be here for you. For whatever you need. You'd do the same for me. You already *do* the same for me." I run a hand over his head, a reminder that when I needed him, he didn't hesitate to help. "In case I haven't been clear, I haven't done anything I didn't want to do. Not once. Not even close." I brush water from his dark brows before it trickles into his eyes. Then I force myself to utter the words we've both been avoiding. "I know you're leaving on Tuesday. I hope we stay in touch this time. But even if we don't, I won't regret a single second I spend with you while you're here. No matter how we spend it. Okay?"

His jaw twitches as he blinks away the water in his lashes. For several seconds, he studies my expression. His own expression is *so* serious I start nursing weird anxieties about an impending revelation that's going to shake up everything I thought I knew about him and us and why we're even standing in this shower together.

"You really assume everyone who loves you will leave you for someone else," he says, which is . . . not what I expected. For a lot of reasons. I start with the assumption.

"If not for someone else," I say, "then for the mountains and the fjords."

"That look in your eyes. The instinct to shut a part of yourself off, or to reconcile yourself to something less than you deserve. It's not about the mountains."

With great effort, I withhold a sigh. He's right. I have some deeply embedded insecurities to work on, but this is not an either/ or conversation.

"But you *are* leaving?" I ask. "And you don't plan to return?"

He slides his arms around me and pulls me against him. I nestle into his embrace, letting my cheek rest on his shoulder as he kisses my forehead. It's like we're swapping leads in a dance, as he takes on the role of comforter while I become the comforted, but it all happens so organically we don't need to know any steps.

"I make it a point to avoid plans," he says, which so obviously skirts my question, I almost call him out on it, but he's had a hell of a day, burying his dad, confronting his mom's withering coldness, facing an onslaught of conservative value bullshit, and then running fifteen miles shoeless in a torrential rainstorm.

Also, I don't want to keep thinking about his departure.

Even though I can't help it.

"Try living with someone who sees the future," I say. "Avoiding plans can be challenging when you know what's coming."

"You mean when you *think* you know what's coming."

"Eliot—"

"I'm serious." He draws back and holds my face between his hands, rubbing my cheeks with his thumbs. "I don't know your exes but I know *you*, Imogen. And nothing you say will ever convince me you're destined to be second best at anything."

"But you haven't—"

He sets a finger against my lips, halting me with a faux-stern look.

"We have the whole day together tomorrow," he says. "We're getting up early. I don't care what it takes. Corn shucking. Square dancing. Cupcake making. Mini-Ironman. Super mini-Ironman. We'll play a round of golf if we have to, and I *really* suck at golf. We're not quitting until you know you're not destined to be second anymore." He gives me a pointed look before quoting back at me, "Not at anything. Not to anyone."

I think about the guy with the mustache and the caved-in roof. I think about the speech Greg made when he told me about the other woman he'd been seeing, how he'd always known something about our relationship wasn't *quite* good enough. I think about sixteen other similar breakups. I think about countless lost games and contests, thirteen birds, and the word *complicated*. I think about how Eliot avoided confirming his impending departure. But I also think about how he snuck in the word *love*.

"Okay," I say. "Let's knock one out of the park."

# HEARTBREAK #13

Lucky number thirteen didn't turn out to be so lucky. It doesn't matter how we met or how long we dated or how good or bad the sex was. It doesn't even matter who he left me for. (Some woman named Mary Jane he'd hooked up with at a recent college reunion.) The most notable thing about our relationship was that he broke up with me while we were stuck at the top of a Ferris wheel. The Ferris wheel we only rode together because—despite a lifelong fear of heights—I believed all the rom-coms that had assured me Ferris wheels were romantic. Instead, for me, the ride turned out to be the place where I spewed regurgitated cotton candy from two hundred feet in the air while my newly ex-boyfriend uttered the less-than-supportive phrase, "And *this* is why we'd never work long-term."

I blamed his inability to keep his dick in his pants.

He blamed my inability to keep food in my stomach while I was freaking out about the dizzying view and being dumped for a woman named after a shoe.

The moral of the story: never trust a rom-com.

Also: if you're going to vomit while stuck on a fairground ride, aim for the asshole next to you. Not the unsuspecting people below.

No amount of apologies could make that day less mortifying. Though, admittedly, now that the sting has worn off, sometimes the memory does still make me laugh.

# Seventeen

## SUNDAY

$\mathcal{E}$liot wasn't kidding about getting up early, a task he manages with much more grace and goodwill than I'm able to muster. I shouldn't be this grumpy. We were very well-behaved last night, calling a strict moratorium on all fooling around by midnight. We went to bed shortly after my mom got home, staying up only late enough to get a book club report and say good night before heading down to my room. My mom didn't seem at all surprised to find Eliot at our place, which, I guess, I should've anticipated, all things considered.

Now Eliot and I are on our way to his parents' house so he can pick up his belongings, with no need to ever set foot across the threshold again, an achievement we plan to celebrate with a 6 a.m. pancake eating contest at the 24-hour diner a few miles up the coast. Eliot swears it's a guaranteed win if only two of us are competing. I'm far too bleary-eyed to contradict him. Also, I'm looking forward to the corn shucking and the square dancing (neither of which my introverted companion will participate in without serious motivation), so I'm in no rush to nab the first potential win.

As I pull into the long, winding drive that leads to the Swifts' mansion, I notice a sleek black Mercedes parked by the side of the house. Eliot notices, too, scrubbing a hand over his face and muttering a barely audible *hmmm*. He's in Antony's sweats again. The hoodie is at least three sizes too big with an obscure band logo on the front and the pants are rolled at the waist to prevent them from falling. His dad's clothes are in the trash.

"Your mom?" I ask as I park my piece-of-shit Honda next to the very not-piece-of-shit Mercedes.

"I thought she was heading back to Portland last night. Guess she's sticking around until we meet with the lawyer tomorrow."

"We can check back later. See if she's out."

Eliot considers, peering out my dingy windows toward the house.

"You still have your keys, right?" he asks.

I pull them from my pocket, secured to a key chain with a chipped resin bird that draws a sweet, subtle smile from Eliot. I am nothing if not on theme.

"Let's go for it," he says. "Quietly. So she'll never even know we were here."

We sneak in through the side door and climb the back stairs—aka "the servants' stairs"—to the top floor where I found Eliot the night he returned to town, having chosen the suite with the fewest personal memories. The suite he used as a kid is on the second floor, still tastefully but impersonally decorated with heavy colonial furniture and dark plaid coordinates. The room's size and elegance left me awestruck the first time I saw it. As I got to know Eliot, I understood that an enormous four-poster bed and a private bathroom were small compensations for the loving homelife he lacked.

We make it to the fourth-floor guest suite without incident. I shut the door and he tosses his belongings into a ragged duffel bag, pausing only long enough to change out of Antony's oversized sweats into a pair of ripped jeans, an illegible print concert tee, and what was probably once a forest-green thermal, now faded and frayed at the cuffs.

I wander over to the window while he packs up the last of his toiletries and winds the cord of his phone charger, waggling it at me as if to note its importance. The view through the fourth-floor window is incredible. Even in the dim light of early dawn, I can see at least a mile up and down the coast, with the immaculate lawn stretching from the house to the shore, and two boats neatly moored to the floating dock, one for sailing, one for rowing. Or for spilling one's soul to one's two best friends.

"I always thought it was a shame that this became a second home," I say. "Though I suppose I'm more sensitive than most to seconds." I glance around the room with its handcrafted woodwork and high, peaked ceilings. "There's so much space. Someone should be living here. Filling the rooms with memories. Laughter. Love."

"Maybe the new owners will use it more often than my parents did." Eliot sweeps a stack of paperbacks off the bedside table and into his bag before sitting on the side of the bed and lacing up his dusty hiking boots. "Or maybe someone will rezone it and replace the house with condos. God knows the property is worth more than the house."

I fight off a frown, but not well, and Eliot notices, giving me a curious look.

"I know you hate this place," I say. "And it was never a home for you, but it's a beautiful house. Antony always comments on it when he visits. He says there aren't many places this old on the West Coast, not in this condition, anyway." I run my hand along the highly polished chair rail, trying to recall where else I've even seen a chair rail, let alone admired one this beautiful. I don't know a ton about old architecture, but my brother sure does, and his enthusiasm is infectious when he starts rattling on about ogees and dentils.

Eliot steps up behind me and wraps me in a hug.

"Our memories are here." He pats my chest, intuiting the other reason for my contemplative mood. The larger, more meaningful reason. "And here." He pats his own chest. "But if you like, we can sneak a souvenir on the way out." He tightens his embrace and holds me for a minute, both of us looking out the window.

I know that for Eliot, the sooner he says his final goodbye to these walls, the better, but to me, this feels like the end of an era. For the last six years, I've been able to come here, immersing myself in the memories, letting the happiest ones rise while the hardest ones softened over time. I've relived silly croquet games and picnics on the lawn and hours spent reading side by side in the rowboat. Now all of that's going to be gone.

I don't say any of this, of course. There's no point. But as we sneak back down the stairs and toward the side door, I request a detour through the immaculate, ready-for-sale kitchen, where I dig through the cabinet with the coffee mugs.

"Didn't I already give you the one with the finch?" Eliot asks.

"Yep." I find the one I'm looking for and hold it out. "I want this one, too."

It is, of course, the mug with the painted swift, though I don't let myself dwell on what it means that I can keep the mug but not the man. If I give it more than a moment's thought, I'll burst into tears here and now, which is the last thing either of us needs.

"Are you going to take something?" I ask.

"We took my grandmother's yarn already. That's enough for me."

"What about photos? Didn't you say there are more in the attic?"

"You saw that slide show. Would *you* want those photos?"

"I don't know. The baby one was cute. You sure you don't—?"

"Eliot?" a familiar pinched voice calls from the foyer. "Is that you?"

We freeze for half a second, wide-eyed with panic, as though we're stealing something far more valuable than a mug and discussing something far more nefarious than photographs. Then I grab Eliot by the wrist, he shoulders his duffel, and together we run, flinging open the back door and flying across the lawn.

Breathless. Laughing. Free.

❧

One might assume it's impossible to lose a pancake-eating contest against an opponent who's determined to lose, but even Eliot is learning to rethink that assumption.

We each ordered a standard stack of three pancakes. Eliot got his with a double side of bacon, partly to slow his eating of the main dish, and partly to refuel after last night's insane run. The waitress set down Eliot's plate first, noting that his was the one with the bacon. As she started to set down my plate, she slipped on spilled ice and my plate spun to the floor, scattering my breakfast. She quickly cleaned up the mess and scurried to the kitchen with a promise to bring me a replacement order right away.

Eliot offered me his pancakes while we waited, giving me a head start instead of letting me fall behind. As he slid the dish my way, he knocked over the pepper shaker. The shaker was full but the lid wasn't screwed on, leaving us with a plate of peppered pancakes. This would've been great if we were writing tongue twisters, but it helped neither of us get going on our contest. Also, I hate bacon, and a *lot* of bacon grease was on that plate, so those pancakes would've been hard for me to stomach anyway.

We flagged down the waitress to request a second replacement dish.

Round two started on even footing, but only until the kids behind me started fighting about *Frozen* characters. The fight grew more vehement, sobbing ensued, and the decapitated head of an Elsa doll landed in the middle of my plate, its shedding blond hairs impossible to pick out of the syrup I'd already poured. The kids' parents apologized profusely and we requested another pancake order. Elsa's fate remained uncertain.

We'd barely begun round three when Rusty—the impossibly chatty teen boy I work with at the hardware store—entered the diner with his parents, spotted me across the room, slid into the booth beside me, and launched a Q&A about how inventorying works, since we have one ahead of us next week. Every time I raised my fork to my mouth, Rusty asked another question. I lowered my fork so I could answer. On the other side of the table, Eliot tried not to eat his pancakes while also trying not to laugh.

By the time Rusty *finally* left us alone and I could pick up my pace, I swallowed wrong, launching a coughing fit. Then I drank my water too fast, only to have it come out my nose as I continued sputtering, soaking what was left of my pancakes.

Now here we are, Eliot and me, each with a pancake and a half left, but mine are soggy with snot water and he has run out of ways to pretend *not* to eat his.

He shakes his head, frowning at my plate. "Unbelievable."

"I'm used to it." I wipe tears from the corners of my eyes, still recovering from my coughing fit. "You've simply forgotten. You've been gone too long."

"I know," he says, and then repeats in his way, with more weight, "I know."

He wedges his knees around mine under the table, squeezing tight and causing a warm fluttery feeling to expand in my chest. I decide to call that feeling *hope*. And I give no other feelings a right to challenge that call.

# Eighteen

"I can't believe you got me out of bed for this," Franny says to me.

"I can't believe *you* told me this would be fun," Anika retorts.

"Maybe it will be fun?" I grin at her in a deeply unconvincing way. If I was fifteen and I got dragged to something like this, I'd be equally skeptical.

It's just past 9 a.m. Franny, Anika, Eliot, my mom, and I are at McGruder's Family Farm about thirty miles inland, staring at a massive mountain of un-shucked corn. The corn can probably be processed by machines but today it will be handled by a motley crowd of about three hundred people, including families, couples, clusters of friends, and a few late arrivals who glance around as if on the lookout for familiar faces. Apparently, McGruder's annual corn shucking contest is a popular event. Who knew?

"How are *you* so awake?" Franny asks me as she takes another sip of coffee.

"I've had a busy morning," I tell her. "This is contest number three."

She raises a curious eyebrow, so I tell her about the pancakes, and about the hour Eliot and I spent at the driving range before picking up my mom and heading out here. We played a version of *HORSE* where we tried to hit various targets on the green. Despite Eliot's determination to lose the game by dropping his club, hitting the ball with his eyes closed, setting aside the club to kick the ball, and completely muffing several shots, our game came to an abrupt halt when I took a wild swing and smashed a light. I paid the damages while the unnecessarily stern pro shop attendant requested we take our immediate leave and never return. No blue ribbons were awarded. No glittering trophies were handed out. No gold medals were looped around my neck. But Eliot and I laughed so hard, and our morning together was so full of joy, it felt like a win in and of itself.

As I take in the crowd around me now, my mom beams at me, rubbing her bony hands together in anticipation, or maybe to cut the slight chill that's in the air. She's the only additional member of our team who looks like she belongs here. Franny's in satin PJ bottoms, a black bra, a men's undershirt, and a vivid yellow woolly sweater-coat, with her riot of copper curls springing out of a sparkly elastic atop her head. Anika's gothed out in umpteen layers of black knits and countless decorative safety pins, her magenta hair dye just starting to fade. My mom is wearing overalls, knee-high rubber boots, and a trio of plaid flannel shirts, along with a busted straw cowboy hat she's somehow pulling off.

"I think this is delightful," she says. "A brisk October morning. Good company. A strong competitive spirit in the air." Her gaze drifts toward a rusted weather vane on the barn roof. Her eyes narrow and she taps her chin, dropping into deep thoughts.

I wrap a hand over her eyes, pulling her into a side-hug with my other arm.

"Oh, no you don't!" I say. "You promised on the ride here. No predictions. No insinuations of predictions. I don't care which way the wind is blowing. You are *not* telling Mr. McGruder a blight is coming. He'll face it if he has to face it."

She flaps her hands, waving me off. "Okay, okay! No blights. I promise."

We all share a laugh. Then we watch as a tall, broad-shouldered man in Carhartt workwear climbs a stack of hay bales with a clipboard in one hand and a megaphone in the other. He's about thirty years old, with an unruly mop of chestnut curls and bright, joyful eyes that crinkle in the corners. He welcomes everyone and introduces himself as Franklin J. McGruder, fourth-generation owner of McGruder's Family Farm and the guy who will be cooking us all his family recipe chili and cornbread while we shuck.

Franny elbows me in the side. "Maybe I *am* glad I got out of bed."

I eye her sideways. "Because you're craving cornbread?"

She tips her chin toward the guy with the megaphone. "Hello? Hot farmer?"

"I didn't know that was your thing. Or, well, one of your things."

"Oh, please. It's hardly niche. Have you never heard of a roll in the hay?"

Anika crosses her arms over her chest and adopts an aggressive scowl.

"You are *so* embarrassing," she says.

Franny waves off her petulance, her eyes already back on the farmer.

"I know," she says. "But I'm also getting that guy's number before we leave."

Anika continues scowling. Eliot shakes his head at Franny as if to say *some things never change*. My mom smiles benignly, as though she has no idea how Franny's plan will pan out, and maybe she doesn't.

Or maybe she's sticking to her promise to let me enjoy this day without any predictions at all, for which I will be eternally grateful.

Franklin J. McGruder—who, on further review, is very attractive and packs some serious shoulders under his boxy canvas jacket—takes a few minutes to explain the rules, which are pretty straightforward. Teams of two to eight are allowed. We'll each pick a spot in the adjacent empty field, relaying cobs from "Corn Mountain" to our designated area where we'll shuck as much corn as possible from the moment he fires a starting pistol until he fires again at noon, signaling the end of the competition and the start of lunch. At that point, the ears will be counted, assessed for "full shucking" (which he *just* manages to say without the obvious flub), and divided by the number of team members. The team with the most fully shucked ears per member wins what he calls a "solid gold ear of corn" but is obviously a regular ear that's been spray-painted. Considering the hooting and applause that ensues, no one's expecting monetary recompense for their work. Everyone's here for the fun of it, and the prize is perfect.

Each team is given two empty plastic buckets and we all disperse to stake out spots in the field. My mom points toward a small cluster of boulders that would give us places to sit, and Anika starts checking for spots where she gets a phone signal, but Eliot reminds us we're here for the win, planting us as close as possible to Corn Mountain so our fetching trips will be efficient. Several other teams carry tarps, tackle boxes, sun umbrellas, tool belts, and folding chairs, fully prepared for the day's events and making me suspect it doesn't matter where we park ourselves. Franny might leave here with a phone number, but that's the only prize we're likely to take home.

Despite that thought, Eliot rallies our competitive spirits and soon enough, the starting pistol goes off. People all around us run to get corn and my adrenaline spikes. Franny and I join the race, hurrying back to our group with our buckets full. We all dive in, seated on the ground with space for two piles in the center of our circle, one shucked, one un-shucked. None of us has ever done anything like this, but we have an absolute blast, chatting away and egging each other on, swept up in the fervor around us. Anika even joins in the fun, letting her phone idle beside her, and my mom only counts gnarled kernels twice before renewing her promise to stop looking for signs.

As we rip away husks, Eliot scoots in close beside me so our knees touch and he can sneak in a teasing tap-tap whenever he thinks I'm dawdling. He also notes that the corn silk reminds him of my hair when he first saw me last week. I give him a shove for it, and he falls onto his side, but he quickly rights himself, laughing in an un-restrained, gut-busting way that's been coloring the entire day, from the moment we fled from his mother, throughout breakfast, golf, and now peeling corn. It's as if he left the worst of his dark shadows behind when he left his parents' house for the last time. His joy is infectious, and I can't help but draw his face to mine for a quick kiss.

"Are you guys boyfriend/girlfriend now?" Anika asks with her usual bluntness.

Franny gives her a light, disapproving swat on the thigh but she looks our way as if she's as interested in the answer as her god-daughter is. My mom laser-focuses on her work as though she can't hear us, though she totally can and she could probably answer this question better than anyone, but she leaves the floor to us.

"We're . . ." I trail off, hoping Eliot will take it from here. When he gives me a little shrug as if to say *I'll follow your lead on this,* I finish with, "Complicated."

My mom pauses her shucking, only for a second, but it's an *intense* second.

Yet again, I consider asking her to reveal what she knows, but so far I'm enjoying the day's ban on prophesying, even if she needs repeated reminders to keep mum.

"Her last boyfriend was a total dick," Anika tells Eliot, earning her another swat from Franny, a swat that only makes Anika scoff. "What? You thought so, too."

"Who, me, what, hmm?" Franny blinks, all innocence, but her ruse is thin.

Recalling her habitual evasions about my ex, I lower my current cob to my lap.

"You didn't like Greg?" I ask.

"*You* liked Greg," she says. "That's what matters."

"Yeah, but I'm asking what *you* thought of him."

Franny stalls, taking in the faces around her. Anika challenges her with a look. Eliot and my mom slow their shucking, their attention snagged. I wait, holding still.

"Okay, fine!" Franny throws up her hands. "No. I didn't like Greg."

"Because of the cheating?" I ask.

"Yes! Right. That. The cheating. Totally."

Anika scoffs again and Franny shoots her a fierce *shut up* look.

"*And . . . ?*" I press.

She darts a look at Eliot and back at me. "You sure you want me to answer? Now?"

"The relationship's over. I feel no need to defend him. Besides, ever since the breakup, everyone's in the We Hate Greg club. Might as well join the crowd."

Franny glances at Eliot again. As I stare her down, willing her to speak, she grabs a fresh ear of corn and starts whisking off the husk at a punishing rate.

"Okay, yes, I hated the cheating," she says. "But less because he did it than because it went on for *so* long. You guys agreed to be monogamous, right?" She pauses while I nod, confirming her point. "So if he wanted to be with that other woman, he should've had the decency to break up with you. Instead, he lied to you for months. Because he knew he had a good thing going so he drew it out as long as possible."

"A good thing going?" I ask, no longer even pretending to pull at the husk.

"You did *everything* for that guy!" Franny flings an arm toward nothing in particular, now fully invested in her tirade. "And you demanded *nothing* in return. If he needed help with an errand or wanted company for an event or got bored on a weekend, he called you. You were always there for him. And yes, I know none of those are crazy demands. They're things most of us do for the people we care about. But when *you* called on *him*? He only came if it was convenient. If he didn't want to do something, he didn't do it, even if it would've made you *really* happy. He only cared what made *him* happy."

"That's not true," I say, though as I say it, I have to wonder . . .

"You were always telling me about the horror movies you guys watched," Franny continues. "Even though you *hate* horror movies. Yet he wouldn't dream of watching a rom-com with you. You helped him pick out all that stuff for his home renovation. You took his cat to the vet when he was busy. You did all the holiday shopping for gifts for *his* relatives. You watered his plants when he was away on business. You stocked his fridge with his favorite things to surprise him when he returned. You baked for him, like, constantly. You rearranged your work schedule to fit around his work schedule. He didn't even show up on time for your birthday party. We waited for hours before we brought out the cake. And his gift? Perfume. Who the hell thinks perfume is a good gift for someone who *never* wears perfume? It's like he didn't even *try* to know you. As far as I'm concerned, you're well rid of him, and every other guy who came before him."

Rather than argue again, I look at Eliot. He offers me a kind, half-mast smile, one that displays no judgment and only tips slightly into pity. Even that hint of pity makes my gut roil. It lends truth to what Franny's saying. Truth I don't know how to deal with right now, even if it only cements thoughts I've already been considering this week.

"And every other guy before Greg?" I ask Franny, my voice embarrassingly thin.

She reaches over the shucked cobs to give my knee an affectionate squeeze.

"You have a big heart," she says. "Making other people happy makes you happy, even when you're sacrificing things you want. It's beautiful and wonderful and it's one of the things we all love about you, but it's an easy trait for guys to exploit. So . . . well . . ." Her eyes drift to Eliot. "It's nice to think of you being with someone who will care about you as much as you care about him. That's all."

I don't look at Eliot this time, worried he's freaking out at the pressure bomb Franny just lobbed his way, like he's supposed to compensate for over a dozen assholes who came before him, and do it in two days. Also, my brain is still whirring, stuck on the question: am I really *that* pathetic??? *That* willing to let myself be exploited???

I'm still staring at the corn in my lap, searching for an answer that isn't a resounding, emphatic *YES!* when my mom gets to her feet and picks up the pair of buckets, holding one toward Anika and the other toward Franny.

"What do you say, girls?" she asks. "Shall we gather more supplies?"

Anika frowns at our current pile of un-shucked corn. "But we already have—"

"Let's do it!" Franny interjects, already jumping to her feet. She indicates Eliot and me with a look before grabbing both buckets, linking arms with Anika and my mom, and leading them toward the big red barn and the already shrinking Corn Mountain.

Eliot and I sit quietly for a moment, both ripping away husks. I don't think either of us knows where to start, but as the silence goes from uncomfortable to excruciating—

"They weren't that bad," I blurt out. "What Franny said. It's an exaggeration."

"Okay," Eliot says, slow and calm.

"I had a really great birthday with a guy I dated while I was in art school."

"I'm glad. You deserve that."

"And the guy after that loved rom-coms."

"That must've been nice."

"And all relationships involve compromise."

"Of course they do."

"And no one's perfect."

"Not even close."

"And I only did all of that holiday shopping because Greg had to work."

"Imogen—"

"And Franny shouldn't have implied—"

"Imogen." Eliot sets his hand on mine, halting my protestations and drawing my eyes to his. "I get it, okay? I know I've only been in town for a few days, but you're not a stranger to me. Honestly? Nothing Franny said was a huge surprise."

"Because I've always been a doormat?"

"Because you've always been there for your friends and your family, myself included. And because of little things you've mentioned about your past relationships." Eliot flips my palm upward and links his hand with mine. "Also, you told me, yourself, that you often focus on attending to everyone else's needs at the expense of your own. If that meant setting aside your art, chances were high it meant setting aside other things, too." His thumb sweeps across the back of my hand in slow arcs, the same way it swept across my back yesterday in front of the church. I love that this little caress already feels familiar, even though that thought also scares me, the way I already crave his touch. The way I crave so much more than his touch.

"I like being in a relationship," I say. "Not because I *can't* be alone but because I *don't enjoy* being alone. I like sex, kissing, snuggling, and having company while picking up takeout or watching TV. I like being part of someone else's life, knowing my choices affect my partner, being aware of his needs, and feeling that awareness reciprocated, even if it isn't reciprocated equally. Even, I guess, if it's barely reciprocated at all."

Eliot listens to my impassioned speech with all the patience in the world. When I go quiet, he gives my hand a squeeze, circling a knuckle with his thumb.

"You know there's another option, right?" he asks. "An option besides staying single forever or dating someone who expects you to sacrifice your needs for his?" He's looking at me with so much tenderness I can't help but grasp his meaning. Also, I'm not stupid. I know from my relationships with friends and family what sincere mutual care feels like. I've been searching for a romantic partner who can offer me that. It's harder to find than it should be. It's also right here in front of me. However . . .

"I don't expect you to change your plans," I say.

"I already told you. I don't make plans."

"You made plans to leave on Tuesday."

"Hmm," he says, and after a few seconds, he echoes the first *hmm* with another.

I'm still trying to parse the possible meaning of those *hmms* when a trio of kids rushes past us, swinging their empty buckets and shrieking with glee. I watch joy light up their faces, letting it lift my spirits as they carry on toward the barn. When their laughter fades from earshot, Eliot scoots around to face me directly, setting aside my neglected ear of corn so he can hold both of my hands, his knees wedged firmly against mine, a swirl of black ink peeking through a hole in his tattered jeans.

"If you're open to the idea," he says, "I could stay in town for a little while. See where this goes. I can research professional caretakers who might free up a few hours of your time. Help with the dogs while you slow down with the sweater you're knitting *way* too quickly." He sneaks me an almost-smile. "Unless you're trying to get rid of me so you can elope with the bartender and start a drunken cupcake business together."

I try to laugh but my throat's all lumpy and I only manage a garbled swallow.

"I'm not eloping with the bartender," I say.

"Then you wouldn't mind if I extended my visit? At least for a few more days?"

Like he even needs to ask. "Of course I wouldn't mind."

"Well, good." He draws all four of our linked hands against his neck, making a little shelf to rest his chin on while he regards me with his characteristic air of gravity. "I'd like a chance to at least *try* to be the sort of person you deserve in your life. Someone you can turn to the way you let me turn to you. Someone who *does* try to know you, who gives you pencils instead of perfume, who remembers—even if belatedly—that you hate bacon so I order it on the side, in case we end up sharing the only edible pancake again. Someone who takes turns picking out movies and who keeps reminding you how talented you are until the voice in your head that says your art isn't important shuts the fuck up. Someone who makes you laugh. Someone who shows up on time for your birthday party, even if I have to join by video call or fly here from the Arctic Circle."

I let out a breathy laugh, more by habit than because anything's funny.

"As long as you don't plan to run here shoeless the entire way," I say.

"I promise I'd travel with my shoes on." He leans closer, resting his forehead against mine. His beautiful eyes are so close I can see every speckle of amber, rust, and copper amid the darker umber tones, an intricate combination I'd love to paint one day. "I know this isn't easy. I won't pretend I have perfect solutions. Our lives are so different and I'm not sure what's best for either of us. It scares the shit out of me to even think about needing you in my life, especially when that need can get twisted into something ugly if we're not both careful. I'm also not sure how much stillness I can manage." The corners of his lips twitch upward, suggesting he's thinking about the conversation we had in my bedroom, when we were both wrestling with so much more than stillness, when we were about to change everything with a kiss.

"You're feeling restless?" I ask, gently, because I already know.

He concedes with a hitch of his shoulders, lowering our knotted hands to his lap.

"I've grown used to being alone with the earth and the sky. It's where I feel most myself. I can't change that overnight, and I'm not sure I can change it at all. Nor do I expect you to suddenly want a life away from the tight-knit community you love so much." He pauses there, and what would be silence fills with the din of laughter and conversation all around us. They're sounds that make me happy but that probably drive Eliot nuts. "Maybe I'm crazy, thinking about how we make this work past tomorrow. I know I can't offer you a life together where we plan nightly dinners and you can count on me coming home at five-thirty from the office every night. You deserve that life if it's what you want. And I know you can't offer me a life where we ramble around the world together without a plan. But I also know I'm not ready for our next goodbye. When it comes, *if* it comes, I don't want it to be forever. And I want to lay the groundwork to make sure we trust each other to stay connected. Can that be enough? For now?"

I draw in a breath, pressing a palm to my chest as though I can force the oxygen where it needs to go. It doesn't obey, and I end up stuttering through my inhale, hinting at the tears I'm barely keeping at bay. It's those last two words. *For now.* They're the same words my mom uttered when she told me about the grebes and herons.

*We'll let the matter rest. For now.*

The words are so small, so ordinary, but they tie a hundred knots of apprehension in my gut. Despite years of preparing myself for breakups, this is different. This time I can't hold back the parts of myself Eliot once noticed. I can't divest *just* enough to provide an emotional safety net for my inevitable fall. I can't put up walls. Every time I try, Eliot sends a wrecking ball through them. Sometimes with only a hint of a smile.

"You're thinking about your curse," he says, saving me the effort.

I sit upright, sweeping a hand over the field, which is abuzz with noise and activity, despite our little pocket of intimacy. We're surrounded by people with team shirts, gardening gloves, and proper shucking tools. Several groups have piles of shucked corn two or three times the size of ours, and not because they have more team members. A family of four with two tween kids is kicking our asses.

"You have to admit," I tell Eliot. "We have *no* chance of winning this thing."

He tips his chin toward a group of women in their sixties and seventies. They wear matching purple shirts as they pass around a pitcher of what looks like margaritas while amassing a pile of shucked corn that makes ours look like an anthill.

"You don't think we're beating the Mother Shuckers?" Eliot asks.

I squint at the shirts, laughing as I confirm the team's name.

"Shuck, no," I say.

This earns me a smile. It's sweet and kind and it helps me get ahold of myself.

"I remember when we were kids," Eliot says, apropos of nothing, though chances are high he's heading somewhere. "The first time I saw you play badminton at one of my parents' lawn parties. You were *so* determined. You were also *so* bad."

"Thanks a lot!" I give his shoulder a shove and we both laugh, though we only laugh a little, still weighed down by our conversation.

"I was so shy back then," he continues. "Afraid to talk to anyone, let alone join in the games. But there you were, seven years old, smacking that birdie around like your life depended on every point. Your tongue was tucked in the corner of your mouth. Your long braids were swinging in all directions. Your knees and elbows were dirty. You were coated in sweat. I thought you were the fiercest, most beautiful thing I'd ever seen. I was in total awe of you. I've felt that way ever since, and I can't imagine I'll ever stop."

"Eliot," I say, and then I stop there, because I have no idea what I was going to say next. Something about pancakes, golf, flipping coins, darts, trivia, swimming toward shore, drawing, singing, coloring, and all the other contests. But I don't need to say any of it. He already knows, and I can tell from the look on his face, his thoughts mirror mine.

"Maybe your mom can see what's coming," he says. "Maybe you never will be first at anything or to anyone. Maybe—as impossible as this sounds to me—I'll meet someone who will overshadow this feeling I've carried with me since the day I saw you fall flat on your face with a badminton racket flying from your hand and I knew I was in love with you. Maybe your curse is real. And also, maybe it doesn't matter if it's real."

I inch backward so I have a full view of Eliot's face. He doesn't look like he's kidding, though he seldom does, but he's been *so* determined to break this thing. He also knows how much my curse, or at least my belief in my curse, has impacted my life. How it has guided my choices for over twenty years, forming the central question I wrestle with on an almost daily basis. It kept me in relationships I assumed were the best I could do since no one would want to stay with me for very long anyway. It made me willfully blind to problems in those relationships as I clung to companionship wherever I could find it, no matter how brief or how shallow. The constant drone of *you're not quite good enough* has underscored my entire adult life, proven true time and again until I can't have a single conversation with Eliot without assuming our days together are numbered.

And now I'm supposed to be fine with that?

"How could it possibly not matter?" I ask.

He meets my eyes, unblinking, giving me a look that bores its way through my befuddlement as though he's reaching deep inside me to draw out the answer. Like that answer has been inside me for ages. All he's doing is helping it surface.

"Because I don't think your biggest problem is not coming first to someone else."

I stare at him, uncomprehending—or maybe unwilling to comprehend—but after a few seconds, his meaning fully registers. Once it does, it hits. It hits hard. I don't want it to. The point he's making sounds like something people would post on social media with sunset backgrounds and silhouetted women doing yoga poses. I've avoided that shit like the plague. If it can be cross-stitched or written in cursive, I don't want to read it. But under my revulsion for sappy, life-affirming phrases, I know Eliot's right. The only person I can truly come first to is myself. And I haven't tried in years.

"Wow," I say. And in a very Eliot Swiftian fashion, I repeat, "Wow."

"Is it okay that I said that?" he asks.

"You mean suggesting I reframe my entire outlook on life?"

"I mean telling you I'm in love with you."

My brain short circuits. "Wait. What?"

He doesn't repeat himself. He just smiles, barely, and waits.

I shake my head, attempting to clear my thoughts as I replay our conversation, digging for words I missed. By the third time I filter everything through my hazy brain, the words form more clearly. Something about badminton, dirty elbows, followed by a massive life lesson, yes, but also . . . also . . . oh my god. OHMYGOD!!

"Yes," I say while blinking. A lot. "I mean *yes! YES!* Of course it's all right. No. Wait. It's not all right. It's wonderful. It's *everything*. Fuck. I'm getting this *so* wrong. How can I get *this* wrong? And I'll never get a redo. But I love you, too. So much." I laugh, only because I can't seem to control anything right now. My words. My brain. My body. But somehow, I pull Eliot in for a kiss, even as I shake with laughter.

"What's so funny?" he asks.

"Nothing. That just felt *so* good to say. Can I say it again?"

He wraps me in his arms while shining the world's most glorious smile on me. Not a tip-and-twitch. Not a half-master. I might even go so far as to call it a grin.

"You can say it as many times as you want," he tells me.

I know I don't need his permission, but the words unlock something inside me anyway, filling me with elation that's so vast, so bright, so pure, even while I stumble to get the words out again, my heart soaring at the sight of his too-long hidden smile.

"I love you, Eliot Swift. I love you. I love you. I love you."

## HEARTBREAK #1

I was so wrapped up in my feelings about Eliot, I didn't go on my first date or have my first kiss until I was almost twenty, at the end of my sophomore year of art school. I was doing a month abroad in London with a dozen classmates, a bonus course tacked onto the end of the term where we went to museums and wrote papers and got drunk in pubs more nights than not. My roommate told me at the end of the first week that one of the guys in our group—the impossibly cute and popular Tyler Cunningham—was into me. I didn't believe her. No one had ever been "into" me. But a couple of nights later, while a few of us were hanging out in Trafalgar Square long after we had a good reason to be there, Tyler took my hand and led me in a dance that turned into an embrace that turned into a kiss.

It was a *good* kiss. I had no basis for comparison yet, but after several minutes—and several rowdy catcalls from our classmates—my knees were weak. My heart was pounding. My head was spinning. My skin was on fire. By the time he pulled away, all I could think was, *What in the hell have I been waiting for? Kissing a boy is AMAZING!*

We had sex the following week. To this day, I don't know if he knew it was my first time. I didn't want him to. I wanted to seem mature and experienced, or at least like I had *some* clue what I was doing. Turned out, I liked sex as much as I liked kissing. The more time I spent with Tyler, the more I liked him, too, and by the time our course ended, I was giddy about finally having a boyfriend. Spending the rest of our summer apart would suck, but we'd be together in the fall, and we could pick up where we left off.

Tyler, as I soon discovered, had other thoughts.

"Let's not try to make this what it was never meant to be," he said as we waited by the gate to his New York flight, which departed two hours before my Portland flight.

"What do you mean?" I asked.

He took my hand and set it in his lap, seated beside me in our linked-together chairs.

"We had fun, right?" he asked.

"Yeah. Of course. Obviously." I swallowed, bracing myself. "But?"

"But you didn't actually expect this to last past a few weeks, did you?" He laughed as though this was the most ridiculous suggestion ever. As though expecting anything at all was idiotic. "I have a date with this girl Liz on Friday. We've been on and off for years, but I think she's finally ready to be *on*, on." He grinned at me, snagging on something in my expression that made him drop my hand, despite my efforts to look unaffected by his announcement. "It was good, what we had. Don't make it weird."

I smiled, because what else could I do? Admit that I was, in fact, an idiot?

"I won't make it weird," I said. "And I hope things work out with you and Liz."

I sobbed through my entire flight home. The steward kept bringing me napkins. The man next to me moved seats. I texted Eliot shortly after I got to Pitt's Corner. If anyone could help me feel less alone, less convinced my heartbreak was entirely of my own making, less angry and confused about my egregious crime of having expectations, it was Eliot. He would always be there for me. Even if he was half a world away.

Imogen: When are you coming back to visit?
Eliot: When icicles form on Satan's testicles

Turned out, my first heartbreak wasn't actually Tyler. It was Eliot.

# Nineteen

## MONDAY

My alarm goes off, jarring me out of a deep sleep.

"Make it stop," Eliot grumbles against the back of my neck.

"I'm on it." I fumble for the snooze alarm until I halt the beeping.

Eliot snuggles in closer. He's the big spoon again, which seems to be his default position, while I'm curled on my side in front of him, my default position. I'm not sure it's wise for us to have default sleeping positions, but I'm going to enjoy it while I can.

I wrap my hands over his forearm where it rests against my chest, nestling into his embrace so I can drift off for nine more minutes of sleep.

"You shouldn't do that," Eliot says, his voice half-muted with sleep.

"Do what?" I ask.

He shifts ever-so-slightly against my backside. His movement isn't overtly sexual, but his meaning is clear. I obey his request, though I have to dredge up an impossible amount of willpower to prevent myself from pressing against him.

"We don't *have* to keep sleeping," I say. Just in case.

He responds with a low rumbled *mmmm* against my neck. God, I love his *mmms*. I don't know what they mean half the time but they always tip toward the affirmative, like accidental admissions that he's enjoying something. A lot.

Sensing his little wiggle was enough to wake us both up, I spin in his arms and watch as his eyes slowly blink toward opening, his body otherwise unmoving.

After a moment, he gives my nose a little nuzzle. "Good morning."

"Good morning," I return. "Sleep okay?"

"I ate too many cupcakes last night."

"Any favorites?"

He considers as his eyes drift shut again.

"The whiskey ones with the chocolate pudding centers, maybe?" he says. "Not sure we have a winner yet. We should try again tonight. Text me a grocery list later and I'll pick up whatever we need on my way back from the lawyer's."

I tuck my head against his neck so he doesn't see my smile and think I'm getting ahead of myself. I heard what he said yesterday about preferring only the earth and sky for company, but I could get used to this *so* easily. Waking up naked in bed with him, my body pleasantly aching from lots of sex the night before. Planning out our day, knowing we'll circle back to being together tonight without having to sort out precisely how we get there. Even knowing he'll run an errand for us while I'm at work. It's a small thing, but it indicates our lives are entwining, and we can carry a tiny bit of one another's load.

"Maybe we should let the cupcake contest go," I say.

"Let it go?" he asks as if appalled at the very idea. "Why would we do that?"

"Because you conceded that my curse might not be bullshit after all."

"I allowed for the possibility, sure, but I haven't given up trying to break it. If I had, I never would've gone square dancing. Also, I *really* don't want you waiting for me to introduce you to a mystery girlfriend I don't actually have." He plays with a cowlick that curls over my ear. The gentle rhythm of his calloused fingers brushing my skin is soothing and almost makes me glad I gave myself a panic haircut. Almost.

"We do both like cupcakes," I say. "And cocktails."

"You also offered to wear that cute little apron while your mom is at her friends' dinner party tonight." He tightens his embrace and sets his lips against my ear. "Only the apron." His voice rolls through me, low and soft and deep, warming my entire body.

"I forgot about that offer," I say. "What are *you* going to wear?"

"If you're serious about the apron? Anything you want me to."

I laugh at that, killing the sultry mood, but Eliot laughs, too, so it feels okay. I also like that he still wants to break my curse, because it still hangs over us, even while I consider how to start putting myself first after so many years of doing the opposite.

We completely bombed at corn shucking yesterday. The Mother Shuckers took home the golden ear for the third year in a row. We also bombed at amateur square dancing, though I can't recall when I've laughed so hard. Franny got the hot farmer to come with us, because of course she did. She chatted him up over lunch. His family recipe chili and cornbread were incredible. He's also an excellent dancer. The rest of us, not so much, but we all had fun and my mom made it through the entire day without telling strangers to get their brakes checked or wear a helmet.

"Mind if I run a load of laundry this morning?" Eliot asks through a lazy yawn. "If I'm going to stick around for a while, I'll need something clean to wear. Preferably something that isn't Antony's or my dad's."

This time I don't hide my smile. *If I'm going to stick around for a while*. What beautiful words. I might even like them better than *I love you*.

"Make yourself at home," I say.

He returns my smile, but a slight hitch in his breathing suggests his smile is forced. It doesn't take me long to realize why. One word. Two very different definitions.

As his smile fades, I trace the contours of a fish that swims across his collarbone. It's sleek, straight, and narrow, but the undulating fantail gives it a grand flourish.

"What you said yesterday," I begin, slowly, searching for words as I say them. "About how we make this work past today. Any further thoughts?"

He takes a deep breath as he rolls onto his back, tucking an arm behind his head.

"I don't know," he says to the ceiling. "I don't think I can live here permanently."

"But maybe some of the time? A few weeks now and then between trips?"

"Maybe," he says, and again after a breath and a twitch of his brow, "Maybe."

I wrap myself around him—a leg over his hips, an arm over his chest—as I peer through the dim morning light toward an expanse of robin's-egg blue.

"Too many walls?" I ask.

He chuckles slightly, jiggling the arm I draped over his chest.

"I could put up a tent in your backyard," he says.

"We'd have to kill the floodlight on the apartment building."

"Should I get you a golf club and you can have at it?"

"Ha-ha." I smile against his shoulder, happy to take a little ribbing for my appalling attempt to golf yesterday. I like when we refer back to something we shared, and when we talk about something we might share in the future. Though that thought brings me full circle to my initial question. "Without the sarcasm, please?"

"Got it. Real answer. Hmm." He nods, thinking, his gaze still trained upward. "Honestly? Now that my dad's gone and my mom will have no reason to come back here once the house is sold—so I wouldn't be here for them, or for a barrage of expectations I'll never fulfill—I think I could handle a few weeks." He rolls his head toward me. "What about you? Could you handle a few weeks on the road once in a while?"

"Wouldn't that change your brand? *The Sometimes Accompanied Wanderer?*"

"*The Sometimes Accompanied Wanderer,*" he repeats, testing the words on his tongue. "I like the sound of that." He shines a sweet smile on me as he grazes the back of a loosely curled hand down my cheek, over my shoulder and ribs, inching back up to take in the curve of my breast. I love the way he touches me, ever the explorer, even in his early morning drowsiness. "Could you get away? Would your mom be okay?"

"I don't know." I trace the fish again, sweeping along its rigid back and over the showy S-curves of its tail. Stillness and movement captured in one image. How very on point. "Aside from her fall the other day, she's been pretty easy lately. No unannounced sojourns to wildlife preserves. No nights spent on rooftops. No climbing trees to examine wasp's nests or count spots on birds' eggs. I don't think Antony or Lavinia could afford more than a week at a time off work, but if we found someone else who'd stay with her, and who wouldn't take the task lightly, it's possible. For a short trip, at least."

He sweeps the side of my breast again, spiraling inward until he's circling my nipple with a single featherlight fingertip. His touch is lazy and barely even there, but my body comes alive, my skin tingling, my heart rate already picking up speed.

"It's a start," he says, and I have no idea if he's referring to a plan to ensure our lives keep intersecting or if he's referring to my body's response to his touch. Probably the life plan, but as he rolls my nipple between his thumb and forefinger, watching it react to the increased friction, I allow for both possibilities.

My thoughts already straying, I run a hand down Eliot's stomach, gliding from smooth skin into a soft, tight tangle of hair. That's as far as I make it before he halts my progress. Next thing I know, he's pinning my wrist to my side as he rolls me onto my back and hovers over me, overpowering me in one swift movement.

"I thought we agreed," he says, suddenly alert. "It's time to put you first."

"But I can't—" My voice cuts off because he's already traveling down my body, trailing his lips and tongue between my breasts while he shackles my hands to the bed.

"I'm not suggesting you have to finish first," he says, now at the base of my ribs and sliding to my stomach. "But we're damned well going to make sure you start first."

This time I don't argue. I know what those lips and that tongue can do. So I lie back and close my eyes, sparking with anticipation until he releases my wrists to spread my legs with his hands and part me with his tongue. A slow sweep. A quick flicker. A moment of intense pressure at the perfect spot. I arch my back and gasp.

"Mmm," he says, and then, in his Eliot Swiftian way, he repeats, "Mmmmmmm."

And I have a whole new reason for loving his mumbled *mmms*.

Five hours later, after the flowers and the dogs, I'm edging my way between two-tops at Ed's with a tray full of lunch dishes. Amid the din of the lunch rush, I set down plates for the Front Porch Gossip Gang, a group of four spry octogenarians currently relocated from Lyle Lee's front porch to a booth by the windows. They order the same things every Monday. Two soup and sandwich combos, one plate of mac 'n' cheese, and for Lyle, a double order of mashed potatoes with a jar of strawberry jam and an entire tureen of gravy. I don't know where he puts it. He must weigh a hundred pounds, tops.

"So, you and Harris Swift's boy?" He waggles his shaggy gray brows at me.

I make a noncommittal noise while wedging his gravy boat among the plates.

"He sure is handsome," says Octavia Jenkins, the woman on his right.

Dorothy Iverson nods her avid agreement from across the table. She's tall where Octavia is short. Round where the other woman's slim. Her hair is a natural gray and she dresses in soft, earthy neutrals, where Octavia changes her hair color every few months, she adores bold floral prints, and she never leaves the house without ten pounds of bling. The two women look like polar opposites, and they've been vying for Lyle's heart since his wife died over twenty years ago. So far, neither woman appears to hold a clear lead.

"Is it official?" Dorothy presses, not letting me off the hook.

I set a ketchup bottle by her plate, noting four sets of eyes watching me a little too closely. The fourth set belongs to Carl Underwood, a quiet, understated man who's already digging into his minestrone while listening keenly to every word.

"We haven't signed any documents," I say to Dorothy. "If that's what you mean."

Octavia waves off my sarcasm with a light, raspy laugh.

"You *know* what we mean," she says. "Are you dating? Sexting? Sending peach and eggplant emojis? Netflix-and-chilling? Sliding into each other's DMs?"

I'm about to ask how much time she's spending on Urban Dictionary, but before I get the words out, Lyle leans toward me and asks, "Did you kiss him?"

"Um . . ." I stall for time by doling out napkins, trying to decide if there's any point in lying when the truth is bound to emerge anyway. "Yes?"

"I knew it!" Lyle pounds a triumphant fist on the table, after which, a flurry of activity ensues while his friends all locate cash and pass it his way.

*Spectacular.* Great to know the entire town is not only speculating on my love life, now they're placing monetary bets. Maybe Eliot's nonstop travel agenda is worth deeper consideration. I wasn't wild about L.A., but a *little* anonymity wouldn't be so bad.

I manage a polite smile and head toward the kitchen before anyone asks if we've "gone all the way" yet. I could lie, but my cheeks would give me away. They always do.

As I cross the room, my gaze snags on the plastic flower bouquet Ed stapled to the unpainted lattice behind the register. It's been a kind of trademark here, a bold statement about how little Ed cares about the fine art of interior decorating, but as I glance around the room with its otherwise bare walls, I have to wonder . . .

"Ed?" I ask as I reach the prep area and load up my tray with burgers and Cokes, sliding plates off the counter that separates the kitchen from the rest of the diner. "Any chance you're open to reconsidering the dust-coated lilacs behind the register?"

He shoots me a scowl while flipping a grilled cheese. "Is your mom reading my lilacs the way she did my tulips last spring?" He turns away, revealing a few fading burn marks on the side of his face and neck, products of a small grease fire my mom predicted when Ed's tulips poked through the ground a week earlier than anticipated. He didn't believe her, but he didn't *not* believe her, either, readying the necessary safety gear and saving him from what could've been much worse scars. And no more diner.

"No predictions," I tell him. "I just thought it might be time for a décor update."

"Those things are plastic," he barks. "They won't wilt."

Franny sidles in next to me, bumping hips in the narrow space that barely fits two.

"You want to do a live arrangement?" she asks.

"More like"—*oh, god, here we go*—"put up some drawings."

Ed continues scowling from his spot by the grill, but Franny shrieks in my ear.

"Aaaaaahhh! Yes! And not just behind the register, right? Like, that whole wall over there." She flaps a hand at the wall to our right, unadorned aside from some crappy sconces and a thirty-year-old NO SMOKING sign. "There's also the hall to the restrooms. We can even sell the drawings like posh coffee shops do. Make postcard prints. Stickers. Magnets. You could illustrate the menus."

"We're not turning my goddamned diner into a goddamned art store," Ed says, though a twinkle in his pale blue eyes suggests he'd be happy to do just that.

"I don't plan to sell anything," I tell him. "I just need a motivation to draw. A framework to work within. And a reason to put art somewhere besides my closet."

Ed harrumphs, which I take as permission to proceed. After six years of working here, I'm fluent in Ed's harrumphs. Also, that twinkle in his eyes speaks volumes.

"I love this *so* much," Franny gushes. "I *knew* you and Swiftie would be good for each other. Yesterday? I've never seen him smile like that. He was grinning like an idiot every time I looked at him. I don't know what you did to that boy but the black cloud is finally gone. And now you're talking about art again? This is totally his influence, right?"

I shrug, wishing I could say I got here on my own. But I didn't.

"He sees me in a way I want to see myself," I say. "Like I've been looking in a dirty or distorted mirror for a really long time, shrinking further and further away from my reflection. Then he held up a clear mirror and said, 'Actually, *this* is you. Take a look. Because you are worth looking at.' That's a pretty amazing gift to give someone."

Franny goes all moony and presses a fist to her heart, or she tries to, aborting when she realizes her fist is wrapped around the handle of a full pot of coffee.

"You're going to make me cry," she says.

"Really? I never pictured you as the sentimental type."

She waves away her wistful expression with a flap of her free hand.

"You're right," she says. "I'm just happy you're happy."

Ed clears his throat. I turn around to find him holding out the plated grilled cheese sandwich, frowning as though our momentary joy bubble is deeply impeding our work. It's not, and we all know it, but I grab the plate and finish loading my tray.

"What about you?" I ask Franny. "You looked pretty happy yesterday, too."

She bites down a grin before Ed can see it but her eyes are pure euphoria.

"If I'd known I'd find a guy like that hanging out on a farm," she says, "I would've ditched the dating apps years ago and joined the 4-H club, or whatever the adult version is. 8-H?" She laughs as she stuffs creamers and sugar packets into her apron pocket. "Anika even likes him. Not that she'd admit it, but she was curious enough to google him on our way home last night. Apparently, he won an Oregon small business leaders' award and he donates a significant percentage of his profits to one of her favorite environmental charities. She was very impressed. Or at least, she was until she found a link for a charity calendar he posed for last year. He was Mr. November, and while she found the photo 'so embarrassing,' we agreed that his ear of corn was *very* well placed."

A laugh sputters out of me as I shake my head at her. Leave it to Franny to find a hot nude model at a family agricultural gathering. The girl has a gift.

I deliver the burgers and sandwich to a table on the far side of the room, scanning the walls again as I consider what to put up. I could do seaside landscapes or downtown street scenes. I could draw from some of Eliot's travel pics. I could start with a collection of cute cartoon cows. Anything goes, probably. I just need the right inspiration.

On my way back to the prep area, I see someone enter the diner through the corner of my eye. My tray is full of dirty dishes so I don't pause to mention that the tables are all full or point out the miniscule waiting area by the register. It's all pretty obvious.

"Want a menu while you wait?" I call over my shoulder.

"Actually, no," says a familiar voice that stops me short.

I spin around to see Greg standing inside the doorway. He's alone, thank god. He's wearing a suit and tie, so he's probably on a work break. He carries a shopping bag and his stress-ball key chain in one hand, while the other latches the door behind him. His sandy-blond hair is disheveled, probably from the October wind, but disheveled hair suits him, a mild and humanizing disruption to an otherwise carefully assembled appearance. He looks good, but not *too* good. A bit jittery. A little strained around the eyes.

I'm pleased to note that aside from my surprise at seeing him, I'm more annoyed than anything. The affection I once had for him has faded fast, maybe because I tempered it from the outset, bracing for my curse to kick in. Maybe because he didn't treat me well enough to earn it. Probably both, and, of course, because I'm insanely happy with Eliot.

"Wait there," I tell Greg. Then I drop off the dishes and tell Ed and Franny I'll be back in five. And if I'm *not* back in five, she has full permission to come get me.

I slide out the door with Greg and we tuck ourselves against the front of the building. It's brisk outside and I'm not wearing a jacket, so I wrap my arms around my body, though admittedly, my posture might have little to do with the chill in the air.

"What's up?" I ask, which I consider a pretty fair compromise between *Nice to see you* and *Why in the hell are you here?*

"You look good. Your hair. I like it." His hand rises toward my face. I pat down my hair without reply, irritated that he has an opportunity to have any opinions about me at all. He retracts his hand to adjust his tie. "I, um, heard you're seeing someone new."

*Goddammit. This town. Of course he heard.*

"Maybe," I say.

"He used to live here?"

"Yep."

"That big old place out on Harrow Drive?"

"That's the one."

"Now he works for YouTube?"

"Something like that."

"But he's—?"

"What do you want, Greg?" I interject before this goes on all day. He sighs as though my terseness disappoints him.

I try not to care.

"I know we agreed to give each other space," he tells me. "But Alison was over the other night and she asked if I could get rid of your things. I didn't want to throw them out, in case you wanted any of it. So . . . well . . . here." He hands me the shopping bag.

I soften as I take it, knowing now that he didn't come here to probe into my life without him. A quick glance tells me he's mostly returning stuff I didn't need back. A toothbrush. A sweater. A paperback I was only halfway through. The shampoo and conditioner I left at his place because he used the never-effective two-in-one stuff.

"I think that's all of it," he says. "But if you remember something I forgot, you know how to reach me. I don't think I left anything at your place."

"You didn't," I say without having to think about it.

He nods, slowly, as though he's letting the implications of this disparity sink in, though maybe that's wishful thinking on my part. He never noticed the imbalances in our relationship while we were together. Why would he notice now?

I point over my shoulder at the door. "I should get back to work."

"Of course. Yeah. Sorry to interrupt." He steps away, squeezing his key chain.

For a moment, we regard each other without speaking. His eyes fill with either guilt or regret, I'm not sure which. Either way, the compulsion to comfort him rises up inside me, strong and fast.

*Wow.* This will not be an easy instinct to change. But I stand tall without telling him everything between us is fine or that I forgive him or that we're better off without each other and I wish him and Alison well, even if it's all true. Making him happy isn't my job anymore. Maybe it never really was my job. So, I thank him for dropping off my belongings. Then we say goodbye and part ways.

Franny watches me cross the diner toward her once I step back inside. The look on her face tells me she knows Greg's visit has shaken me, though maybe not in the way she thinks. Lyle and his friends are also watching me. Cue the gossip circuit.

"You okay?" Franny asks as I join her in the prep area.

"I don't know." I glance into the bag again. A year-long relationship reduced to meaningless junk. A reminder that happiness can be fleeting. Relationships go downhill. Affection and attraction are seldom carved in stone. "What if I'm fooling myself?"

Franny grabs my arm, spinning me toward her and forcing me to meet her eyes.

"*Please* tell me you don't want to get back together with that guy."

"What? No! Hell no." I gust out a nervous laugh but it fades quickly. "I'm talking about Eliot. Should I be letting myself get this attached to him? If I know it can't last?"

"Oh, Mogi." Franny pulls me into a hug. It's the best thing, ever. "Curse or no curse, Eliot would *never* do what Greg did. He's way less self-involved and way more self-aware. Don't you see the way he looks at you? The way his eyes trail you around a room or the way he lights up every time you're close by? He's crazy about you."

"Maybe so. But you understand why I'm worried."

She drops her embrace but keeps her hands on my arms, watching me with eyes full of concern. It helps, knowing she believes so I don't have to argue the point.

"I do understand," she says. "And, okay, maybe he'll *eventually* meet someone else, but I think that's a *long* way off, and you should enjoy what you have together while you can." She smiles reassuringly, but the effort shows. I suspect she's thinking about her sister and brother-in-law, which makes me think of my mom and dad.

Even if I wasn't cursed, no future together is guaranteed.

"You're right," I say. And then, maybe because I've been spending so much time with Eliot, or maybe because I haven't yet convinced myself, I repeat, "You're right."

# Twenty

I get home shortly before 5 p.m., having stayed late at the diner to make a decorating plan with Ed and Franny, who stuck around for moral support. Despite a *lot* of highly comedic grumbling, Ed not only agreed to let me put up anything—well, anything but naked people—he's also letting me paint a feature wall, bringing a splash of color into the space. I'm already picturing a deep teal blue, the color the ocean turns on a stormy day. Blue is a color that lives in my soul, an effect, no doubt, of growing up by the sea.

The living room is empty and the house is quiet when I walk in the front door, shaking off a chill from a strong coastal wind.

"Mom?" I call. "Eliot? Anyone here?"

No one answers.

I peek into the kitchen, expecting to see cupcake ingredients stacked on the counter. Nothing's there. Just the usual assortment of bins and bread boxes, all in need of replacement. Eliot replied with a thumbs-up emoji when I texted him a grocery list earlier today, but I haven't heard from him since. His appointment at the lawyer's was at 10 a.m. and Portland's only ninety minutes away by car. I assumed he'd be back by now.

I send him a quick text to let him know I'm home from work and thinking about him and I hope he's okay. God knows spending the day with his mother can't be fun.

And speaking of mothers . . .

I search the rest of the house but don't see my mom anywhere. She has a dinner party at 6 p.m. but it's only two blocks away. I doubt she'd leave this early. When I don't find her in the yard or on the beach just past the ugly pea-green apartment building, I open the tracker. It shows that she is on the beach, but about a mile north, near a little wooded area that's full of birds' nests. The sun won't set for another hour, and she's probably fine, but she's so easily distracted these days, anything's possible. I should go collect her before I have to call the fire department to pull her out of another tree.

After sending Eliot another text to let him know where I am, I bundle up and trudge along the rocky beach, checking my mom's location every few minutes to see if she's moving. So far, the little red dot remains stationary. She's probably beachcombing, gathering busted crab shells or shed seagull feathers she can examine for signs. I pick up my pace regardless, my feet skidding on rocks, sand, broken shells, and damp seaweed.

Twenty minutes later, I spot her, but she's not on the beach. Her little white sneakers are perched on a beached log, with her phone and socks tucked inside. She's straddling a piece of driftwood, paddling away from shore with a branch that doesn't seem to be doing much good. She's also belting out a sea shanty, indicating she's in good spirits, but this is *so* not what I want to be dealing with right now. I know she's not trying to prove a point or lock me in Pitt's Corner for the rest of my life, but things like this always happen the second I think about sharing my responsibilities.

"Mom!" I call from the edge of the shore. "What in the hell are you doing?"

She cranes around and waves at me. She's about seventy or eighty yards away, her hair and clothes buffeted about by the wind, her legs thigh-deep in the ocean.

"Do you see it?" she calls back. Then she points at something floating about ten yards ahead of her. Driftwood, maybe. An old fishing buoy. A dead duck. I can't tell.

"Come back!" I yell, both hands cupped around my mouth. "It doesn't matter what it is. Turn around before the tide pulls you out."

She says something else but her voice is carried off by the wind as she turns away from me to continue paddling. Her dismissal irritates the shit out of me. The waves aren't storm-level, but they're not nothing. Most are high enough to crest near the depth where she's paddling. One good swell and she'll be knocked off that log. She can swim, but after her fall, she's not fit for any intense physical activity. She's also wearing a lot of clothes, as always. If the undertow is strong, those clothes could pull her under.

"Mom!" I call again. "If you don't turn around, I'm coming to get you!"

She doesn't turn around, though whether that's because she doesn't hear me or because she doesn't *want* to hear me, I can't tell. Either way, a moment later, a wave hits her log. She wobbles badly. She rights herself before falling, but she loses her makeshift oar. It floats away from her while she reaches toward it with an agonized cry.

I mutter a few choice curses under my breath. I love her spirit of adventure. I despise her total lack of forethought, a feeling that only intensifies as she leans forward and uses her hands as paddles, still determined to reach her target, now without anything to help control her movement and direction.

*Goddammit.* Can she *please* let the floaty thing go and paddle this way instead?

When another wave leaves her scrambling to remain upright, I fire off a text to Franny, letting her know where I am and what's going on. I ask her to get here ASAP with towels and blankets. Also, help if she can find it. If she's busy, she knows to recruit Eugene and Kym or anyone else on the call list. It's a long list, and everyone knows the drill, even if I haven't had to rely on help like this in months.

The message sent, I strip down to my ever-impractical, barely-there underwear—this time a strappy peacock-blue set I put on for Eliot's benefit, back when I thought I'd be ending the day with sex and cupcakes, not with a frigid swim in the ocean.

I brace myself for the cold and walk into the waves. The water's freezing, as expected, but I don't give myself time to react. I plunge forward, head down, swimming toward my mom. It's a hard job. My body's stiff from the cold, and the waves keep pushing me back toward shore. I pop up every few minutes to ensure my mom is still in sight. So far, so good, but when I've closed about half the distance, the wave I was dreading knocks her into the water. She grabs hold of her log but she can't pull herself onto it, weighed down by more sweaters and skirts than anyone needs to wear, ever.

I paddle on but the cold gets to me, despite the adrenaline coursing through my veins. I'm also swallowing too much water, splashed by the waves every time I pause to get my bearings. But on I go, chanting to myself *Hold on, Mom. Hold the fuck on.*

Eventually I reach her. She's clinging to the log like what's-her-name at the end of *Titanic* with only her head, shoulders, and arms out of the water. At least she didn't have to fight anyone for log space. Her teeth are chattering and her skin is blanched. I swing myself onto the log and haul her up so she's draped over it on her stomach.

"What are you thinking?!" I shout, my skin already coated in goose bumps as the wind whips past. "You know this is dangerous!"

"It's important," she pushes through her chattering teeth.

"Not as important as your life."

"But I need to know."

"*Need?* Really? You sure about that?"

"It could mean a twist of fate."

"Whose fate?"

"Whose do you think?" She blinks at me through wet lashes.

I can't help it. I hesitate, glancing toward the floating object. It's not a piece of driftwood or a dead duck. It looks like a chunk of heavy hemp net wrapped around a group of blue and green glass floaters, the kind plastic made obsolete. My dad used to collect them and I've always found them magical. I can see why my mom suspects they hold deep meaning, but as desperate as I am for evidence that a life with Eliot might not be as "complicated" as she once predicted, or that my curse might be breakable after all, we can't stay out here. It's way too dangerous. Fate can deal whatever hand she likes.

"Leave it," I say. "We're heading in."

"But if any of them are cracked—"

"Then they're cracked."

"I just want you to be happy."

"I'll be happy when we're back on shore." I shut her down with a look.

She gazes at the mass of floaters as though it's a lover she's about to part ways with forever. I appreciate her sincere concern about my future happiness but I don't have it in me to focus on the positive right now. Nor do I have the strength to drag my mom to shore without something keeping her afloat, not among choppy waves and shifting currents. So, I slip into the water, telling my mom to hold on tight while I position myself at one end of the log, spin the other end toward shore, and kick like my life depends on it.

I'm not an elegant swimmer, and progress is slow, pushing a heavy log in a direction it doesn't want to go, but what I lack in grace I make up for in determination, the same determination Eliot saw in me before I let my curse—and my relationships—wear me down. Thank god I can still call on that determination when I really need it.

After about fifteen minutes of mostly futile kicking, I see three people run onto the beach. I can make out Franny's wild red curls and Anika's shock of magenta hair, but the salt and wind are stinging my eyes so I can't tell who they're with.

I take a moment to catch my breath. Just enough to ease out my cramping toes now that help has arrived.

"How're you holding up?" I ask my mom.

"C-c-cold. I c-can't feel my feet." She adjusts her grip, her hands clawlike and her knuckles white. She's hugging the log with her face pressed to the top while her elbows, knees, and toes drag through the water, along with the hems of her skirts.

I'm tempted to ask her to kick or paddle alongside me, but I don't think she can manage it. So, I set to it again, my entire body aching. The shore barely seems to get closer. I'm starting to worry that I'll have to haul my mom off the log after all when I notice someone swimming toward us with smooth, strong strokes. I stop kicking and await help from someone who's clearly a much more capable swimmer than I am.

Our rescuer is nearly upon us before I realize who it is.

"Dutch?" I ask as he swims up beside me and grabs the log. "How?"

"Olympic hopeful about ten years back."

"How did I not know that?"

"I'll tell you stories one night over drinks." He winks, or maybe he just blinks, and his ease with the situation knocks my stress level down a billion notches. As I take my first full breath in several minutes, he pats the log. "If you want to ride, I've got this."

I shake my head. "We'll both kick. Let's get her home."

He nods, taking my position at the back of the log while I wrap an arm over the front. Together we propel my mom toward shore at several times the rate I was going on my own. I don't know how Franny thought to call Dutch, or how she got him here so fast, or if she knew he was a powerhouse swimmer, but I'd be sobbing with gratitude if I wasn't using every ounce of energy to kick and stroke, stroke and kick.

When we reach shallower waters, Dutch drags my mom off the log and carries her to shore. Amid a flutter of anxious activity, I find my way to a blanket Franny's holding out for me while Anika hands off towels to Dutch and my mom. She gives me one, too, and within a matter of minutes, we've collected our clothes and we're packing into the cab of Franny's truck, which is parked nearby on the side of the road. My mom and I are in the middle, swaddled in blankets and towels. Franny's at the wheel, cranking the heat. Anika's rubbing my mom's arms, trying to kick her circulation into gear. There's no room for Dutch. He stands beside the open passenger door of the truck, with a towel around his shoulders, holding his wadded-up clothes, wearing only his underwear.

I allow myself precisely two seconds to let the image sink in. Flawless skin. Broad chest. Superhero abs and thighs. Wet white boxer briefs that leave nothing to the imagination. Then I snap back to far more urgent matters as I scooch toward Franny.

"We'll make room," I say.

He shakes his head and points over his shoulder at a cute little yellow bungalow.

"My place is right there," he says. "Go get warm and dry. I'll check in later."

I nod, shivering despite the heat blasting from the vents in the dashboard.

He taps the roof of Franny's truck, twice, like a signal for us to drive on. My brain is still addled from cold and panic but as Anika grabs the door handle, I find my voice.

"Dutch?" I say, and he leans low to meet my eyes. "Thank you."

As though he's taking an order at the bar, he shines his megawatt grin on me.

"You got it."

An hour later, the four of us are drinking hot cocoa in my living room. Franny, Anika, and I are wedged together on the ugly mustard-colored sofa. My mom's in her usual recliner, snuggled tight in an afghan, no longer up for attending her friend's dinner party and pouting because I didn't let her finish her quest. I promised her we'd borrow a rowboat tomorrow and see what we could find, but we both know the chances the floaters will still be there are slim to none. My fate is sealed, whatever it may be.

Anika has control of the remote, and she stops on a sci-fi show, answering my mom's questions about unfamiliar vocabulary and devices. Oddly enough, for a woman who lives a life rife with paranormal activity, sci-fi isn't her jam, but Anika is super into it, and she and my mom soon get going on a conversation about black holes and the time-space continuum, so I catch Franny's eye and nod toward the back door.

We head out to the backyard and park ourselves in a pair of lawn chairs. Like everything else my mom owns, the chairs are old. The crisscrossing canvas straps are frayed and they always leave check marks in my ass and thighs, but tonight they feel as cozy as anything, a reminder that even a butt imprint can feel like home after a long, hard day. A dozen wind chimes made of sea glass and sand dollars tinkle and clink behind us as wind rustles the grass below our feet. It's overdue for a mow, but I like the sound. For a quiet moment, I let myself imagine the apartment building at the other end of the yard doesn't exist, and we have an expansive view of the sea and the sky.

"Thank you for coming so quickly today," I tell Franny. "I'm not sure I would've made it all the way back to shore on my own. Or home after if she couldn't walk."

Franny reaches over and gives my arm a squeeze. "It takes a village."

"No kidding." I smile, grateful for the millionth time that I live somewhere people care, even if I get irritated at the lack of privacy. "How did you know to get Dutch?"

"Total stroke of luck." She takes a sip of her cocoa and licks melted marshmallow off her upper lip. "He was grabbing his mail when we pulled up. I told him you were fishing your mom out of the sea. He was the first one to reach the beach."

I nod over my steaming mug, my mind whirring with thoughts of handblown colored glass, a sweet yellow beachside house, a guy who was in the right place at the right time, and an unforgettable phrase blown away on the wind. *A twist of fate.*

"I'll have to find a good way to thank him," I say.

Franny shoots me a look, making me burst into awkward sputters of laughter.

"Not *that* way," I say. "I meant I'd offer to clean his house or something."

"He keeps that bar spotless. I think he can take care of his own house."

"Fine. I'll bake him a pie."

"Is that a euphemism?"

"That is definitely *not* a euphemism."

Franny takes another sip of her cocoa, or more accurately, her mug of melted marshmallows. Very little cocoa is in that mug. While she tips back her head to gaze up at the stars that are starting to appear, I check my phone again.

"Anything?" Franny asks.

"Not yet. His mom probably guilted him into having dinner with Portland's elite."

"Wouldn't he have let you know?"

"Maybe. Unless his phone died again."

Franny's eyes slide sideways to mine, full of skepticism.

"I know, I know," I say. "But he's used to being on his own. Things most of us take for granted about firing off texts all day aren't part of his thinking. I'm sure if I told him I expected to hear from him by a certain hour, he would've reached out by now."

Franny's dubious look lingers as she tucks a fluttering spiral curl behind her ear.

"I'm still going to give him shit about it," she says.

"Please don't. God knows what stunts his mom pulled today. I bet she showed up at the lawyer's with an itemized list detailing every possession's value, displaying more interest in porcelain figurines than she ever did in Eliot. And he'll already feel guilty for not being here when I needed help." I take another sip of cocoa. Slowly.

Franny's expression doesn't budge. "You going to tell him who *was* here?"

"No reason to hide it." I say this with conviction, but another glance at Franny makes that conviction die away. I turn my gaze on the ugly green apartment building while the wind plays with the mismatched chimes, centering us midway between the worst of Pitt's Corner, and its most magical. "It would be so easy, wouldn't it?"

Franny chokes out a laugh. "Dating a guy who lives nearby, holds down a steady job, likes Pitt's Corner for some inexplicable reason, and nails a three-second smolder as though he can get you off with a look? Yeah. I'd classify that as pretty easy."

I roll my eyes. "Well, when you put it *that* way . . ."

"What way would *you* put it?"

"I don't know." I frown, still haunted by the glass floaters and an unconfirmed sign that my life might be about to take a new direction. "You're right, of course. Dutch is here. He's a solid, good guy. He's reliable. He's easy to talk to. He makes me laugh. He isn't hard to read. I wouldn't have to wonder if he was wishing he was somewhere else or if I was holding him back from the life he really wanted. Even his house was pretty, like a little Lego house with little Lego flowers and smiling Lego people."

Franny laughs again. "You forget to mention he's insanely hot."

I groan as I throw my head back. "I tried *so* hard not to notice today."

"*He* didn't. Dude totally checked you out the second you hit the beach. Nice call on that underwear by the way. For a girl who spends her life in boyfriend jeans and rumpled thrift-store sweaters, you have excellent taste in lingerie."

I cringe at the thought of an urgent rescue turning into a hasty exchange of lusty glances.

"Am I crazy?" I ask Franny, my gaze still skyward.

"For which part? Staying with Greg instead of dating Dutch or for trying to work out a future with the Un-lonesome Wanderer instead of dating Dutch?"

"The second, obviously. Your opinions on Greg have already been noted."

She shoots me a half-hearted sneer before finishing off her marshmallows.

"Truth?" she says.

"Please." I scoot up in my chair, bracing for words I might not want to hear.

Franny sets her mug on the ground before tucking her knees against her chest and spinning toward me, watching me for a moment as though she's assessing how much truth I can handle right now, a kindness after yesterday's cornfield revelations.

"One." She holds up a finger. "I think if you wanted to date Dutch, you would've done it by now. He's given you plenty of openings. You haven't taken them."

"Fair." I nod in agreement, though I suspect I'll give this more consideration in days to come, as I reflect on why I stayed with Greg for so long, and how I got in the habit of giving the men in my life more agency than I gave myself. "Number two?"

Franny raises another finger. "I think you're scared and that fear is making you look for ways out, but you don't actually want a way out, just a way to be less scared."

"Wow. Well put. I'm really getting my money's worth. Is there a three?"

"Three." She raises another finger. "If anyone told me ten years ago that the great love of my life would be a stubborn, anxious girl who rattles off sci-fi factoids, panic texts me on the regular, leaves hair dye all over the bathroom counter every month, steals my favorite clothes and ruins them before I can get them back, despises my cooking, and periodically tells me she hates me? I would've told them they were crazy. But I'd do anything for that girl. We love who we love. Easy has nothing to do with it."

"God, you're good." I tear up a little as I choke out, "Is there a four?"

"Four." This time she doesn't hold up another finger. Instead, she reaches over and takes my hand, linking her fingers with mine and giving them a powerful squeeze. "I've known you and Eliot my entire life. While I somehow missed all the silent pining back in high school, now that I see your connection for what it is, I think either one of you would take a single day with the other rather than a lifetime with anyone else. So, my final vote? No, you're not crazy for pursuing a relationship with Eliot, even if that relationship is really, *really* hard. Because, frankly? Easy has never been your style."

I have to smile at that, thinking back on our school years, and the intense effort I put into every club I joined, every grade I scrambled for, every contest I entered or sport I played. All the years I spent striving for unattainable firsts, followed by the pursuit of a challenging career, the voluntary caretaking of a uniquely complex parent, and the management of way too many jobs to do any one of them as well as I'd like to.

"You know I love you, right?" I ask Franny.

"Of course you do. I am *very* lovable." She gives my hand another squeeze. "But so are you. We're in this for the long haul, you and me. Even if Swiftie rides off into the desert sunset by month's end and you shack up in the Lego house with Poseidon."

"I was thinking more Aquaman."

"Yes!" Franny bursts into a joyful laugh that shakes her curls. "*That's* who I was trying to think of. Oh my god. Did you see the pecs on that guy? I know you recently reunited with your soulmate and I am one hundred percent Team Eliot, but *come on*. I think your mom full-out swooned when he swept her off that log and carried her to shore like an imperiled damsel in a period drama. If you don't jump him, maybe she will!"

We share another laugh, knowing full well my mom might blush and stammer while being rescued by a handsome, almost-naked man, but she has no interest in dating, especially not a man half her age. She has other priorities, with her nature walks and her visions. Sometimes I also catch her rereading my dad's favorite Shakespeare plays, the tragic, messed-up ones that gave Antony, Lavinia, and me our names. Her relationship with my dad wasn't easy, either. He was intensely opinionated, he worked crazy hours, and he had a lot of dark, impenetrable moods, but she loved him so much. I don't think any prophecy in the world would make her think there was another man for her.

My phone *finally* buzzes.

Eliot: Sorry. Should've texted earlier. Rough day
Imogen: You OK?
Eliot: Been better. You find your mom?

I scroll up to realize my last text was just before I left the house in search of my mom. I assumed I'd fill him in on the rest when I saw him.

Imogen: Yeah. She's back home. Where are you?

The ellipses appear but he doesn't text back right away. Instead, after a moment, a photo comes through. The bow of a beautiful, well-polished wooden rowboat, a stretch of dark sea, and a single hanging lantern in the top corner of the shot.

"Oh, shit," I say as I register the location.

"Eliot?" Franny asks.

"I don't think today went the way he thought it would go." I knot a fist in my hair as dread coils in the bottom of my stomach. I could be wrong, but I can think of only one reason he'd be at his current location. "Can you stay with my mom for a while?"

# Twenty-one

By the time my feet hit the first worn planks of the floating dock, I can already make out Eliot's slumped form in the moored rowboat. He's facing the open sea, lit by the string of hanging lanterns that cast this area in a soft, warm glow that wobbles with each breeze, making every surface dance. His tattooed hands are linked behind his neck the way they were at the funeral, with his elbows propped on his thighs, his gaze cast downward, and his spine deeply rounded. It's a familiar sight, despite a few key differences. Eliot always used to come here when he needed to think. It was as close as he could get to being alone in nature while still at his parents' house, a goal he might be trying to achieve right now.

The boards creak beneath my steps, announcing my approach, but Eliot doesn't turn to face me. Nor does he look up as I stop beside the boat, watching it rock in the mostly gentle waves, with only an occasional light swell rolling through. The surrounding cove was constructed to calm stormy waters, reshaping the earth to control the ocean. One day, even if it's centuries in the future, I hope the ocean gets her way again.

"Thanks for coming," Eliot says without looking up.

"Of course." I nudge the nearest hitching post with the toe of my battered Converse. "I thought you might want company, but would you rather be alone?"

He lets out a humorless breath of laughter. "Question of the century."

"I can give you some time and come back later if you'd prefer?"

He takes a deep breath. Releases it. Then he scoots sideways on the bench, making room for me to step into the boat and join him. As I take a seat, he lowers his hands to his lap. I reach for the hand closest to me, knitting our fingers together, resting the little knot on my knee, and wrapping it with my other hand.

For several minutes, we sit side by side, rocked by the waves without saying a word. It's so peaceful here, with the waves lapping the shoreline behind us and the world fading into darkness beyond the lanterns' glow, but a tempest brews beside me, held tightly within a man who's accustomed to shouldering his burdens entirely on his own. I understand why, but I also remember how he looked when he showed up on my doorstep Saturday night. And what he said about his fear of needing support. He didn't say he didn't want it. He said he didn't *know how to* want it. And so . . .

"Your mom didn't get the house?" I ask, hoping it's a gentle lead-in.

Eliot shakes his head. Then he blows out a painfully slow breath as he finally raises his head, looking out toward an unseeable horizon.

"I felt *so* good when we left here yesterday. Like I could finally let go and move on. Never again would I have to question whether my desire to return had anything to do with my dad's bullshit about the life he thought I should live. If I came back, I came back for you, and for Franny, for the choices *I* wanted to make, not the ones someone else thought I should make. But the old man had one more card to play, and he played it."

I glance behind us toward the towering mansion with its corner turret, its green tile roofs, its grand bay windows, and the ornate widow's walk Franny loves so much.

"Only the house?" I ask.

Eliot shakes his head again. "The house, the furniture, the art on the walls, those stupid jeweled eggs. My mom gets a chunk of money and a share of his business, plus whatever personal goods she kept here. My uncles get the vintage convertibles my dad kept in the garage so he could show them off at house parties. He never even drove them. Just shined them up and displayed them, like everything else." His jaw clenches as though he's biting down on a hard nut that refuses to crack.

I allow him a quiet moment to collect himself as I consider the implications of his inheritance. I don't have much experience with stuff like this. My dad didn't make a will, though there was nothing to inherit. Just a shitty station wagon and a mortgage. Eliot's dad probably lined everything up years ago, always aware of what he owned and ensuring it wouldn't get into "the wrong hands."

When Eliot's jaw stops twitching, I ask, "Is your mom going to fight it?"

"There's nothing to fight. He planned out everything. Crossed every *t* and dotted every *i*, like always. He made sure the only way I could deny ownership was by beating him to the grave. The house is paid for in perpetuity through a trust. The taxes. The maintenance. A significant allowance for repairs or renovations. He even budgeted for a caretaker to see to the upkeep. I don't have to do a thing. But there's one kicker." He *finally* meets my gaze, his eyes haunted and hollow. "I'm not allowed to sell it."

"But if it's yours . . . ?"

"You should've read his letter, Imogen. That fucking asshole. *I know you think you don't need a home, but you can't wander forever.*

*You need a place where you can build a life and a family.*" He scrubs his face with his free hand, shaking his head as though he can shake off his thoughts. "He went on and on about what I don't know yet but I'll learn in time, as though any day now I'll realize I've been wasting my life, but gosh, I sure will be grateful I can come back here and walk in my father's footsteps, because he knew what was best for me when I couldn't possibly figure it out for myself."

A wave rocks the boat. Eliot and I release our handhold to brace ourselves. As the rocking eases, I wrap an arm around him and lean my head on his shoulder. I'm still not sure how much personal space he needs right now, but when he reaches across my lap and takes my other hand, I decide my embrace is welcome.

"I know I sound like the world's most privileged jerk," he says. "I inherited a fortune and I'm complaining about it. Cry me a river, right? But it isn't a house. It's a trap. A power play. A means of forcing me to admit my dad's way of life is the only way of life, one with an impressive house, a high-paying job, a country club membership, and a nuclear family I've never wanted and have surgically ensured I'll never have. The kind of family he only ever managed in name while he screwed every secretary and shipped me off to camp every summer so I wouldn't be 'underfoot.'" He shakes his head again, gazing into the darkness with his brows pinched together behind his glasses. "I can walk away tomorrow, like I did ten years ago, but this place will follow me now. I'm tied to it. I'm tied to him. To his way of living. And I can't do anything about it."

Another wave rolls through but I don't release my embrace. I hold on tight, willing Eliot to feel my love, to know he doesn't have to face any of this alone if he doesn't want to. I'm not sure what else to do. Or what to say. Saying "it's only a house" or "let a caretaker deal with it and forget you even own it" won't help. Eliot's a different man than he was this morning. His joy is gone, his laughter, his brief but beautiful lightness, and I can't bring any of it back with trite reassurances.

My thoughts turn to what Sophia said after the funeral. How Mr. Swift thought love was about giving people things he thought they should have. Maybe he didn't *mean* to make Eliot feel trapped, but I don't think that's what Eliot needs to hear right now. I think he has a right to be angry and we need to give space to that anger.

"Is your mom here now?" I ask.

Eliot shakes his head, still staring off toward the sea. "I texted you right after she left. We spent hours with the lawyer, digging for loopholes that didn't exist. It was past four when we got here. I told her to take whatever she wanted. I didn't care if it counted as 'personal goods.' I'm not about to limit that to clothes and a toothbrush. Also, I'm allowed to dispense of the furnishings as I see fit. Just not the house itself. My mom packed what she could fit into her car, set aside the rest to get later, and headed home."

I almost say *Sounds like we both had fun evenings with our moms*, but this isn't the time and place to bring up my own family drama. First things first.

"So we're alone?" I ask.

"Just you, me, and the ghosts of three generations of Swifts wondering what the hell I'm doing with my life if I'm not planning my first dinner party so I can show off my fabulous new home and possessions." He lets out a strangled laugh that fades into a sigh.

I stand and offer him my hand. "I have a better idea."

He takes my hand but remains seated. "Backyard tent?"

"More like another contest."

"You thought of a way to break your curse?"

"Maybe. Or maybe I'm trying to break yours."

Twenty minutes later, we're on the expansive back lawn where we used to play badminton and croquet. We set up four bases and a pitcher's mound using embroidered throw pillows. We couldn't find any baseball equipment in the garage so we removed a collector's bat from a glass display case in Mr. Swift's office. It's been signed by several famous ballplayers and is probably worth a fortune, but to Eliot and me, a bat is a bat. He's at home plate, practicing his swing. I'm at the pitcher's mound, readying my pitch. I played softball for three years back in grade school. Despite an unbroken losing streak, I have a decent arm. Eliot has never played, and I suspect he'll rack up strikes, but I'm prepared, with a basket full of gilded, jeweled eggs at my feet.

"Ready?" I ask as he settles his stance.

"My mother would kill me if she saw what we were doing."

"She didn't set them aside. They're yours to do with as you like."

"Then why do I still feel like I'm going to get in serious trouble?"

"Consider this step one in shedding that fear. And in using your inheritance in ways that make you feel good, even if they're not the ways your dad intended. *Especially* if they're not the ways your dad intended." I toss the egg from hand to hand, waiting for a cue to throw while quelling my own anxieties about this idea. I don't want to know how much a Fabergé egg costs, or how rare they are, and I'm secretly praying these aren't the real thing. Selling even a knock-off would at least buy me a new set of lawn chairs and a shower curtain with all of its grommets, but these eggs aren't mine to sell. Also, this feels important. So when Eliot readies the bat and gives me a nod, I go ahead and pitch.

He completely muffs the first two throws, but with a sharp *crack*, his bat makes contact with the third. The egg shatters. Bits of gilded enamel and tiny seed pearls go flying. It's both horrifying and exhilarating. We stare as the dust cloud fades and the final remnants of the egg settle between us, sparkling in the grass.

"Was this a bad idea?" I ask when Eliot remains frozen in place.

"I don't know." He blinks at the shards by his feet. "I got grounded for a month when I accidentally cracked one of these as a kid. Destroying it on purpose feels weird."

"Good weird or bad weird?"

He continues blinking for several seconds, his silence underscored only by the nearby sound of soft waves. Then he pushes his glasses up his nose and readies the bat.

"We should probably give it another shot," he says. "You know. To be sure."

"Your eggs. Your call." I dare him with a look, getting into the competitive spirit. "This time, if you hit one, don't forget to run."

He nods and steadies his footing. I wind up and throw. With another ear-piercing *crack*, the egg splits apart, though only into a few pieces this time. As those pieces arc through the air, Eliot drops the bat and rounds the bases. I urge him on, hooting and cheering until he slides into home plate feetfirst and lies panting on his back.

"You okay?" I call from the pitcher's mound.

"Yeah. Just . . . yeah." He covers his face with both hands, muffling what could be either sobs or laughter or a combination of the two.

I give him a moment to experience whatever it is he's experiencing. Guilt. Relief. Shock. Amusement. Horror. Then I jog over to join him, nudging him with a toe.

"Home run, Swift. You should be proud."

"I can't believe I did that." He slides his hands down his face, staring up at me. "Eighteen years spent tiptoeing around this house, afraid to leave behind so much as a fingerprint, and I just smashed the shit out of two precious pieces of art."

"Hell yeah, you did. Want to do it again? We have at least ten more."

He blinks up at me, considering, his face still awash with incredulity, but with another shake of his head, the tiniest hint of a smile starts to form.

"Actually," he says, "I think it's your turn."

For the next half hour, we alternate turns pitching and hitting. I'm by far the better ballplayer, and as the bucket of eggs turns into glittering detritus that speckles the lawn, I consider the possibility that I'll beat Eliot at this ridiculous game, and maybe we'll both break a curse tonight. However, as is always the way of these things, when I'm down to my last three turns, I drop the bat for no reason whatsoever. I also have an ill-timed sneezing fit, trip over the pillow/home base plate as I swing, pause to blink away a bug in my eye at the wrong moment, and get distracted by a skunk that scurries across the yard from out of nowhere, causing me to strike out all three times. Not that it matters, because I think Eliot was always meant to win this particular game, annihilating the final egg with a swing he propels with twenty-eight years of unaddressed resentments.

I wait at home plate as he jogs the final stretch and falls into my awaiting arms. We hold each other tight, bathed in moonlight, serenaded by the sea. Neither of us makes a move to release our embrace. Instead, what begins as a congratulatory hug turns into something much more desperate, and much more conflicted. We cling more tightly with every second that passes. My sweater twists into knots in Eliot's fists. His cheek crushes against mine as I press it there with a hand splayed wide on the back of his head.

While we clutch at each other, cheek-to-cheek and chest-to-chest, my memory fills with images of blue and green glass floaters, and a twist of fate I can neither verify nor deny, even though I knew, as soon as Eliot confirmed he'd inherited his parents' house, that he wouldn't be able to stay in Pitt's Corner. The same way I knew when I spotted my mom paddling out in the ocean that I wouldn't be able to leave.

*But you know he'll leave?* I asked her last week.

*Yes,* she said.

*And I'll stay.*

*Yes.*

Her prediction about Eliot has also come to pass. Thirteen birds in an early morning fog. A shift in the wind. *A change. A shuffling of expectations. A surprise. An unexpected loss. A severing. A transformation.* As is common with her predictions, I could interpret the words any number of ways, but I can't dismiss any of them. Nor can I dismiss the notion that what happens next will absolutely be *complicated.*

"I love you so much," I say against Eliot's shoulder.

He rests his chin on my head. "I love you, too. I always have."

"Because I was such a terrible badminton player?"

"Because I knew my life would be infinitely better with you in it. Sorry I let myself forget. Scratch that. Sorry I *made* myself forget. I won't do it again. I promise."

I draw back far enough to look at him, to see the conflict playing out in his beautiful brown eyes. He's trying to figure out how to tell me. But I already know.

"We didn't break my curse," I say.

"What about the cupcake contest?"

"I don't really want to enter once you're gone."

He goes dead still, his gaze locked on mine.

"Imogen," he says, but he stops there. If he was a different man, he'd soften the truth with a sweet lie. He'd tell me he's only *thinking about* leaving. He'll figure out a way to get excited about the house. He just needs a few days on his own and he'll be back. But he isn't a different man. If he was, I wouldn't love him this much.

"When you told me you could stay for a while, you made it clear you could only stay because you thought you were free of all this." I flap a hand toward the house. "You don't feel free here anymore, and until you find another way to feel that freedom, you'll only build more resentments, so . . . you need to keep moving."

His lips press together as a pair of deep creases appears between his brows. For what feels like an eternity but is probably less than a minute, I watch him chew on the inside of his cheek, flickering through a dozen expressions without speaking.

"I don't want to be this afraid of stillness," he says at last.

"I know."

"I don't want to hate walls, or noise, or plans, or routines, or the tight-skin claustrophobia I feel when I'm around too many people for too many days in a row."

"I know that, too."

"I don't want to be someone who only takes from you. I want to give back as much as you need. Or more. Lots more. I want to be able to offer you a life together."

"Maybe one day you can. Maybe today just isn't that day." I put on a brave face as I say this, but inside I feel completely shattered, as though I, too, have flown through the air until I met the swing of a bat, and my pieces will never come together again.

Eliot brushes my bangs off my forehead, though my cowlicks refuse to budge.

"I'm an absolute disaster right now," he says. "I can't dump that on you."

*Actually, you can,* I think, but then I recall our conversation yesterday, and my tendency to attend to everyone else's needs while ignoring my own. I hope one day soon I can stop doing that, but today isn't that day for me, either.

"Guess we both have some work to do," I say.

"I guess we do." He cradles my face in his hands, planting sweet, slow kisses on my cheeks, nose, and forehead. Then he pulls me into another tight embrace.

I bury my face against his shoulder as I battle a powerful instinct to beg him to stay, to let us work out our problems together instead of apart, but I'd be fighting an unwinnable battle. I still have my limitations. He still has his. I don't have any answers yet for when to keep pushing against those limitations and when to accept them for what they are and make the best of things, though maybe there is no answer. Maybe life is made of best guesses, a constant balancing act of hope and doubt. But I know that if I tried to keep Eliot here, he'd be miserable, and I'd be focused on trying to lessen his misery. I also know we both want to be together. But sometimes wanting something—even with your whole heart—isn't enough to make it the right thing to want.

As we loosen our embrace, Eliot looks around at the beautiful destruction strewn across his lawn. I suppose I should call it that now. Not *his parents'* lawn. *His* lawn.

"We should probably clean this up," he says.

"Let's leave it. I know a good housekeeper who can take care of it later."

He shakes his head at me. "Only if you let me triple your wages."

"Screw the wages. Look at this lawn." I bend down and pick up a faceted blue gemstone. "I bet a jeweler would pay serious money for even one of these."

Eliot curls his fingers over mine so the gem nestles inside both our hands.

"Then it's yours," he says. "Do anything you like with it."

A swell of gratitude rises in my chest, warm, but complicated.

"You sure?" I ask, knowing there isn't a chance in hell that I'd sell this gemstone. Not if it's the last souvenir I'll ever acquire from my time with Eliot.

*The last souvenir.* A thought that eviscerates me.

Eliot nods, squeezing my hand with his, looking as wretched as I feel.

"I am sure. The only thing I have any use for in this place is whatever's in that kitchen." He tips his chin toward the only illuminated window in the house, taking a play from my book by diverting our mutual agony toward a much lesser problem to solve. "I haven't eaten all day. Any chance you can join me for dinner?"

I take a deep breath.

I swallow the monster of a lump that has formed in my throat.

I pocket my precious souvenir, pushing it down deep where it'll be safe.

I replay Franny's words of wisdom. *Either one of you would take a single day with the other rather than a lifetime with anyone else.* We might only have a single day now. Maybe even less than a day. But that isn't nothing. It's actually quite something.

With that thought, I pull myself together and link my arm through Eliot's.

"Why, Mr. Swift, I'd be delighted to join you for dinner."

# Twenty-two

*E*liot doesn't want to spend a second longer than necessary inside the house, so once I confirm Franny's okay to stay overnight at my place, we raid the Swifts' kitchen and make ourselves a picnic dinner with fancy cheese and fancy crackers and a variety of ridiculously flavored relishes, along with a bottle of wine. We carry everything out to the rowboat, where we collapse the hinged bench and make a bed of pillows and blankets.

As we eat, drink, snuggle, and stargaze, Eliot tells me more about his day with his mom, and I tell him about my day with mine. I don't leave out Dutch's timely rescue, even though doing so leads me to reiterate my statement that I have no intention of "eloping with the bartender" while Eliot's wandering the globe again.

"I'd understand if you did," he says. "Not that I wouldn't be insanely jealous, but he seems like a good guy. And I can't offer you the support you deserve right now."

"Even though you offer me kindness, laughter, stories, love? Encouragement for me to chase a dream again? A solid Ironman joke if you ever think of one?"

"I'm pretty sure you'll think of one before I will."

"Maybe," I say, and then repeat, in my best Eliot Swift imitation, "Maybe."

Despite my attempt to make him smile, he frowns up at the stars, his forehead furrowed with creases I could map in my sleep by now. We're lying side by side in the rowboat, tucked under rumpled blankets and rocked by the soft rhythm of the sea. The wine bottle's empty, set on the dock with our glasses and picnic leftovers. The air smells of salt and seaweed. The waves lap the shore with their gentle *hush-hush-hush*. We talked out the possibility of a long-distance relationship already. Eliot didn't think it was a good idea. Not when he doesn't know when or if he'll return, and not when he worries he'll be a burden on me with little to offer in exchange. I have my own reasons for accepting that when he leaves, he'll leave as my friend and not as my lover or boyfriend. Still, it's hard. So fucking hard. All the potential. All the love and desire. Where does it even go?

Feeling a need to be as close as possible in our dwindling time together, I roll toward Eliot, resting my head on his shoulder and my hand on his chest. The movement draws his eyes my way, and he holds my gaze for a long moment, his eyes full of sadness and regret, but also tenderness, warmth, and love. So much love.

"I'm sorry we didn't break your curse," he says.

I muster a smile. A thin one. "I had a hell of a time trying."

"Best five days of my life."

"Even though they included a funeral?"

"Even though." He takes a breath and releases it slowly. I hate that even this is something I'm going to miss. Watching his chest rise and fall as we lie together. The simple beauty of being so close to someone I notice how he breathes. "Remember how I told you at the bar that I didn't know what I was running away from?"

"Of course. Did you have an epiphany, too?"

"Sort of. Maybe. Today, when I read my dad's letter, I thought *this*. *This* is what I'm running away from. I'm running from his assumptions and expectations. But as I sat with the idea, I realized it's not that simple. I *know* my dad's assumptions are baseless. I stopped entertaining his expectations years ago. So my need to get as far away from this life as possible must have another root cause." He wraps his arm around me, drumming his fingers on my bicep while he thinks. And thinks. And thinks. "I wanted something from my dad. Approval, I guess, or something like it. I feel like a child for wanting that, but I can't seem to stop. Even now." He looks toward the house as though he can see his dad standing at a window, gazing out upon his realm under stern, silvering brows. "I think maybe that's what I'm running from. From wanting something I wish I didn't want. Something I know now for certain that I'll never have."

I watch his face flicker through a dozen indecipherable expressions until the creases between his brows ease and his fidgeting hand goes still.

"Something like approval?" I ask. "Something like . . . love?"

"Hmm." His lips go tight and the creases reappear as he repeats, "Hmm."

I wait, in case he wants to disagree with me, or in case he feels like he said enough and he doesn't want to talk about this anymore. When he doesn't offer up an argument or shift the subject, I decide this is the right time. So I tell him what Sophia told me at the funeral. That his dad watched every video. That he called his son brave and brilliant. That maybe he wasn't skilled at showing his love, but he felt it. I even suggest that this house, which Eliot will always view as a trap, was given with good intentions. Misguided ones, sure, and if he knew his son at all, he would've understood that it was the worst possible choice, but Eliot's father did love him. In his way.

Eliot listens to everything I tell him, quiet and still as the sea continues rocking the boat and a canopy of stars glitters above us. He doesn't say anything when I finish. He just blinks toward the stars, his forehead furrowed and his mouth twitching ever-so-slightly. He swallows, and swallows again. I'm about to ask him if he's okay when a tear slides down his cheek. Just one, but since I've never seen him cry before, that single tear says more than hours of sobbing might from someone else, someone who isn't so accustomed to keeping his emotions locked inside so only he knows they exist.

"Fuuuuuuuuuuuck," he whispers to the night sky. Then he rolls into me, drawing his legs and arms toward his chest and tucking his head against my collarbone.

I wrap my arms around him, half expecting more tears to come, but his breathing remains even as I hold him, praying with my whole heart that he knows he's not alone. He might spend the rest of his life climbing mountains and camping in deserts. His desire for space and movement are built into his soul. I know that. But I no longer believe he doesn't get lonely. I think he needs people, too. I hope one day that thought doesn't fill him with fear. I hope it brings him comfort, and I hope that thought brings him back.

Eliot's the first to stir as morning light tints the sky with the barest hint of gray. The stars are gone, replaced by a cloud cover typical of coastal weather systems. We get our glimpses of the sky, but they rarely last long. So many good things in life never do.

I pull the blankets tighter around my neck, snuggling against Eliot. We wake up face-to-face this time, proving that four nights together is too short a time span in which to develop default sleeping positions. It's too short a time span for a lot of things.

I expect to see Eliot blinking away sleep, as terrible at mornings as I am, but he appears to be wide awake, his lashes free of crusty bits and his glasses on.

"Did you sleep at all?" I ask.

"Not much. I've been thinking."

"About your dad?"

"About how I want you to have it."

Still drowsy, all I can do is blink at him. "You want me to have what?"

"I can't sign the house over to you. It'll stay in my name, and I'd need to sign for any major renovations or additions, but you can liquidate the assets. If you sell some of the gems on the lawn, the art, the wine, the first edition books, the furniture, you can afford the help you need for your mom. You might also be able to quit one or two of your jobs. Spend your Friday nights out having fun instead of delivering pizza. Draw pictures for the asshole who told you he was in love with you but didn't stick around long enough to take you on a single proper date." He nuzzles my nose, *almost* smiling.

I continue blinking at him like an idiot. "You . . . you want me to have *all* of it?"

"Not sure the house is worth as much to you as the contents," he says, which I guess means yes. "I know you want to stay with your mom, but you'd have a place to go if you wanted time away. Maybe you can turn the house into an artists' retreat or a dog hotel. Rent it out if you want. I don't care what you do with the place, as long as it makes you happy. And if it makes you happy, maybe it can make me happy, too."

My brain spins, unable to make sense of what he's saying. He's so calm about it, so easy and certain, but if I understand him, if this is real, then what he's offering me is life changing, and I have no idea how to reply. *Thanks, pal! I'll get right on that wine auction and set up an Airbnb listing!* I need something more. Much, *much* more.

I scoot up in the boat and crane around to peer past the shore-line and the open lawn toward the beautiful house I used to think belonged in a fairy tale, with its turret and balustrades. I'm struck once again by how many memories we made here. With what Eliot's offering me, I wouldn't need to let them go. As badly as I could use the money from selling some wine or antique furniture, *this* is the thought that overwhelms me.

Eliot scoots up behind me, wrapping me in his arms and resting his chin on my shoulder with his cheek against my ear. As with his first night back, I don't know what he pictures when he gazes across this lawn. His memories aren't as happy as mine, but as I imagine dogs playing in this yard or painters setting up easels or families using the suites, with a new generation of kids leaping off the dock together, I see a future full of joy. And suddenly I wonder if my mom's prophecy wasn't about Eliot. It was about this house, though maybe the two are even more inextricably linked than I thought.

"You're sure?" I ask, barely getting the words out.

"You'll change it. You'll give it new associations. It'll be good for both of us."

"It's . . . so much."

"Use what you need. Give the rest to charities, especially if they're charities my dad never would've supported. Food banks. Planned Parenthood. Homeless shelters. Voting reform. Let's spend his money where it should've been going for years."

We go through several more rounds of this conversation as I try to accept the reality of what he's offering and what it could mean for me, and for my mom, and even for Pitt's Corner if I can bring new business into town or redistribute some of the Swifts' wealth. It seems impossible, but Eliot's determined to see the idea through.

Eventually I acknowledge that anything I do with this house or its contents will require work. Eliot's not giving me easy handouts.

He's taking a step toward finding peace with his relationship with his parents, and he's offering me a step toward putting myself first. It's those steps that might help us find a way back to each other one day.

So, I accept.

# Twenty-three

## HEARTBREAK #18

Eliot stays in town through the rest of the week, sorting out legalities, which include starting the process of rezoning the house for business use should I decide to open a dog-friendly bed-and-breakfast, an idea we agree would be kind of perfect, even if it would make his mom furious. (Especially if it would make his mom furious.) He also hires a company that sorts out estate sales and auctions, working on commission since neither of us has any funds with which to pay up front. We then set up a joint bank account so any resulting income doesn't funnel only to me. This is a selfish move on my part. If Eliot ever decides to return to Pitt's Corner—whether that's in a month, a year, or a decade—I want to make sure he can afford the trip. Also, we agreed. For every dollar I spend on the house conversion or my mom's care, we donate at least two to charity.

In the evenings, we bake more cupcakes. I do a few drawings and make good use of my lingerie collection. We take a trip to the cemetery so Eliot can say a new goodbye to his dad, a goodbye that's a little more peaceful than the one he said on Saturday. With Franny's inestimable help, we also host an ice cream eating contest at Ed's and organize a town-wide tug-of-war. We even figure out how to hold a worm charming contest, which involves trying to coax earthworms from the ground using vibrations, sound effects, and for those who prefer such methods, verbal encouragement.

As we entrench ourselves in plans for the house and continued efforts to shed my curse, Eliot shakes off the worst of Monday's quiet restlessness, but it doesn't go away. I often find him standing apart from the crowd, looking off toward something on a distant horizon, unable to stand still. Meanwhile, I lose every contest, proving some limitations can't be overcome by willpower alone. Not for either of us. And our goodbye still looms.

On Saturday morning, ten days after arriving, Eliot packs his duffel bag with his meager belongings and I drive him to the bus station, the same station we sat at years ago while I sniffled into his oxford shirt and he tap-tap-tapped his khaki-clad knee against mine, assuring me everything would be okay. This time he's in busted-up jeans and the blue fisherman sweater I finished yesterday. At least I only used a single color of yarn on this one, but my needlework is still full of knots and flaws. Eliot swears the flaws make him love the sweater more. For today at least, I decide to believe him.

We sit on a bench in front of the station, our hands knotted and my head on Eliot's shoulder. I've held myself together all week by focusing on tasks and reciting self-assurances that this goodbye will be different. We're older now. At least a little bit wiser. Eliot knows what he's running away from, and that he might not be un-lonesome after all. I know my curse doesn't mean I can't love and be loved. It just means my life will be complicated. Though Eliot has rebranded it with a better word. Unconventional.

"I won't ghost you again," he says.

"Okay." I nod against his shoulder, my voice already breaking.

"And I'll get help. Someone I can talk to about stillness and running."

I nod again, unsure I can open my mouth without sputtering.

"You'll make art and call that number for help with your mom."

I nod a third time. It's all I've got right now. My body feels weird, like I'm no longer solid. Like I'm made of the tears I've been holding in since I saw Eliot sitting in the rowboat, gazing out at a dark sea, a wreck of the man I saw earlier that day. If someone put a pin in me right now, I'd pour onto the cement, leaving nothing but a puddle of unshed tears and an Imogen Finch–shaped skin. It wouldn't even have good hair.

"I won't always have cell service," Eliot says, filling the silence by correctly sensing that I'm incapable of speaking right now. "But I'll be in touch every time I'm in a city. Send me anything. Photos of your artwork. Stories about what you and Franny are up to. Iron-man jokes. And I'll post new videos so you can see where I've been."

I inhale a shaky breath, rallying to say something. Anything. Eliot's doing all the work here. We can't have a repeat of our last parting when all I did was blubber at him. I swallow a few times. Take a deep breath and let it out. Close my eyes and clear my head.

Just when I think I might manage a few words, engine noise breaks through my spiraling thoughts. Eliot's bus pulls around the corner and into the station, parking in the loading bay only a few yards away. Its headlights look like widespread, squinting eyes, as though it's daring me to oppose it with a look. I've never hated the sight of a vehicle more. And anything I might've offered to the conversation vanishes from my mind.

Eliot squeezes my hand, likely intuiting my thoughts. Some of them, anyway.

"I'll send you pencils," he says. "And I won't miss your birthday."

I manage another nod, and even eke out a breathy, "What can *I* do for *you*?"

He kisses my forehead and the knuckles of our linked hands. I risk a glimpse at his beautiful face. The intense warm brown eyes, open wide to the world. The weathered skin. The nose and chin that blend his dad's sharply angular features with his mother's distinctive softness. His expression is pensive, as it so often is, while I wait for him to tell me to stop obsessing about my curse or to take back the reins of my own life.

"What can you do for me?" he echoes. "How about . . ." He pauses. Thinks some more. "Every once in a while, tell me how deeply unattractive you find that bartender?"

I snort out a laugh, which unleashes the tears I've been holding back. In an instant, I become a blubbering, shuddering, uncontrollable mess. Without hesitation, Eliot pulls me to him so I can sob into his ugly blue sweater and fall apart in his arms.

"I love you so much," I sputter. "So, so much."

"You have no idea." He presses a kiss to the top of my head. We stay like that for a minute, maybe two. Everything else seems to happen in three seconds' flat.

The bus driver calls for boarding.

Eliot and I release our embrace and stand.

He picks up his duffel bag and slings it over a shoulder.

We approach the bus.

He gives the driver his ticket.

He pulls me into one last hug.

He promises he'll stay in touch.

He tells me he loves me.

I tell him I love him, too.

I wipe away tears with the back of my hand.

He boards the bus, turning to wave from the top of the steps.

The doors close.

I step back, pressing a hand over my mouth as though I can hold back my sobs.

The bus pulls away.

And he's gone.

# Twenty-four

## OCTOBER

*I* spend a solid week pining. I drink everything out of the mug with the swift on it. I listen to countless terrible pop songs about heartbreak. I wear a ratty T-shirt Eliot accidentally left behind until I'm forced to admit it needs to be laundered. I officially meet the job requirements my various employers set for me, but barely.

Eliot texts when he reaches his stop in B.C. and again before he heads back out on his hike. He tells me the guy who was holding his gear has a good lead on a therapist who will work remotely with Eliot as he continues his travels. Eliot's feeling optimistic. I'm feeling like he's about to get smothered by an avalanche and I'm about to begin nightly visits to his widow's walk while sobbing toward the sea.

Really, I just miss him. My crappy twin-size bed feels too large now. Even my tiny shower feels big. Or maybe it's my heart that has too much empty space.

Franny invites me to a Halloween party at Franklin J. McGruder's farm, hoping to snap me out of my self-indulgent lethargy. In a tradition I've been upholding for over twenty years, I dress as a woman who was first at something. I've been Annie Edson Taylor (first woman to go over Niagara Falls in a barrel), Sophie Blanchard (first woman to pilot a hot-air balloon), Marie Curie, Edith Wharton, and one year I even went as Laika, the first dog in space. This year, I'm dressed as Gertrude Ederle, the first woman to swim the English Channel back in 1926, and she swam it faster than every man who preceded her. My black tank top and spandex shorts work as a vintage bathing suit, and all I had to add was a swim cap, a pair of goggles, and a fluffy robe since it's only forty-five degrees outside. Franny is dressed as a chicken, wearing a clunky, bright yellow foam mascot outfit she borrowed from a fast-food place a few towns away.

"Why a chicken?" I ask as we head into the barn, where dance music's throbbing and a tightly packed crowd is milling. "And why *that* chicken?"

"Franklin isn't into costumes, even though he hosts this party every year, but he agreed to wear his farmer gear. This was the closest I could get to a couple's costume on short notice. It was either this or half of a cow costume from Anika's school's production of *Into the Woods*. I decided a whole chicken was better than half a cow."

I can't help but laugh. This is *so* Franny. She could've put on a sexy yellow dress, picked up a cheap boa, face-painted a cute little beak, and shown up here looking super-hot. Instead, she got the mascot costume and is now elbowing her way through the crowd toward the makeshift bar while I follow in her substantial wake.

"Eliot would hate it here," I say as I take in the noise and lack of personal space.

Franny glances over her shoulder at me. "What's the latest?"

"He's finishing his B.C. hike. Said he'll be out of touch for a couple weeks."

"And then?"

"And then . . . he'll figure out what happens then." I shrug, but Franny catches something in my expression that makes her stop short. She spins toward me, sloshing a guy's drink when her giant foam tail feathers clip his elbow. He barks out a few choice words, but when his gaze lands on Franny's gorgeous face, he melts into a puddle of apologies, one of her many superpowers.

"We *never* would've dragged Eliot to this party," she says to me.

I sigh before I can stop myself. I love parties. I love the pomp and circumstance of Halloween, how even as adults we seize the opportunity to be someone else for a night. I love dressing up as women who inspire me, the smart ones, the strong ones, the brave ones. I love dancing and being around big crowd energy. This year, I wouldn't have minded setting aside what I wanted to do for a chance to be with Eliot. In fact, I would've loved it. But a few months from now? A year? Would I be back in the same pattern as always? Doing whatever my partner wants instead of asking if we could do what I want? Would I even suggest taking turns or finding compromises that suited us both?

Eliot's working on his personal challenges. I should be, too.

"All right, Rockwell." I link an arm through her wing. "Let's get our groove on."

We dance. We drink. We play games and talk to people we've never met before. I explain my costume more times than I can count. Franny and Franklin make heart eyes at each other. For several hours, the sting of Eliot's absence fades, subsumed by music, laughter, conversation, a substantial amount of mystery-ingredient green punch, and the visual distraction of costumes coming apart as the night wears on. In short, I have fun.

When Franny drops me off at around 2 a.m., my mom is waiting up on the living room sofa with the TV on but the sound muted. Two steaming mugs of tea are on the coffee table. Two mugs that would only be steaming if she knew when I was about to walk in the door. This is not the first time she's been spot-on about such things.

She looks up as I step into the room.

"It was great," I say through a smile. "Exactly what I needed."

She pats the sofa next to her. I take a seat and lean my head on her shoulder. She wraps an arm around me, completely unfooled, and holds me while I cry my eyes out.

# Twenty-five

## NOVEMBER

Eliot: How are the interviews going?

Imogen: Slow. My mom's being VERY particular

Eliot: She didn't like the birder? Seemed like a perfect fit

Imogen: It was, until the poor woman misidentified a simple robin

Eliot: So she lied about being a birder?!?!?!

Imogen: I don't think she lied. I think she's a really bad birder

Eliot: Right. Not a perfect fit then. And the retired RN?

Imogen: She suggested my mom get a brain scan

Eliot: The tarot reader?

Imogen: Total chaos. Two prophesiers do not an ideal partnership make

Eliot: The woman who used to coach Outward Bound teams?

Imogen: She told my mom her wardrobe was impractical

Eliot: And that was the end of that?

Imogen: My mom has a unique take on what's "practical"

I kick my feet up on the empty lawn chair. It wobbles under the added weight. I tried to buy a new patio set with some of the funds

that have been coming in from gradually liquidating the Swifts'
most valuable assets, but my mom wouldn't have it. These chairs
were meant to be ours years ago and they're still meant to be ours.
So here I am, making a checked pattern on my ass while I sip a beer
and continue working on the Find More Time for Myself plan. And
the Stop Pining for My Absent Soulmate plan.

> Imogen: How was the flight?
> Eliot: Crowded. Not sure why so many people want to be in
>     Iceland in the winter
> Imogen: Why do you want to be there?
> Eliot: One day I'll show you. Easier than explaining

I warm at the thought, even while I can't imagine myself trek-
king across Icelandic plains with Eliot. However, we're both making
changes, so who knows? Maybe one day.

> Eliot: Did you get my package?
> Imogen: Three minutes into this text convo and you're
>     already bringing up your package? Where's your sense of
>     foreplay?
> Eliot: You did have a way of making me impatient
> Imogen: A 21-year wait to admit you liked me was hardly
>     proof of impatience
> Eliot: It was, however, proof of total idiocy
> Imogen: Total but also mutual
> Eliot: I won't wait 21 years to tell you anything ever again. I
>     promise
> Imogen: Low bar, Swift
> Eliot: Speaking of bars . . .

A soft laugh slips out of me as I consider my reply. I could say I have a new favorite cocktail, one Dutch only makes for me. I could say the bar now hosts a weekly trivia night and Franny, Franklin, and I seldom miss it. I could say I've stopped thinking of Dutch as an unattainable fantasy and now think of him as a very real friend. But I know what Eliot's ellipsis implies, even if it's implied in the guise of a shared joke.

> Imogen: Remember that repulsive homunculus who works at
>    O'Malley's?
> Eliot: You're a kind, kind woman, Finch
> Imogen: I do my best. And yes, I got your package. Thank
>    you for the Canadian flag pencils. I used them to draw
>    these . . .

I send him a picture of cute cow drawings.

He replies with a smiley face emoji.

We text for another half hour or so. I tell him I picked out a paint color for the wall in Ed's diner, and that I have two new dogs to walk, both of whom I adore. He tells me about his first few sessions with the therapist. It wasn't a good personality match, but he got a referral for a grief counselor. He was shocked by the suggestion, discounting grief as his central issue, but upon reflection, he realizes it might be a good fit after all.

# Twenty-six

## DECEMBER

"Where the hell is he?" Franny leans forward to peer at my laptop screen.

"Give him a minute," I say. "He's probably having tech issues. He'll be here."

It's Christmas Eve. We're in the front parlor of Eliot's house.

*Eliot's house.* Wow. That thought still doesn't sit quite right.

My laptop is perched on a folding table while Franny and I sit in heavy chairs we dragged in from the dining room. The rest of this space is empty, other than the fireplace, the chandelier, the rug that covers most of the polished wood floor, and a photo of the three of us we put on the mantel for inspiration. Eliot's planning to join us via FaceTime from Gaborone, Botswana. After a few weeks in Iceland, the Kalahari called him back. The video he put up on his channel last week was phenomenal.

He was right. I would love to draw those trees. And those meer-kats.

My laptop screen flickers and the window opens, showing us Eliot's face. My hand flies to my chest, where I swear my ribs are puls-ing with my heart. I haven't seen him since he boarded his bus two months ago. His hair has grown out but he remains clean shaven. He's wearing The Sweater, even though he's probably roasting in it.

"Merry Christmas!" Franny shouts as he waves at us.

"Merry Christmas," he says back through a light buzz of static before leaning in and squinting at his screen. "Where are you guys?"

I pick up the laptop and walk it in a slow circle.

"All the porcelain is gone," he says, his voice full of wonder. "And the chintz!"

"We're going to make this the reception room," I tell him.

"The permits came through?"

"We got the okay to proceed yesterday, though we still have to go through several rounds of inspections and approvals." I swap an eager grin with Franny. Over the past few weeks, she became a full partner in this venture. She's putting her house up for sale and moving into one of the fourth-floor suites so she can be on-site manager while I continue living with my mom. Anika's thrilled. She gets to live in a turret. I'm thrilled because we're fencing off half of the back lawn to make a dog run. "Antony's coming out next month to give us renovation pointers. Not that we're making structural changes, but he can help sort out appropriate décor. Lavinia's even working on a grant to support writing retreats for her Oxford colleagues. It's going to be amazing."

"What does your mom have to say about it?" Eliot asks.

An amused snort slips out of me. "Thankfully nothing."

Eliot laughs. The sound breaks my heart and puts it back together again.

"I don't mean prophecies," he says. "Is she okay with you being around less often while you get the bed-and-breakfast up and running?"

"No major crises lately," I say. "Agatha's helping."

"The latest candidate for the companion position?"

"Yep." I nod, grateful I can finally report something positive on this front. "She made it past an interview, a nature walk, a family dinner, and a road trip to look for river otters in Klamath County. She even loves reality TV. So far, so good!"

Eliot beams at me through the screen and my heart does that break-and-mend thing again. God, I miss him. Even while I'm elated he's in my life again and we've been staying in decent contact. Franny and I are also starting a business, I'm making art again, and my mom has part-time care. None of this would be happening without Eliot, and yet, there's a painful irony to those words I can't ignore. *Without him.*

"Where are you heading next?" Franny asks.

"A fishing village on the Gulf of Thailand. Population thirty-seven. Right on the coast. A couple I met last week told me about it. I can rent out a hut. Daytrip from there while I start training for the Great Wall Marathon."

"Sounds fantastic." I force a smile, masking a break in my voice with a cough.

Outside of Eliot's screen view, Franny takes my hand and gives it a reassuring squeeze. The Great Wall Marathon is in May. Half the population of Oregon runs. He could easily train here. I don't know when this will get easier.

I don't know *if* this will get easier.

Franny catches Eliot up with a few local anecdotes. He tells us about his latest trek through the desert. We hold up mistletoe and kiss the screen. All too soon, Eliot says his internet service is spotty and he should go before we get cut off.

Franny and I shout out overlapping *I love you*s.

"I love you, too." He blows us a kiss.

The call ends.

# Twenty-seven

## JANUARY

Imogen: Why did the swimmer/cyclist/runner lose the
    Ironman race?

Eliot: I give up. Why?

Imogen: Because she didn't tri hard enough

Eliot: That was TERRIBLE

Imogen: Told you. Niche genre

Eliot: Very niche. Happy New Year, Finch

Imogen: Happy New Year

Imogen: ♥

# Twenty-eight

## FEBRUARY

Imogen: Tell me to go home

Franny: Go home

Franny: Why am I telling you to go home?

Imogen: I'm at O'Malley's

Franny: And?

Imogen: And I've been here for three hours

Franny: Still not a cause for concern

Imogen: And it's Valentine's Day and I'm about to make bad
decisions

Franny: Are you sure those decisions would be bad?

Imogen: I don't know. Let me ask the bottom of my glass
again

Franny: Got it. Don't leave. I'll be there in ten

Imogen: Aren't you on a date with Franklin?

Franny: He'll understand. Just hold tight

Franny bustles into the bar about twenty minutes later. Adjusting for
Rockwell time, that's a pretty quick turnaround. I'm nursing my fifth
whiskey on the rocks while playing with the necklace I made from

Eliot's blue gem. Dutch has stepped away from my company to pull beers for a pair of dude bros who look like they just got their first chin hairs. His forearms still look good when he pulls a beer.

His everything looks good.

Franny slides onto the stool next to me, her overcoat open atop a sexy red minidress. She takes in the look I'm giving Dutch as she breathlessly swivels my way.

"Scale of one to ten," she says without preamble. "How badly do you want this?"

I twist my little blue pendant between my thumb and forefinger while I watch Dutch. His ridiculously handsome grin. His easy, confident way of moving through the world, every gesture, every word so self-assured. It's deeply compelling, how he anchors the space he's in. The way he might anchor me, too, if I gave him a chance.

"Nine?" I say, but without conviction.

"And how long has it felt like a nine?" Franny asks.

"I don't know. Since halfway through drink number four?"

"And has it felt that way because it's what you want, because you're drunk and horny, or because you're missing you-know-who and you need to fill the void?"

"All three, maybe?" I reach for my whiskey but Franny slides it away, shooting me a look that says she's unwilling to let whiskey be the deciding party. God, I love her.

"You know I've always assumed you and Dutch would at least hook up at some point," she says. "I'm glad you're finally thinking about it."

My inner turmoil eases a little. "Are you really?"

"Seriously? Look at that man." She tips her chin in his direction. "He's also kind, and fun, and he has saved us both a fortune in bar tabs. If he hadn't so obviously fallen for you shortly after moving to town, I would've made a pass at him ages ago."

We share a smile at that. We both know she's happy with Franklin, but her admission helps me feel less weak for letting lust and loneliness muddle my thoughts.

"But?" I ask, because if there wasn't a *but*, she wouldn't be here right now.

"But I think your heart is still elsewhere."

"You mean with the guy who dumped me for a mountain range?"

She scolds me with her eyes, in a patient but parental sort of way.

"I *mean* with the guy who made choices he thought would be best for both of you, all things considered. And you agreed with those choices."

I feel a deep frown settle onto my face as I grow more muddled than ever.

"What if he was always meant to leave?" I ask, still haunted by my curse, and by the stupid glass floaters with the fate they carried out to sea. "What if we were only ever meant to have those ten days in October together? What if he came back into my life at a time when I needed him, and a time when he needed me, as a friend, not as a soulmate? What if the only way we'll live happily ever after is if we live our 'ever afters' apart?"

Franny's brows lift. "Is that how you *really* feel?"

"Yes," I say before I can overthink it. Or because I've already overthought it.

"You think of Eliot as a friend? *Only* as a friend?"

"Mm-hmm," I mumble, a little less sure this time.

"And you'll be happiest apart from each other?"

"Yes? Maybe? Seems like the obvious conclusion to draw at this point."

"So if he walked into this bar right now, you'd still pick Dutch?"

I glance at the door. At Dutch. At the door again.

"Um . . . I *think* so?"

Franny's skeptical expression doesn't soften. In fact, her brows seem to have inched higher and she might even be laughing at me now.

"Then why did you text me to tell you to go home?" she asks.

I groan as I slump onto the bar, burying my face in my loosely folded arms. I'm such a mess, composed entirely of contradictions, and I can't blame it all on the whiskey.

"You tell me." Franny sets a firm hand on my shoulder, drawing my eyes to hers. "If you're ready to give things a shot with Dutch, I'll leave you to it and I'll blow up your phone tomorrow until you give me every last smutty detail. But if the idea of waking up with someone besides Eliot doesn't feel right, then my truck is parked outside."

I consider my options, albeit with a hazy, alcohol-infused imagination. I do want to do more than occasionally flirt with Dutch over the bar, and I can't wait forever for Eliot, but Franny's right. I texted her for a reason. I'm not ready. Not yet, anyway.

I flag Dutch over and ask for the bill. He tells me it's on the house, flashing me a brilliant grin that nearly undoes me, conjuring images of the breakfast in bed he once offered me, and everything that might precede that breakfast.

I shoot a *save me from myself* look at Franny.

She shrugs while stifling a laugh at my expense, a laugh I fully deserve.

"Thanks for the drinks and the company," I say to Dutch. "I'll see you around?"

His grin widens. "I'm not going anywhere."

I smile back. I can't help it. It's a nice thought, and one that stays forefront in my mind as Franny and I tell Dutch *Happy Valentine's Day* and we head out of the bar.

# Twenty-nine

## MARCH

On the first clear day after nearly a month of sleet and rain, I pack a few of the dogs I still walk for Vera into my hatchback and drive them out to Eliot's house so we can give the newly completed dog run a try. The run is awesome, a big open space where the dogs can enjoy agility equipment and an elaborate doghouse that Rusty—my chatty coworker from the hardware store—made to match the house, complete with a green tile roof and a fancy balcony that's soon occupied by a very contented dachshund.

Inside the main house, we sold the expensive art and replaced it with works from local artists. The first edition books are gone. The shelves now contain pulp fiction and books about the history of Coastal Oregon, as well as maps of the area for hiking, fishing tours, and other recreational activities. The dining room, living room, front parlor, and office have been converted into public spaces. We kept most of the furniture but updated linens and smaller furnishings, while Franklin helped us develop a farm-to-table breakfast menu. Our website and reservation system went live last week, and signage goes up next month, with a grand opening planned for June first. It's all happening.

My mom finds me out with the dogs. I brought her over this morning before picking up the dogs so we could spend the day here together.

"You look happy," she says as we watch a herding dog circle two terriers.

"I am happy. Or mostly happy." I can't help but smile as the elderly chocolate Lab I adore wanders over for a scratch behind the ears, groaning when I hit the good spot.

"Has Eliot seen all of this?" My mom takes in the lawn with a glance.

"He's offline. Somewhere in the Andes. We'll touch base in a week or two."

She nods as her every-color eyes study me a *little* too closely.

"And the handsome man who walked you home on Friday night?" she asks.

I restrain an eye roll. My mom knows Dutch's name. She also knows that while he did, in fact, walk me home after he closed up at the bar on Friday, that's *all* he did.

"I'm still not ready," I say. "And not just because of Eliot. This time on my own has been good for me, away from the temptation to orbit around someone else. I've unearthed buried ambitions. I'm less obsessed with my curse. The ugly little voice in my head has finally grown quieter, the voice that keeps telling me *Accept whatever affection you can get for as long as you can get it because you'll never come first to anyone.*"

My mom nods as an ocean breeze flutters a few loose strands of her graying hair.

"Maybe I never will come first to anyone other than myself," I continue. "Maybe no one does. I'll always share Eliot with Mother Nature, though let's face it, she's a hard act for anyone to beat." I fix my mom's collar where it pokes out under more layers than I can count. "You shared Dad with the sea, and with Shakespeare, and even with his depression. He shared you, in his way, and neither of you was fighting a curse."

"True." She looks out toward the ocean. "Very true."

"I'll never shed *all* of my insecurities or know precisely which of my choices make me lose too much of myself in service of others, but I don't want to enter another relationship assuming I'm a placeholder ever again. When I'm absolutely certain I'm not doing that, and when I'm no longer comparing the guy I'm with to the guy I'm *not* with, then I'll do more than accept a walk home."

My mom nods thoughtfully as she takes a deep breath of warm spring air. I take one, too, inhaling the scent of cut grass and briny kelp. For several minutes, as dogs frolic and light dances on the waves beyond the lawn, I let soft-focus childhood memories flicker through my mind. The games. The laughter. The countless ways we shaped each other's lives, even before we knew we were doing it. I'm so grateful this place didn't get bulldozed and turned into condos. Maybe this weekend I'll put up a badminton net.

My mom lets out a tiny gasp. I turn to see a ladybug land on the Labrador's head. Before the dog can shake it off, my mom eases it onto her finger and peers at it closely.

"Eleven spots." Her eyes widen. "*Eleven*, Imogen. That means—"

"Don't." I flash her a palm.

"Even if—"

"Doesn't matter."

"But you—"

"Still no."

"And he—"

"Mom. Please." I plead with my eyes, but she's not looking at me. Her gaze is locked on the ladybug, while her slender finger trembles beneath it.

"Oh, Imogen," she says, rasping and breathless. "But surely . . ."

Her intensity unnerves me. Her insistence that I know. As with the ducks and the floaters, my willpower wavers. What if she knows Eliot will return? Or that I'm destined to be with Dutch? Or that my curse is about to break? Hearing something like that could save me so much worry and doubt. So much longing and confusion.

Then again . . .

"How about we agree that if I hit a point where I can't handle not knowing, I'll tell you. Otherwise, whatever eleven spots mean, you can keep to yourself."

"Okay," she says. "For now."

# Thirty

*I* can't remember the last time I was this soaked. I also can't remember the last time I laughed this hard. Dutch is holding a large but useless golf umbrella over our heads as we run through a downpour together, the puddles deep and the rain pelting us sideways. I'm woefully underdressed in a tank top and shorts. It was eighty degrees without a cloud in the sky when I got to the bar tonight. Now it's cold, dark, and so very, very wet.

"Why doesn't your mom warn you about weather like this?" Dutch asks.

"She usually only predicts weather patterns when destruction is involved," I say, my voice raised above the thrum of the rain. "Let's take her silence as a good sign."

Dutch laughs as we splash through another ankle-deep puddle and carry on toward my house. We're completely drenched by the time we jog up to my front door, me in my summer clothes, Dutch in his usual black tee and jeans, both of which now look painted on. He holds the umbrella over our heads as I fish for my keys in my pocket. I appreciate that he's trying to keep us dry. He didn't have to walk me home at all. In fact, he didn't have to do a lot of things. Teach me how to carve intricate cocktail garnishes out of citrus rinds. Close up early when the deluge hit and I said I should head home. Wait for me all this time, even during the months when I gave him no reason whatsoever to hope.

I look up, keys in hand, to see him watching me patiently, holding the umbrella over my head while rain runs down his face and over his broad shoulders. His blue eyes sparkle as his lashes flutter against the rain. His ever-present smile forms dimples in both of his cheeks. His hair cowlicks over his temples, perfectly framing his broad forehead.

It strikes me in this moment that I have no interest in walking away. I don't know if my feelings changed in an instant or over several weeks of trivia games and trying out new cocktail recipes and playing pool together, but this doesn't seem like a bad decision anymore. I'm not sure it even feels like a decision. It just feels . . . right.

"Dutch?" I take a step toward him.

"Yeah?" He takes a step toward me.

"Can I kiss you good night?"

A swoon-inducing grin stretches across his face as he tosses the umbrella aside and sweeps me into his arms.

"I thought you'd never ask."

# Thirty-one

## MAY

*E*liot runs his marathon in China. He crosses the finish line in four hours and seventeen minutes, which is utterly bananas to me. I ran track in high school but I topped out at the mile. There are very few things I want to spend over four hours on, and running is not one of them. He FaceTimes Franny and me after the race, all sweaty and tired and proud and beautiful. I wish I didn't notice the "beautiful" part, but I do.

I'd planned to tell him about Dutch, but our call is so brief, just long enough to say a few emphatic congratulations before he logs off to clean up and celebrate with fellow runners. It's just as well. Dutch and I have only been dating for a couple of weeks. A movie one night, a nice dinner out on another. Breakfast in bed. (Okay, *breakfasts* in bed.) We're still figuring things out. It'll feel more like a relationship—more like something worth talking about—by the time Eliot and I set up a longer chat.

At least, this is what I tell myself.

I spend the following Friday through Sunday at Eliot's house, working through final details of the bed-and-breakfast with Franny while Agatha does a trial weekend with my mom, sleeping over in

Lavinia's room. They have a three-thousand-piece jigsaw to assemble and a new season of *Good People, Bad Choices* to watch. Between budget spreadsheets, website tweaks, and test-cooking our breakfast menu, I keep a sharp eye on my phone. Neither Agatha nor my mom text. At all. When I head home Monday after work, they're laughing about something they swear I had to be there for.

I worried that I might be jealous, that *not* being needed might sting, but it doesn't sting at all. I feel nothing but joy as I swap greetings with Agatha and my mom before heading downstairs, where several unfinished drawings await my attention.

# Thirty-two

## JUNE

ranny gives my hand another encouraging squeeze as we sit before my laptop, waiting to launch our video chat. We toasted the grand opening of the B&B two weeks ago. This call has another purpose altogether, one I was afraid I'd chicken out on. Again. Franny's here to make sure that doesn't happen.

We agreed. If I don't tell him, she will.

"He might be seeing someone, too," I say.

"He might be."

"And I'd be fine with that."

Franny side-eyes me as she mutters an unconvincing, "Mm-hmm."

"I'd *have* to be fine with that," I amend.

"Okay," she says, equally unconvincingly.

"Otherwise I'd be the biggest hypocrite, ever."

Franny doesn't bother with a half-hearted affirmation this time. Instead, we both glance at my screen where the time shows we're four minutes past our scheduled call. I float a hand over the keyboard *again*, but I don't make the connection.

"I *really* like Dutch," I say. "And I don't even own a pair of hiking boots."

Franny renews her side-eye. "You could be ready to marry Dutch tomorrow and Eliot could be playing only-one-tent with a hot, hiking-boot-collecting mountain-climber who catches fish with her bare hands. This would still be hard for both of you."

I nod before taking my umpteenth bracing breath (and before permanently expunging Franny's only-one-tent image from my memory). Then I tighten my grip on her hand, corral my nerves as best I can, and make myself connect the call.

Eliot picks up on the first ring. He's in a stretched-out, hasn't-been-white-for-years T-shirt, sitting in front of a yellow stucco wall. A black-and-white cat lies on the windowsill over his left shoulder and the back end of a vivid turquoise bike rests against the wall to his right, the rest of it out of frame. He looks like he's been dropped into a painting, one that comes to life when a broad smile brightens his face as our camera turns on and we wave hello.

We swap the usual greetings. Franny sets a light mood by telling Eliot about Franklin's next calendar shoot and Anika's costume plans for her first Comicon. I relate my progress with the art I'm making for the diner. Eliot tells us about his transcontinental train ride from Tai'an, China, to Oviedo, Spain, where he's planning to start his next multi-week trek. They're good updates, and ones I'm grateful to share and hear, but at the first obvious break in the conversation, I turn the topic to our weekly trivia game, which gives me the opening I need to say the last possible thing I want to say right now.

"About Dutch." I pause, breathe, squeeze Franny's hand. "We've been spending a lot of time together. And, well . . . we started seeing each other. Not just as friends."

Eliot's forehead furrows and he runs a hand down the short

beard that's grown out in recent weeks. After an agonizingly drawn-out pause, he nods and lowers his hand.

"Okay," he says. And then, as he does, he repeats, "Okay."

Seconds pass. They are *long* seconds. I almost ask if he's seeing anyone, but he just traveled thousands of miles on his own to spend the next month wearing out the soles of his boots with only his backpack for company. Pretty sure I already know the answer.

"Are you happy?" he asks, and for some reason the question guts me. Maybe because no other guy has ever asked, not like this. Not like the answer *really* mattered. Not like it was the only question that was even worth asking.

"I am happy," I say, and I mean it. Even though the instant I say it, I can't help picturing an alternate universe with an alternate happiness. One in which Eliot found a way to stay with me, or I found a way to go with him, not necessarily all of the time but at least some of the time. And the instant I picture that alternate universe, I start fleshing it out by imagining nights under the stars, useless but wonderful games, laughter in bed, reading side by side in a rowboat, knitting terrible sweaters he wears no matter the temperature, swimming under waterfalls, making sexy cupcakes, adopting homeless dogs, erecting a tent together as I somehow learn to enjoy camping, and holding each other like we'll never, ever let—

"I should probably go," Eliot says. "It's good news, Imogen. I'm glad for you. Really. I just need some time to sit with this before I can . . . anything, I guess."

"Okay," I say, though my voice comes out so thin even I can barely hear me.

Franny graciously wraps up the call by wishing Eliot well on his trek and suggesting we all talk soon. We share a hard goodbye, but not a forever goodbye.

"That went pretty well," she says once we're alone.

"It did," I say, and even go on to describe how glad I am that I was honest and he was honest and sure, my news surprised him the same way it would surprise me to find out he was seeing someone, like of course it'll sting for a while but by the next time we talk, we'll be like old friends again, joking and laughing without any under-currents of hurt, guilt, anxiety, or awkwardness. The worst is done. The rest is clear sailing.

Franny listens with her usual patience, but she doesn't say any-thing. She doesn't need to. We both know I'm not actually trying to convince *her* of anything.

And therein lies the problem.

# Thirty-three

## JULY

"I'm so sorry," I say. "I'm getting this all wrong. I've never done it before."

Dutch's brows rise as he takes a bite of his ice cream cone. Not a lick. Not a nibble. A full-on, tooth-chilling bite that leaves a formidable dent in the scoop.

"You've never had ice cream?" he teases.

I bump his hip with mine as we walk along the beach together, our hair tussled by the ocean breeze, our shadows elongated by the evening sun.

"You know what I mean," I say.

He nods. Takes another bite. Watches me sideways as I lick chocolate off my knuckles. Dutch has the right idea, fast-tracking his dessert while I remind myself to never again get a double scoop in the middle of a heatwave.

Also, breaking up with someone is *hard*. I have a new respect for all of my exes.

"So you think he's coming back?" Dutch asks.

"Not necessarily." I say, still losing the battle with my melting ice cream. "It's distinctly possible that he won't come back, and eventually I'll accept that reality. My heart will firmly label him *friend* and I'll move on."

"But you haven't moved on yet?"

"Apparently not." I give up on the chocolate dripping off my knuckles so I can look Dutch in the eyes, even though doing so ties knots in my gut. I like him *so* much. He's fun and sexy and . . . uncomplicated. Though I guess that's the problem. I like complicated. I fall in love with complicated. "There's a lot I'm really unsure about right now. How to move on. *If* I'll move on. But I've spent most of my dating life, maybe *all* of my dating life, being treated like my partner's second choice. I don't ever want to do that to someone else, not if I can help it. You deserve better. We both do."

Dutch reaches into the back pocket of his cotton shorts and offers me a napkin, smirking a little as I wipe at the ice cream that has made its way to my tank top and cutoff shorts and even my sneakers. Because of course it has. Once again, I have managed to turn what should be a serious, heartfelt conversation into a ridiculous mess. Only three things are preventing this moment from being a total disaster. One: Dutch's impossibly gracious goodwill. Two: no Ferris wheels are involved. Three: my terrible haircut has finally grown out. It's a small win, but it's a win.

"Think you might feel differently in a month or two?" he asks.

"A year or two, maybe. A month or two? Unlikely. Meanwhile, the great love of your life might walk into the bar any day now. If she does, you should be available."

He smiles, but in a conflicted way I'm not used to seeing on him. Then he takes my dripping cone and makes fast work of the rest while I clean up at the ocean's edge.

"Can I still hang out at O'Malley's with you?" I ask as I rejoin him.

"Always," he says. "Though I *might* have to start charging you."

He flashes me a cheek-to-cheek grin, at ease with himself and his surroundings, even during the kind of conversation that often brings out the worst in people. It's one of the things I will always like about him. One thing among many.

As his grin fades to a gentle smile, he offers me his elbow. I take it, pulling it close against my side. We carry on down the beach. Together, but also not.

# Thirty-four

## AUGUST

t's perfect," Eliot says through my phone.

"Ed thinks he looks too grumpy."

"As I said. It's perfect."

I'm standing in the diner. The sun is setting outside. Franny and Ed went home as soon as we closed up after lunch hour, leaving me to hang my drawings on my own. As promised almost a year ago now, I wanted Eliot to be the first to see everything together.

I painted the feature wall a deep sea blue. A local artist made frames from driftwood gathered along the nearby shoreline. Inside the frames are local portraits. Lyle Lee and his friends in the center. Franny and Anika to their left. My mom and Agatha. Kym and Eugene Green. My pizza coworkers. My hardware store coworkers. Vera and her roommates. A dozen other diner regulars. The dogs, of course. Dutch, who I skimmed over with my phone, even though Eliot knows we broke up last month. I also snuck in a small sketch of Eliot, because I've come to think he does belong here. At least a little bit.

This is my art. It's also my family. My big, beautiful, extended family. The people who hold me up when I falter. The people I love so deeply, even when they annoy the crap out of me. When I look at them all together, drawn in my hand, my heart feels full. Even if I never see Eliot in person again, I'll be forever grateful he reminded me to stop listening to the bullshit. He made an effort to know me. He put a pencil in my hands.

"Told you you were brilliant," he says.

"Gotta admit," I say. "It feels amazing. Planning it. Making it. Sharing it."

"Good," he says. And again, after a moment, "Good."

I slide into a booth so I can rest my phone against a napkin holder and get a better look at Eliot's face while we chat. He has a light scruff this time, only a week or so of growth. A strong tan. A shaggy mop of loose dark curls that tip onto his forehead. The same impossibly tender eyes behind his hot nerd glasses.

"Can I ask how you're feeling about . . . other things?" he asks.

I shift in my seat, approximating a shrug, even though I'm far from ambivalent.

"It was the right thing to do," I say.

Eliot gives me a look that suggests I'm not answering the question he asked, but he doesn't press me. Just like I don't press him to say *Dutch* instead of *other things*.

"I don't know how I'm feeling," I say. "Any pointers on how to thrive while being alone?"

He lets out a breathy laugh as he scratches at his collarbone where the undulating fishtail peeks above the neckline of that damned fisherman sweater he keeps wearing.

"Yeah, well, about that," he says. "My new counselor. I'm *finally* getting somewhere. She got me to start talking about what I want instead of constantly talking about what I don't want. Reframing what I'm running away from into what I want to run toward. So far I only have one answer, but it's an answer that rings true every time I say it. And every time I say it, it also feels less frightening to say."

"Do I want to know what that answer is?" I ask.

The softest, sweetest, most beautiful smile stretches across Eliot's face.

"Oh, Finch," he says. "I'm pretty sure you already know."

# Thirty-five

## SEPTEMBER

"Don't tell him," I beg Franny.

She holds up both hands. "I won't. I swear."

"It has to be a surprise."

"You made that very clear." She wedges her hands on her hips, leaning back against the island in Eliot's kitchen. Six of our eight suites are occupied this weekend, but we're sneaking in a personal gathering while most of our guests are out and about for the day. "You *really* don't think I can keep a secret, do you?"

"Let's just say secrecy hasn't historically been your greatest asset."

She huffs in mock offense before turning away to jam candles into my cake.

"Maybe I'm better at secrets than you think. Everyone has the potential to grow, Mogi. Look at *you*. You've made it eleven months without dating any assholes."

"Ha-ha." I attempt a sneer but it quickly fades into a laugh.

Eleven months. It's been eleven months since Greg and I split and Eliot Swift came back into my life. The "surprise" is that when he calls today, I'm asking if I can join him for a few weeks. I don't know how he'll respond, but I've prepared a very convincing argument, complete with artistic goals, personal-growth goals, a physical fitness plan, extensive research on hiking equipment, and a promise that I won't cling and he can still have plenty of alone time. At this point, I'd do just about anything to hold him again, and to feel him hold me.

Anika steps into the kitchen, her hair now dyed a vivid turquoise-to-green ombré.

"Is it time yet?" she asks.

"Almost." Franny shoves in one more candle before giving up on trying to fit all twenty-nine. "Just waiting for Eliot to call and for Franklin to get here."

"Where is he, anyway?" I peer out the window at the backyard, where several dozen friends have gathered, all in breezy summer clothes, while my mom looks like she's bundled up for a hard winter, as always. "Wasn't he here earlier with the chili?"

"He was." Franny darts a fleeting glance at Anika. "I sent him for ice cream."

"We have tons of ice cream." I march over to the freezer.

She beats me to it, jamming it shut with her hip.

I back away, eyeing her suspiciously. "What the hell, Rockwell?"

She blinks at me with ridiculously fake innocence. "What do you mean?"

"I mean I was with you yesterday when we bought—?"

"The wrong flavor," Franny says while Anika says, "The wrong brand."

I look back and forth between them. "What are you two—?"

"Where are you guys?" Franklin's deep voice cuts in from the foyer.

"Kitchen!" Franny yells back, still blocking the freezer while exchanging another collusive glance with Anika. "Have any trouble finding Imogen's gift?"

"It was right where you said it would be." Franklin steps into the kitchen, tall, broad, packed into a white tee, and nearly filling the doorframe he passes through. He isn't carrying ice cream or shopping bags or a gift-wrapped box. But he's not alone.

He's not alone.

"Oh my god." My hand rises to my mouth as tears fill my eyes, welling up so fast they're already streaming down my cheeks as I struggle for breath.

"Happy birthday," Eliot says.

*Eliot* says this.

Eliot Swift.

The real, in-the-flesh man, himself. His dark hair forms a shaggy mop, curling over his forehead and ears. He's wearing a thinned-out gray T-shirt and banged-up jeans that are probably the same pair he wore last October, now with even more holes. His inked forearms are bare and his hands are shoved in his pockets. He's smiling so slightly anyone unfamiliar with his usual range of smiles would miss it entirely. And his face . . .

I've never seen anything more beautiful in my entire life.

"Y-you're . . . here," I stammer. Then my breath catches and I end up making a garbled half-choking/half-sobbing sound before dissolving into awkward convulsions.

Eliot steps forward and wipes tears from my cheeks with his calloused thumbs. As I sputter before him, locked in place by the shock of seeing him, I become vaguely aware of shuffling noises as Franklin, Franny, and Anika slip out of the kitchen, with Franny sneaking me a wink as she sidles past. I guess she can keep a secret. She's never going to let me hear the end of it. And I've never been more elated to be proven wrong.

"Hi," Eliot says once we're alone, still wiping away my torrent of tears.

"Hi," I manage. Sort of.

"God, it's good to see you."

"I was—I thought—I didn't, I mean, call, plan, where, how?" I shake my head. Attempt to order my thoughts. "I thought you were in Spain. Or Portugal."

He points over his shoulder with his thumb. "I can go back if you'd prefer."

"No!" I shake my head. Hard. "Stay. Please. *Please,* stay."

His smile widens a little. "Only if you have a room available."

"Can you handle walls or should we see if the rowboat's free?"

"I can handle a few walls." His smile widens further, but after a moment, he bites it down, shifting his stance and his shoulders. Eliot is *not* a shifter. He doesn't shuffle or stammer. Yet here he is, twitching before me as though he's mustering the courage to ask me to a high school dance, which is a crazy thought considering how high school went down for both of us. "My being here won't make things uncomfortable for you, will it? Not that I'm expecting dueling pistols or anything . . ." He cranes around to peer out the window at the crowd gathered on the lawn.

I smother a smile while his back is turned. This man has been cliff diving and outrun avalanches, but he's worried about a guy I broke up with two months ago.

"He's in Sacramento at a family wedding," I say. "He took a date."

Eliot stops shifting as he turns my way, though his eyes are tinted with wariness.

"It's a good thing," I assure him. "I want him to be happy. And he's a catch. You know, to anyone who can overlook his vast catalogue of physical imperfections."

Eliot gusts out a light laugh, though it comes out more like an exhale of relief.

"And you?" I ask. "Any updates on relationship status I should know about?"

Eliot shakes his head. Then he pats his chest. "I gave this thing away over twenty years ago. Whatever's left is useless for anyone but you."

I don't even try to hold back my tears at that. I let them flow as I fling my arms around his neck and cling to him with all my strength. He hugs me back, holding me close while I cry out my relief, my wonder, and my profound gratitude that he's here. He's *here*. He's actually here. And that thought alone makes all others fade to black.

I don't know how long I cry, or how long we hold each other, making up for months of distance between us, but eventually I remember the milling crowd on the other side of the windows, and the cake with its candles waiting to be lit. Eliot gives me a quick summary of how he and Franny arranged my "birthday gift" and how he wouldn't have missed being here for anything. He looks around as he says this, and while it's clear he still has a difficult relationship with this house, he smiles as he takes in the food prep spread out on the counter, the chipped bird mugs we hung on the wall, the notes and photos on the fridge. Also, the children and dogs out on the lawn. This is a house that's being lived in, that's being enjoyed, and Eliot will surely sense that.

Linking my hand through his, I lead him out onto the lawn, where everyone greets him as though he's part of the family, subjecting him to more hugs in a few minutes than he has probably received in the rest of his days combined. Sure, he only spent ten days here back in October, but he's been in my heart ever since, and everyone here knows it.

He does have a place in Pitt's Corner, whether he wants it or not.

At the perfect moment, Franny brings out my cake and everyone sings "Happy Birthday," Eliot included, as he once promised. We catch up on recent days. We eat. We laugh. We tease each other mercilessly. We pet the dogs. We watch a quartet of kids play badminton, grinning as one of Ed's great-granddaughters completely muffs a swing and tumbles to the grass, leaping back up with a look of fierce determination on her face.

Later, as my friends drift away, and as Franny and Franklin volunteer to take care of the cleanup, Eliot and I wander out to sit at the end of the dock, kicking off our shoes so we can dip our feet in the ocean. It's cold, but it's home.

"You doing okay, being here?" I ask.

"I am." He glances behind him. "I knew you'd change it for the better."

*Same,* I think, because I'm pretty sure we're not talking about the house.

"My dad had one thing right." Eliot threads his fingers through mine and rests our linked hands on his thigh. "I do need a place to return to, a place to build a life, but that place doesn't come with a deed or a mailing address." He caresses my knuckles with his thumb, making his meaning clear. "It's taken me a while to get here, to say my dad did anything right at all. But I've given it a lot of thought, and if you're open to the idea, I think I could learn to be still. As long as I can be still with you."

I fight back another swell of tears. "Really?"

"Well, not that I can be still *all* of the time."

"But some of the time?"

"Definitely some of the time."

"I can work with that." I bring our linked hands to my lips and plant a kiss on the back of Eliot's hand, where a pair of inked birds now perches on the octopus tentacle that undulates along his forearm and wraps his index finger. "Also, I bought a backpack. A big outdoorsy one with strap-on camping gear I don't know how to use. And I renewed my passport. So if *you're* open to the idea, I could join your next trip for a few weeks."

"Only a few weeks?"

"To start. To see how it goes before I circle back home."

Eliot nods, considering. "I can work with that, too."

I lower our hands so they rest on Eliot's leg again. We sit quietly, shoulder-to-shoulder, as the sun dips lower and the *hush-hush-hush* of the ocean welcomes her in. Even in her contained state, bound by the cove that calms her rage, the sea makes her feelings known. I take solace in that thought. In knowing her spirit can't be suppressed.

After several minutes, a ladybug lands on my knee. I pick it up and examine it.

"Eleven spots," I say.

"Eleven, huh?" Eliot peers closer.

"According to my mom . . ." I take another look at the ladybug, but I don't count the spots again. I didn't actually count them the first time, nor have I asked my mom to tell me what eleven spots mean. Right now, on the first day of my twenty-ninth year, I have everything I need with which to live my often complicated, forever cursed but mostly happy, deeply unconventional life. And whatever future awaits me, or awaits Eliot, or awaits us both together, I want to reach that future because we get there of our own accord. Not because we're standing by, waiting for it to unfold for us.

"Well?" Eliot prompts. "Does it mean something?"

"Yeah," I say. "It means anything we want it to."

My smile unfurls. Eliot's does, too.

I blow a light gust across my palm.

The ladybug flies off, taking her secrets with her.

# Acknowledgments

One might think writing the book is the hardest part. Then comes the blank acknowledgments page. Here I am, desperate to pour out my gratitude to the many, many people who have helped my work reach this point, hyperaware that the list goes well beyond the names I know and the people I've interacted with most directly. Trying to name everyone would invariably lead to accidentally leaving off names of people who deeply deserve my gratitude. So, in broad strokes, to my friends and family; to the authors and readers who've cheered me on, boosted my work and morale, and provided essential support during my deepest bouts of self-doubt; to the countless individuals who spread joy about books on social media and within your communities; to everyone at Bradford Literary and St. Martin's Publishing Group, THANK YOU. I mean those words as much as I mean every *I love you* I say to my dog. And I really, *really* mean those I-love-yous.

A special thank-you to a few key people . . .

To Jennie Conway, who was my first editor on this book, and who helped give the story its initial shape. I hope by the time this reaches print, you're precisely where you want to be, doing things that bring you tremendous joy.

To Sallie Lotz, my current editor, who was the first person to read a full draft of this story and who returned that draft to me with such profound care and brilliant insight, I knew it had landed in the best possible hands. I also knew you'd make the work stronger every step of the way. I have, *predictably,* been correct on this front.

To Laura Bradford, my agent, for finding the ideal home for my work.

To Kat Conley, for being the first to read a few messy chapters as I sorted out the voice and the story idea, and saying, "Yes! There's something here! Keep going!"

To Ellen, Kristen, Emily, Brook, Rona, Jen, Kelsey, and Jodi, for keeping me going in a year where momentum was elusive and emotional turmoil was my super-annoying daily companion. I'm here because you're here, and this book wouldn't have been written without you.

To the exes who inspired the heartbreaks in this story, none of which is entirely invented. Thanks, I guess?

To the dogs. This one's for you, for being an integral part of my personal HEA.

To anyone and everyone who's been knocked down so many times, reaching for happiness, or when your own personal version of success has come to feel impossible. Wait for sunset. Dip your toes in the ocean. Find a ladybug. Count the spots. Let it go. That's when the magic begins.

## About the Author

Tallulah

JACQUELINE FIRKINS is a writer, costume designer, and lover of beautiful things. She's on the full-time faculty in the Department of Theatre & Film at the University of British Columbia, where she also takes any writing class they'll let her into. When not obsessing about where to put the buttons or the commas, she can be found running by the ocean, eating excessive amounts of gluten, listening to earnest love songs, and pretending her dog understands every word she says.